Let's talk about delusions. You're a lawyer. And you think this is a court of law. But it is not — ABSOLUTELY NOT — a place of justice. There is only one place in this country to find justice. And that is on the street. You're doing what you believe is right. BUT SO AM I.

ABOVE THE LAW

Dexter Dias

Seal Books

Seal Books and colophon are trademarks of
Random House of Canada Limited.

ABOVE THE LAW
Seal Books/published by arrangement
with Doubleday Canada
Doubleday Canada hardcover edition published 1999
Seal Books edition published August 2000

ISBN 0-7704-2850-9

Seal Books are published by Doubleday Canada, a division
of Random House of Canada Limited. "Seal Books" and the
portrayal of a seal, are the property of
Random House of Canada Limited.

Cover illustration by West Stock
Cover design by Susan Thomas/Digital Zone

PRINTED AND BOUND IN CANADA

*All characters in this publication are fictitious and any resemblance
to real persons, living or dead, is purely coincidental.*

TRANS   10   9   8   7   6   5   4   3   2   1

For my mother

And for Katie

per sempre, cara

PROLOGUE

There was a soothing quality to the sound of the cash-counting machine, a low, soft whisper, as it fanned through hundreds upon hundreds of used £50 notes, which briefly reminded Roots Johnson of the Jamaica of his youth.

He leaned forward a few inches so that the wooden back legs of his personalised director's chair just left the ground, then he allowed his fingertips, many shades lighter than the ebony skin on the back of his hand, to hover over the shuffled notes. Cool air rose casually from the machine and he remembered the refreshing onshore breezes that blew on to the beaches around Montego Bay at this very time, the middle of the afternoon. He remembered how his father often pointed to the slowly moving branches of the palm trees and said to the then four-year-old boy that these were not really palms, but the arms of his African forefathers, dragging the coming night over the island from the depths of the Caribbean with an invisible net. At first, this vivid thought had scared the boy — to think that these ancient spirits stood guard everywhere around his homeland, constantly watching him — but as Roots grew into his teens, pride swelled in his chest, and he became fiercely loyal to everything about Jamaica. For his ancestors were not ordinary men, working in chains in the plantations. Quite the reverse. They were 'Maroons', fearsome runaway slaves, who fought the British from the mountainous interior of the island, and who were never anything but free men until Jamaica's independence after the war.

So when it was time for the boy to adopt a street name, there was no debate. Johnson's boy became 'Roots', for the roots of their family were indeed planted deep in the Jamaican soil. There was no official ceremony — everyone just called him Roots from that day some two decades before. And they showed him 'nuff respec' ', for the twelve-year-old boy had just killed his first man for the posse.

These bitter-sweet thoughts of his youth evaporated abruptly when the casher was suddenly still. With a slight ache in his chest, which he recognised as his longing for home, Roots looked around at the dark room, the latest in a long line of such dark rooms, which had been his shelter — never his home — in the intervening two decades. The sound of the rain outside depressed him. London. A Yardie 'lab'. The subterranean base for his trafficking operations, in the basement of a Victorian terrace in that basement of London south of the river. The other London, the touristic, theme-park capital of historic sites and relatively safe suburbs, had always been to Roots Johnson as removed from the London in which he conducted his 'runnings' as was the tropical isle of his birth.

To his left were windows, or rather what was left of the cracked glass, boarded and barred to keep out vagrants. A 'jamb', a stolen piece of scaffolding, constituted a second line of defence behind the reinforced steel door, to deter soldiers from rival posses from smashing their way in with nine-mils blazing. Ripping off the don, Roots Johnson, could conceivably secure their street rep. But no one had yet tried it. For the word on the street was rarely wrong, and the gospel was that going after Johnson was as likely to get you covered in blood as in glory. Around the walls of the lab were banks of microwaves, which could be used to cook up narcotics, not that Roots ever got high on his own supply. It was bad business. It set the wrong example to his young soldiers. And, anyway, he didn't like it. On the concrete floor were various mattresses, cheap but comfortable, upon which several other members of Roots's crew slept, cradling their semi-automatics like long-lost lovers.

Roots sat in his director's chair surveying this, the nerve centre of his operation, and thus of his life. It made him sad. For despite his undoubted intelligence, and the hopes of his mother, the life of Roots Johnson had come to this: white powder, laundered money and guns. He found that he was increasingly tormented by thoughts of another life — a family, children, a legit career. Perversely, he relished this pain, for it told him an important truth about himself. Fate might have decreed that he end up a dealer — The Dealer — but that wasn't necessarily his true nature, his only nature. That other self lay hidden and protected within his chest. He had not let it die.

A ringing.

His 'burner', his illegal mobile phone, began to ring. Most of his crew continued sleeping, but one, the youngest, a youth wearing an Arsenal shirt, stirred. Roots put the burner to his ear and listened. His rule was never to speak first. Let the other man speak. Words were always cheap. Sometimes treacherous. They were confessions, they gave you away. So he listened.

"It's me," the voice said.

Still Roots listened.

"Johnson, are you there? There's a problem."

Roots grunted. He knew that if the caller described the situation as a problem, it was likely to be a catastrophe.

"Where?" Roots asked.

"St Margaret's junior school. It's right next to the senior—"

Roots clicked off the burner. All the while his youngest spar, Peckham, had been watching him with growing concern.

"Is what happ'n, baas?" Peckham said.

It made Roots smile to hear this English homeboy, as Yardies called Jamaicans who had been born and raised in England, trying to speak patois.

"Sleep now, Peckham," he said.

"But, Don, there some problem, I'm your man."

Roots smiled again. Peckham was not much older now than Roots had been all those years ago when he had killed his first rival. Despite running with Roots's crew for half a year, Peckham had never even fired a gun, as far as Roots knew. The youth spent his time playing computer games, especially Street Fighter and Gangbuster, and arguing with the other soldiers about the merits of the Arsenal back four. Roots wanted to keep it that way. Peckham was his lucky mascot. Business had taken off since he had been around — the turf had spread, competitors had been dealt with.

"I is ready, ya know," Peckham said.

"Get some of that beauty sleep," Roots replied.

"You saying I need it?"

"You saying you don't?" Roots said.

Peckham laughed and lay back down on his mattress. Roots removed the steel jamb and was about to open the steel door when he hesitated. He debated with himself as to whether he would need a gun. Scattered around the room, like cast-away toys in a nursery, were Glocks and Uzis and Brownings and Macs. But despite this lethal array, Roots left the lab without 'packing'. He left unarmed. It wasn't his style.

St Margaret's junior school was that rare specimen: a private prep school on the edge of a rough run-down borough. With green fields and trees behind the high fence, it was like a verdant, wooden fort besieged on all flanks by urban desolation.

To the right side of the compound, the classroom in which Nicki Harris sat was a prefab near the playground. Local kids from the tower blocks that mushroomed around the privileged school had broken into the premises one weekend and had fire-bombed the old form room. As compensation for the disruption, the class were being allowed by their teacher, Mrs Jeffries, to paint a picture of whatever they wished, in a hopeless effort to make the place appear anything but what it really was: a draughty caravan for kids. Nicki decided to draw a policeman.

The girl was only eight years old, but she already knew that the vast majority of her school-mates were jerks. It was no surprise — she had seen their parents, as they waited outside the school gates, leaning against their Range Rover Discoveries, Cherokees and Fronteras, rows and rows of them like a squadron of tanks. Her parents could never have afforded to pay Nicki's fees, but she had always been a smart kid. She had sat the entrance exam and been awarded a scholarship. She had agreed to go to St Margaret's to please her parents and tolerated being teased about her prissy uniform by the other kids on the estate. None of her class-mates lived near her. But they did invite her to birthday parties with clowns and magicians in the leafy roads of the exclusive conservation area in which most of them lived.

The teacher leaned over Nicki's desk as the child coloured in the policeman's blue uniform. Nicki held the crayon in her fist like a dagger.

"Haven't you finished yet?" the teacher asked.

"It's the wrong shade of blue," Nicki complained. "It's supposed to be serge."

"Serge is the uniform's material, not the colour, isn't it?"

Nicki shrugged.

"Why don't you draw your mother for a change?" the teacher asked.

Nicki shook her head. "Mum doesn't like being pho-toed. It's the same sorta thing, isn't it?"

"Same sort of thing, Nicola," the teacher corrected. "No East Enders grammar at St Margaret's, thank you.'

Nicki sighed.

Just then, the school bell went. All around Nicki in the prefab, kids itched to dash out.

"Remember," Mrs Jeffries shouted, "it's country danc-ing after playtime."

"Swing you pants," Nicki whispered to Candida Lloyd, who was condemned to sit next to the sharp-witted kid.

"I — like — dancing," replied Candida, enunciating every word like Audrey Hepburn after Rex Harrison had finished with her.

"Yeah, but no one likes dancing with you," Nicki said.

"You're pathetic, Nicola Harris. But you're doing remarkably well. Considering."

"What?"

Candida stood up, ran her delicate hand through her blonde hair and stuck her nose in the air, its natural posi-tion. "Considering where you live," she whispered. Then she left.

Normally, Nicki could take the snide comments about her background. It went with the territory. It made her tough. She never told her parents. But on this day, it wounded her. For she knew that her mother was at home, laid low with flu, but would still have to drag herself around to the 'village', as the conservation area was laughingly called by estate agents, to do some cleaning for people like Candida's parents. And she would find time to mend the puncture on Nicki's bike, even though Nicki was perfectly prepared to wait until the weekend for her dad to do it when he came off nights.

The other girls began to leave the classroom, and Nicki was soon alone. Her eyes misted up as she wrote five letters above the policeman's picture: M-Y D-A-D.

Nicki Harris was the last girl to enter the playground.

Roots saw the car immediately. The white saloon was parked in a side street opposite St Margaret's, but not too near the mouth of the junction. It was a perfect spot from which to see and not be seen. On the same side of the road as the car was the secondary school, where three hundred of the most privileged, most highly achieving girls in London made the journey from childhood to adolescence in a grey uniform and a pink blouse and a guaranteed Ninety-Five per cent exam pass rate. The rain had just stopped and the dull light of the late winter afternoon and the low, dirty clouds made Roots pine all the more for just one more Jamaican Technicolor sunset and a long draught of white rum. Thick globules of rain ran down the windscreen of the saloon car and, as they did so, they mixed with the grease and the pollution, so that some of them suddenly stopped halfway down the glass, defying gravity. The windscreen wipers left an oily smear across the glass. But this was not enough to conceal the huge man sitting in the car. Finally, the rain stopped.

Roots nodded briefly at the driver, but there was no response from the white man. His eyes, somehow even darker than those of the Jamaican, Roots always felt, burned into him. This was a man who spoke to you without the need for words. His face was creased with life. Roots had often wondered who would win if they ever went at it. One on one. Hand to hand. It would be too close a thing to call. He got in the car.

As soon as the passenger door shut, Roots realised that the man had been sitting in the cold without the heating on. This didn't surprise him. This white man did things differently to the others. Both men stared straight ahead, saying nothing for some seconds. Roots noticed that his breath began to form a small oval of condensation on the windscreen in front of him. There was no such mark in front of the driver.

"He's here," the white man finally said.

"Who?" Roots asked.

"Your man."

"I have lots of men, Hogarth," Roots said, trying to conceal his irritation. But the fact that Hogarth had summoned him here, to a school, had begun to make him worry.

Just then, Hogarth noticed someone through the gloom. Roots saw him too. Another Yardie, strutting across the road, into the alley near the senior school. But he gave off a different vibe to Roots: instead of the smart casual clothes that Roots preferred, this youth was street-sharp. He was so covered with gold it was a wonder he could walk. Rope-like chains hung from his neck, and each of his wrists sported a thick amulet of the type last popular in ancient Rome.

"That bwoy drip with cargo," Roots said.

Hogarth did not reply immediately, for just then two teenage girls, sixth-formers possibly, appeared in the alley. Hogarth turned his head slowly, mechanically, towards Roots.

"Now do you see?"

Roots cursed to himself. He forced himself to watch the other Yardie, Earl Whitely, to take in every gesture, every movement. Earl was so wrapped up in the fresh-looking girls in front of him he didn't appear to think for an instant that he was being watched. This made Roots doubly furious. Not only was Earl running around behind his back, dealing on his own, he was also being careless as he did it. Hogarth looked out of the side window, where there was nothing but an old wall.

"Where's your gun?" he asked Roots.

"What gun?"

"You haven't got a gun?"

"Do you ever see Don Corleone with a gun?" Roots replied.

Hogarth looked back, now uneasy. It was the first hint of emotion he had displayed.

"Earl's beginning to talk," he said.

Roots glanced at the youth, now furiously chatting up the girls, smiling his broad, perfect-tooth smile. "Earl always talks."

"No," Hogarth said simply. "To Internal."

It was now Roots's turn to show how he was feeling. He felt his fine lips come apart, and a small gasp of incredulity escaped.

"Yes," Hogarth said.

One of the girls now looked towards the school gates and palmed Earl something. Her hand lingered just a moment too long in Earl's, white palm on black, and Roots knew that the deal had been done. Coke for cash.

"Earl's meeting them again tonight," Hogarth said. "So we've got to do it now."

"I still haven't got a gun," Roots said. "Don't you have no back-up?"

Hogarth considered this for a moment, looked solemnly down, at the steering wheel, towards his lap. He was deciding something. Then he forced his large frame lower, crumpling his heavy overcoat as he reached under his seat. He rummaged around, saying nothing, until finally he pulled out a dusty gun. He offered it to Roots.

"We've got to do it now."

Roots ripped the gun from Hogarth's hand. Primed it.
Jacked in a cartridge. Then he offered it back to Hogarth.

"So wet him."

"I thought you were the one dealer with rules,"
Hogarth said. "At least, that's your rep."

"It ain't just a rep."

"No? Well, rules without punishments are just bullshit,
Johnson."

Roots stared back at the white man, and he felt that
uncontrollable blood rush in his head that he had first
experienced in downtown Kingston when he had killed
his first man. "You dare talk to me about rules, Hogarth?"
he spat out. The gun now shook fractionally in his hand,
not from fear but from rage.

Hogarth curled his long, thick fingers around the customised handle grip. For an instant, nothing separated
Roots from Hogarth, black man from white, except a narrow length of gun barrel. The two men stared hard at each
other. It was a test of wills, of resolve. But the issue was
left undecided, for at that moment Earl scoped them. His
eyes lit up with fear and he set off at a desperate run. The
two girls ran too when they heard the double slamming of
the saloon doors.

Roots and Hogarth pounded along the wet pavements
after their man, but Earl was younger than both of them,
and in a straight race could easily have outrun them. But
he could not outrun a bullet. He veered across the road,
heading straight for the junior school playground. With
an expert kick, he booted open the gate, and, barely
breaking his stride, sped into the playground. The gate
continued to swing back and forth on its rusting hinges
in the Yardie's wake. Roots and Hogarth were closing in,
one moment Roots ahead of the white man, the next their
positions reversed. Roots couldn't co-ordinate his breathing; it was as if he was constantly chasing his breath as

well as Earl Whitely. Suddenly both men were brought to
a shuddering stop.

There Earl stood, in the middle of the playground, surrounded by children. And they were screaming. The
teacher, Mrs Jeffries, lay over as many of them as she
could, but she could only manage two or three. The rest
were frozen in place around Earl. A human shield. He
stood side on and aimed, Yardie style. The gun turned
through ninety degrees. He fired.

The bullet ripped through the air, crunched into the
concrete of the playground. Roots and Hogarth dived out
of the way on the road side of the gate. Roots gashed his
knee; a fold of skin now hung loosely with the ripped cotton of his trousers.

Still Earl continued to fire. Children screamed. But one
of them was still and silent. The girl furthest away from
Earl, closest to where the nine-millimetre bullets were ripping up freezing concrete. Nicki Harris.

Nicki stood alone by the swinging gate, the drawing of
her father clutched preciously in her hand. She hadn't
wanted to be with the other children, not after what
Candida Lloyd had said. So there she was, alone, miserable
and more frightened than anyone ever deserves to be.
She clutched at the swinging gate, holding it in front
of her, trying to close her eyes tight. But she couldn't
help staring through the mesh of the gate at the man
with the gold and the gun. She refused to scream or to cry
like the other girls. She was a policeman's daughter. The
girls always said she was different. Now she was going to
prove it.

Using his lateral vision, Earl spotted an opportunity.
On the other side of the playground was a red-and-
white barrier of some kind, like the entrance to a carpark.
Maybe for staff. His pursuers were cowering behind the
brick gateposts. Now was his chance. He sprinted crazily

across the wet pavement and hurdled the barrier, firing another shot.

Shards of broken concrete fizzed at Nicki and rattled against the metal mesh. One piece hit her on the chin. It hurt like nothing she could remember. But she didn't cry. Instantly, the girl decided that she couldn't stay where she was. She also saw her chance. She ran out of the open gate and into the road. There were two men lying on the ground outside. It was strange, but she couldn't stop. She just ran, with her drawing in her left hand and her right hand scrunched up as if she hoped it would make her go faster.

Earl discovered that he had jumped right into a dead-end alley. There was no option, he had to backtrack. If his pursuers caught him here, it would be a turkey shoot. He leapt back into the playground, and then turned sheer left and into the road, much further up from the other men. He ran for his life, skidding, slipping, banging against cars. He glanced back and made to fire again. There they were, burning down the road after him. Side by side.

Roots now saw Earl clearly. Perhaps fifty yards separated the two men. Hogarth too, at Roots's side, had a clear view. They instinctively crouched as Earl turned, still running, and fired at them. A windscreen right next to them shattered and a myriad of fragments showered upon them.

Earl turned back. He smiled, and was about to fire again when he noticed that one of the men had a gun. He couldn't keep his head still. He was running too fast. In his mind, in his near-hysteria, the gun appeared to move from the white man to the black man and back again. Perhaps it was two guns. No. Just one. Earl aimed. Suddenly, from between two parked cars, a girl dashed into the middle of the road. Earl pulled his shot, violently lifting his arm, so violently that the amulet from his right wrist flew off and clattered and rolled on the road. But still something crazy happened.

A shot tore through the air anyway. He hadn't fired it. He *knew* he hadn't.

One minute Nicki saw the man with the gold chains, then instantly, as if by magic, she saw the two men behind her, only now they weren't behind her but in front of her, even though she had made no attempt to move. She saw the man with chains again. And she knew — London wasn't falling around her, she was falling. She saw the school, the sky, the tarmac, the school, the sky, then finally felt the tarmac underneath her. The fingers of her left hand slowly opened, like the petals of a flower, and the drawing of her father was released into the gentle breeze.

By the time Hogarth and Roots stood over her, Earl had faded further and further into the distance. The two men saw one side of her head, still fragile, still beautiful. But from the other, where the bullet had exited, was the black-red of real blood. Roots was horrified and tried to cradle the girl, but Hogarth held him back. When Hogarth spun him around in order to drag him away from the body, Roots was suddenly inches from Hogarth's face. What he saw terrified him. For there was nothing there.

Part One

CHAPTER ONE

Darker than the girl's blood in the twilight, the river threaded its way through the centre of London. The City rose imposingly from the lengthening shadows as a million shimmering lights competed with each other to make the definitive statement about corporate identity.

And in one of the teeming office blocks, in one small room of one floor, unnoticed by the rest of London, a woman in her mid-thirties stood quite still for an instant and looked down at the Thames. She had an attractive face, and was certainly more attractive to other people than she ever believed herself to be. She had large, watery blue eyes, a fine nose and thin lips — the type of woman for whom make-up was rarely necessary.

From her vantage point on the fourteenth floor, the river was little more than a purple-black thread pulled by the tides through the heart of the City. She carried a brown cardboard box in her arms, stacked untidily with an array of personal possessions, as behind her in the cramped cubby-hole office a maintenance man unscrewed her name-plate from the door.

"Look how long you've been here," the blanched, overweight man said. He held up the six-inch rectangle of brass, upon which was engraved: ANDREA CHAMBERS.

"What do you mean, Jim?" Andrea asked.

"The wood."

The oak was two or three shades lighter behind the plate. It was as if old Jim had taken a fine brush and lacquered the rest of the door with a dark varnish. "Ten years," Andrea said.

"Won't be the same without you over here," he said. His ruddy complexion grew redder, as if he took Andrea's imminent departure as a personal loss.

"I'm only going across the floor."

"Yeah, but you'll be a partner."

"I won't change."

He looked at her, unconvinced, wiping the sweat from his brow with the back of his hand. "They'll change you," he said. "I've seen them. Twenty-five years. One minute they ask about your kids. The next they don't even look at you when you deliver the internal mail."

Andrea smiled a little. She knew the truth of this inexorable law of legal London: partneritis. The propensity to pomposity that going on the letterhead produced. She briefly reached out with her left hand, holding the box firmly under her right arm, and took Jim's hand. "Thanks for the warning." She added as he smiled back, "Can I keep it? The plate?"

"'Course," he said. "I was only going to chuck it in the bin."

They laughed together, and then it was time. Andrea looked back once more at the view she had seen virtually every working day of the last decade, one that she loved — not so much because of the river, impressive though that was, but because from her vantage point she could see South London. She had read in a weekend supplement about how in Zen philosophy it was said that the man might look at the mountain, but really it was the mountain that looked at the man. This was how she now felt: she looked at the city and somehow the city looked back at her. And this, too, was her experience of her career in the law, a constant merry-go-round of judging other people as they in turn judged you.

She walked out of the office and into the open-plan area. In the large, wall-less space, boarded only by the plate-glass windows on either side of the building, several dozen desks congregated in clusters around the various supporting pillars. VDUs, printers, miles of cables, multi-function telephones and headsets defined the working environments of PAs and the lesser lights of the law firm — the apprentices, the articled clerks. Muted strip lighting in crinkled plastic panels in the ceiling cast down an even, ergonomically efficient light; wrist supports on desks helped prevent Repetitive Strain Injury; the latest sight-savers shielded users from harmful radiation from the PC screens. Everything was designed to promote efficiency in the workplace and, as importantly, to prevent employees from suing the firm.

Andrea now passed the one aberration in this harmonious business environment. In the centre of the workspace was a huge tank of water, supporting itself on four crude cast-iron legs. The whole thing was something of a monstrosity, but it was the most treasured possession of the senior partner, so everyone pretended to love and admire it. Everyone except Andrea.

As she bent fractionally and looked at the grey-green water, other aspects of the office were distorted like the rooms in a house of mirrors, sometimes grotesque, sometimes funny. It was bizarre to see a self-important new recruit, an Oxbridge double first, sporting red braces, swept-back Hugh Grant hair, a receiver at each ear, conducting an intercontinental conference, while from Andrea's point of view a brilliantly coloured Korean fighting fish swam right past his nose. Andrea smiled and moved around the fish tank, and her image briefly flashed across his VDU. The articled clerk looked round.

"Miss Chambers," he whispered respectfully.

"Andrea," she whispered back.

He nodded nervously, unconvinced, and she understood. To an articled clerk, an equity partner was not of
the same species, but some kind of higher life form, supe-
rior and mysterious, the product of a decade of seventy-
hour weeks. Andrea walked on and finally 'crossed the
floor'. There was now a corridor which led off the open-
plan area, with conference rooms walled with mahogany
on one side and, on the other, what was for many lawyers
their final destination before retirement, pension and
death. Here another man, one she had never seen before,
was expertly engraving her name on the door. Not on to a
brass plate, but actually on the thick wood of the door.
The craftsman had a small pile of tools at his feet, what he
needed to lay on the gold leaf once he had finished her sur-
name. For an instant, Andrea's heart sank. To change an
equity partner you needed to change the entire door.

Over the years she had been into numerous
such offices, but it was different now that she was
entering her own. The room was at least ten times
the size of her old cubby-hole. On each side were floor-
to-ceiling bookshelves, and the end of the office was a
plate-glass wall of React-a-glass, which she knew
would darken in sunlight and clear as darkness
fell. She put her box on the desk, an extravagance of
power furniture, as large as the bed in her spare room
at home. She briefly rummaged inside and took out a
framed photograph. It was of a younger Andrea, from
perhaps a decade earlier, surrounded by children. A
kid's party. Hats and balloons. She wondered what the
woman in the photo would have made of this room.
She didn't have the chance to decide on an answer.
Just then another woman staggered into the room with
another box, this one overflowing with legal briefs.

"Where shall I file these, Andy?" the woman asked.
She had a trace of a Liverpool accent and was not the usual

blonde babe in her mid-twenties to be found in commercial law firms all over the City. This woman was thick-set, with short dark hair.

"Floor's fine, Siobhan," Andrea replied.

Siobhan dropped the box immediately. "Thank Christ for that," she said. The box landed with a muted thud, the impact cushioned by the thick pile of the carpet. She looked down at the carpet in amazement. "Jesus, that's softer than my bed."

Andrea smiled, then realised that she was still holding the photograph in her hand. She casually put it in the top drawer of her desk. It was not for public consumption. Siobhan was now captivated by the vistas of London that spread out beneath Andrea's window: St Paul's, the Bank of England, the heart of the City. She dashed forward and leaned her body right against the glass.

"A room with a view," she opined.

"Our old room had a view."

"Yeah, but that was South London. South London doesn't count."

"Thanks," Andrea said. "I used to live in South London."

Siobhan didn't appear to hear. "I'll miss sharing an office with you," she said.

"No you won't," Andrea replied.

Siobhan looked around. "What's the matter with you? Fishing for compliments?"

"No."

"Yes you bloody well are. Well, since it's the day of your coronation, I'll give you just one. You know that no other associate would ever put up with a sarcastic bitch like me as an articled clerk. So, yes. I'll miss sharing an office with you, Andy."

Andrea moved a couple of steps closer. "No you won't," she insisted.

"Have you gone soft or something?"

But there was no need for Andrea to reply. At that instant, two men struggled through the door with another, albeit smaller, desk.

Andrea took Siobhan's hand. "We're in this together, remember?" she told her amazed assistant. "I got a promotion. You got a promotion. I only accepted the partnership on condition they took you on when your articles end."

For once, Siobhan was choked and did not reply immediately. But she recovered her composure and put on what Andrea called her Scally scowl. "Shit," she said. "And I've been having interviews behind your back with all our competitors. God, think of all the grovelling I didn't need to do. What a bummer."

"You're right," Andrea said.

"Eh?"

"You are a sarcastic bitch," she continued.

The two of them hugged, but they broke apart when a man in his late fifties burst into the room. He wore a three-piece suit, Chester Barrie, Savoy Taylors Guild stuff, Church's brogues, and a striped college tie. Although he was greying around the temples, he had kept his body in good shape.

"Where's that memo, girls?" he said.

Siobhan immediately blushed. Andrea glanced at her and realised that she had forgotten.

"What memo?" Andrea asked.

"The memo. *The* memo. Hong Kong contract."

"I'm sorry, Mr Chambers," Siobhan began.

Andrea interrupted her. "Actually, it's my fault, Dad," she said. "I told Siobhan I'd do it."

Siobhan looked across at her in amazement. But Gordon Chambers appeared to be taken in.

"Don't expect any favouritism, young lady," he admonished Andrea. But he broke off as his attention was drawn to three men in dark suits striding through the open-plan area, directly towards Andrea's new office. As they passed successive work stations, people stopped what they were doing, became silent, or began whispering behind their hands. The men, two burly white men and a lithe black man, walked purposefully, looking neither to left nor right. A white man at the rear of the group was weighed down with a large briefcase.

"Who are they?" Siobhan asked Andrea.

Andrea shook her head.

"Let me handle it," Gordon said.

As the men approached, one or two people from the open-plan area hesitantly followed in their wake, but leaving a gap between them as if to make good their escape if necessary. They had now reached Andrea's office. Gordon edged in front of the box of files on the floor, full of ring binders annotated in thick black marker pen: OFF-SHORES; DERIVATIVES; HONG KONG.

The first man, the black man, began to speak. "Miss Chambers? Miss Andrea Chambers?"

"Yes?" Andrea could feel the muscles in the back of her neck tensing up. She glanced again at the files on the floor. She was convinced she had complied with the tangled web of regulations that now governed financial products. But she wondered if she had missed something.

"SFO. We've had a tip-off."

"Serious Fraud Office?" Gordon demanded, aghast. "What sort of tip-off?"

The black man nodded to one of his burly associates. The man with the briefcase laid it on Andrea's desk and snapped open the locks. There was some kind of recording equipment inside. The man pressed a button. Suddenly, to Andrea's astonishment, loud reggae music pounded out. It was a ghetto-blaster.

"We've been told it's your birthday." The black man smiled.

In a flash, Andrea's office was filled with other lawyers, paralegals and admin staff. They all chorused happy birthdays. The men adopted a triangular formation in front of Andrea's desk and began to strip very slowly, the black man in front, enticingly unbuttoning his white shirt to reveal his 'six-pack' of ab muscles. Bottles of champagne were popped open and everyone began to have a great time, except Gordon. Especially when one of the men's ties was swung in time to Bob Marley around the stripper's head like a lasso and then flew through the air and landed on the senior partner's shoulders. Andrea and Siobhan now had a glass of champagne each.

"Wonder who arranged all this?" Andrea asked.

"Don't ask me, gaffer. We don't grass in Liverpool," Siobhan replied.

"When they said they were SFO," Andrea said, "it nearly scared me to death."

"They *are* SFO," Siobhan said, laughing. "Strippers For Older women."

"Should be SFOW, then."

"Jesus, Andy. They're strippers, not rocket scientists."

Old Jim entered with a tray of canapés. He pushed his sweaty way through the milling group of lawyers, not bothering to offer anything to anyone. Finally, he dropped the tray on the desk and went up to Andrea, kissing her on the cheek.

"Twenty-one, isn't it?" he asked.

"Yes, I started here when I was eleven." She grinned back.

Gordon now moved a little way from the throng and positioned himself against the plate-glass window. He began to tap on the side of his empty champagne glass with a cake knife.

"Ladies and gentlemen, ladies and gentlemen," he shouted above the gossip. "Can I have your attention for just a—" He didn't complete his sentence for the room suddenly became silent. After all, it was the big boss talking. Gordon paused for a few seconds, building the expectation like an expert orator. "Unaccustomed as I am to making speeches . . ." he said. There were good-natured groans around the room. "I hope you'll bear with me while I make a brief announcement."

"Pay rises," a voice shouted from the throng.

"Yes, thank you, Siobhan," Gordon said.

People laughed.

"Was it that obvious?" Siobhan whispered to Andrea.

"No comment," she replied.

"Bloody lawyer."

Gordon was getting into his stride at the front of the crowd. "Today is a historic day for our cherished law firm. Ten years ago, my dear daughter left the rarefied world of the criminal Bar to become a City solicitor. To work for her old dad."

There was a polite round of applause. Siobhan didn't join in. Instead, she looked at Andrea, astonished. It was clear she didn't know that Andrea had once been a barrister.

"In those ten years," Gordon continued, "this firm has gone from strength to strength, and although we still have a long way to go before we can dream of entering the hallowed company of the 'Magic Circle' City firms, we are on the right track."

There was more applause at this, more enthusiastic than before. As Andrea gazed at the lawyers around her, she knew why there had been this increase in volume. This progress directly affected their lives. If the firm continued to climb its way up the legal ladder, salaries would rise, bonuses would grow, people could start to dream of grander homes, better schools for their kids, small villas in Tuscany.

"And today," Gordon announced, running his hand through his greying hair as he reached the nub of his speech, "another member of the Clan Chambers finds her way onto the letterhead. So, please," he said, looking about, "please raise whatever's in your hand and toast my newest partner."

There was a rapturous round of applause, and like the Red Sea parting the striped shirts, braces and Chanel for Women's suits moved before Andrea, so that a small passage opened between her at the back of the room and her father at the front. Gordon beckoned her forward, and she knew that she could not refuse — this was his moment as much as it was hers. The clapping continued as she moved forward, and words of encouragement and good luck were passed on to her from both sides. By the time she reached her father, he had put down his champagne glass. Not knowing or caring what the appropriate public behaviour was, Andrea hugged and kissed him. She could see that the old man, feared negotiator though he might be by repute in the City, had moist eyes. His voice was breaking as he spoke in a low whisper to her. It reminded Andrea of how he used to speak to her when she was a girl and used to wait up in bed for his return from the office, no matter how late it might be.

"I wish your mother were alive to see this," he said.

"I know," she replied.

She felt her father trembling, and she wished that he'd told her that he loved her.

"She would've been so proud," he whispered.

"Of both of us," Andrea replied.

When they broke apart, Andrea saw that the gap in the crowd had closed behind her. It appeared to her that now, confronted with the faces of fifty or sixty people, the room was becoming smaller. She couldn't tell if the group was closing in on her and Gordon or whether it was her imagination conjuring it. The faces began to blur the one into the other, and the gathering now seemed to consist not of individuals, but of one multi-headed organism. From many points within the creature came the same shout: "SPEECH, SPEECH."

Andrea froze. Suddenly her breathing became very fast and loud inside her head.

"SPEECH, SPEECH," continued the cry.

Andrea felt her head shake as if to say no, though she could have sworn that she had not ordained this. She felt herself coughing, spluttering. A hand grabbed her waist. She broke free, even though it was just her father.

"SPEECH, SPEECH."

But at the sight of Andrea's reaction, the cries died away. Now there was a heavy, embarrassed silence in the office. People stood about, trying not to look at Andrea, but they couldn't help doing so, and this made her feel infinitely worse. The awful impasse was breached when Siobhan grabbed a sausage roll and prodded one of the exotic dancers.

"Hey, Lionel Blair," she said. "Start dancin'."

The music started up again and people pretended to look away. Gordon put his arm around Andrea's shoulder. Siobhan rushed up.

"Is Andy OK?" she asked.

"She'll be fine, thank you," Gordon replied.

But Andrea knew what had happened, and that she could not possibly control it. It was precisely what had happened to her a decade before, in those days when she was still technically a barrister, the last time she had set foot in a courtroom.

CHAPTER TWO

Blue-and-white swathes of police tape blew slowly back and forth in the night breeze around the site of Nicki Harris's death. Bits of rubbish blew slowly around the pavements, and apart from the ticking-over of idling car engines all was quiet.

From the direction of the senior school an unmarked car pulled up. Two 'suits' got out, two members of CID. The first man, the driver, was the more expensively, but not necessarily the better, dressed of the two. His suit had the sheen of an Armani off-the-rack, or perhaps a very good imitation. His blond hair was swept straight back and he had a gold signet ring on the little finger of his right hand. Determining his age was not an easy task, since although he had the jauntiness in his walk of a man in his twenties, his face seemed more worn by life than that, more used. Perhaps he had just seen more than an average twentysomething. As soon as he slammed his door, he spat something on to the road and kicked it under the car with his shiny shoes.

Darkness had closed in completely. The winter city sky was illuminated only by the fluorescence of millions of artificial lights. More immediately around St Margaret's were many police vehicles: area cars, marked vans with riot shields, 'nondies' — nondescript or unmarked cars. Some had swirling lights which bathed the scene in red then blue. Many uniforms were there, ostensibly for crowd control, but in truth, on this late winter's night, there was scarcely a crowd over which to exercise control. It was just too cold and too miserable.

"Fucking sugarless gum," the first CID man said. "Tastes like shit. Like that alcohol-free lager. What tosser's going to drink alcohol-free lager?"

"I drink it," his colleague said, joining him from the passenger's side.

"Yeah, but you're a bloody college boy, ain't you, Kelso?"

His colleague did not reply. They slowly began to walk towards the police tape. The second man was shorter than Stevie Fisher, and had dark hair. With his steel-rimmed glasses, he gave off a studious, even contemplative air. The sort of kid who was always asking questions the teacher could not answer in class.

"You're a lucky bastard, Kelso," Fisher said.

"Kelsey."

"First day, juicy murder."

DC Mark Kelsey slowed to a halt and took in the circus of men and vehicles and lights and tape around the crime scene.

"This is what the job's all about, Kelso," DS Stevie Fisher continued. He breathed in deeply, smiling. "Makes you glad to be alive."

Further in the background, a line of six uniforms knelt shoulder to shoulder on the cold, wet tarmac and began an inch-by-inch search of the area.

"Poor bastards." Fisher laughed, displaying anything but sympathy for the boys in blue.

From behind the tape, a WPC approached them. Her red hair was pinned tightly back and she wore her point-ed cap low over her forehead.

"ID on the kid correct?" Fisher asked her.

The young woman's face, framed by the front of her cap, her flame-red hair and the dark serge uniform, appeared ghostly pale. She was so upset that she could not find the words to reply. She bent down so that she could get under the tape, but as she did so the tape got caught up in her coat. She lashed out at it and burst out crying. Kelsey moved swiftly forward and unhooked the tape, freeing her.

"Come on, Jen," Fisher said. "It's just a job, remember?"

"She was only eight," she sobbed.

"It's still just another job," Fisher insisted.

Kelsey's attention had been drawn to a piece of paper that had blown face up in the gentle breeze. He moved a couple of paces towards the roadside drain in which the paper had been trapped. Slowly, he squatted down and reached for it.

"Oh, Jesus," he said.

Fisher rushed over, leaving the WPC in his wake. In Kelsey's trembling hand was a child's drawing of a policeman with the two words written above the cop's helmet like a crown: M-Y D-A-D. The picture was splattered with blood.

The hunted Yardie, Earl Whitely, ran through a litter-strewn alley between the back gardens of two sets of terraced houses. Though his lungs were about to pack up and screamed to his brain that he should stop, his mind was frozen. His legs were weak now, and it felt as if he were running through water or sand, but still he kept going. He had just one thought. The one place in the area where he hoped to find sanctuary, somewhere to rest up and try to take stock. He crashed into a row of corrugated metal dustbins, and a cat, which had been nosing around behind them, ran off in shock. Earl got to his feet once more and saw the block of flats.

The building was separated from the alley by a wall skirting the carpark that surrounded the building to one side. Earl looked around. At the end of the alley was the main road, and his instincts told him that he should not risk so public a place. He would have to jump the wall. It would normally have been easy, but the muscles in his legs were the consistency of jelly. He decided to give himself ten seconds. Rest up. Regain his cool. That was what had kept him alive. In the circles he frequented, without that icy deliberation he would have no life. He slumped behind the rubbish bins and closed his eyes.

As soon as he shut his eyelids, the horror of the shoot-out at the school rose in his mind. It was bad. The worst. A girl had been shot. Probably killed, but he couldn't be sure. This would change everything. The shit would hit the fan. No one could stop it. A schoolgirl gunned down. His eyes sprang open and he cursed himself. What the hell was he doing? Lying against a wall in a stinking alley when they were probably looking for him already. He must have been crazy. He scrambled to his feet.

He leaned against the wall opposite, feeling the black, slimy wetness, and reached up with both hands. It was too high — his fingertips just made it to the top of the wall. He would have to take a run at it. He stepped back and leaned against the other wall, gauging where he would plant his right foot halfway up the wall to lever himself upwards. He fixed his eyes on the spot. In an effort to reassure himself, he swiftly remembered the many high walls, higher climbs, he had successfully nego-tiated when he had got away with burglaries, commercials and domestics — and sometimes he had had guard dogs snapping at his heels. This wall would be no problem.

He took a deep breath.

He lunged forward. Planted his foot, sprang upward, grabbed at the top of the wall with both hands. Made it. But it was too greasy. He briefly glimpsed the other side of the carpark. The rear of the flats. Perfect — quiet, safe.

And then it slowly disappeared from his view as he slid back down the wall. In his scrambling, something fell out of the rear of his waistband on to the cobbles beneath, clattering as stone met metal. Earl squatted back down in the alley. Picked up his nine-mil and checked that the safety was on. There was nothing for it. He would have to hold it in his hand as he attempted to scale the wall. He wiped his precious gun against his Calvin Klein classic-fit chinos. It left a dark, oily smear. He didn't care. He could always get another pair of CKs. He could never replace so sweet a trigger. He might have been born with it — the balance, the smoothness of the action. The nine-mil was his best friend, the only thing in the world that he truly trusted.

He leaned back again. With greater effort he launched himself at the opposite wall, and this time his foothold was perfect. Up he sprang, and even with the nine-mil in his right hand he managed to lever himself over the wall, falling softly into the plastic refuse sacks at the rear of the carpark. He quickly and expertly slid the gun into the rear of his waistband and sauntered towards the stairs that led to the first-floor balcony.

What Earl did not see was a woman in a house on the other side of the road. Watching him. Even as he banged on the door to the second flat in, the woman was dialling the police.

Earl pressed himself up against the door to the flat. "Calvin?" he hissed, as he held open the letterbox. "Calvin, it's me."

He heard nothing inside the flat and his heart plunged. In the flats on either side there were signs of life — television, people talking loudly — but in his friend's flat absolutely nothing. Cold sweat dripped from his temple. He shook his head, causing small droplets to spray off him, and began to devise a back-up plan. Perhaps he should take a minicab out of the area. But what if there were roadblocks? The Tube was too far away and too dangerous. There were security cameras on the platforms, and he couldn't be sure if that teacher in the playground had made him for a positive ID. As he bent down, peering through the partially open letterbox, squeezing his eyes tight, trying to focus, someone grabbed him from behind. Earl spun around, reaching for the gun in his waistband.

"Is what you trying to do, rude-boy?" Calvin joked.

Earl let his right hand drop as he squatted against Calvin's door. When Calvin saw the gun, his eyes narrowed. He didn't speak but fumbled with the bunch of keys he snatched out of his jeans pocket. The door key shook and he couldn't quite get it into the lock with one hand; he put a second hand on the first to steady it and the tip of the key slid in. The door burst open and Earl scrambled in. Calvin looked left and right, saw nothing, no one, and slammed it shut.

Once inside, he turned on Earl.

"What the hell're you doing?" he shouted.

Earl was bent double with the stitch that had been gnawing at his side ever since the shoot-out. He shook his head in fear as he looked up at Calvin.

"Earl—"

"Not here, man." Earl gestured towards the living room.

Calvin stepped past him, his anger now taking over from his fear. Earl followed the teenager into the ramshackle room, an adolescent jumble of music equipment, half-finished meals, dirty cups, clothes discarded on the floor. He reached for the remote control to Calvin's hi-fi and switched it on. He pumped the volume control and a rare-groove melody flooded the flat, not angry gangsta rap but smoother lover's stuff, more Calvin's style. Earl still had the nine-mil in his hand. Calvin marched up to him and hissed under the throbbing bass, "I don't want no piece in my gaff."

"Nah, man. Listen," Earl protested.

"Ain't nothing to listen to. No guns. Not here."

"Calv, there ain't no time, man."

"You hearing me? I know you's is Jamaican, but you better check out some plain English, Earl. I don't want no guns here." Calvin grabbed Earl's hand, the one that still clutched the gun. He hoisted it, so that the gun now occupied the space between the two youths.

"Calvin, I'm going down, star."

Calvin stared back impassively.

Earl continued, "Calvin, they going to be after me serious."

"You're full of shit."

Earl began to lose it. "This ain't no game. A kid, Calv. I think a kid got killed."

Calvin's grip on Earl's arm began to weaken. "What kid?"

"Like I know. Nah, just some kid. A girl. At the school."

Calvin wrenched the gun from Earl's hand. "You idiot. You fucking—"

"Nah, I didn't do it."

"Then who?"

Earl looked down.

"Who?" Calvin persisted.

Earl closed his eyes. Blinked. Sweat still ran down his face, down his pinched cheeks and high cheekbones. Both youths were seventeen. Calvin's skin was more of a rusty hue than Earl's chocolate brown. Both sported the 'fade' haircuts of London black youth, short and sharp, streetwise, with attitude. When he looked up at Calvin, Earl's eyes were wide, almost yellow. "Calv, hear me out, spar. If they nick me? See Roots Johnson."

"But you said you didn't do it."

Earl reached for the remote. He turned the music up. "Roots Johnson, Calvin." He took a small slip of paper with an address on it and shoved it into the battery compartment of the remote.

"Why?"

Earl moved even closer, almost nose to nose. "If Johnson don't bail me, tell him I'm going to the three dons."

"What?"

"The three dons," Earl screamed.

Calvin snatched the remote from Earl. In an instant the music was off, and the boys looked at each other in the sudden unreal silence. Calvin was about to speak when from outside the flat came a faint droning sound. Earl glanced round, began to panic. The drone became a wail. Of sirens. Police sirens. Earl collapsed on to Calvin's broken sofa.

"Oh, shit. Oh, shit," he sobbed.

Calvin looked down at the gleaming nine-mil in his hand. He glanced at the back door, then rushed to the window, edged back the dirty grey netting of the curtain and saw a convoy of police vehicles with lights blazing. He still had the gun. He looked at Earl, but his friend had his hands pressed to his ears, trying to keep the noise out of his head. Calvin rushed to the back door and undid the bolts. A gust of cold air blew in from the carpark. He turned his shoulders, coiling his body, then hurled the gun with all the fear and rage he possessed way out into the rectangle of night. He watched it arc almost in slow motion through the air, tumbling end over end, until it landed in the refuse sacks by the alley wall. From the front of the flat, the sirens were now so loud it seemed they were in the room. Earl still had his fists on either side of his head, like a boxer covering up. Calvin tore them away.

"Say nothing," he shouted at him.

Earl stared back, wide-eyed, his mouth open, salivating uncontrollably.

From outside there was shouting now: "Armed police. Throw out your weapons."

"We're going to die," Earl sobbed.

"Say nothing, man," Calvin shouted at him.

There was now a banging on the door. First a gentle knock, then a monstrous thud, and the door flew off its hinges. Armed policemen in flak jackets followed the truncated battering-ram into the flat. With semis and dragon lights they looked like soldiers from a futuristic war. Calvin shot to his feet and raised his hands in the air. A cop smashed him in the gut with the butt of his weapon. Pain exploded in Calvin's head and his legs gave way. He saw that Earl had been clubbed off the sofa and now lay on the floor as well. A dozen gun barrels were pointed at them.

"Fucking groids," someone shouted.

"Child killers."

"Let's shoot them in the eyes."

"Cuff the groids now."

Huge gloved hands spun Calvin on to his front and he felt Quikcuffs cutting into the flesh of his wrists and ankles. He saw the same happen to Earl before they were carried out of the flat like pieces of meat.

He closed his eyes as the men bore him down, the hard concrete of the steps inches from his face.

CHAPTER THREE

Roots Johnson watched from behind the iron railings of a basement flat as above him, at street level, a convoy of police vehicles screamed through the streets of South London like an army of occupation. There were motorcycle outriders in front of and behind the two Transit vans, and behind were marked area cars with sirens blaring and lights spinning, their drivers focused and composed, 'dominating' the road as they had been instructed to do in advanced driving courses. Roots knew that the officers sitting in the front passenger seat were likely to be armed, with a heavy piece of firepower just out of view below the dashboard. He watched, captivated. He remembered when as a boy he had seen a similar convoy racing through the streets of Kingston, but in jeeps and fortified land cruisers, manned by agents with sunglasses and crew cuts. One of the first American DEA raids to hit Jamaica. That was when his father was still alive.

The convoy soon passed and the street was filled with that intensified silence which follows chaos. Roots shook his head and sighed. Arrests, or at least an arrest, had been made. He wondered if it was Earl. He turned slowly and walked down the broken, uneven steps, past black plastic refuse sacks, a twisted bike frame, rags, aluminium cans. He was confronted by a steel door. There was no handle, no keyhole, no lock visible. He ran a plastic card through a thin groove to one side. There was an electronic bleep and the door sprang open.

The scene in the lab was much as it had been when he left earlier. Three or four Yardies lay prone on mattresses. With the noise of the door opening, they began to rouse themselves like bears with sore heads. Peckham was already up. Watching the cartoon channel on cable with a cup of something and a doughnut. He brushed some sugar granules off his Arsenal shirt.

"You seen them, Don?" Peckham asked. "Five-O all over the turf like a rash."

"I seen them," Roots replied.

He stepped over one of his sleeping soldiers and lowered himself into his director's chair. Next to the chair were two books: *Transactional Analysis* and *How to Make a Million in Music*. Peckham zapped off the TV, looked at Roots's knee.

"Don, you is bleeding, ya know," he said.

Roots nodded. Peckham crossed to the bank of microwaves on the far wall and reached for a small medical kit. He opened it, but in the dim light of the lab couldn't find what he wanted. He switched on a small light on a desk with two computer VDUs.

"Hey," the largest Yardie shouted from a mattress beneath the window, "cut that light."

"Get up, Lifer," Peckham told the huge man.

Lifer, who had been sleeping in his wrapround shades, glanced at his watch. He shook his huge shaved head. "Is still early, ya know." Then he spotted Roots sitting in the chair. "Yo, the don is back in town."

"Street report, Lifer," Roots said.

The huge man hauled himself up, leaving a crater in the mattress. He was the size of an American fridge. One with double doors, jammed full of sixteen-ounce steaks. Below his shaven head a tiny rat's-tail of hair tried to escape the rolls of fat that constituted his neck. He wore the 'colours' of the crew: American baseball shirt, baseball cap the wrong way round, loose trousers, a kicking pair of designer trainers. On his chest hung a thick medallion of solid gold, forged into a dollar sign.

"Nah, Don, that consignment of steel come," Lifer said. He kicked a wooden crate on the floor, a veritable arsenal of assault weapons: Uzis, Glocks, 'matics, Berettas, Brownings. He picked up a semi in each hand, postured with them as if they were fashion accessories.

"So now we wet the Mashango?" he said.

Peckham had made his way to the foot of Roots's chair. He inspected the gash on his knee.

"Cut bad," Peckham said.

"I'll live," Roots replied.

Peckham showed the small bottle of iodine to Roots. "You or me?" he asked the older man. Roots took the bottle.

"Don, when we gonna hit the Mashango?" Lifer pressed.

Roots slowly unscrewed the cap and then straightened his leg so that he could see the damage. He poured a small amount of the dark, evil iodine directly into his open wound. Peckham winced and looked away.

"Hear now," Roots said. "There's gonna be no more posse killing. Not for now. Not until I say."

Lifer loomed above him, blocking off the little light that emanated from the desk lamp and the flickering VDUs. "So what we gonna do?" he asked.

"We gonna think," Roots replied.

"Think?" Lifer said, aghast.

Roots nodded.

"Oh, Lord," Lifer shouted. "Now I feel sick, ya know."

With great exaggeration, he pretended to go weak at the knees and collapse on the nearest mattress. It broke the tension and the half-dozen men in the room laughed. Lifer reached behind him to a fridge under the computer desk.

He opened it and grabbed a six-pack of Red Stripe. He began flinging the cans around the room like missiles.

Roots reached for a corked bottle under his chair. He lifted it up and inspected the label: Corton 1985. He took out the cork, sniffed it expertly, held the bottle up to toast his crew, then put the neck to his mouth and drank heavily.

At that moment, his burner rang. He took the phone from his jacket pocket and listened.

"Mr Johnson?" asked the woman's voice at the other end.

Roots listened.

"Mr Johnson, it's Vanguard Records."

"Yes," Roots said.

"I'm ringing you back again," the woman said, "about your proposal."

"Yes," Roots repeated.

"I was wondering, could you come to meet us? I'm working late in the office if that's convenient."

Roots looked around at his crew, at the guns, and he thought again of the dead girl. He wondered where the white man, Hogarth, had gone.

"Is now convenient?" the woman asked.

"Yes," Roots said.

The kitchen was lean, cream, simple. The brochure that had been shoved through Andrea's Hammersmith letterbox had promised that the Shaker design would evoke the spirit of the pioneers and the prairies. In fact, the showroom was in Brentford, just beside the M4 flyover.

Andrea stood with Siobhan, peering at the dark, viscous sludge at the bottom of the dish.

"I just can't get it to rise," she moaned. She had crammed herself into a tight cocktail dress of midnight blue and a pair of strapless Italian shoes. "No matter what I do, it just stays there. A soggy lump."

"Yeah, I have that problem," Siobhan agreed. She paused, looked mischievously at Andrea. "With men."

Andrea burst out laughing.

"What the hell? It's meant to be your birthday," Siobhan grinned. "Who says you've got to cook?"

"Good point," Andrea said. "I must speak to my lawyer." But the smile disappeared from her face when there was a loud burst of guffawing from the dining room next door. The guests were waiting for dessert.

"Look, they're middle-class foodies, right?" Siobhan began. Andrea nodded. "That means they'll eat any old shite, Andy." She took the ladle from Andrea's hand and gave the gunge a stir. "Tell them it's chocolate soup. Delia's," she said.

Andrea's face lit up. "You are a gen-I-us." She pulled open a drawer, found a red sieve and put it over a glass bowl. As Siobhan held it in place, she began to pour.

"I didn't know all that," Siobhan said.

Andrea slowed down. "Know all what?"

"That you were a barrister."

Andrea tried to smile, and patted her hands nervously on the sides of her dress. "In another life," she said.

Just then there was a call from the other room. "Andy? Andy, darling?"

"His Master's Voice," Siobhan joked.

"That's what he likes to think," Andrea replied.

She walked through the arch, held the bowl aloft to the gathered guests and announced, "Chocolate soup."

Cameron, sat at the head of the table, queried, "Choc soup?"

"Colombian," Andrea replied confidently. "Delia's."

There was a small round of applause. It began with Jemma, the aerobicised New Labour MP, was taken up by Pippa, who was equally well toned but didn't seem to do very much at all, and was finished off by Pippa's husband,

Peter, whose ample frame burst out of his three-button suit at every opportunity. Cameron, an outdoor type, ruddy, sickeningly healthy, pulled up the sleeves of his thick Shetland jumper and eyed Andrea. She winked at him and they smiled conspiratorially at one another.

Jemma leant forward in her Christian Dior two-piece. Her hair was immaculate, never seemed even to move, yet Andrea could remember a time during her revolutionary phase at college when Jemma had a nose-ring.

"Oh, come on, Cameron," Jemma cried. "Drugs are the greatest threat to this country today. And the government's new drugs czars are determined to—"

"Drugs czars?" Cameron replied. "What do you lot know about drugs?"

"I smoked at the LSE," Jemma said, indignant.

"But you never inhaled," Andrea said.

There was laughter from everyone except Jemma.

"Come on, Andy," Jemma tried to continue. "As a mother. Don't you think we should strengthen the drug laws?"

Andrea looked back and was about to reply when Cameron intervened. "Oh, Andy isn't really into things *politique* any more," he said.

Andrea stared back at him. It was, she knew, her deadly look. Fair warning to him that there'd be serious arguing that night before bedtime. "No," she said. "I just cook for Cameron like a devoted woman should."

"Don't be sarky, Andy," he told her.

"Then don't put words in my mouth. That's my job. I'm the lawyer," she said.

She began to ladle the sludge out into their hand-painted bowls, for which she had bartered viciously in Assisi on holiday the previous year. An uneasy silence fell over the party. It was broken only when there was a monumental banging from the front hall. Cameron, trapped at the top of the table, began to stand up, although Andrea was nearest.

"I'll get it," he said.

"He's such a hunter-gatherer," Andrea whispered to Siobhan. The two women laughed. Andrea left the room first.

In a moment she was out in the hallway, with its boxed radiators and heavy, smoky mirrors. Ahead of her lay the front door, solid wood until halfway up, when it became predominantly stained glass, an art nouveau design of flaming flowers and abstract blues. It was the first thing Andrea had noticed when she came round with the estate agent a decade earlier.

She put on the chain. On the other side of the glass she could just discern a large, dark shape, silhouetted by the streetlamp. She slid the end of the chain to its limit and then fractionally opened the door.

In the darkness stood an attractive man in his sixties, with a black wrinkled face and a wild white beard. Particles of ice shone brilliantly in his hair. His eyes were fixed with worry.

"Rufus," Andrea said, shocked, and yet pleased to see him at the same time.

"Come now," the old man replied.

"Why?"

"Calvin needs you. He's been arrested."

"Calvin?" Andrea asked.

The old man did not reply. He simply nodded.

"I'll get my coat," Andrea said. She turned round quickly, undoing the chain, opening the door wider. "Come in," she told him.

"I'll wait here," the man said.

As the door opened, Cameron appeared in the hall. The two men stared at each other, but said nothing.

"I've got to go," Andrea told Cameron.

"Why?" he asked.

"My grandson," Rufus said.

*   *   *

Fifteen minutes later, Andrea's car, a cramped Korean hatchback, sped along the Embankment. The illuminated bridges of West London shot by to her right, reflected grudgingly by the sullen black water. Rufus sat to Andrea's left, arms crossed tightly, refusing to wear a seat belt.

"Are you sure it was murder?" she asked. "I mean, he was arrested for that?"

"That's what he tell me."

"How long's he been in custody?"

"He didn't say."

"Who was the victim?"

"I don't know."

"Didn't you ask? Jesus, Rufus, they might've interviewed him."

The old man stared hard at her. "I wanted to ask. I didn't have no time to ask. That bwoy *is* my grandson, you know."

A silence fell between them, and Andrea continued driving. She turned right across the river and drove into South London. There was little traffic and they made good progress. She jabbed at the wiper switch, just for something to do to break the silence. The wipers arced across the glass in front of them.

"I'm sorry, Rufus," she said finally. She could feel his eyes, large, slow and beautifully brown, studying her. She prodded her hair in a nervous reaction. "I know, I look crap and they charged me seventy quid for the cut. The bastards."

There was another pause. Then Rufus said, "You always look beautiful to me, darlin'."

"You old smoothie."

"But my eyes. They ain't so good no more."

Andrea laughed.

But the smile soon faded from Rufus's face. "You gonna get Calvin out?" he asked.

Andrea glanced at him. "I don't know," she said.

She pulled the car to a stop on the opposite side of the road to a police station. Earlier in the day this building had resembled a typical London station, with the pointed blue lamp outside, the thick grey stone walls, steps leading up to the glass entrance. But now there was pandemonium outside. A series of crowd control barriers was positioned on the pavement outside the entrance. Somewhere in the low clouds, the searchlight of a helicopter swirled, while its blades cut the air and made it virtually impossible to hear. Andrea and Rufus got out of the car. As they did so, a van with sniffer dogs, trained Alsatians, pulled up. The dogs dragged their handlers along the kerb, rising on their haunches and barking at the helicopter above.

"Is it Crufts already?" Andrea shouted to Rufus, leaning right over to his ear so that she should be heard in the din.

"I hope them dogs has eaten," he shouted back.

The helicopter moved off and the dogs turned their attention to Rufus and Andrea, barking in particular at the elderly black man. Andrea took Rufus's arm and the two of them crossed the road. They slipped through a gap in the barriers and began to walk tentatively up the station steps. But their way was blocked by two men in suits, DS Stevie Fisher and, slightly behind him, DC Kelsey. Fisher raised his right hand.

"Sorry, luv," he said to Andrea. "The shop's closed."

"But my grandson," Rufus protested. "He's inside. Calvin Patterson."

"You got any ID, Gramps?"

"ID? How you mean, ID?" Rufus cried. "He's my grandson. My blood."

"We can do a blood test, then. Can't we?"

Rufus stood defiantly in front of Fisher. "I want to see my grandson."

Fisher sneered back. "Well, I don't want you to see him, Gramps."

Andrea stepped between the two men. She tried to affect a smile, though it pained her even to look at the arrogant young detective. "Look, Officers," she said. "I'm Calvin Patterson's . . . er, lawyer."

"I heard he didn't call no lawyer," Fisher said.

"No," Andrea continued. "He called his grandfather. This gentleman. And he called me." She took a professional card out of her coat pocket. "I'm Andrea Chambers. Partner in the firm of—"

Fisher scrunched the card up in his hand. "Honoured, I'm sure."

Andrea turned to Rufus. "Look, perhaps it's best if you wait in the car," she whispered.

"You'll be all right?" he whispered back. "I ain't scared of no policemen. I know my rights."

She took his hand, squeezed it, smiled. She went closer so that the cops couldn't hear what she said. "If I scream, come running."

Rufus grinned and looked at Fisher, challenging him. "Tell Calvin I love him," he whispered to Andrea.

She nodded. She left Rufus at the foot of the steps and walked up to the glass doors that formed the entrance to the police station. Above the doors was the Metropolitan Police shield.

Once she had announced who she was, she was let through into the custody area at the rear of the station. Here she encountered the familiar sights and sounds of a custodial institution. Strip lights flickered, phones rang unanswered, men in uniforms walked with purpose in and out, and from the cell area behind the front desk came the desperate cries of an unseen prisoner: "You bitch, you bitch, you bloody bitch." A world of keys and chains and uniforms and the smell of stale canteen food, a male world that had always unnerved Andrea. Behind the counter she was somewhat surprised to see an Asian duty custody sergeant, with a neat side-parting haircut, a thin moustache and a precise, deliberate way about him as he paused to think for a moment before he filled in yet another form.

"I'm here for Calvin Patterson," she said.

The sergeant looked up, his forehead crinkled with surprise. "He didn't want a lawyer."

"He will want me," Andrea said. She handed over her card.

As he studied her details, another uniformed officer rushed into the custody area. He was an older man, perhaps in his fifties, with a shock of silver hair. Andrea could just discern little shoots of stubble on the man's chin. It had obviously been a long day.

"This is Patterson's brief, Super," the sergeant said.

The superintendent gazed at Andrea and she felt uneasy, painfully aware that under her camel coat was a tight cocktail dress, not exactly appropriate attire for the cell block. The super stared without saying anything.

"I want to see Calvin Patterson," Andrea said.

"Not now," the super replied.

Andrea shook her head slightly. "I'm not making myself clear. I'm his lawyer. I want to see him. He has that right."

"Right?" the super scoffed. "Of course, he has all the rights in the world. But I have an eight-year-old girl lying in a morgue. She has no rights, Miss . . ." He took the card from the sergeant. "Miss Chambers."

The mention of the age of the victim was like a blow to Andrea. She tried to regain her composure. She had to do the job Rufus had entrusted to her.

"I want it endorsed on the custody record, then. I was

refused access to my client."

"I've authorised that both suspects remain incommunicado pending swabbing for gunshot residue," the superintendent said.

"Gunshot residue?" Andrea asked. "No, something's wrong. Calvin wouldn't have gone near a gun."

"Then he'll have nothing to worry about, will he?" the man replied. "Nor will you." He turned to the sergeant. "Where's Fisher?"

"In the incident room, Super."

"Jesus *Christ*." The superintendent stormed back in the direction from which he had arrived.

Andrea was left standing rather foolishly in front of the desk. She tried to assimilate every new revelation, to grasp what she was dealing with, but it didn't make sense. Something dreadful had happened, and she began to doubt whether after all this time she was fit to cope with it.

"You can wait over there," the sergeant said. He nodded towards a bare wooden bench against the far wall. "If you're really nice to me, I might be able to get you a cuppa." He smiled and whispered, "We'll get you in soon enough, Miss Chambers. Look, it's a murder. People go crazy for a bit. But then it all settles down."

"Yes," Andrea replied.

"It always settles down," he repeated.

CHAPTER FOUR

In the incident room on the other side of the custody suite, Stevie Fisher stood over one of the dozen cluttered desks. On the wall were charts with pins marking observation points, aerial photographs of the patch, mugshots and notices. Rubbish bins were stacked high with Styrofoam cups, computers were left on, cursors blinking. Seated at the desk was an immensely overweight detective. He scribbled on the back of a postcard and then paused.

"What's the matter, Brigson?" Fisher asked.

"I can't do it with you watching. I can't make it as funny as you." He gazed up at Fisher and offered him the pen. "One of your famous dedications, then, Stevie?"

The offer flattered Fisher hugely, and he snatched the pen with a flourish, glancing behind him at the studious Kelsey, who was reading through the *Journal of Psychology*. Fisher picked up the postcard and wrote, reading out the words as he completed them.

"Welcome to the rest of your life. Signed: All your pals in CID." He looked at Kelsey for congratulation, but Kelsey continued to read, pretending not to hear. As Fisher paced across the room, a phone rang on Kelsey's desk. Kelsey went to grab it, but Fisher got there first, put the receiver to his mouth and said, "Wrong number."

"What are you doing?" Kelsey asked.

Fisher held the postcard right in front of Kelsey's face. "Teaching you. About the unit. Our . . . traditions.

Whenever we get a result. And the slag goes down. We send a postcard to their prison. Just so they don't feel lonely."

"You're all heart," Kelsey said.

Fisher ignored him. "This slag was importing horse. Turkish. Good heroin. We got him twenty-four years. Not strictly a Yardie gig, but they're all connected now. We share intelligence."

"I'm surprised you have enough to share," Kelsey said.

Brigson laughed, and Fisher glanced round at him with a lethal scowl. The smile instantly disappeared from Brigson's face.

"Where's the guvnor?" Fisher asked. "He needs to sign it."

"Still out on the prowl," Brigson replied. "But World of Pies was open." With this, he raised a bulging white paper bag, made almost transparent in places by the greasy pastries inside. "They got this new pasty. The Steak Stonker."

"Does the word BSE mean anything to you, Brigson?" Fisher asked.

"Actually, BSE's not a word," Brigson said. He took a large bite from a half-demolished pie on his desk. "It's an acronym, Steven."

Fisher was about to reply when the superintendent stormed through the swing doors to the room.

"What the hell're you lot doing?" he shouted. "Get down the crime scene."

The three detectives shot to their feet.

"We just got back from there, Super," Fisher said. "To interview the two bodies."

"There's going to be no interviews until the DCI returns. Now get back down the school and find me that bloody bullet."

Before anyone had an opportunity to make further comment, the super rushed out of the door.

"Welcome to the Yardie Unit," Fisher told Kelsey.

He drove both Kelsey and Brigson down towards St Margaret's. Most of the shops had metal grilles pulled down over their glass fronts, some even had solid corrugated screens. Every now and then there was a gap in a terrace where a business had gone bust or been condemned or demolished or burnt, probably in an insurance scam. There were flashing lights on some arcades, indicating that minicabs were available, their drivers leaning against the bonnets, chatting. If there were people around, they generally kept to themselves. If they loitered, they were likely to be pushers or prostitutes.

"This ain't the London I grew up in," Fisher said. He surveyed the street cabaret contemptuously as they drove slowly through. "Bit bloody different to that seat of learning you been skiving off in, Kelso."

Kelsey didn't take the bait and sat quietly in the passenger seat.

Brigson leant forward from the rear. "So it's true? The force paid you to check out all that young totty in college?"

"Something like that," Kelsey said.

"Bloody hell," Brigson replied. "I'm going to apply."

"Oh yeah?" Fisher laughed. "What're you going to study? Advanced pie-making? Anyway, you got to take a bullet or something first. Like our hero Kelso here. Get some sick leave."

"You took a bullet, Mark?" Brigson asked.

"Two," Kelsey said. "When I was at Vice."

Fisher pointed to a small corner shop, barred and boarded. "See that? Used to be Cohen's jewellers. My dad bought Mum's engagement ring from old Isaac Cohen. Last year? Two blaggers hit the place. Shot Isaac in the face. Unloaded both barrels of their sawn-offs. It was all on the security cameras. We never caught them. The community out there bloody well knows who did it. They won't tell us." He paused, then added, "Bastards."

There was silence in the car until Fisher turned the corner and neared the school. He pulled up at the police tape. But as soon as the three detectives got out of the car, they were surrounded by a scrum of both print and TV reporters who had gathered. As Fisher pushed through the mêlée of microphones and notebooks and flashbulbs, he smiled. He enjoyed it. Questions were hurriedly fired from all directions.

"Is it a cop's kid? Have two black kids been arrested? Are they Yardies?"

The three detectives bent down so that they could squeeze under the tape and into the relative peace of the cordoned-off area. Fisher saw that Kelsey was shaken by the media onslaught.

"You got to use them or they use you, Kelso," Fisher assured him. "That's what the guvnor says."

Kelsey walked a little more quickly. "So what's he like? The guvnor?"

"Hunts. Alone. Makes it happen. Like one of them wolves what's left the pack. These are dark times, Kelso."

"Kelsey."

"We get the heroes we deserve," Fisher said. "God, what'd they teach you at Vice?"

"That the Porn Squad was bent."

"Yeah, they committed the copper's two biggest sins. Bent and stupid."

By now they had reached the centre of the area. On the tarmac a scene of crime officer, a SOCO, was arranging white masking tape over a chalk outline. The SOCO stood up, having completed the job.

"Oh, Christ," Kelsey said.

There on the cold tarmac, in the gloom, was the outline of Nicki Harris's body. A crowd of gawpers had now gathered around the limits of the police tape, attracted by the TV vans, the arc lights, the police vehicles. Fisher nodded towards two black youths. They wore thick bubbled jackets and sported exotic bandanas.

"Mashango warriors," Fisher told Kelsey. "Look at them. Jealous as hell. Here's a killing they didn't do. Bit of catching up required. My money's on one of the other posses. Collect all twelve and get a set of steak knives free."

"I thought there were eighteen," Kelsey replied.

Fisher began to head into the crowd, calling over his shoulder, "Tell him, Brigsy."

As Fisher disappeared, Brigson said, "No, there're eighteen families what run Jamaica. A dozen major criminal posses. Five dons. Or were. Till three got snuffed."

Kelsey was only half listening. He carefully watched Fisher sparring with the two black youths. "What's he doing?" he asked.

"Bit of business," Brigson replied.

One of the youths appeared to palm Fisher something, and then the two Mashango vanished into the night. Kelsey kept his eyes fixed on what was going on, until the red-headed WPC they had encountered earlier approached him. She held up a clear evidence bag.

"We found a bullet," she said.

As Kelsey took the bag, he saw that the squashed stub of lead was finely traced with blood.

Andrea sat in a cold, sparse interview room. The dark wooden door was partially open, so that she was constantly aware that an armed policeman was propped on a chair directly outside, a dull gunmetal semi-automatic across his knees. She sat at a table, which dominated the small, square room. A shelf of recording equipment ran along the end of the wall. A stained institutional carpet led from

Andrea to the wall opposite the door, where there was the thick mottled glass of a security window. The room stank of stale coffee, a hundred stubbed-out cigarettes, sweat, people in confined spaces, under pressure.

She thought briefly of old Rufus, sitting in her car opposite the station, and she wondered how to tell him that his beloved grandson had been arrested in connection with the murder of an eight-year-old girl. She stood up as she heard the pounding of feet, marching directly towards her. The armed officer outside the door stood, placing both his hands carefully on his gun. Then, before she knew it, the door was flung fully open and two officers in white shirtsleeves hauled a young boy into the room. The boy's rusty skin sweated and he was cuffed and chained like an animal. He wore a white boiler suit made of paper. Andrea knew that meant his clothes had been sent for forensic analysis.

"Undo him immediately," she said.

The first jailer held Calvin upright. "Yeah? On whose authority?"

"I'm his lawyer," Andrea said.

Calvin, whose gaze had remained resolutely on the floor, now glanced up. For an instant his large almond eyes made contact with Andrea's, but she saw nothing in them, no recognition, no warmth. It frightened her more than anything thus far that evening. The policeman undid the shackles. When he was free, Calvin rubbed his wrists and looked at the first cop.

"She ain't my lawyer," he said.

The cop noticed Andrea's discomfort and smirked.

"What did you say?" Andrea asked.

"I said," Calvin repeated, this time more scathingly, "she ain't my lawyer."

"And who's she?" Andrea asked quietly.

Calvin now affected a broad Jamaican patois. "De

bloodclot cat's mother."

Andrea saw both the officers smirk. She knew instantly how to decode it: a white woman like this, she can't handle a Yardie. She looked down, and felt deep inside herself the wound that not just Calvin's words but his demeanour had caused her. Then she quickly looked up. Right into his eyes. Before she knew what she was doing, some more elemental instinct had taken over, and she slapped the boy on the cheek.

"What the fuck?" the first officer shouted.

Andrea wasn't interested in the reactions of the police. She stared at Calvin, and he could not hold her burning gaze. "He's my son," she said softly.

The two policemen began to edge out of the room. "You've got a few minutes," the first spluttered. "The DCI's returned. He wants to speak to you both."

Andrea looked at the officer, and so steady and focused was her gaze that he knew to shut up and leave. It always amazed her how men simply crumpled when confronted with a woman's anger. Now that she and Calvin were alone in the room, she went over and shut the door. Calvin stood at the window.

"I don't want you here," he said.

"You need me here," she replied.

"I can handle it."

"Like you handled your way into a murder arrest, Calvin? Is that how well you can handle it?"

Just then there was a faint knocking on the door and Andrea's head snapped round to see the Asian custody sergeant. He had two cups of tea in white Styrofoam beakers in his hand. They were wrapped in white paper bags. "Just thought you could use these."

Andrea nodded, a grin flashed across her face and she took the cups. The sergeant closed the door behind him and again mother and son were alone. She put the cups down on the table in the centre of the room and noticed that one of them was leaking. She took a tissue out of her coat pocket and placed it under the cup.

Calvin couldn't help but laugh. "It's only a cup of tea, for God's sake."

"Shame to waste it," Andrea replied.

"Don't tell me: waste not, want not."

"Or words to that effect." She offered the other cup of tea to her son and he came over, cupping the warm Styrofoam in both his hands as the curls of steam played off its surface. They sat down, on opposite sides of the table.

"I'm only here to help," Andrea said. Calvin didn't look at her, but concentrated intently on the watery tea. "You think I want to be here, Calvin? Well, I don't. I don't even do criminal law any more. But you need me here." Still he refused to meet her stare. She took a sip. "You need someone," she said. "The girl was only eight."

With these words, Calvin finally glanced up. His wide eyes blinked slowly. Andrea could see that her son was in pain but wasn't sure how to reach out to him. She was out of practice.

"It's a mistake," Calvin whispered.

"Of course it's a mistake."

"Then I'll be released."

Andrea's head dropped and she let out a sigh — not a reaction to her son but exasperation at the legal struggle that she knew lay ahead.

"What?" he asked with concern.

"It just doesn't work like that, Calvin."

"Then how does it work?"

The thought that shot into her mind was: Sometimes, it just doesn't work at all. But she stopped herself from scaring her son further. She was anxious enough herself.

"I need to know," she said. "What happened.

Everything. Especially about this other boy."

"Earl?"

"Who is he?"

"He's just my friend," Calvin said unconvincingly.

Again there was pounding in the corridor outside. This time it was louder. More men, walking even more quickly, directly towards Andrea and her son. She glanced over at Calvin and saw that he had narrowed his eyes. He bit his lip and stared hypnotised at the door.

"Say nothing," Andrea whispered, but he didn't appear to hear her.

A group of men burst into the room and fanned out around Andrea and Calvin. At the centre of the group was a huge man whose shadow fell over Andrea as she sat at the table. His eyes were deeply set in his imposing face and did not move, or blink, as he slammed a still-wet photograph on to the desk between Andrea and her son.

"DCI Hogarth," he said, so softly that it chilled Andrea.

Hogarth slammed another photo on to the desk, this time right under Calvin's nose. Andrea looked at the black-and-white image: the prostrate figure of a dead girl.

"On or off?" Hogarth said to Calvin. The DCI glanced at the tape recorder. "Your call, Calvin. On or off?"

Andrea stood up. "You . . . you can't bypass his rights," she objected.

Hogarth slowly turned back towards her. At his full height he was well over a head taller than Andrea. He looked down coldly, disdainfully, with hardly a gap between his lips as he spoke. "I want to bypass his going to prison," he said. "Now Calvin's probably a good lad — which means I can't say he's a bad lad. But his friend Earl is a killer. And Earl Whitely will shop him. Without blinking. Without remorse. Even for fun." Hogarth turned back to the terrified boy sitting beneath him. "So, son. It's your call. On or—"

"No," Andrea insisted.

"Off," Calvin shouted.

Andrea slumped down again in her seat. She tried to see past the bulk of Hogarth's body as he leant over the table and spoke right into Calvin's face. But Calvin wouldn't meet her eyes. He was lost in Hogarth's presence, looking helplessly at the huge detective.

"A murder's been committed, son," Hogarth said.

"He's not your son," Andrea protested.

Hogarth turned on her in a flash. Now he gritted his teeth, spat out the words. "No. He's yours. And he's in my nick arrested for murder." He turned back to the boy. "And murder's like no other crime, Calvin. You must understand that right now. It's . . . alive. Like a forest fire. And it'll consume everything in its path. So I'm giving you a chance. Right now. To get out of the way. A cop's daughter is dead, Calvin. Her name is — was — Nicki Harris. Eight years old. Do you know where she is now? On a slab. With a bullet hole in her head."

"I don't know nothing," Calvin said.

Hogarth banged his fist on the table. "Yes you do." He picked up the photo of the dead girl and raised it to Calvin's eyes. "The bullet deflected off her palate. Bounced around her skull. Exploded out of the back of her head."

"Stop!" Andrea shouted.

"Do you want me to stop, Calvin?" Hogarth demanded. The boy was frozen and made no response.

"Calvin!" Andrea shouted. "For God's—"

"Did you see that?" Hogarth pressed on. "Did you see Nicki die? A crime's been committed, son. There will be punishment. That's the law. That's . . . nature. Action, reaction. Right and wrong. But just now, it's you who's looking at a dirty prison cell for the rest of your life. So what did Earl Whitely tell you, Calvin? Was he boasting about shooting the girl? That's what your friends do, isn't it?"

"No!" Andrea shouted.

"They boast about killing people, don't they, Calvin? Tell your mother. Tell her about the guns and the killings."

Andrea tried to get up, to put an end to the madness. But the room began to blur in front of her. Wherever she looked, Hogarth appeared to be there. She felt a vice on her chest, compressing her body, refusing her air. Convulsions in her midriff bent her double, but still she fought for breath, tried to look up to see her son. Then she glimpsed him, throwing the Styrofoam on to the floor, sending splashes of tea across the carpet. In a flash he sped past Hogarth and held the bag over Andrea's mouth. He made her ventilate into it. Even through the pain, Andrea could feel her son's arms around her shoulders.

Slowly, her breathing normalised.

Calvin glanced up at an astonished Hogarth, who had backed off a couple of paces.

"Please," he said. "Leave us alone."

CHAPTER FIVE

Roots Johnson drove his white Golf GTi slowly through fashionable central London streets. Even though it was after normal business hours, this trendy area of media London was still buzzing. Lights still blazed in the offices of post-production companies, animators, casting agencies and record labels, as people toiled to meet impossible deadlines or conversed with the other side of the Atlantic. At street level, small cafés were open, and would remain open to serve cappuccinos and jet-black espressos into the small hours, while a throng of beautiful people gathered around the entrances, drinking on the pavements despite the cold weather. It was a million miles away from the South London Roots more usually frequented.

His young spar, Peckham, sat next to him in the passenger seat. He had an *A to Z* on his lap, but was rather more preoccupied with checking out the trendy women outside the bars and clubs. "Did you see that sister, Don?" he asked admiringly. "Longer legs than the Arsenal centre-halves. And they're tall mothers, ya know."

"Just read the map, Peckham," Roots said patiently.

"I'm reading, I'm reading," Peckham assured him. Then he broke off. "Oh, Jesus. Girl, they can't be real."

"Peckham."

The youth glanced down at the map. "Yeah, turn right — nah, nah, left here, left here."

Roots spun the car left and into a quieter street.

"Why I'm called Peckham?" the boy asked. "I'm from Dalston, Don."

Roots eased the Golf into a parking space. "Ya, man, but Peckham is worse, ya know." Roots grinned.

"Baas, I want a proper street name. I don't want me slave name no more. I'm a Yardie, too — seen?"

Roots laughed loudly, as he always did when this black British youth from North London tried out his patois. "No, sir," Roots replied. "A Yardman is born in the Yard. And there is only one Yard, you hear. And that is my blessed isle, Jamaica."

"Yeah, yeah." Peckham grunted miserably. "Shining like a jewel in the Carib-be-an. I heard it all before."

Roots looked out and saw the offices he had been seeking. There was a brass plate outside the black-painted door, with dusty railings on either side of five steps that led up from street level. The sign said: VANGUARD RECORDS.

Peckham looked about, confused. "Don, what is with this record stuff?"

"That's a secret between you and me, Peckham."

"Yeah, but it's a shit secret if I don't understand it."

Roots opened the driver's door. "You see that sign? That's the future."

"Whose future?"

"Ours." Roots paused. "In music."

The boy didn't appear to take it in. "Look, I can run drugs good as any gangsta. Seen, last week? Your mule what got shaken down by the police? Wouldn't happen to me. Five-O ain't never gonna catch me. He sidesteps, he spins, he shoots, he scores. Boom."

Roots's face filled with rage. He could feel his cheeks flushing with blood and didn't know what to do. He leant into the car, snatched the *A to Z* from the boy's grasp and flung it violently into the rear. These uncharacteristically petulant actions frightened the boy into silence. The two looked at each other until Roots spoke once more.

"Believe me, Peckham. You don't want to be no gangsta. I never going to let you run drugs, so forget it."

Peckham looked back with wide, sad eyes. "So what can I do, then?"

Roots tapped the roof of the car. "Guard my chariot good." He peeled a £50 note from a thick bundle in his trouser pocket and handed it over to the boy. "I won't be that long."

He shut the car door gently. He had decided to wear a Ralph Lauren jacket to go with his black shirt. With great deliberation, he smoothed the jacket out, took a deep breath, and then walked up the five steps. He pressed the grimy white button of the entryphone. He could faintly hear a buzzing inside the building.

"Yes?" came a woman's voice.

He bent forward so that his mouth was closer to the speaker. "It's, uh, Mr Johnson. I hope it's not too late."

"I'm on the phone to New York," the woman replied. She buzzed open the door.

Roots pushed the large door fully open with the tip of his index finger. Inside was a corridor with dirty walls, which had once been white. But the paint was old and peeling, and curls of it lay on the wafer-thin carpet. On the left-hand side was a locked door; to his right he could hear the woman's voice. He headed for it. As he turned into the doorway, he saw her for the first time. A little older than him, perhaps late thirties, a face that was once obviously striking, with unusually high cheekbones, but lines and wrinkles were beginning to dominate it. Her hair was shoulder-length, an indeterminate colour between red and brown, as if it had been coloured and styled too many times. But when she looked at him, with the phone receiver balanced expertly under her chin, he saw what had to be her real glory: large, cow-like, slow eyes, so gentle and warm that when she smiled at him he couldn't help smiling back. She gestured for him to enter and sit on a leather chair in front of her modernistic steel-and-wire desk. The whole office had a hi-tech designer feel, and yet it all seemed jaded, more eighties than nineties. This feeling was confirmed to Roots when he glanced at the framed discs and awards on the wall. They all related to the eighties. Finally, the woman put down the phone. She stood, reached over the desk and offered her hand. Roots stood and shook it.

"Hi, I'm Katherine Hamilton," she said. "Welcome to, er, Vanguard Records."

"Thank you," Roots replied. He noticed that she had an open bottle of champagne on the end of her desk. There was a glass in front of her, which was empty. She saw him noticing these facts; it appeared to unnerve her.

"Louis Roederer?" Roots asked.

"Yes," she said, impressed.

"Vintage?"

"Sadly, we haven't quite sold enough records for vintage." They both laughed. "Can I offer you a glass?"

Roots accepted.

She found another glass behind her desk and poured. "I was very interested in your business proposal. We're only a small indie label these days, but we have a good track into the States." She gestured to the accolades on the walls. "Past triumphs."

Roots toasted her deftly with his glass. "To future glories, then."

She toasted him back. "I'm looking for a new street sound. Something raw. Authentic. Something true. You say that you have these kinds of contacts."

"Nothing happens on the street without me knowing. But my . . . expertise really is in finance."

Katherine nodded and took a sip of champagne. "So how long have you been in music?"

Roots smiled. "Well, my mother used to play the gospel organ. On Sundays. Back home in Jamaica when I was a kid."

"Oh, I'm sure that can't have been too long ago." Katherine laughed.

Roots realised that he was enjoying himself. He liked her. He was beginning to sense that she liked him, and he liked that just as much. He spotted a silver-framed photograph on her desk. There was a bright, happy child in the snap, messing about in the snow in a Technicolored ski jacket. When he saw her, he couldn't help remembering the dead girl, lying on the cold tarmac outside St Margaret's. He wondered about Hogarth, where the detective had gone. All he wanted to do was sit in a darkened room and grieve. When he looked over at Katherine, he saw her glancing with affection at the photograph, but he sensed that the sentiment was tinged with pain.

"Pretty girl," Roots said.

"My daughter." Katherine emptied the rest of her glass. "She's in Canada. With her father."

"Looks cold."

"Freezing."

Roots leaned back in his leather seat, thinking again about the dead girl's face as she had appeared almost asleep, with the road as a pillow.

"Do you have kids?" she asked quietly.

He shook his head. "I would have liked a daughter," he said. "Or a son."

"Well, there's time," Katherine replied.

He nodded, but he was unconvinced. He knew how time was the one commodity that his peers did not possess. His mind flashed with an echo of the pain that the dead girl's family would be in at this very instant, and the knowledge that, though he principally blamed Hogarth, he had to take his share of responsibility. He looked up at Katherine and he saw a decent person. A member of that other species of human beings, through whom he moved every day to ply his trade, to do his deals. He was unclean, he could not mix with such people. He carried the cancer of his chequered life around with him like a contagion. He stood up.

"I'm sorry," he said. "I'm wasting your time."

Katherine shot to her feet on the other side of the desk. "No, no. We haven't even started to discuss business." When he shook his head, she continued, "Mr Johnson, I see one hundred people a month, and most of them are charlatans. But I'm too long in the tooth now not to spot someone who is genuine. If what you say about your contacts is true, and I have no reason to doubt it, then with those contacts and our marketing expertise, well . . . Look, I'm an instinctive person, which" — she sighed in embarrassment — "normally gets me into trouble. But I just want to talk."

Despite himself, Roots was won over by her earnestness. "Perhaps tomorrow, then?" he said.

"Tomorrow's good. When?"

"I don't know."

"Any time's good." She smiled. "Look, I'll walk you out."

They were silent until she swept past him, the empty glass still in her hand, and opened the door at the end of the corridor. She leaned against the yellowing wall as he passed by, inches from her. He tried to respond to her warmth.

"Nice meeting you," she beamed.

"You too."

"Does, uh, your mother still play?"

"She passed on," he said simply. He eyed the empty

glass in her hand. She toyed nervously with it. "Do you always drink champagne?"

"What's wrong with champagne?"

"You tell me," he said.

Roots Johnson looked deeply, unswervingly, into her eyes, and she returned the gaze with equal intensity. Something passed between them, and they both felt it, an unspoken chemistry.

"I *really* like champagne," she said.

"No you don't," he replied.

She half laughed, looked at the glass, then back up at him. "Why are you here?"

"I want to invest in music." The words rang hollow, and he knew that she had grasped the lack of conviction. So he told her the truth. "I'm sick of what I do."

"And what's that?"

He nodded slowly. "Accounts," he said.

She nodded. "That must be interesting."

"That's one word for it," he replied.

"Tomorrow, then?"

Roots nodded and started down the steps. He heard the door close behind him, and by the time he reached the door of the Golf he could make out Katherine's silhouette moving through her office. Peckham had the car stereo on at full volume, and the thud-thud of the bass shook the car on its tyres. But before he could open the door and scream at him, his burner rang. He stood against the driver's door and watched Katherine moving casually around the office, filing papers, then switching off lights. He put the cellular to his ear.

"Johnson?" the man on the other end whispered. Roots listened without replying. "Johnson, it's Hogarth."

"Yeah."

"Johnson, we need to meet."

"Yeah." Roots paused. Katherine had put out the final

light. For some reason he didn't want her to see him standing in the road. He spoke quickly into the phone. "You know where. Soonest time."

He clicked the phone off and opened the car door. Peckham's head bobbed as he absorbed the deafening vibes into his head. Roots turned the volume right down. "I got some business," he told the boy.

"So? I come with you."

"This ain't no business for no youth." Before Peckham could protest, Roots peeled another £50 from his roll. "Get the crew some rations."

Peckham grabbed the note and held it up to the overhead light. "It ain't a fake."

Roots got into the car and gunned the engine. "Did you hear what I—"

"I'll get Ronald McDonald's, innit?"

Roots turned out of the side street and into a busier thoroughfare.

"Don?" Peckham asked. "Can you drop me here? I know a girl in the next flats who keeps asking me to check her."

Roots glanced into the rear-view and then indicated left. He pulled into the kerb at the next junction. Peckham stretched out his Arsenal shirt and then popped the two notes into his padded jacket. Even before the car was at a standstill, he jumped out.

"Don't be long," Roots called out of the car.

Peckham smiled broadly. "I never is," he joked.

"Hey, Peckham," Roots shouted. "Look, all round here is Mashango turf. So you watch your back and get back to the lab direct, you hear?"

Peckham pretended to cuss, Yardie style. "Is you my old man now, or what?" he laughed.

Roots watched while Peckham swaggered down the street and then turned off towards some council flats set back from the main road. He worried for the boy in a way he had never worried for any of his other soldiers. When he considered it, it was perhaps Peckham's cheekiness and his boundless optimism which attracted him. In Peckham, Roots Johnson saw a shadow of his teenage self, or more accurately, the youth he might have become if the killings back home had not started.

He turned the ignition key and slowly moved off into the traffic for his meeting with DCI Hogarth of the Metropolitan Police.

CHAPTER SIX

Back at the police station, Fisher and Kelsey waited in the incident room for DCI Hogarth to decide on the interview teams for the two detainees. The bullet found outside the school had been rushed to the ballistics lab at the Home Office's forensic science service, but it was of course late in the evening, and the police would have to wait until the next day before they received a preliminary indication as to the progeny of the bullet. Many of the other detectives from CID were down at the scene, co-ordinating the legwork with the uniformed branch — the canvass, the door-to-door quest for witnesses.

Kelsey sat at his desk, diligently tapping away at his computer's keyboard as he logged on to the database his "actions" thus far in the investigation. Fisher, for his part, sat on a swivel chair on the opposite side of the desk, with his large feet on top of a pile of Kelsey's scientific journals. He flicked through one of them distractedly.

"So you're really into all this social psychology stuff, Kelso?"

Kelsey grunted, and kept typing.

"So what is it, then? Can't all be mumbo-jumbo if you studied it for a year."

Kelsey's fingers came to a stop. He adjusted his wiry glasses and stared with his deep blue eyes at the other officer. "It's the psychology of group behaviour that really interested me," he said.

Fisher ran a hand through his blond hair. "Yeah? What groups?"

"Any."

"That's why they transferred you to the Yardie unit, then? Gangs and all that."

Kelsey nodded. "Those with uniforms and those without."

The comment was lost on Fisher, who looked around him to ensure that the two of them were alone. The large room was silent and still except for the humming of computer towers and the flashing of screen-savers. Fisher carefully took an envelope out of his pocket and slid it across the desk towards Kelsey. The other officer picked it up, opened it gingerly and then put it flat on the desk again. There was a fold of used notes within.

"I don't understand," Kelsey said.

"Oh, well, college boy," Fisher said, getting to his feet and beginning to stride around the well of the room, between the desks, "let Prof Stevie Fisher explain." He picked up a pen and wafted it around like a pointer. "You see, Kelso, Joe Public pays us to police the mean streets of Gotham City. But Jim Public, Joe's naughty, naughty brother, pays us . . . not to. Look on this as a professional gratuity."

"That's what you were doing? Shaking down those Mashango?"

Fisher pointed with his pen at a row of mugshots on the wall, a collection of the squad's target criminals. "Those Mashango can afford it. Christ, one of them got shot last month, and he had BUPA. Can you believe that? So don't fret about the dosh. Take it."

"I can't," Kelsey said.

Fisher came closer. He glanced at Kelsey's VDU and prodded the power-saving button. The typing shimmered and then disappeared. Fisher sat on the desk above Kelsey.

"Let me tell you a story. Once upon a time, ages ago, there was this bloke. He was in a specialist squad. It doesn't matter which one. Well, he reckoned he was better than his mates. More what you might technically call honest. But do you know how many doorways we all go through? How many bullets we dodge? You can't have eyes in the back of your head, but you can have your mates. So this bloke gets shot. In the neck. Big bastard mystery. Three CID right behind him, saw FA, nothing. A tragedy for our times. Considering that he left two kids. One was four. The other only . . . let me see . . ." Fisher paused, affecting to download this detail from his memory. "Yeah, eighteen months."

"But my kids are . . ." Then Kelsey realised. "How did you know?"

"How'd you think? Look, I know people who know people at Vice who know . . . you. We're one happy family." He shoved the envelope towards Kelsey again. "So don't ruin the party."

"I can't."

"It's a trust thing, Kelso. I've got to be able to say to the rest of the lads: Yeah, this young recruit is kosher. In terms of social psychology, you're behaving in a very unkosher fashion."

Kelsey's head dropped and he closed his eyes.

Fisher whispered, "We've all eaten of the tree of knowledge, Kelso. Except Brigson, who stuffed his fat face. Don't worry. No one will know."

"I will," Kelsey protested.

"You can take it to your grave with you, can't you?"

"What if I said no?"

"We all say no. At first. Shows you're a good bloke. Then you'll say yes. We all say yes. It shows you're a good member of the team. We're all in this together. One goes down, all go down. This ain't a democracy."

With this, Fisher picked up the envelope, opened

Kelsey's fingers with his other hand and then closed them around the white paper.

"Welcome on board," he said.

Just then, Hogarth stormed into the room, his cellular in his hand. Fisher skipped off Kelsey's desk and stood upright in his boss's presence.

"Want us to go two and two on the Patterson and Whitely, guv?" Fisher asked.

Hogarth shook his head. "I'm releasing Calvin Patterson."

"Guv?" Fisher protested.

"We've got nothing on him."

"So?" Fisher said, confused. Abject lack of evidence was not necessarily an impediment in Stevie Fisher's legal universe.

Hogarth shook his head. "I don't want other lawyers sniffing around this investigation. I just want Earl Whitely in here. Alone. Do you understand?"

"Yes, guv," Fisher said.

"Besides, I've had a little . . . chat with our Calvin. I don't think he knows anything. I want to get him out of the nick."

A few minutes later, an astonished Andrea sat with her son on the same hard wooden bench in the corner of the custody suite as they waited for the custody sergeant to book Calvin out. Andrea's breathing had returned to normal, and Calvin's original grunge clothes had been returned to him. The Asian sergeant had provided them with fresh cups of tea.

"Thanks," Andrea said to the boy. "You know, for the bag." She tried to tease a smile out of him. "Some mothers get flowers for their birthdays. I get a bag." She paused. "I think I prefer the bag."

Calvin nodded distantly, only half listening. Andrea

tried to assess what he was looking at, but he was so lost in thought that it was impossible. Every now and then pairs of uniformed officers came in or out of the area. Someone shouted constantly from the cells, and even when this man screamed no one but Andrea appeared to notice. Here she found herself again after all these years, deep in the looking-glass world of the law. She knew that whenever you stepped through one of the portals of criminal justice, whether it be a court or a police station, the real world effectively disappeared. Now she inhabited that strange realm of accusation and denial, of claim and counter-claim, where the truth was usually irrelevant. Calvin had still not told her what he knew, no one had told her why he was to be released, but unquestioningly she sat and waited for the next act to begin. She just wanted her son out.

"You've put on weight," she said.

He looked at her, and finally seemed to snap out of his reverie. "So have you."

They both laughed. She couldn't remember the last time she had laughed with her son. When they spoke again, they were both quieter. There was less tension in the air, as if the interference down a telephone line between them had disappeared.

"You never come home," Andrea said. "Not since you moved into that bedsit."

"Yeah, well, that's my home now."

"Six months, Calvin. That's too long."

Again Andrea became aware of the ritual that the difficult years had erected between them. The cut and thrust as mother and son tried to get close, but never too close. Too close was uncomfortable, too close meant having to deal with the past.

"Know what I miss?" Andrea said in a lighter mood. "I miss kicking your butt at dominoes."

"I'm not a kid any more," he snapped, more as a reaction

than anything else, a stock response to any of his mother's reminiscences. "Anyway, I used to let you win."

"No, I used to let you let me win."

"I never understand what you're saying."

"Of course you don't. I'm your mother. So by definition you speak English and I speak some obscure strain of Serbo-Croat." She thought she saw the hint of a smile around the edge of his mouth. Then it grew. She decided to take a risk. "How's college?"

It was a mistake, one she regretted immediately.

"What college?" Calvin almost boasted, as if he would enjoy the discomfort the sentiment would cause.

"Oh, Calvin. Please tell me your father's still checking up on you."

"Yeah, he is." Calvin paused, to sharpen the next words it seemed. "When he's not knocking off a new bit of skirt."

The sentence hit home, and Andrea could not help but retreat into herself. As a silence fell between them, she reprimanded herself for exposing herself to yet more emotional buffeting. But she knew that she could not help it.

The sergeant returned to the custody desk and Andrea walked across the room to him. Calvin turned and put his feet up on the bench defiantly.

"I've checked with DCI Hogarth and the super," the sergeant said. "You can take him home."

Relief washed over Andrea's face. "Thank you, Sergeant—"

"Miah," he said. Then he whispered, "I'd keep an eye on him."

Andrea turned around and saw to her horror that her son was lounging flat out on the bench. "Easier said than done," she whispered back.

"Hey, Mr Patterson," Miah shouted. "I need your autograph over here." The sergeant waited until Calvin lounged over. "Please check that all your property's been returned and then sign here." He indicated both a plastic bag with the boy's possessions in it and the appropriate boxes on the custody record.

Calvin just signed.

"Don't you want to check?" Miah asked.

Calvin looked up with a surly expression on his face. "I trust you. You're a cop."

With that, the boy spun around and sauntered out of the station. Andrea smiled apologetically at the Asian officer and then hurried after her son. One part of her wished to express the anger she felt over her son being arrested without charge, but that could keep. For by far the overwhelming feeling that flooded over her as she walked with Calvin into the icy night air was relief. Simple relief. She wasn't sure why her son was free again. For the moment, she didn't care what the reason was. He had been in trouble, and she had been there for him. In the emotion ledger that all parents and children secretly keep, this would appear in Andrea's credit column and she knew it.

Rufus was waiting on the other side of the road. The old man repeatedly crossed and uncrossed his arms across his chest to keep warm, but this stopped when he saw his grandson. He rushed across the road towards the boy. Calvin pretended to remain cool, sauntering for a bit, until he could control his excitement no longer and he rushed to Rufus's open arms. The two hugged each other.

"Come, now," Rufus said, kissing Calvin's cheek. "We go home. My home."

"Thanks for being here, Gramps," Calvin whispered back.

Andrea watched this mutual display of unbridled affection. It wounded her deeply, and even though she tried to smile she hated herself for feeling this way. It was the most natural thing in the world for grandfather and grandson to love each other, but she knew that the past excluded her from sharing the moment. They still lived in the shadow of too much pain, and just at that moment Andrea was miserable, because she couldn't see how that sullen cloud could be shifted.

She joined the two generations of Pattersons. She had taken out her car keys and she jangled them noisily to stress the point she was about to make. "I could give you a lift home."

Calvin's head was still buried in the grandfather's shoulder, but Rufus turned and looked at her, his eyes moist and wide. "Thank you, darlin', but we can walk." He broke apart from Calvin, looked his grandson up and down with pride. "He's a strong boy. I think he can walk a mile if his old grandfather can."

"So long as I can sleep in tomorrow," Calvin laughed.

"Sleep? All you do is sleep. A generation is sleeping its youth away."

"But it's so cold," Andrea said.

"And it's your birthday," Rufus insisted. "Go. Have fun. Before them guests of yours eat everything."

Andrea sighed and laughed to herself. It seemed inconceivable to her now, as she stood in the crystalline night outside a fortified police station, that she had during the course of this same evening been worried about a chocolate soufflé. She wondered if the party was still in progress. While she was lost in speculation, Rufus had clapped his large hands around Calvin's shoulder and had continued talking. Andrea caught the tail-end of it.

"And then we'll go fishing," Rufus finished.

"You're always fishing," Calvin said.

"Yeah, and one day I'm going to catch something," Rufus said, bursting into fits of laughter.

"I'll believe it when I see it," Calvin said.

Again, Andrea found herself awkwardly standing and watching as grandfather and grandson continued their sparring routine. She felt decidedly surplus to requirements, wondering if they would even realise if she just melted into the night, not to see her son for another six months.

"Well, I'll be off," she said.

Rufus sped up to her as fast as his arthritic knees would allow. He clasped her in one of his spontaneous bear hugs, towering over her, and she realised again that, even though he was a pensioner, he was still a strong, magnificent man.

"Oh, thank you, darlin'," he said. "Ain't no one in this whole wide world I coulda trusted like you."

Andrea could faintly smell the warm, alluring smell of Jamaican rum on his breath, and she could feel the hard outline of the small glass bottle in the upper pocket of his coat.

"I'm glad you called me," she whispered.

"We'll sort that bwoy out soon enough," Rufus whispered back.

Andrea noticed that Calvin now stood with his hands buried deep into the long pockets of his baggy grunge trousers. He stared intensely at the pavement as he shuffled from foot to foot, ostensibly in an attempt to get warm. She remembered when he was a boy, how he'd do just this while they were out shopping, when he wanted a Bounty bar or a Marvel comic. It reassured her that he hadn't changed in this respect at least. She waited for the request, but when it came it was not one that she had anticipated at all.

"Earl hasn't got a lawyer," Calvin said.

Andrea stared back with a growing sense of foreboding.

"Earl won't ever have a lawyer," the boy continued. "The police won't ever let him have a lawyer." He tilted his head meaningfully at Andrea and paused, awaiting a reply.

Andrea froze. But from the inside. A different kind of chill that originated from somewhere in her gut and spread outward. "Oh no, Calvin, please," she said.

"You're a lawyer," he replied.

"Not a criminal lawyer. Not any more."

"You came for me."

"You're my son."

"And Earl's my friend."

"Calvin, please—"

"Jesus," he shouted, losing it. "You never do anything for me. Well, fine. I'll go to Dad. I always have to go to Dad."

Andrea saw red. She tried not to rise to his bait, but it was useless. "That's so unfair, Calvin."

"Is it?" he said.

"All right. All . . . right," Andrea shouted. She caught her chest beginning to tighten and she paused for a moment, tried to relax. This was the trump card that her son could always play against her, and she simply had no answer. She knew she had to go back into the police station. She glanced across the road, and in the icy night the yellow lights of the squad rooms burned eerily. Shadows flitted across them and a police dog barked. She would have to enter alone. To represent someone she had never met, someone arrested for the murder of an eight-year-old girl. Her stomach turned slowly. "I'll do it on one condition," she said.

"What?"

"You tell me the truth."

"What truth?" Calvin asked.

"All of it," Andrea insisted.

She watched motionless as her son walked right up to her. He looked around, suspiciously towards the brooding police station, briefly towards Rufus, now with a hint of shame, and then settled on Andrea. He had taken her arm, but more roughly than he could have realised, for his nerves and his fear were clearly in control.

"Did they say why they were releasing me?" he asked her.

"Not clearly," she replied.

Then he said, practically thinking aloud, "So the gunshot residue tests must have come back negative?"

"Yes," she said immediately. Then she picked up the unspoken nuance of his question. "Why? Shouldn't they? Calvin, look at me. Calvin, you're scaring me now."

Her son paused, then gazed up at her with the almond eyes she had fallen in love with the moment he had been placed in her arms as a child. It crushed her to see that cherished look in this dreadful place.

"He knows," Calvin said.

"Who knows?"

"Earl knows. Who did it."

Andrea was frightened. A terrible realisation crawled slowly over her body. She looked at her son, and despite every maternal instinct she was compelled to ask herself if Calvin was also involved in the murder of Nicki Harris.

A few seconds later, on the other side of the road, there was movement outside the police station. Andrea saw that DCI John Hogarth was leaving.

CHAPTER SEVEN

The derelict site was right on the river, little more now than a wasteland of strange lumps of bricks held together with cement, broken-down fences, high, razor-sharp and rusting, and the shells of the various rooms, with black, empty holes for windows. It was a total mess. Everything of the remotest value had been ransacked, stolen or destroyed for the sheer hell of it. But to Roots Johnson, this site was the very foundation of his dreams.

Roots sat on a broken wall now, a short distance from the black water's edge, gazing across to the other side of the Thames, the north bank, where there were more lights, buildings, warehouses and offices, but all these had roofs. He had put a holding deposit on the property, and was serious about buying it. It didn't bother him in the least that there was nothing here except the remnants of yet another mobile phone empire that had gone bust. It had been a school prior to that, and as he stretched his long, muscular legs out in front of him, and rolled his head in an effort to relax the tension in his neck, he imagined that he could hear the ghostly voices of preceding generations of children playing all around him. His eyes shot open. His body recoiled. There rising in front of him was the image of the stricken girl, smiling at him, reaching out for help. Roots Johnson put his head in his hands.

Then he heard someone moving in the ruins behind him.

"You're late, Hogarth," Roots said.

The crunching of Hogarth's huge feet moved closer, but Roots continued staring out at the oily waters as a fine spectral mist shimmered just above them.

"I don't know why you insist on meeting here, Johnson." Hogarth now moved in front of Roots and looked down at the black man.

"Because it's mine," Roots replied.

"So?"

"So one day, right here, I'm going to start building. This, Hogarth, is going to be the greatest studio for black music in Europe."

The detective shook his head pityingly. "Don't give up the day job." It was said with the habitual unswerving conviction that accompanied all of Hogarth's pronouncements. "I'm not joking, Johnson."

"You never joke, man." Roots stood to eliminate the disadvantage he felt by having Hogarth tower over him. He looked into his cold eyes. "Why you never joke, Hogarth?"

"I don't find life amusing," the policeman said.

Roots nodded his head slightly, but he wasn't agreeing.

"You got rid of the gun?" he asked.

"Forget about the gun," Hogarth scoffed. "The gun's my affair."

"Jesus, you still got it?"

"Think clearly, Johnson. What do you think's going to happen? Someone's going to arrest me?"

Roots felt his teeth grind. He had wanted the meeting to be a quest for clarification, the forging of a plan of action, but here they were in a dick-swinging competition. It annoyed Roots. "Last week. One of my mules got shaken down. By one of your men, Hogarth." He looked at the DCI, but there was no trace of emotion. "His name is—"

"Leave him to me," Hogarth said.

"You knew already?"

"No. But I know my men. I know them better than they know themselves. I know who it will be." Hogarth's rough hand rubbed his large chin. "Leave him to me."

"Now, I'm gonna ask you again, what's you cut, Hogarth?"

Hogarth used the sole of a plate-like shoe to push over a teetering wall. A cloud of dust mushroomed above the bricks briefly, then disappeared. "I don't want your money, Johnson. Why can't you understand that?"

"Ya, man, I understand it. But I don't believe it none."

"You're doubting my word?"

"I doubt everything," Roots said. His gaze was iceberg cool, but deep within him there was a faint glow of satisfaction.

"When are you hitting the Mashango?" Hogarth demanded.

"I'm not hitting them."

"What?"

"Don't you think there's been enough killing? The child, for Christ's sake. A civilian."

Hogarth folded his hands behind his back and walked slowly away from Roots. He stepped slowly over the rubble now, as if walking on eggshells, until he was right at the edge of the water. Then he turned round and said, "There are no civilians. Not any more."

"It's getting outta control," Roots said. "I've had enough. I want out."

Hogarth said, "There is no out. For either of us."

"Why not?"

"It's gone too far. The plan."

"The plan?" Roots shouted. "Oh, I know, this plan that says I'm supposed to get protection? From the police? From other posses? Well, that plan ain't working, DCI."

"You're just upset about the girl. I'm upset about the girl."

"Yeah? Well, you don't look upset, Hogarth."

Hogarth looked down, picked up a stone, and threw it so far Roots could barely make out where it disappeared into the river, though he heard the splash. Hogarth was silent for a moment, as if finally he had discovered some feelings.

"Look," he said. "Two years from now — less? — the international cartels will be on-stream in Britain. Do you know how they see us? As an emerging market. These are the only people to scare the CIA in twenty years. But the American market is saturated, so they want a piece of us. And your lot will be history. Unless you make a stand now. Show your strength. Convince the cartels they'll have a real war here."

Roots remained unconvinced. This was always the gap in the puzzle as far as his assessment of Hogarth was concerned. He had met one hundred cops over the years who had wanted a skim. He could understand that, as much as their greed and betrayals revolted him. But with Hogarth there was something that didn't make sense. "Why'd you care about . . . my lot?" he asked.

Hogarth shook his head. "I don't."

"Then who do you care about?"

Hogarth grabbed Roots's coat. "I have a kid," he said. "She's eight years old too."

Both of them were silent, and at that moment the human cost of their plan weighed heavily upon Roots Johnson's shoulders.

"Most decent folk," Hogarth said, "they want to live in Enid Blyton England. Where the international Mafia, the cartels, the mobs are a myth. They pay me to keep it that way."

"No matter the cost?"

Hogarth was troubled by the question, and his granite face appeared to crack into something more vulnerable for the first time Roots could remember.

"No matter the cost," Hogarth said. "That's why I know you've got to hit the Mashango."

Roots tried to look away, but as he gazed around the site he again believed that he heard the playful laughter and screams of children.

Further upriver, Rufus and Calvin made their way slowly home along the south bank. The old man walked perfectly upright, with his arms crossed tightly over his chest. The teenager, three or four inches the smaller, appeared shorter still, marching with his head down and his eyes fixed on the sparkling paving slabs beneath his feet.

"You worried about that ruffian friend of yours?" There was no reply to the old man's question, but he continued. "I don't understand you, boy. Disgracing your mother, hanging out with those gangsters." Calvin did not appear to be listening, so Rufus stopped walking abruptly, causing the boy to turn towards him. When he did so, Rufus fixed his large hands on Calvin's shoulders. "Bwoy," he shouted in a thicker patois than normal, "you come from a proud island people, you know. You act as if you forget this. But we are Jamaicans. And we are proud. Decades ago, runaway slaves fought the British back home. They brought us over in boats from Africa as slaves, but we left Jamaica for Europe as free men."

"I know, I know, Gramps," Calvin said sheepishly. "We were Ashanti warriors."

Rufus shook his head solemnly. "Yes, yes. Youth today know everything. So tell me, then. When the black man first comes to England?"

"Slave trade?"

"You see?" Rufus shouted, horrified. "You all go to bad because you been deprived of your history." He drew Calvin right up to his face, to his wild white beard.

"The black man first come to these here islands not as slaves, Calvin Patterson. But as conquerors. With the Roman army."

Though Calvin was frightened by Rufus's intensity and passion, he couldn't contain himself any longer. "Think she'll get Earl out?"

Rufus stepped away from Calvin angrily. "*She?* You call her she. Your mother is a living, breathing saint. And you call her *she*?"

"*She* walked out on me," Calvin said quietly.

Rufus did not reply. He was sick with worry for the boy. He desperately wanted to tell him the truth about what had happened ten years ago, but it was not his place to do so. Instead, he resolved to show the confused youngster all the love he could muster, even though he could see that Calvin was speeding away from the family, in the same way that Rufus's own son, Calvin's father, had done in his time. Perhaps that's the way of things for young black men in this country, he thought. They're not wanted here, so they expect nothing in return. A generation shorn of their history, their culture, their family — rootless, adrift. It was, Rufus knew, a tragic waste.

Grandfather and grandson continued walking, but now in a brooding silence. They walked through near enough the same streets that Earl Whitely had run through earlier that evening. It was all Calvin knew of the world, and to him it was home. But to Rufus, this land was a foreign land, even after forty years; this was not and could never be his real home. As he walked through the rubbish strewn streets, bounded by graffiti-daubed walls and intimidating estates, the old man yearned more than usual for a long, slow Caribbean sunset, for rice and peas, and for an altogether gentler way of life. Rufus Patterson had never abandoned his most treasured dream: to return to Jamaica one more time before he died.

Soon they arrived at a junction and some traffic lights that Rufus recognised with concern. A series of scary, half-lit alleys ran off from the main road in several directions, and he concentrated on one in particular, which backed on to Calvin's flats. He noticed that the boy's eyes had lost their street-cool indifference; now they were wide and sharp and scanned everything. He tried to follow where Calvin was looking, but the old man's eyes had deteriorated rapidly since he had retired from the post office some years ago — it was sheer vanity that prevented him from wearing his ugly prescription glasses. Consequently, the alley behind the flats and the carpark bordering it were little more than a blur to the old man, no matter how hard he squinted.

"Gramps, I need a slash," Calvin said.

"We be home in five minutes, son."

"Can't wait," the boy said as nonchalantly as he could.

Calvin began to wander behind some rubbish bins at the mouth of the alley. Rufus walked into a brighter pool of orange light on the main road to wait, but drew a sharp breath when he saw the front of the flats. On the first-floor balcony, by Calvin's front door, stood a man in dark clothing. He moved as quietly as he could to the carpark wall, edging marginally forward to get a better view. In the cold his arthritic knee cracked and he was sure that the man must have heard it, for the sound of the cartilage clicking burst like a firecracker in his head. But the man on the balcony did nothing. A couple of steps nearer and Rufus saw who it was: a single uniformed policeman. He began to edge back along the wall, but more quickly now, towards the mouth of the alley. From the direction in which Calvin had gone, he heard a clattering.

"What you doing?" he hissed to his grandson.

"What d'you think?" came the reply.

"Hurry now. The police is at your door."

"Watch them, then. I'm out in two secs."

Calvin used the opportunity to jump over the wall and into the carpark itself. He busied himself by reaching around between the mess of black refuse sacks against the wall. He was very glad that it was so dark that he could not see what he was groping around in. He held his breath, not just to avoid the odious smells, but in anticipation. It had to be there, but he couldn't find it.

"Calvin," Rufus hissed again.

Calvin kicked over a larger sack in desperation, and felt the smooth metal of the nine-mil's barrel. He tucked the gun into the rear of his waistband as he had seen gunmen do a dozen times at gigs. Then he hauled himself up and over the wall, using the sacks for a leg-up. When he thudded down to earth in the alley once more, he froze in abject terror. He hadn't put the safety on. In fact, he wasn't even sure how to make the gun safe. With the impact of his landing, the semi could have gone off in his trousers. He chuckled shallowly to himself: so that's why they shoved it down the rear of their waistbands. It couldn't blow your balls off from there. He exited the alley, pretending to do up his flies.

Rufus eyed him suspiciously. He sniffed the air around the boy. "Son, you tread in something bad?"

Calvin smiled back nervously. "Let's go home," he replied.

As they left, Calvin cast a casual glance at the policeman outside his front door. He didn't recognise the uniform from earlier, and the man appeared bored and half asleep. He took his grandfather's elbow as they walked, but with every step the boy could feel the smooth outline of the gun in his waistband, and he realised that his wise old grandfather was probably right: that night, he had trodden in something bad.

Chapter Eight

Andrea was led by the Asian custody sergeant through the security doors and into the cell area. On either side of the narrow corridor were cells, all but two of them unoccupied, with their doors open a few inches. The confined space and the shiny, smooth stone floor created a gauntlet of metal bars and cold brick, an echoing tunnel, in which her heels resounded loudly and her breathing could be heard clearly. It was an eerily lit place, with little or no natural light, but with electric bulbs everywhere, behind protective mesh. They would be on twenty-four hours a day. For his part, Sergeant Miah appeared to glide along in front of her effortlessly. This was a journey he completed a dozen times each working day. When they reached a final metal grille, he stopped and jangled his keys till he found the correct one. He turned and smiled, his neat moustache curling over his top lip.

"I hope you don't mind me saying, Miss Chambers, but you seem rather young to have a son Calvin's age."

The door slid open and they continued to walk.

"I met his father in the early eighties. At the LSE," she said.

"Early eighties? I was at Brixton then."

"During the riots?"

The sergeant nodded, then turned away. It appeared to be an uncomfortable memory. "We pulled a thousand black kids in three weeks," he said. "I can't tell you how many called me scab. Race traitor. House nigger."

"I'm sorry," Andrea said.

"Yeah, I was," Miah replied. "I was just doing my job."

Suddenly, as they passed the nearer of the two locked cells, something flew violently at the bars. Andrea automatically shifted her weight away from the cell. And then, with her back against the hard door of the cell opposite, she saw a man's desperate yellow eyes between the bars.

"Give us a fix," he cried, and it was the cry of someone in excruciating pain. "Jesus, I'm dying."

The sergeant was firm, as you might be with a wilful child, but concerned at the agony in which the prisoner cowered. "Behave, Irish," he said softly.

"Sarge, the ants. They're crawling over my face."

"Try to sleep, son."

The sergeant moved back to Andrea and then ushered her past the cell, with his arm around her shoulders. She didn't mind, was even grateful that his body was physically between her and the man in the cell. As they continued to the end of the corridor, she could hear the pitiful weeping of the incarcerated addict behind them.

"Withdrawing?" she asked, really for something to say to cover her nerves.

"Into a place we cannot imagine," Miah replied. "I'll call the doc if it gets worse."

The sergeant stopped as they reached the final cell on the left. Once more he jangled his chain and searched for the correct key. Chalked on a blackboard on the wall outside the cell was one word: WHITELY. The wicket gate, the square peep-hole cut into the centre of the door, had been pulled up. Miah manipulated it and it slid vertically downwards like a guillotine finding its mark. Andrea had to steel herself as the door slowly opened.

Miah whispered, "There's a panic button inside."

The door opened further and more of the dank walls of the cell were revealed. Andrea found that she was not breathing, her entire body tense, on hold, expecting the worst, entering this hateful place for she knew not what. She was confused as she edged into the cell, as at first she could see no one. It was only when she was fully inside that she saw him.

There was a frightening bang as the cell door slammed behind her.

Miah called through the wicket gate, "Remember the button."

Andrea glanced round, but no sooner had he said it than he was gone. Suddenly there was laughter in front of her and her head spun around. There, sitting cross-legged on the wall bed at the end of the cell, was Earl Whitely.

"Remember the button," he laughed at her.

"Mr Whitely?" she stuttered.

He sprung up from the bed in one lithe movement. "Don't panic. Don't panic."

He came closer. The cell now seemed infinitely small to Andrea as the Yardie circled around her.

"Mr Whitely? Earl? I'm Calvin's mother."

Earl looked her up and down lasciviously, smelling her hair, taking all of her in, even her ankles. "I can live with that," he said.

She turned quickly so that she could look directly into his face. He was darker than her son, though of about the same age. In contrast to Calvin's innocent almond eyes, this youth had stunning saucer-round eyes, which perfectly matched his high cheekbones. He was much taller than Andrea and, compared to the boy she still imagined Calvin to be, Earl Whitely was unmistakably a man. His skin was deep in hue, glowing, a dark coffee.

"Earl, this is important," she tried to impress upon him. "Calvin says you and his father is separated."

"Yes."

"So you got a boyfriend?" he asked.

"What?" Andrea was aghast.

"Figure you must like black men. Well, sister, I may be many things, but one t'ing I is for sure is black."

Andrea moved quickly so that she had her back to the cell door. She was as far from him as she could be, and with her lateral vision she spied the protruding red button with which she could summon Miah. Earl moved steadily in on her, landed an arm on either side of her head, his body inches from her.

"Leave me alone," Andrea shouted.

He shook his head. Winked. "They're taping," he whispered so quietly that even in such close proximity she could barely hear it.

He let his arms drop down to his side and tilted his head apologetically. She wondered if his performance had truly been just that, an act. They were silent for a few seconds.

"Calvin says you know who did it," she whispered.

He shook his head.

"Earl, help me. They're trying to send you to prison for the rest of your life."

With this he exploded, hissing to her, "I ain't got no life. Unless you get me out. You gonna get me out?"

"Then I need to know—"

"Whether I did it, huh?"

"No. Not as a lawyer."

"How 'bout as a mother? You need to know if I shot that girl as a mother? You want to know whether your son hangs with a child murderer? Or don't you care?"

"I'm only here because Calvin said—"

"Calvin said, Calvin said. That bwoy know shit. And you know shit."

"God, I must have been crazy even to see you."

"Yeah, run back to your boy. Before he gets even blacker on your ass."

"I better leave."

Andrea turned and banged with her fist on the cold cell door. Earl was right behind her. Breathing on her as he spat out words.

"Yeah, you better leave. You all better leave. Cause you're looking at a dead man. You understand? This ain't England. Your England. In these cells, your England don't exist. It never has. In here, you's dead. You's died and gone to hell."

There were marching feet outside and Andrea pressed herself against the door, straining her neck muscles to peer out of the wicket gate, but the corridor was too long. The marching grew louder. It appeared to be two men, not one. She kept banging on the door. But now she was aware that Earl had stopped talking. She glanced around and saw that the hard, streetwise Yardie had crumpled into a squatting position on his haunches. There were tears in his eyes, which he fought back. Her eyes sped around the room — the plastic mattress, the disgusting toilet bowl, a leaking tap. She glanced from the wretched young man to what could be the surroundings for the rest of his life. From above his hair appeared to be cut in a similar fade style to her Calvin's, and she imagined her son in the same cell. Her heart ached.

"Miss Chambers, Miss Chambers," Earl cried.

She squatted down next to him. The echoing feet outside grew louder.

"I . . . I never shot no gun. I ain't never shot no girl," he said, verging on hysterics. He looked up at her with wild eyes. "And . . . and they — you gotta believe this — they're going to kill me."

Andrea was shocked, frightened. "Who?"

But before Earl could reply, the keys were in the lock and the door flew open. Andrea glanced up to ask Sergeant Miah for a few more minutes, but instead of the

Asian officer Stevie Fisher filled the doorway in his flash suit. Earl stood defiantly to meet him.

"We rechecked your GSRs, Earl," Fisher said.

Andrea stood too, between the two men. She saw that Miah was behind Fisher in the corridor.

"GSRs?" she asked.

"Gunshot residues," Fisher smirked. "Doesn't your brief even know that, Earl? No? Well, here's the good news: you're positive. We're going to charge you with Nicki's murder when the DCI returns."

Fisher stepped back out of the cell and Miah shut the door. As he did so his eyes met Andrea's briefly, but he averted his gaze. The Yardie staggered back and slumped upon the wall bed.

"You *did* fire a gun?" Andrea demanded, fury driving her towards him. "You lied to me?" He did not reply. "I came here to represent you and you lied to me? Your legal representative?"

Earl put his hands over his ears, not wanting to hear any more. But at the same time he shouted back, "You can't represent me. No one can represent me. They won't allow anyone to represent me."

Andrea didn't believe him. She was not about to be taken in again. She banged hard on the cell door and shouted to the retreating officers, "Sergeant Miah, Sergeant Miah."

A minute later she burst out into the cold air. She was on the point of tears. This was why she detested the criminal law. Why commercial practice, for all its mind-numbing paperwork and oleaginous entrepreneurs, corporate bullshit, naked greed and ambition, was infinitely preferable to the real-life pain of crime. She pulled her coat tightly around her and felt the ice underfoot as she made her way down the steps at the front of the police station.

A crowd was gathering outside the station. Her car was

surrounded front and back by media trucks, full of equipment and support personnel. She stepped more slowly down to pavement level, and then had to find a way through the crowd control barriers. Word had got out, or word had been put out, that suspects in the Nicki Harris murder were in the police station. Andrea spotted a small gap between the barriers and moved towards it. But the wall of people separating her from the road would not yield. All around her were hateful, staring faces, strange and shrivelled in the cold.

"Are you the brief?" someone asked, but she could not see the questioner.

Andrea didn't know what to do. She didn't want to lie, but nor did she want to admit it, given the hostile vibes coming off the crowd.

"Nigger-lover," a man whispered.

Andrea searched the front of the crowd for his face, but all their features appeared to melt into one another in the misty darkness. Someone spat at her. He didn't hit home. He didn't have to.

She pushed hard into the crowd until a space appeared between one man's arm and the next woman's midriff. She forced herself sideways, squeezed through as best she could until she was suddenly beyond the group and in the road. She hurried across the road, fumbling at the same time for her car keys. Lights burned from the open back doors of the media trucks parked in front of and behind her hatchback. She slotted in the keys, opened the driver's door, jumped in and then over-revved the engine, grinding the gears as she manoeuvred the car out of the space. One or two of the demonstrators now followed her car, one man banging on the side of her window. She glanced at him in the rear-view as he shouted after her, but she could no longer hear anything.

Her eyes misted up. Even though the road was

completely empty, Andrea flicked on her indicator and parked in a side street. The energy had evaporated from her body and she slumped forward, her forehead against the hard, smooth plastic of the steering wheel. She squeezed her eyes tightly shut, but the images that flashed through her mind became more vivid, the hateful words shouted at her louder. She reached under the steering wheel and found two pieces of rock-hard chocolate under the dash. She wolfed both of them down. Then the weight of her cellular in her left pocket gave her an idea. She flicked it on and dialled home.

"Cameron?"

"Andy? Where are you?"

"On the way home."

"Are you OK? Is Calvin?"

"Yes. No." She paused. "Oh, God, Cameron. It was awful."

"Just come home, Andy."

She turned on the engine, at the same time propping the phone under her chin. "Cameron, just speak to me."

"Are you driving and calling?"

"Yes."

"Why?"

"I don't want to be alone."

From inside the police station, Hogarth had watched impassively as Andrea was swallowed by the crowd. He stood at the squad room window, and once Andrea had disappeared into the throng he pulled once on the blind cord. The world outside disappeared. Behind him could be heard the background hum of computers. A phone rang briefly, a steady ring denoting an internal call, and then was silent. Hogarth turned around, still in his heavy overcoat. Standing uneasily in the centre of the room was Fisher.

"Yes, guv?" Fisher said nervously.

Hogarth stepped between the desks and power cables until he was right next to Fisher. "Why did you join the force, Stevie?"

It was clearly just about the last thing Fisher had expected. His mouth fell foolishly open as he scrambled around for words.

Hogarth continued, "The pay? The uniform? Fighting the good fight?"

"Well, all the—"

"Me?" Hogarth said. "I just defied my dad. He wanted me to go into the army. Like him. But I thought: Hang on. We've got to win the war against ourselves first, haven't we? Broke his old heart." When he finally looked up at the younger man, his eyes were cold. "One of Roots Johnson's mules got taken down. Know anything?"

Fisher's cheeks reddened. A fine film of sweat gathered on his upper lip. "Er, no, guv."

Hogarth sighed, and when he spoke he was barely audible. "You didn't ask when. Or where." The DCI spotted a nervous tic at the side of Fisher's mouth, and he knew he had his man. He grabbed him roughly, backed him through the gap between the desks and slammed him against the wall.

"Guv, please—"

Hogarth slapped Fisher hard on the right cheek. He yanked his groomed blond hair so that his lily-white throat was exposed, then inspected Fisher's nostrils as if he were assessing a horse.

"You police the streets, Stevie. But I police you." His voice did not rise above normal conversational volume. "You think you're fireproof? Getting thank-you shags off domestics for putting their old man inside? Shaking down dealers. Tasting the product? And then you lie? To me? What do you think I'm trying to do here? If you're bent for the job, that's because the system stinks. But if you're bent for yourself? Then you're pond-life. You're a slag. Worse than the rubbish we go after — because you hide behind the uniform. And a real man would not do that."

By now Stevie Fisher was almost in tears. His body trembled and Hogarth could sense his subordinate's fear. His throat was still arched backwards, the neck muscles still taut. Hogarth knew that he could break this man, but he needed him. It sickened him to the pit of his stomach, but weak men were necessary to him to accomplish his plan. Weak men were fearful. So despite his instincts to rip out Fisher's throat, he began to stroke the man's hair.

"I'm going to give you a chance, Stevie," he said, letting go. "Because the squad takes sinners. This squad needs sinners. But with the right sorts of sins. It's up to you. If you want, I'll transfer you out. And I'll see that you push pens like all the other wankers till you're pensioned off."

"No, guv. Please."

"Or you'll do what I say. Everything I say. Anything I say."

Stevie Fisher blinked rapidly, stared fearfully at his boss, and finally nodded.

Roots Johnson could not get the chill out of his bones. Even though he returned to his lab with the heating in his Golf on at full blast, and even though small beads of sweat formed on his forehead, the Yardie don still shivered. As he entered the street in which the lab was located, he realised that he was hungry. He had not, in fact, eaten since breakfast.

He entered the lab looking forward to the takeout that Peckham would have bought the crew — so long as it wasn't a greasy burger. He hoped the boy would have been sufficiently influenced by the don to try West

Indian — Roots could almost taste the patties and jerk chicken. Inside, the other Yardies were checking out the racks of designer clothes at the far end of the lab. Lifer tried unsuccessfully to squeeze himself into a virgin-wool Armani jacket. Roots looked all around before he spoke. It worried him that there was no smell of food hanging in the air.

"Where's Peckham?" he asked.

The rest of the crew stared blankly back or shrugged.

Earl Whitely was let out of his cell by Stevie Fisher. The youth stretched out his arms, as if such a thing had been impossible inside the cell. He yawned casually and looked about. He was about to speak when the sight that met his eyes froze the words in his throat. Half a dozen white men in trousers and shirts were lined up in the corridor, three on each side. They all had truncheons.

Suddenly, from behind him came the ripping sound of thick tape. Earl tried to look round but huge white hands in clear surgical gloves held his head still, the palms clamping his head fast, compelling him to stare at the wall at the end of the corridor. He began to struggle, but more hands grabbed at parts of his body, his arms, his legs. The enclosed world of the cell area suddenly spun about him, and then he was staring up at the ceiling. The tape was lashed painfully across his mouth. Earl gazed frantically from right to left, from left to right, but all he could really see were feet and legs. His T-shirt was ripped off his body, and now there was a sickening sound that made him struggle even more, though he could not move as feet and knees pinned him to the hard floor. Every time he wriggled, his vertebrae scraped along the concrete. The noise grew louder, and he realised that it was the truncheons as they were hammered against the wall. It was a riot of noise, echoing, swirling around him, and in an awful flash everything went dark. He felt a heavy boot across his eyes. He could smell the rubber of its sole. But he could see nothing. And then he heard a voice in his personal blackness, so deep, reciting the words so slowly that it seemed to take for ever.

"Roots Johnson knows what you're up to," the voice said. "And so do I." The huge boot pressed more firmly across his eyes and his forehead. But it was expertly done and did not restrict his breathing. "We couldn't decide. Who should kill you."

The boot was lifted from his face and Earl saw the huge figure of DCI John Hogarth towering above him. He could hear his own pained breathing — mortified, hopeless, urgent. Hogarth swooped down, and now all there was in the world was Hogarth's face, and the hissing words, and the spittle raining down on Earl with each word, and all the time the drumming, the hammering of the truncheons, grew louder as the air was pressed from Earl Whitely's body.

"You wanted to grass me? To Internal? When will you learn, Earl? You're all alone. There is nothing but me. And this cell block. Do you understand? No one can help you."

CHAPTER NINE

The next morning, Andrea lay beneath her sweat-drenched duvet pretending to be asleep. Cameron was already up and marching around the bedroom brushing his teeth, which was a capital offence in their household since it was always Andrea who had to wipe the dribbles off the floors. Even though she held the square French pillow tightly over her head, she could just make out the murmur of the breakfast news on the television.

"Andy, Andy, it's your case," Cameron spluttered.

It drove her nuts to think that at this very moment little globules of foaming fluoride-enhanced toothpaste were heading towards the new 'Golden Biscuit' carpet, which they still hadn't paid off. She clamped the pillow more tightly over her head. Cameron came over to the bed, and she could feel the hard mattress yield a fraction as it took his thirteen stone. It was an especially hard orthopaedic mattress which Andrea had agreed to buy to help support Cameron's dodgy back, the legacy of a misspent youth playing rugby. He pulled at the duvet.

"Andy, your case is on the box."

"I'm asleep," she groaned.

"No you're not."

"I'm dead."

"You just look it," he said.

"No, last night I died and went straight to mother–son hell."

She was aware of him skipping off the bed, rushing into

the en suite bathroom, gargling, while at the same time zapping the volume control on the TV. With Cameron out of the room, she peeked out from under the pillow across to the small portable perched precariously on the cherry-wood chest of drawers. The brightness of the morning light stung her eyes and announced to her, joy of joys, that the new day had decided to greet her with a throbbing headache. On the box, a dyed-blonde reporter in a tight Burberry spoke earnestly into the camera.

". . . sources close to the inquiry confirm that the police have charged a young black man, thought to be an illegal immigrant, with the murder of eight-year-old Nicki Harris. Police refuse to release his name, but the suspect will be brought before magistrates at a high-security court this afternoon."

Cameron rushed in, wiping his face with a disgusting purple hand towel, embossed in one corner with his college coat of arms. He wore a blue silk dressing gown that was fraying at the sleeves. As far as Andrea could remember, he had always had it, ever since she had met him a decade before.

"Give me the remote," she said.

"Yeah, let's check the Sky report. Bound to be more dirt." Cameron eagerly handed her the remote control.

Andrea simply zapped the TV off.

"Hey!" he protested.

"They would say that, wouldn't they?"

"What? And I was watching that."

"A young black man. And you were meant to be brushing your teeth. Or those you have left, dribbler."

Cameron joined her on the bed. She lay back against the headboard. "Translate, counsel," he said.

But as Andrea told him what was on her mind, the jocular banter in which they engaged most mornings, as a form of foreplay, appeared distinctly unfunny. The cloud that had hovered over her last night from the moment that Rufus had banged on her front door now returned. She pulled the top of the duvet up to her chin defensively.

"I just mean, think about what they said. Young black man. Not young white man. But young black man."

"Oh, he was a white Yardie, was he, Andy?"

"No, but . . . Look, black man kills black girl? Sad. But it happens. Same black man kills white girl. Whoa. Hold the front page. Major media story. It just pushes all those buttons."

Cameron slowly got up from the bed. He wandered over to the curtains, his dressing gown trailing behind him. He carefully tied the curtains back on either side. He never did this. This was Andrea's job. As he spoke, he stared out of the window at the gardens beyond. "I thought you said, last night, that this Whitely guy lied to you. And he tested positive for gunshot residue."

"He said they were going to kill him."

"Who?"

Andrea paused. She didn't want to get into this, not when a throbbing head made her thinking fuzzy. But she knew Cameron well enough to realise that he would not let it rest.

Right on cue, Cameron repeated, "Who?"

"I think he meant — I know it sounds crazy — but I think he meant the police."

Cameron finally turned around. "Not if I could get to him first. For Christ's sake, Andy, she was eight years old. Eight. And you said he was a complete bastard to you."

"That's not the point."

"Then what is?"

"Race."

"Bollocks."

"Look, you don't understand."

She regretted it the moment she said it, and sure enough

it set Cameron off. "Oh, how could I possibly understand? I'm just a marketeer, who must be a racist because I don't happen to like the fact that a black gunman — there, I said it — shot a white schoolgirl in cold blood. Call me old-fashioned, but I think he's a total shit. And if he's convicted, I wish they could hang him. Which really pisses me off, because I don't actually believe in hanging . . . Which" — he came closer, more sheepishly, hands held up — "which makes me realise that you're probably . . . er, right."

He knelt beside her on the bed, while Andrea fumed silently, her arms tightly crossed over her chest.

"There," he said, submissively. "I shall throw myself at your divine feet and be your devoted sex slave all day."

Andrea turned away from him, tried to look out of the neat square lattices of the windows, but she couldn't control the smile that tickled the corner of her mouth. She grabbed his pillow, which was scrunched up next to her, then spun around and belted him with it. Cameron dived on her and tried to pin her to the bed, but she used her thighs to spin him over, then pinned his arms back behind his head. They were both breathless and smiling at each other, and she fleetingly wondered if there was time for a quickie before work. She glanced at the clock on her bed-side table, and saw her mobile. It reminded her instantly of the crowd outside the police station, the hatefulness, the name-calling, how she had needed to speak to Cameron from the car. Her smile faded.

"What?" he asked.

She shook her head. "God, it came back to me in about a microsecond why I left the Bar. And gave up crime."

"Your dad needed you."

"That was just an excuse." She let go of his arms and rolled off him. "All the lies. All the bloody lies, Cameron. And the pain. Real pain, seeing-a-dead-child kind of pain. And every time that DCI slammed another photo of that poor girl in front of Calvin, I knew I was getting further and further out of my depth."

"That DCI sounds a scary bloke."

"Scary? God, he was Keyser Sose."

Cameron laughed. "Can I have the TV on again? For the weather?"

Andrea found the remote buried in the folds of the duvet. She clicked the set on. As the screen crackled with static and the picture came into focus, she held Cameron's pillow tightly in both arms and rested her chin on top of it, loving the fact that it smelt of him. "Calvin's still in the frame as an accessory on the Nicki Harris," she said. "I just know it."

"How?"

"Look, a black kid's killed a white schoolgirl. Do you think people really care which black kid gets life for it? Or how many?"

"And how would you feel? If Nicki Harris was your daughter."

"Terrible. Sick. Devastated. But all I know is that I have a son. And he's moving in this Yardie world I know nothing about."

"So what're you going to do?"

"Find out about it," Andrea said.

Calvin slowly roused himself from a fevered sleep. In those instants while he drifted from dreams to consciousness, the world immediately around him was alien. He knew that he was sleeping on something hard, his neck was stiff, and he imagined that he was still in a police cell. Then he heard a reassuring voice.

"You awake, boy?" Rufus called.

Calvin's eyes shot wide open and he saw that he had been sleeping on Rufus's sofa, right in the middle of his grandfather's kitchen-living room. His fingers fumbled with the old sheets, then under the cushion he had rested his head upon, panicking until he found it. The gun. Earl's nine-mil. Relieved, he shoved the gun further down the side of the sofa and then closed his eyes again and nestled into the warmth of the cushion.

With his eyes still closed, he said, "You awake, Gramps?"

There were several clanking and stirring noises from the kitchenette as Rufus replied, "Couldn't sleep no good. That draught keeps coming in the windows, you know. Now, what you want to eat for breakfast?"

At the mention of food, Calvin's stomach rumbled. He was starving. He slowly eased his neck up from the cushion and rolled his head. "A Big Mac, innit?"

"No, no," the old man said, "this is a Jamaican household. You got to eat a proper breakfast, son. Now, I'm making up my special porridge."

"What? The one with rum in it?"

Rufus laughed. "Don't be cheeky, huh? You is cheeky just like your father." He poured some milk into a pan on the stove. "You heard from him?"

Calvin stood up, and shook his head. "He's still Stateside."

"Then how was he gonna get a lawyer for your gangster friend, Earl?"

Calvin replied sheepishly, "Mum didn't know that."

Rufus tutted loudly to himself, and battered whatever was in the pan as if it were to blame. "You don't treat your mother good, son. You can have lots of friends, but you only ever get one mother."

Calvin didn't reply to this. He had heard Rufus's entreaties on behalf of his mother so often before. The boy was wearing a pair of boxer shorts and he shivered as a gust of wind rattled the wide expanse of window in the high-rise flat. He pulled on his thick, wiry jumper, not bothering to put his T-shirt on underneath it. He walked a couple of steps behind the sofa and looked out of the window, at an identical tower block opposite. An Alsatian dog, locked out on a balcony twenty floors up, barked its head off. Below Calvin, South London spread out in concrete grey — railway lines, carparks, scrap yards and dismal kids" playgrounds. An InterCity hurtled towards central London, full of commuters with jobs, from the suburbs and shires, for whom this landscape in which Calvin had grown up was little more than a blur.

"How long d'you work for the GPO?" he asked Rufus.

"Thirty-five year," Rufus replied proudly.

Calvin shook his head and whispered under his breath, "Shit." His grandfather was the finest, most loyal, hardest-working human being he knew. All over the flat was the paraphernalia of his obsession — fishing — with nets and rods everywhere. Calvin thought it unfair. How could his grandfather have worked his guts out for thirty-five years just for this?

"What you say?" Rufus asked, craning his head to one side, so that his right ear, in which his ailing hearing was marginally better, was pointed towards his grandson.

"I just said, last night? The police kept calling me and Earl 'groid'."

Rufus was unsure if he had heard the boy correctly. "What foolishness is this?"

"Groid, you know, like negroid."

For an instant Rufus stopped stirring the porridge, and the old wooden ladle hung there in midair, dripping a thick white milky gunge. He blinked slowly, and his normally bright eyes appeared to Calvin to be wider and sadder.

"Gramps, I did what you always tell me to do. I tried to be strong. And I kept telling myself: Gramps says it's their problem. It's their fault. Not mine. But it didn't work. It always feels like my fault. And it always is my problem. They make me hate them."

Rufus looked up, concerned. "Hate? What good your hate does anyone?"

"I don't know. But my generation. We're going to fight back."

Rufus now came out from behind the stove and approached the boy. "Ah-ha, that's why you all have them guns?"

Calvin was stunned. He glanced over at the sofa, but the gun could not be seen. Yet somehow the old man knew. He looked guiltily at him.

"Calvin Patterson," Rufus continued, "I changed your nappies, and wiped your nose, and did your teas one hundred times. There ain't nothing I don't know about you." He moved behind the sofa, saw a rod on the thin, wan carpet, picked it up and flexed it. When he spoke again it was more quietly, and his eyes shone with tears. "You're all I really got in this country, Calvin. Your father never visits me, now he's a big-shot businessman. You're all I got to show for all these years. Make something of yourself, boy. Not for me, but so that you are something that your grandmother would have been proud of." He glanced across at the mantelpiece, where there was a picture of a striking black lady in an auxiliary nurse's uniform. The old man sniffed, turned and checked on his porridge. "See now? My porridge go burn."

Calvin felt disgusted with himself. His relationships with his mother and his absentee father were too complex, had been too fucked up over the years, to allow him to know how he felt about his parents. But for Rufus he felt nothing but love, and to see the stoic old man on the verge of tears drove a knife into his young, and usually impregnable, chest. He rushed up to Rufus and hugged him. He took the ladle from the old man's strong hands and took over the stirring.

"It's ruined," Rufus said.

"Nah, I like it burnt, ya know," Calvin replied.

"You is a dirty liar." Rufus leant over and kissed the boy. "But I love you, son."

"I love you too, Gramps."

The old man nodded. "So you'll take that gun outta my house?"

Calvin protested, "Earl told me to hide it. He said it might help him."

"A gun never help no black man I heard about," Rufus said sternly.

"But it might be evidence. Promise you won't tell Mum. Earl wants to play it his way."

Rufus walked over to the small fold-up table, on which he had a vice for making his own bait and artificial flies. He sat down and began to strip a multicoloured feather.

"Porridge is ready," Calvin announced.

"I ain't hungry," Rufus replied, deep in thought.

"Gramps, you won't tell Mum about the gun?"

"Then you better give me a good reason why not."

Calvin turned off the stove and joined his grandfather at the table.

Chapter Ten

John Hogarth finally returned home as the morning rush-hour traffic began to build. He had been on the go for over twenty-four hours, but the length of time did not concern him unduly. In his many years as a police officer, he had stayed up for longer continuous stretches on several occasions. But he could not remember when he had last felt so exhausted. The reason, he knew, was simple. It sickened him to think that he had become a policeman precisely to protect girls like Nicki Harris, and now she was dead.

The house was on the edge of Hogarth's patch, and in purely statistical terms it was in one of the less crime-ridden areas of the division, with fewer burglaries, street muggings and vandalised cars. But crime was still bad. It was still the major preoccupation of his wife and her group of ladies who lunched. It made neighbours regard Hogarth as something of a hero, their hero. It often made him feel a fraud. Karen had often begged him to move further out of London, or at least to the south-west, to Richmond or Wimbledon. But Hogarth lectured his men about the policing advantages of living on the patch, of knowing the people. His style had always been to lead by example, and he regarded it as hypocritical to move out himself.

The street comprised two rows of identical mock-Tudor houses, with little squares of lawn out front, and a driveway for off-street parking. The neighbourhood consisted mainly of lower-tier management or small business owners, a sort of

tribe whose ignorant bigotry and small-minded avarice normally made Hogarth feel sick. He had always striven to see
the bigger picture, to dream bigger dreams, and now he was
a DCI he was finally in a position to do something about
them. It was a test of nerve. He didn't intend to fail.

He noticed that the curtains were drawn and that the
papers, the *Telegraph* and the *Mail*, were still on the
doorstep. He opened the door, bent down to pick them up,
and entered. It was dark indoors.

"Karen?" he called.

There was no response. He turned to his left and stood
in the entrance to the living room, but could see little in
the murk. Then suddenly there was a pounding of small
feet down the stairs on the right-hand side of the hall.
He turned around just in time to see his daughter leap on
him. Abby was a frail girl, with something of her father's
intensity, despite her youthfulness. With the physical
exertion of jumping upon her father, she began to cough
dryly. She joined her thin arms round his neck and he
swung her round.

"Hello, angel," he said. Then he really looked at her,
and even though she looked nothing like Nicki Harris, his
heart ached. "You really are my winged angel."

"Daaad," she protested, although it was crystal clear to
Hogarth that she loved his attention.

He put her down. "Where's your mother?"

"In bed," Abby said, matter-of-factly, adding, "Again."

Hogarth noticed that the girl had an old sheet draped
over her school uniform. There was a faint Hindu mark in
the middle of her forehead. "What's going on, Abby?"

"We're studying Dipawali," she yawned. "It's so boring."

Hogarth squatted down to her level. He gently put
one of his huge fingers under her chin, forcing her to
gaze at him. "It's really important, Ab. To understand.
Other people."

"Yes, Dad," she said.

Her reply was a little too regimented for his liking, and he hoped again that he had taught his daughter to agree with him through understanding rather than fear. He checked her forehead with the back of his hand. She was running a higher temperature than usual.

"Have you taken your medicine?" he asked.

Before she could reply, there was the honking of a car horn from outside. Abby rushed to the door and reached up to open it. The morning breeze blew the door further open as she pulled on her mac, and Hogarth could see one of their neighbours smiling and waving from her lurid-coloured 'people carrier' outside. It was the school run.

"Bye, Dad," Abby said, and then dashed out, slamming the door behind her.

Hogarth was alone again in the hall. He whispered after her, "Perhaps you should stay home."

He waited in the half-darkness of the hallway until the sound of the vehicle containing his daughter had faded. Then he steeled himself for the meeting with his wife.

The bedroom was in total darkness, and had the still, stuffy smell of a room that had not been aired. In the shafts of light that poured into the room from the corridor, Hogarth could discern his wife's outline curled in the sheets. He approached her slowly, remarkably quietly for a man of his immense stature, but then he had crept up upon things all his life. On reaching the side of the bed, he bent down and felt under the frame. He found it immediately. A bottle. Valium, tranqs, drugs by any other name, but a medically approved way for women of a certain age to escape from the disappointing reality of their lives, or at least to desensitise themselves to it. The bottle was half empty. Next to the bed, strewn carelessly across the floor, were glossy travel brochures for exotic holidays. In the dim light, Hogarth could just discern some of the names:

Fiji, Martinique, the Seychelles. He kicked the magazines under the bed. He knew this was a dream holiday they would never have. At least, not together.

"John?" Karen whispered.

Although still wearing his heavy coat, Hogarth crumpled on to the bed next to her. She rolled over and put the light on. As she spoke, he determinedly did not look at her.

"John, what is it?"

"A cop's daughter," he said.

She moved over and hugged him tightly, even rocked him like a huge child. For as a result of their years together, and the repeated horrors of his job, they had unwittingly created a shorthand between them, a way of ventilating the dreadful thoughts that assailed his mind without his having to describe them in depth. He found, however, that now he could not return her affection, even though he needed the intimacy, the concern of another human being. Their love was used up. How, he did not truly understand, but that was the fact, and John Hogarth dealt with facts. He took the bottle of pills and put them in his coat pocket as he stood up.

"You don't need these," he said.

"Yes I do."

"Why?"

Karen was hurting so much that she couldn't contain herself. "Because I don't have you," she said.

Hogarth reached behind him and pushed the door further ajar. He turned to go, not able to watch her grief. But her words stopped him.

"John, what happened to you? You just can't speak to ordinary people any more, can you? No, you spend your life with criminals and cops and you've forgotten how to come home. Even when you walk right through that door after your shift, you're not home, John. You're not really here. You're still stuck on this ice-cold, far-off planet. And you're there all alone, John. All alone."

For his part, Hogarth recognised the truth of this. But as he had discovered professionally, in the face of the absolute truth there was often nothing of significance to say. "I'll make some tea, then."

"John, please," Karen cried.

"Do we have any milk?"

"John," she wept, "please don't go."

But it was too late.

Later that morning, Hogarth had showered and shaved, and stood in front of his squad, about to brief his men. The incident room was packed. There was a haphazard semi-circle of chairs, upon which a dozen men sat, but there was not enough room for all of them and other detectives stood behind, amid the desks with steaming cups of coffee and tea. At the centre of the group, standing at the blackboard, was Hogarth. He was about to begin when DS Stevie Fisher skulked into the room. Fisher knew that his late arrival was not lost on the boss.

"Sorry, guv," Fisher said. He waved a couple of sheets of shiny paper in apology. "Faxes."

Hogarth did not respond. He paused until the excited hubbub died down. He surveyed his men — they were precisely that, all men — and he tried to imagine them not just as detectives on a mean pay scale, but as his troops. He knew that the secret war he had been waging must now inevitably enter a critical stage, for the shooting of the previous day was a point of no return. John Hogarth had read many textbooks about the theory and practice not just of policing but of warfare, because that was precisely how he saw the invasion of drugs into his beloved London. He had read about the great generals and the decisive battles of history: of Alexander, of Hannibal and Scipio, the

Peloponnesian wars, Napoleon's brilliant retreat at Austerlitz, and, even more stunningly recounted in Tolstoy's *War and Peace*, the Russian Kutuzov's retreat past Moscow. In particular Hogarth had devoured time and again, sometimes in one sitting, Sun Tzu's *Art of War*, the ancient Chinese handbook, thousands of years old. It was all a painstaking preparation for the greatest contest of his life, if only he could keep his nerve. Hogarth understood that sometimes civil populations had to be sacrificed, or at least parts of them, that the populace itself was sometimes the most potent weapon, to enrage, to incite, to create the iron will necessary for a successful campaign. All this he understood, but now as he stood before his men, he could not get the spectre of an eight-year-old girl out of his mind. He scanned mentally through every ruthless theory of warfare, but none consoled him one jot.

The men were becoming uneasy, glancing at one another, as their boss stood silently before them. Finally, it was the obese Brigson who spoke. He put up his fat hand gingerly. As usual, it contained a half-eaten pie.

"Guv? What's the position regarding Earl Whitely?"

Hogarth ran his tongue over his bottom lip and realised how dry it had become. Again, this was not usual. It was as though his body and his mind were rebelling in a dozen ways, each designed to give him away, and he were struggling to contain them.

"Since we . . . spoke to him last night . . ." Hogarth began.

The lads jeered. Or rather, all of them did except the newest recruit, Mark Kelsey. Kelsey intrigued the DCI, and he had specifically endorsed the youngster's application to his squad. Kelsey had taken two bullets, and yet had the strength of character not to bitch about them but to learn from his wounds. He had the focus and tunnel vision of a pilgrim, the conviction of an inquisitor. He reminded John

Hogarth of himself, a decade and a half before.

The jeering continued.

"Keep it down," Hogarth said. "Whitely's up before the beak at fourteen hundred today. He won't apply for bail. But if any witnesses come forward, if they contact the inquiry line, I want them brought in. Down here. In the nick. No cosy statements in their homes with tea and chocolate Hobnobs."

The men chuckled sycophantically. Kelsey made a written note of the order.

"Stevie," Hogarth continued, "you check the CPS aren't going to balls up the bail app. Speak to the case lawyer, not to one of the minions. To the case lawyer. Lay down the law. Get Kelsey to help you. Brigson, you check the—"

"Pie shops," Fisher interjected.

Again, everyone laughed. Hogarth allowed them their moment. Then he asked, "How many crazies since breakfast?"

Fisher moved through the crowd till he was in the space between the chairs with Hogarth. He said, "Five frothing-at-the-mouth confessions since it was on the news. One says it's the beginning of the race war. Another says it's the end of the world. A divorcee's named her ex — and his bit on the side. This Greek café owner's faxed the nick." At this, Fisher held up the fax with which he had entered the room. "Says it's his Turkish neighbour."

Brigson clambered to his feet, and with the hand that did not contain the pie pulled a fax out of his inside jacket pocket. "Funny," he said. "But the Turk says it's the Greek geezer."

There was a riot of laughter now and Hogarth decided not to control it. He turned to the board behind him and searched for the magic marker so that he could write up a list of priority tasks. To his surprise, the laughter behind him rapidly evaporated of its own accord. An absolute silence fell over the men, so much so that Hogarth could clearly hear the door close at the back of the room. When he turned around, he was confronted by two deadly serious men. They stared at Hogarth, but said nothing. Hogarth's heart jerked in his chest, but he swallowed hard and fought to control the blood racing through his veins. He threw the marker at Fisher.

"DS Fisher will write down what is known about Earl Whitely," he said. "Please give me a moment, lads."

As he moved steadily through the men, he heard mutterings and whisperings as they assessed the two new arrivals. He gestured with his eyes at the new officers, and they knew to go outside. Once in the corridor, the smaller of the two, a sturdy man with a black moustache, spoke. He was balding, with a prop-forward kind of build and a Brummie accent.

"DCI Hogarth? I'm DSu Mason. Internal Complaints Unit. And this is DS Woodbridge."

Hogarth nodded briefly at this taller, younger man. Woodbridge was red-headed, with a rash of freckles over his face. He carried a thick file.

Mason continued, "We've come about Earl Whitely."

Hogarth looked deeply into Mason's eyes and tried to gauge his latest opponent, for since ICU were on the case he knew that Mason would have to be an adversary. Mason couldn't hold his stare, and this pleased the DCI. The contest would be challenging, but he could win it.

Mason coughed nervously, looking beyond Hogarth and at Woodbridge. "We've come to question you about Earl Whitely."

"I've been expecting you," Hogarth said.

CHAPTER ELEVEN

Andrea sat behind her desk with a steaming cup of hot Parisian chocolate. Across the desk were three men, two Hong Kong businessmen and their Chinese-American attorney, all immaculately dressed in classic but understated dark suits, intensely gazing upon her. She knew that they awaited her next answer. But her mind was still locked in that bare cell with Earl Whitely, her thoughts kept drifting to Calvin, to where he was, to what he was doing, and, most importantly, to what he might have done. Although she faced into the body of the office, she was aware of the huge field of glass that constituted the wall behind her. She could feel the chill on the back of her neck. It set her teeth on edge.

"We're on target. We've still got to close the deal next Thursday?" she said.

"Wednesday," the attorney said curtly.

"Yes, uh, Wednesday. And your clients will be in Las Vegas."

"Los Angeles," the younger of the clients replied.

The senior man, who wore thick black-rimmed glasses, and who had a lightening streak of grey in his otherwise black hair, sat silently. This silence was even more off-putting to Andrea, and she ruffled files on her desk.

"Yes," she said. "That's right. I've got a memo — somewhere."

She opened the top drawer and then was thrown off balance completely, for there was the photograph of herself, more than a decade before at the children's party. Her eyes fell sadly upon the younger, less stressed, evidently more hopeful woman she once was, surrounded by children, all Calvin's young friends. Calvin had a thick brush of wiry black hair, and with his little barrel chest amply filled out his 'Tigger is Tuff ' T-shirt. He didn't know it, but she still had it washed and folded neatly at the bottom of her wardrobe at home. Of course, Calvin's father Lawrence was not around; then again, he rarely was. He had claimed to be a thoroughly modern black man at the LSE, but once Andrea was pregnant he treated her increasingly like a 'baby mother', and slept his way around the campus while offering to provide her with token subsistence from his grant. She had never taken a penny from Lawrence; she was too independent or, as her father had said, bloody-minded. It made her cringe now to recall the Marxist revolutionary claptrap that Lawrence had spouted in those days, and how she had fallen head over heels for it. This vanguard of the proletariat, this future leader of the Black Nation, was now a successful capitalist businessman, importing and exporting God knows what, while being driven around in a Daimler by a white Albanian chauffeur. To Andrea's intense annoyance, Lawrence rarely spent time with Calvin, and it pained her to think that the boy somehow blamed her for this fact.

"Is your father available?" the older client asked sternly. He slowly removed his glasses, folded them, then put them in his inside jacket pocket as though he no longer even wished to see Andrea.

"Yes. No," Andrea replied. "I mean, I can handle your contract. Don't worry."

The older man stood up. The other two immediately did so too, and Andrea was compelled to follow suit.

"Worry?" the old man said. "In the current political climate in Hong Kong, Miss Chambers, I do nothing but worry. But worrying is good. Worrying means that I am careful. We pay your father's firm to do the worrying for us on the European tranche of this intercontinental deal. We did not anticipate that we would have to worry about *you*. Good morning."

The man bowed shallowly, with all due courtesy, as he delivered the most humiliating snub she had experienced in ten years of commercial practice. In a flash, the party turned and left the room. Andrea was left alone, standing at her desk, her top drawer open, gazing down at the photograph of Calvin. At that moment, Siobhan entered the office with a thick bundle of papers in her hand.

"Andy, here are the LA photocopies." Then she looked around. "Hey, where did they go?"

"To see Daddy," Andrea said sarcastically. She slowly sank back into her chair. The postmodern contraption of rolled steel and wires and black leather creaked. "God, I hate this bloody chair. It's like sitting in a shopping trolley."

"Want to talk about it?" Siobhan asked.

Andrea shook her head. "Do you think you could do me a favour? I just need to be alone for a few moments."

Siobhan dropped the photocopies on her smaller desk in the far corner of the room. "If anyone calls," she said, "I'll be feeding your father's fish."

Andrea smiled back, and then waited until Siobhan had quietly shut the door behind her. When she was once more alone, she picked up the phone. It rang a couple of times before Rufus answered it.

"Hi, Rufus," she said. "How are you?"

"Better for hearing your sweet voice, darlin'," he laughed back. "But me nets is all tangled."

Andrea looked around her empty office. "Yeah, I think I know what you mean. Look, can I have a quick word with Calvin?"

"I'm afraid he's gone."

"Do you know where?"

"When's the last time that boy tell you where he goes?"

"Thanks. I'll try again later."

"Any time, princess."

Andrea put the receiver down and slowly closed the top drawer.

Lifer entered the Yardie lab with a huge plastic takeout of goat curry. The vast man ate as he walked, though it must have been difficult for him to see exactly what he was eating since he still wore his wrapround shades, and the lab was almost pitch black. The last of the brilliant morning light vanished when he kicked the security door shut after him. The thud of steel briefly roused two other soldiers asleep on mattresses. Roots Johnson sat in his director's chair, trying to read a book about the music business, but he was in truth too distracted.

"What news of Peckham?" he asked.

"No sign, Don," Lifer replied. "Not in them clubs uptown. Nowhere." He took another mouthful of the curried goat and then spoke as he munched. "See, Don, how much you give Peckham last night?"

"A hundred," Roots said.

Lifer shook his head knowingly. "Maybe he party on it."

"No," Roots said firmly.

"Don, English is not like us. A hundred's a good party for an English boy, ya know."

"Peckham's not like that."

Lifer tossed the partly eaten tub of curry towards a wastepaper bin at the far end of the lab. The skin on his forehead crinkled into thick folds, and even these seemed fat. "What now? No one can say anything 'bout Peckham?"

"No," Roots said. "Not behind his back."

"Uh-huh, then why don't you make this Peckham your lieutenant? Why keep me? But remember good, Don, who was by your side all through the turf wars? That boy, he ain't even killed a man."

"Any fool can kill a man, Lifer."

Lifer picked up a Mac pistol from the cutting table in the middle of the lab. He primed it, gazed down the front sight, targeting an area on the wall above and behind Roots's head. Roots did not flinch. "We ain't gonna agree on that, Don," Lifer said.

Roots was about to reply when he noticed something on the entry screen, which gave a hazy view of the street outside the lab's door. There was a boy, a teenager, checking a piece of paper, as if he were checking an address. The boy came down the stairs so that he was directly outside the lab, but still he seemed confused. There was, of course, no handle on the steel door. Roots glanced at Lifer and flicked his eyes towards the door. His lieutenant understood immediately. He moved with surprising grace, Mac in hand, and then leant against the wall next to the door in wait. Roots checked the blurred image on the screen, and when the boy turned around to look back up to street level, he nodded at Lifer. The Yardie flung the door open and in a flash had the end of the Mac's barrel under the chin of the youth, his monstrous hand clamped on the boy's mouth. Such was Lifer's strength that as he hauled the boy into the darkness of the lab his feet barely touched the ground. Another soldier kicked the door shut behind him as the boy was thrown at Roots Johnson's feet. Three deadly weapons were aimed at his head. Lifer moved behind him, and removed a gun from the rear of the boy's waistband.

"Look, Don," Lifer said. "One of them gun enthusiasts."

Other Yardies laughed, but Roots was deadly serious. He felt he had seen the boy somewhere before, but for the moment he could not place him. But the fact that this kid had Roots's address was a gross breach of security. He had to get the boy to talk.

"Name?" he asked.

The boy looked up from the floor, but was too terrified to speak. Lifer, who was directly behind him now, hovering like a grossly distended shadow, pulled at the boy's hair.

"You answer when the don questions," he shouted.

"Calvin. Calvin Patterson," the boy said.

Roots joined the palms of his hand together, extending his long fingers into a steeple. He let the tips of his index fingers come to rest under his chin. "Why do I know the name Calvin Patterson?" he asked.

"I'm a friend of Earl's," Calvin spluttered.

Lifer yanked Calvin's head again. "Ah, we got Earl's girlfriend, ya know."

"Let him go, Lifer," Roots ordered.

The huge man let go of Calvin and the boy slumped prostrate on the floor. There were still three guns pointed at him. Roots Johnson sat impassively, deep in thought.

"I've come about Earl," Calvin ventured.

Roots could see that although the boy was probably as frightened as he had been in his entire life, he was dealing with his fear. He fought it. This courage impressed him.

"Earl Whitely ain't my problem," Roots said.

"Look, he said if he's in trouble, the don's the man to see."

"I know he's in trouble."

"Big trouble," Calvin said.

"He deserves it," Roots replied harshly. He could see that his acidic final words frightened the boy, made him blink, flinch just a fraction, but enough for Roots to divine what was going on. He didn't have anything against the youth, so he tried to speak in a calmer voice. "Tell me how you and Earl are friends."

"He does lyrics sometimes. On my system. I'm an MC."

Roots nodded, filed away this information. Perhaps one day, if his move into music came off, Calvin Patterson and Roots could do some business. But he decided that Calvin needed to know the truth. "You know that Earl is a dealer, too?"

"He's just my friend, and the police have got him inside. He said you'd help him with bail money."

"No, Calvin," Roots replied. "He hoped I'd help him."

The boy looked down at his trainers for a moment, and screwed up his face, as if he were trying to drag up some scrap of information from a deep vault in his memory. Roots closely observed the change in expression, the easing of the lines on the boy's forehead, as something clicked. Calvin looked up.

"Earl also said that if Roots Johnson wouldn't help him out of this, then he would go somewhere else."

"Where?" Roots asked.

Calvin glanced around nervously at the three guns. "To the three dons," he said.

There was suddenly absolute stillness and silence in the room. Roots Johnson rose very slowly from his chair and took three steps forward, so that he was now above the youth. The anger surged from deep inside him, and he knew that, when he responded, he would be rough with the boy, that he had to be rough. His patois broadened as he spoke.

"You been thinking all dis some kinda game, haven't you? But this ain't no game. People die. People die horribly. And right now? I dunno if you're gonna see Earl Whitely again. But I hope you do. 'Cos I want you to tell him from the don: Roots Johnson don't deal with dealers who deal to school kids. Do you understand?" He grabbed Calvin's neck, forcing the boy's left ear to his mouth. Then he whispered, "That's the rule."

From behind the boy, Lifer shouted maniacally, "Let's do him now, Don. Let's wet this boy."

Roots held Calvin fast, almost in an embrace. "That's the rule," he whispered again. "Do you understand the rule, Calvin Patterson?"

"Let's kill him, Don," Lifer shouted. "Let's kill him now."

In an interview room in the police station, Hogarth sat at a table, with the burly DSu Mason directly opposite him. DS Woodbridge was silhouetted with his back to the window. Shredded light came through the blinds. As the two men at the table talked, the red-headed Woodbridge fidgeted absent-mindedly with his file.

Hogarth methodically attempted to assess Mason, all the time listening to the superintendent's words, but probing for any emotion that lay behind them. He had been told that Mason was formidable in his job with Internal Complaints. The ICU, referred to by many as the "rat squad', was the highest-ranking, most resourced team of internal investigators in the Met, even more powerful than the CIB, the Complaints Investigation Bureau. Hogarth had learnt that years ago Mason had transferred from the West Midlands Organised Crime Strike Force, and in a unit accused of widespread corruption and criticised by the highest courts in the land, he had been 'fireproof', untouchable and untouched, with a blemish-free record. This was not an opponent Hogarth could roll over easily.

Mason stroked his moustache instinctively, then continued, "All I'm saying is that my job is to listen. To all sides. Not to judge. Not till I get all the facts. To treat all parties equally."

"Criminals and cops?" Hogarth said. "Just the same? No matter how bad the criminal? No matter how good the cop?"

Mason sighed and ran his hand across his balding scalp. Hogarth saw minute beads of sweat amid the fine, wispy hair. It was not hot in the room — if anything it was colder than in the rest of the building, even the cells. Hogarth had organised it that way. He had wanted suspects to get a jolt when they finally entered this room for interview. He wanted to use every advantage to disorientate them, to throw them off their practised lies. Most crimes were solved with confessions, not with forensic pyrotechnics, but with confessions, admissions of guilt and atrocities, made here by the psychopathic and the penitent alike to DCI John Hogarth. To this extent, Hogarth had always seen himself as a confessor. It was strange, then, that he was being interviewed in his own lair. But the cold sweat on Mason's scalp encouraged him. Mason sighed and decided to try another tack.

"Look, off the record, OK?" he said, and Hogarth nodded. Mason leaned back in his chair, revealing more clearly how his portly stomach pulled at the straining buttons of his shirt. "Look," he said, "I know what it's like dealing with . . . these people. You don't think we used to get slags like this up in the old West Midlands? Well, we did. They come here illegally. Break all our laws. Then demand all the protection our laws can provide them. John, I understand your position. But try to understand mine."

He paused. He wants some kind of minimal agreement, Hogarth thought. Some recognition of common ground, us against them. Some concession. He stared back blankly.

Mason tried again. "John, my job is to protect the good name of the police. Not the individual policeman. But the police. The institution."

"The myth," Hogarth said.

Mason shook his head. "Earl Whitely was lifted two weeks ago. For arranging an importation of drugs. Customs found stashes of cannabis concealed within a sound system he had transported from Jamaica."

"You surprise me," Hogarth said.

"No. This will surprise you. Our darling Earl is batshit scared of being sent back to Kingston. He ripped the grass off one of the Trench Town posses. So deportation equals death in Earl's fertile imagination. So Earl, bless his cotton socks, is prepared to deal. With us. With me." Mason paused again. But still Hogarth was silent. "Earl will give up a corrupt senior officer if he's allowed to walk on the ganja rap. A walk back on the London streets, take his chance here."

"Of course," Hogarth said casually, "he said who the cop was?"

"Not till he gets a deal in writing. But he gave us a taster, a titbit to keep us hungry. Said it was all linked to three murders. Three different posse leaders."

"Three dons?"

"Whatever the hell they call themselves now. Look, think about how it looks from the outside."

"Are you outside?" Hogarth said coldly. "Or inside?" When he saw with satisfaction that Mason hesitated, he added, "Or don't you know?"

Mason looked away an instant to compose himself. "Earl gets lifted. He's willing to sing about someone senior in the force. We arrange a second meet with him for last night. Only laughing-boy doesn't show. Where is our star witness? I ask. We seek him here, we seek him there. Then: lo and behold. We discover that you've nicked him on a murder on what appears to be flimsy evidence. Now as a reasonable man, I've got to ask myself: Is this a coincidence, or is this—"

"Justice," Hogarth said.

"Yes, well, you see, justice to me is a little like the tooth fairy. Sounds nice. But you know it doesn't exist. When you grow up. So if I was a *bent* copper and I wanted to shut someone up, I'd nick him on something big. Scare the sweet bejaysus out of him."

"But are you?" Hogarth asked.

"What?"

"A *bent* cop?" Hogarth got to his feet, so that his intimidating bulk towered over the still-seated man, one arm on either side of the table with Mason between. He continued, "You see, if you were a corrupt cop, sir, and your neck was in the noose? Then what you'd do is kill a little piece of shit like Earl Whitely. But if you were *bent*, sir, then *this* is what you'd do."

Hogarth held out his hand and Woodbridge advanced, as if on cue. He handed Hogarth the file that he had been handling all along. Hogarth slammed the file on the table in front of Mason. Black-and-white photos splayed out across the shiny surface until they practically covered the entire table. They had the quality of surveillance photos, with digital times and dates at the bottom. Sometimes the target was obscured by unknowing people. But mostly the photos had been expertly and successfully executed. They showed Mason, in obviously gay drinking clubs. Drinking with young boys. Confronted with these images, Mason's head dropped.

"Each to his own," Hogarth said. "That's what we say, eh, Woody?"

"Yes, guv," Woodbridge agreed.

"Woody was on firearms training with me," Hogarth added. "Didn't he tell you?" When Mason did not reply, Hogarth picked up one photo at random, examined it closely, nodded. "I can understand if you want to explore your . . . feminine side. Or have it explored. Leaves more women for us real men. We don't object to that, do we, Woody?"

"No, guv."

Hogarth slammed the table with his fist, causing Mason

to jump. "But I do object to you coming on my patch with your lily-livered equal-opportunities psychobabble, and trying to lecture a real policeman, who's trying to do something about all this . . . shit we're sinking in. Well, there's a new policing out there. By new policemen, who are sick and tired of taking the fall for it all. Sick of presuming the slag're innocent when we know they're guilty. Sick that this country's become the Legoland of law enforcement. Oh, you've blown away a serving officer? Go straight to your heated cell. Get clothed. Get fed. Get healed. Then adios till you're ready to do it again." Hogarth paused. He was practically breathless now. But he slammed the table again to ensure that Mason was looking up at him. "Now it's up to you. You can report me and investigate this Earl Whitely crap about the three dons. Or you can go home quietly, like a good little boy. And listen to your YMCA records till it's pension time, and never cross me again. Because if you do, sir," Hogarth finally whispered, "I'll kill you."

Suddenly, there was a rap on the door and the beleaguered Mason almost had a coronary. Hogarth glanced over, and saw Stevie Fisher.

"Guv," Fisher called urgently. "You've got to come. *Now*."

In the Yardie lab, Calvin sat on a broken wooden chair directly in front of Roots Johnson. The three other soldiers stood in a tight arc around the boy's back, so that Roots had an uninterrupted view of the youth, as if he were a model in front of an artist, for study, a life drawing.

"Music is your t'ing?" Roots asked. The boy nodded, but his fear had worn him down by now and he did not reply verbally. "So when's your next gig?" Roots continued.

Calvin began to speak, stopped, licked his dry bottom lip. "Tonight," the boy replied. "I'm clashing with this crazy guy."

"Most of them are crazy enough," Roots said.

"Yeah, but this guy? He's on everything and off his head."

"Got a handle?"

"The Mashango Warrior," Calvin said. Roots nodded. "Know him?" Calvin asked.

"Good MC. Bad man," Roots replied.

Then Lifer pointed to the CCTV screen. On the hazy VDU, Roots could see a motorcycle courier in red-and-black leathers, with his helmet still on but the visor up. He stood outside the steel security door, confused.

"I have a parcel for Mr Johnson," he shouted hopefully.

Roots burned with fury. Two security violations in one day. He would have to consider finding a new lab. But this thought was immediately superseded in his mind by the more soothing one that if he could get out of the business, he would not need another lab. He nodded at Lifer, who placed the Mac in the corner behind the door. He slowly opened it, filling the door frame with his bulk so that little of the courier could be seen.

"Give it up," Lifer growled.

The courier had a pasty white face and a matchstick body that the leathers did little to ameliorate. He spoke in the officious tone of a tax inspector. "You've got to sign. And print your name," he told Lifer. He handed the Yardie a clipboard. He tried to glance around Lifer and into the lab. Lifer roughly grabbed the pen from the courier's glove and then, holding it in his fist like a stick, drew a huge 'X' right across the page, ripping the paper. The courier tutted, not knowing how close to serious, incapacitating injury he was. He handed a package over.

"No chance of a tip, then?" he asked, hopefully.

Lifer slammed the door in his face. He carried the parcel, which was about the size of a large shoebox, across the lab and to Roots. He drew a lock-knife from one of his pockets, cut the tape on the back of the envelope and handed the package to Roots.

Roots knew that his face expressed grim foreboding, but his crew were watching him intently and, in addition, he had the boy before him. He had to keep his cool, had to perform, but even as he removed the unusually heavy shoebox inside he had guessed the worst. He took his time to undo the coarse string tied around the box itself, all the time praying, actually praying as he had not since he had been at his mother's graveside in Jamaica as an adolescent. He looked around at the men, who were captivated. Lifer edged slightly forward for a better look. Roots Johnson silently promised himself that if what was inside was not what he thought, then he would definitely get out of the game. He wouldn't toy with it, wouldn't dabble, he would be out. He slowly removed the lid. There was something still wet inside. A faintly recognisable shape, wrapped in an Arsenal shirt.

Roots screamed deep inside himself, though he uttered not one sound.

Hogarth's car skidded to a halt by some waste scrub on the fringes of his patch. A WPC was already unfurling crime scene tape, and several other uniforms held back a growing crowd. Hogarth marched the short distance across the uneven, overgrown ground, strewn with bicycle wheels, illegally dumped refuse sacks, pram frames. A pathologist in white overalls was already on-site, whispering into a hand-held tape recorder as Hogarth joined him. The doctor's face was drained of blood. Hogarth had never seen him look so shaken.

"Both . . . both feet," the pathologist said into the tape, "severed. At the ankles. Ligature marks. Jesus. Jesus Christ."

He dropped the tape and it almost fell on the black

youth's body. Hogarth bent down and picked the machine
up. He carefully handed it back.

"Ligatures consistent with hanging upside down," the
path ologist stammered. "Both hands, too. Sev-severed. At
the wrist."

Stevie Fisher now joined the two men above Peckham's
body. "Guv?" Fisher asked. "Guv, what is it?"

Hogarth briefly shut his eyes and uttered a short, silent
prayer over the tragic figure of the young boy, as he had
done over every corpse he had come across in his work.
Every one, he realised, except that of Nicki Harris.

"Guv?" Fisher repeated. "What the hell is it?"

"A challenge," Hogarth said.

Roots Johnson now stood over Calvin, the feared Yardie
on the verge of pitiful tears, but none of them fell, not
outwardly.

"Peckham was my spar, Calvin. Do you know what that
means to a Yardman? He was . . . he was like my son. And
he died. Alone. In a way you cannot imagine. The
Mashango kill him. So now I have this duty to speak to
these men who do such a thing. Tonight you sound clash
against their Warrior. If the gig goes on? The rest of his
posse will be there. Celebrating. Bragging. And then it's
either they kill us or we kill them. Now you can walk
away, you can run when I release you, and there will be no
gig. But I've checked you out down here in the lab, and
you don't act like a boy who runs. Peckham was like you,
Calvin. He did nothing. He was a black boy who was born
on this island, not mine. And they killed him. Now you
can run, and then I might not find the Mashango tonight.
But I'm asking you to help me, and I can give you no rea-
soning why you should — except this: I'm hurting real
bad right now, Calvin Patterson, and you can help me out.

And if you do? I'll see if I can help your spar, Earl."

Roots held his hand out, with the palm uppermost. Lifer slapped a gun into it. Then Roots held out Earl Whitely's nine-mil towards Calvin. The boy hesitated, then finally he accepted it.

CHAPTER TWELVE

The South London Central Magistrates' court, known in the trade simply as Central or Central Mags, was one of the new high-security courts that had sprung up in the course of the previous decade as a response to two things. Firstly, the fortified building, with its extra-thick walls and shatterproof glass, was designed to cope with the threat of terrorist attacks on the mainland, and to deal with people accused of security offences. Secondly, the proliferation of gun-related offences and internecine wars between and amongst the new classes of gangs, posses and criminal organisations had created the need for courts that could effectively be turned into armed fortresses. All this was incorporated into Central's design.

Less than two hours after he had gazed upon young Peckham's partially dismembered body, Stevie Fisher entered Court 1 in Central Mags with Brigson and Kelsey. Two AFOs, Authorised Firearms Officers, guarded the door in flak jackets, with large semi-automatics cradled across their chests. They whispered into the mouthpieces of their headsets periodically, relating the state of activity outside the court to the command office. Huge grey screens had been erected directly outside the courtroom itself, creating a security tunnel through which everyone had to pass and identify themselves. A bored uniformed officer sat at a desk between the screens, checking people off. He was in shirtsleeve order, since the court building was suffocatingly hot despite the crisp winter's day outside.

Fisher held up his warrant card. "DS Fisher." He attempted to continue into the courtroom itself, but the desk officer stopped him.

"You've got to sign here," he told an increasingly irritated Fisher.

"Whitely's our body," Fisher replied.

"I don't care if he's your best friend, you've still got to sign in."

Fisher leant over and his swept-back blond hair fell forward over his eyes as he did so. Behind him, Kelsey and Brigson smiled at each other.

"When's the show start?" Fisher asked.

The desk officer shrugged. "Don't ask me. I'm only collecting autographs."

Once the three men were in the courtroom, another uniform came up and patted them down. Sniffer dogs eagerly dragged their handlers along as they checked the various rows of seats, and court staff waited nervously at the front for proceedings to begin. The press contingent sat on the left-hand side, comparing notes. But the court itself, the architecture and the décor, was exactly like hundreds of similar Magistrates' courts around the country.

The three detectives sat in a designated police row, near the dock. Kelsey gazed around, his eyes wide, in awe at the tumult. For his part, Brigson sheepishly opened the brown paper sack he had been carrying, stained as it was with grease.

"What've you got this time, Brigsy?" Fisher asked.

Brigson hesitated.

"Jesus, I'll find out Brigson," Fisher continued. "I am a bloody detective."

Brigson looked sheepish again, then said, "Pickled eggs."

Even Kelsey had to laugh at this.

Stevie Fisher shook his head. "God, it's as though Delia

Smith never existed, innit? Why can't you eat doughnuts like cops are supposed to?"

"They're too fattening," Brigson replied.

With that, he popped a whole egg into his mouth. Then he nearly choked. There was growling behind him. The three men swivelled around to see a sniffer dog with its teeth bared.

"I'm sorry you had to see that," Fisher told the dog.

From the front of the court, there was a rapping sound and people began to get to their feet even before the usher shouted, "Court rise". The stipendiary magistrate, the 'stipe', briskly entered from a side door at the front. He was a man in his late forties, with horn-rimmed glasses, a receding head of greasy brown hair and an old-fashioned three-piece suit. Ackroyde was patrician, not so much upper-class as officer-class, a tough, irascible man, who got the job done — and the job was to process and sentence and lock up or bail a conveyor-belt of some of the most dangerous criminals in Europe as they passed through his court. He bowed shallowly to everyone and sat down. The rest of the court did likewise.

From the right, another door opened, one that led from the cell area below into the dock. Two huge sumo-like jailers escorted a man into court in chains. It was Earl Whitely.

The usher stood below the Bench, and in front of the dock, inspecting her clipboard. "The first case in your list, sir," she said. "Earl Alphonse Whitely."

The court clerk, an unnaturally cheerful-faced Asian man in a suit, which barely contained his middle-age spread, stood immediately below the stipe. He turned to his left and stared at the dock.

"Are you Earl Alphonse Whitely?" he asked.

Stevie Fisher craned his neck forward for a better view. Though he sat at the end of the row and nearest to Earl, the bulk of the jailers obscured his head from sight.

Earl stood statue-still in the dock. He did not speak.

The clerk attempted to repeat his question, but the stipe interrupted. "You must answer," he hissed at Earl in an icy whisper. Then Ackroyde noticed something about Earl that infuriated him. "Why is this man wearing a hat in my court?" he demanded.

Fisher glanced at Brigson; both of them were on edge.

The bigger of the screws cleared his throat. "It's some kind of religious thing, Your Worship. He's a Rasta-far-on."

Earl still said nothing. The screws now stepped back and behind their prisoner, as if they were trying to escape Ackroyde's venom. Fisher now saw Whitely's face. He looked at Brigson.

"How bad?" Brigson whispered.

"Ten rounds with Tyson bad," Fisher replied.

The stipe's radar-like hearing had detected some noise in his hallowed courtroom. "*Silence!*" he shouted.

Fisher and Brigson lowered their heads like reprimanded schoolboys.

The clerk said, "Sir, Mr Whitely has been charged with murder and this is the first appearance."

"Is he represented?" Ackroyde asked.

"No, sir."

Ackroyde once more addressed Earl. "Mr Whitely, I have to tell you that you are facing a most — the most — grievous charge. Are you sure you don't want a lawyer? If you can't afford to engage one, the Legal Aid scheme will provide one for you." Still Earl stood impassively. "Do you want to say anything? Anything at all to me? You see, I have the power to remand you in custody. To take away your freedom. Do you understand?"

Now a CPS rep, a lawyer for the Crown Prosecution Service, stood. Or appeared to stand, since he was barely five foot five tall. Fisher could see that his brown suit was crumpled badly at the back. "Sir, the Crown asks for a remand in custody for seven days anyway due to the serious nature of the offence and due to the fact that there are outstanding enquiries to be made. We strongly believe that the defendant would interfere with those enquiries."

"Has he been interviewed by the police?" Ackroyde asked.

The small man glanced down at the pile of papers in front of him. "I think he refused."

"You think? Can anyone tell me definitively whether this man can actually speak, for heaven's sake?"

There was silence in court, and as Ackroyde tapped his pen angrily on the Bench the tension grew. Brigson made eyes at Fisher, indicating that he should say something. "Sod off," Fisher mouthed silently.

"Right," the stipe said. "I want a preliminary psychiatric assessment. Is Probation represented in court?"

A woman in a long knitted cardigan-like jacket and greying hair stood in the row next to the CPS rep. She made a note of Ackroyde's request.

The stipe again turned to the prisoner, and spoke now as if to a small child. "Mr Whitely, I'm going to remand you — that is, keep you in custody — for a week. I want to find out more about you, and I'm going to do it for your own protection." Then he said to the jailers in a different, colder voice, "Take him down."

The larger screw tugged on the handcuffs and began to push an immobile Earl towards the door and into the pit of the building.

"Thank fuck for that," Fisher whispered.

The second screw joined the first in ushering Earl away, and now Earl took his first couple of steps. But suddenly he flung himself back against the smaller jailer, and began shaking his head back and forth rapidly, screaming all the time. With every sinew of his young, athletic body, Earl

dragged the jailers to the front of the dock, where he
shouted, "I want me brief. Andrea Chambers. I want me
brief. Andrea Chambers. Andrea Chambers."

Stevie Fisher's head dropped a second time. "Where's
the guvnor?" he asked Brigson.

In police divisional headquarters, a sadly familiar scene slowly
unfolded. Nicki Harris's parents were facing up to the cameras.
The press conference had become an almost obligatory stage in
the investigation of high-profile murder cases, and if it rarely
achieved its supposed purpose, the obtaining of further
actionable clues or evidence, John Hogarth knew that it was
indispensable in the general battle against crime. As he stood
quietly at the very rear of the room, separated from Dawn
Harris and her husband by a sea of TV crews and cameras,
Hogarth knew that conferences such as these bought time for
officers like himself, who were in the field. They created sympathy for the victims, admiration for the police, but most of all,
by showing the grieving, desolated family, they conveyed the
starkest message: This could happen to you. And it was the
subliminal message that accompanied such conferences which
interested Hogarth as he gazed up at the inquiry number on
the boards behind the Harrises. There was the Met logo, massive free publicity, a jingle that went: We are all you've got.
That's what Hogarth wanted the citizens to understand.
Between them in their cosy living rooms and this conference
table lay one thing: the police.

As the officer in charge of the Nicki Harris murder
inquiry, Hogarth should have been up front, available for
questions, but he had, of course, been called out on young
Peckham's murder. So Hogarth's superintendent, Mitchell,
the uniform who stood above him in the station political
hierarchy, conducted the conference. This was another
thing to which Hogarth objected: having members of the
uniformed branch above CID squads, the line managers, to

whom the men in the trenches had to report. It was unnecessary, unrealistic, and, Hogarth knew, it didn't achieve its purpose. It didn't stop corruption.

There was a flurry of flashbulbs, exploding like firecrackers around the room in front of Hogarth. The curtains around the auditorium had been drawn to prevent glare on the lenses of the television cameras, and the Harrises were bathed in a pool of artificial light. Hogarth remained in the shadows at the rear.

The seated Superintendent Mitchell finished his introduction by saying, "So the murder inquiry number is the one you see behind me. Now, please, do not shout out questions while Nicki's father makes a brief statement."

To Mitchell's right sat PC Peter Harris, and next to the PC sat Dawn. She was a smallish woman, Hogarth observed, but with a strong face, the type of face he had seen rarely among citizens and cops and criminals, the three categories into which he divided the world. She wore thick glasses and her mouth was set, her hands clenched on the table — not as if in prayer, but almost as if she were trying to control them, to stop them reaching out and tearing at the world that had taken her daughter.

Peter Harris was in his constable's uniform. "We were just an ordinary family," he began in a weak voice, glancing down at some papers in front of him, reading from a prepared and approved script. "An ordinary, loving family in an ordinary home, in an ordinary part of London. I might be a serving officer in the Metropolitan Police, but before . . . this . . . happened, Dawn and me were just like any other happily married couple with an eight-year-old child."

To reinforce this point, after he had looked down at his script again to ensure that he had picked the right moment, Harris woodenly put his arm around Dawn's shoulder and hugged her. This interested Hogarth greatly, for Dawn was ice. She did not respond, but stared out into the room unrelentingly.

"Me and Dawn thought the world of our Nicki," Harris continued. "We lived for Nicki. She was our life. That's why we've agreed to make this appeal. To anyone out there who knows, er, anything."

Dawn could contain herself no longer. "Please," she said intensely. "Someone. Help us."

Harris appeared to have been thrown entirely off his stride, like a bad actor who had forgotten his lines. The superintendent, seeing this, piped up again.

"Ladies and gentlemen, DCI Hogarth and his team will treat each and every call in the strictest confidence. They will—"

Dawn stared into the cameras and yet through them, beyond them, right to the back of the room. So much so that Hogarth felt every word she now uttered like a punch. He sweated and recoiled a fraction as she shouted, "Someone out there must know something." She picked up an enlarged school photo of Nicki and rested it on the desk, saying, "This is my daughter. This is my Nicki. Someone must know something about her death."

Hogarth's forehead dripped with sweat, and at that moment he became aware of his cellular phone flashing in his hand. He stepped quietly out of the conference room and into the corridor, fronted with sheet glass, which gave on to the main road. Cars drove past unheard outside as the DCI turned the phone off mute.

"Guv?" he heard Fisher say. "All is not well on Waltons mountain. Earl Whitely's been remanded for seven."

"So?" Hogarth said.

"So now he's asked for that Andrea Chambers and the stipe's listed the case again for tomorrow. But she might not go to see him in prison. He did sack her."

"She'll go," Hogarth said. He lowered the phone, pursed his lips. His mind raced.

"So what do you want us to do?" Fisher continued.

"Go to the ballistics lab. Find out what they're saying about the Nicki Harris bullet."

"But, guv, Andrea Chambers will have to go to the Young Offenders this afternoon. I know people inside the YOI. I could—"

"I'll deal with her," Hogarth said.

CHAPTER THIRTEEN

Andrea and Siobhan walked into the open-plan area of the law firm, sharing a joke about the dinner party the night before.

"I can't believe that lot are your friends," Siobhan said. "I mean, that Peter and Pippa. They're brain-dead. Pod people."

"No, their little Petey's got into Mensa." Andrea smiled.

"Oh yeah? When's the kid get out, then?" Siobhan replied.

They both laughed. Each had a small paper bag, incriminating evidence that they had been on a bun-run to the bakery across the main road, and that their working lunch was going to consist of a nourishing assortment of wicked cream cakes. But as they sauntered back, the path to Andrea's office was blocked by Gordon Chambers.

"Where have you been?" he demanded.

The smile withered on Siobhan's face, but Andrea tried to ease the tension. "Would you believe the law library?" she ventured hopefully, the chocolate éclair still in her hand. But her face became serious when she saw the thunder on her father's normally benign features.

"Imagine my surprise," he said coldly, "when I was in conference with what were supposed to be your clients, your extremely important Hong Kong clients, Andrea, when my attempt to persuade them not to go to our rivals was interrupted by a phone call."

"I'm sorry," Andrea said, suitably penitent.

Gordon ignored her totally. "And this call is from a Jamaican gentleman. A man who insists on talking to me. Who shouts down the telephone wires, and I think I do him justice: 'I want me brief.'"

"Oh, God, Dad. I'm so sorry."

"Don't be sorry, Andrea. Be careful."

There was a moment's silence between them. Andrea regretted that she had caused her father this irritation when she knew he had enough woes in the running of the firm. But she was also embarrassed. She felt as if she were again thirteen years old and was being scolded by her folks in front of her teenage friends.

"Look, darling," Gordon whispered. "It's the firm's reputation I'm worried about." He glanced past the fish tank and around the open-plan area, where secretaries and paralegals watched the confrontation from a safe distance. "Yes, get back to work," he said patiently. Siobhan excused herself. Gordon waited until the tap-tap of keyboards began again before he continued. "Andrea, I'm not having a go at you for the sake of it. But we have some very unhappy — and very rich — Hong Kong clients."

"They don't want me," she said quietly.

"Yes they do. But they want the old you, the one who attended to every detail."

"OK, point taken."

Gordon began to wander over to the fish tank, and she followed him as he peered into the murky waters, in which exotic rainbow-coloured fish darted about. He sprinkled fish pellets on the surface.

"Darling, aren't you getting a tad out of your depth?" he said. "With this crime thing?"

Andrea didn't know how to respond, unsure whether it was a trick question. "Leading question," she replied breezily.

"Look, unless you say no, I'm going to call Mary Williams. Mary's just won that explosives appeal. This murder would be right up her street."

"No," Andrea said firmly.

"If you handed this Yardie thing to Mary, no one would think less of you."

"I would."

"Andrea, I'm not one of those wise old fathers who thinks he knows best. As you know, your mother had the monopoly of wisdom in the marriage. But . . ." He hesitated and glanced around nervously, even though it was his law firm, even though his name was on the door. Public displays of emotion were not one of Gordon's strongest suits. "I'm just worried about my daughter," he whispered to her. "Is that so criminal?"

Andrea took his hand, concealed as it was by the fish tank from the prying eyes of the staff, who were pretending to work. "Thanks, Dad," she replied. "But I'll wrap up warm and I'll be back from the prom by midnight."

Gordon let go of her hand. He looked at her earnestly. "It's not a prom you've got to go to, Andrea. It's a prison."

An hour later, Andrea parked in the large carpark of the West London Young Offenders Institute. The public entrance to the building was user-friendly, with a disabled ramp and potted plants, and the complex, built in the eighties, was of warm brick rather than grey concrete slabs. But there were security cameras and razor wire strewn across the top of walls. As Andrea got out of her car, carrying her briefcase, a chill ran through her body, for she knew that this was the sort of place that Calvin could easily have been in now, if the police had not released him from custody the night before. She thought back to her life as a criminal barrister, and realised that the soul-destroying reality of such places was still imprinted on her mind. For any way you sliced it, this YOI, like most of the other youth remand facilities around the country, was just a prison for kids, replete with potted plants and teenage suicides.

Blinkered by her sense of foreboding at the prospect of the meeting with Earl Whitely, Andrea did not notice another car that pulled into the rear of the carpark. It had tinted windows, across which windscreen wipers leapt three times as a jet of screen-wash cleaned the glass. Inside the car, Hogarth watched fascinated as Andrea disappeared into the legal visits entrance to the YOI.

She walked through a bricked archway and up to a glass security booth on the right-hand side of the entrance. A prison officer in a dark uniform sat at a control desk behind the glass, reading a battered paperback, creasing the spine so much that the pages could have fallen out at any moment. The man pretended not to look at Andrea, though one lazy eye glanced at her briefly before it returned to the page.

"Proof of identity?" the screw said.

"My name is Chambers," Andrea said. "Andrea Chambers. I phoned about an hour ago."

"Proof of identity?" he said in exactly the same fashion.

Andrea fumbled around in her bag and discovered to her horror that she had forgotten her business card. The screw shook his head knowingly.

"We take VISA," he said wearily. "We take MasterCard. We take American Express."

Andrea looked up incredulously, and she fleetingly noticed her surprised face reflected in the glass. Things had changed since she had practised criminal law. She opened her purse and offered her only credit card with pride. "I assume you'll take the Co-op Animal Card." She slid the rectangle of plastic into the shiny metal tray that ran under the glass.

The screw looked at the lions and giraffes printed on the front of the card and then, as he wrote down Andrea's name, asked, "They let you buy things with this?"

"If you're nice." Andrea smiled. "Now, I'd like to see Earl Whitely."

The screw slid the card back and then resumed his reading. Andrea waited, unsure whether there was some other procedure to complete, but before she could ask the huge electronic doors that constituted the first barrier of the security labyrinth growled open. Andrea stepped inside and waited as the door closed slowly behind her. She was now in a kind of airlock, surrounded on four sides by identical pairs of heavy glass-and-metal doors. Immediately, another pair of doors, this time to her left, ground open. Again she stepped through. Now there was a staircase. With no instructions, but equally with no other alternative, she climbed it. Then there was a solid steel door. On the brick wall next to it was a red buzzer. Someone had scribbled in crude red Biro on the brick above it: PRESS ONLY ONCE. ONLY ONCE.

Andrea reached for it, then stopped, rubbed her sweating palm on her jacket, then pressed. But nothing appeared to happen. She could hear no noise, and could not see into the next corridor. She was tempted to press the buzzer again, but noticed again the insistent instructions in Biro. There she waited for three long minutes, looking desperately around the dismal place, finding it hard to breathe, until finally there was the faint clinking of keys somewhere beyond the steel door. Three minutes — it couldn't have been much longer than that, she decided. It horrified her to think that kids were sentenced to spend months and years of their young lives in such a place.

A large, red-faced jailer opened the steel door. "You only pressed once," he said as he let Andrea through.

"It said only once," she replied.

"Yeah, but most lawyers, they never obey the rules."

He let her through another door until Andrea's field of vision suddenly opened up from the hitherto confined spaces on to a large, echoing hall and a sea of tables. Each table, and there must have been close to one hundred, had a pair of chairs, all of them arranged exactly the same, one nearer the jailer's desk, where Andrea now stood, and another directly opposite, nearer the back wall. Another jailer, much smaller, sat at the desk with a huge register on the table in front of him. He was a gaunt man, with almost bluish grey hair.

"Whitely you want, isn't it?"

"Yes," Andrea said.

"They're bringing him down from his luxury penthouse," the seated man said. The other jailer, who had let Andrea in, appeared to be his subordinate, and he laughed sycophantically. He ventured into a small office behind the desk and brought out a half-consumed cup of tea.

"Glad I reserved a table," Andrea said, trying to relieve the tension between her and the uniformed men. Neither responded. She lifted her briefcase so that she could carry it with both arms across her chest. "Sit anywhere, then?" she said more quietly.

"Table seventy-two," the older jailer snapped at her.

Andrea began to pick her way through the rows of empty tables. On the opposite side of the room, another door opened. Two other jailers brought in a young black man, whom Andrea didn't immediately recognise, for he wore a baseball cap with a large peak low over his eyes. She had begun to make her way towards the boy when the greying jailer shouted at her again.

"Table seventy-two. Seventy-two."

Andrea turned, found the table, but didn't sit. She put

her briefcase on the small, square wooden surface and waited until the youth was led to her. She tried to make contact, but he looked resolutely downwards, even when the two accompanying screws had joined the others.

"Earl?" Andrea said. "You wanted to see me?"

Andrea could see the white peak of his cap, now pointed almost vertically down towards the ground, but she could not see his eyes. His nose looked swollen, and she saw that his dark skin was discoloured, bruised to a kind of plum colour. It was difficult to gauge from the angle of his face, but his cheeks appeared swollen, as if he had stuffed something inside his mouth on both sides. Then a tear rolled slowly down the left-hand side of his face.

"Earl?" she said. "What is it?"

He finally looked up and took his baseball cap off in one movement. Andrea felt her stomach turn. For his face — and it barely looked like a face any longer — was one large welt. And there was worse. Where just the previous night she had seen his neat Afro hair, in a precise fade style, now there were holes. Singed holes. There were small, almost circular burn marks on his scalp.

"Oh, Christ," she whispered. "Oh, Earl, what did they do to you?"

Earl slumped down into his chair miserably. "They hurt me, Miz Chambers," he said.

Andrea rushed round to the far side of the table and took his hand. Though it was much larger than hers, it trembled.

"Stay on this side," the older screw shouted. He began to approach Andrea rapidly.

"I want a doctor," Andrea shouted back. "I want a doctor right now."

"Stay on this side," the man repeated.

Andrea's stomach was knotting with fury. "I don't care. You call a doctor right now."

"Tell her," the screw said to the seated Earl. "Tell her."

The boy looked down at his feet again now that the jailer was upon him.

"Tell her," the screw said.

"Earl?" Andrea asked gently.

Still fixed on the floor, he said, "I've seen a doctor."

Andrea's head snapped round at the jailer. "He looks like this? After? You animals."

The three other jailers had now advanced and surrounded Andrea intimidatingly, crossing their arms across their huge chests. But it was the smallest, oldest jailer who did the talking.

"Animals? We didn't kill a schoolgirl."

"He's presumed innocent, for Christ's sake," Andrea shouted.

"So were the Wests," the man replied.

"I want to see the governor. Now."

"He's not here."

"So who's in charge?" Andrea demanded.

The older jailer looked at his colleagues. "Well, me, I suppose," he said. They all laughed at this, at Andrea. Then the man put his hand on Earl's shoulder. "Do you want to see the governor, Mr Whitely?" he asked sarcastically.

Earl still refused to raise his eyes. "No sir," he said.

"There, counsel," the screw told Andrea. "Problem solved."

Andrea went right up to the man, face to face. "I'm going to give you so many problems about this, the whole Home Office won't be able to solve them."

"We'll see."

Andrea detested the man's smugness, the arrogance of his certitude. But she also felt helpless as she stood surrounded in the visitor's hall. In this closed world of doors and chains and cameras and keys, she knew she was as helpless as Earl Whitely, as any prisoner. Within these walls, the word of men such as those confronting her now was the law, the only law, and she knew it. "Look," she said, "I want a private consultation with my client."

"Oh," the man said sarcastically. "Why didn't you ask?"

Two minutes later, Andrea and Earl were locked into a small, urinous-smelling room that was situated in one corner of the hall. The door was solid stripped wood at the bottom, but the top half consisted of plate glass. This meant that although the screws standing guard outside could look into the room and maintain their observation of lawyer and client, Andrea was pretty sure that they couldn't hear what was being said. Nevertheless, she and Earl spoke in whispers, Andrea standing with her back to the door to shield Earl, who sat wretchedly in a basic wooden chair.

"Why did this happen?" Andrea whispered. She spoke angrily at him, even though her ire was properly directed at his attackers.

Earl shook his head.

"Come on, Earl. You've got to talk to me. It's your only chance. You asked for me. Well, I'm here. So help me help you."

He stared up at her, and his simple, plaintive eyes reminded her that even though he was charged with the most serious crime in the criminal lexicon, he was just a boy, not so very different to Calvin.

"The po-lice want me quiet," Earl finally said.

"About the shooting?" she asked.

As he stared unblinkingly at her, with his long, curly eyelashes, she realised that he was assessing her, but in a different way to the previous night in the police station. He was unsure if he could trust her.

She tried to allay his fear, came closer, for the first time moved from the door. She squatted in front of him. "Earl,

I won't tell anyone."

He shook his head.

"Why won't you trust me?" she asked.

"'Cos I never trusted no one."

"Earl, you've got to start. Now."

His doubts remained, and they appeared to circle before his eyes, confusing him, causing him to speak falteringly when he began again. "And the police want me to consent. To the burial. To the girl's burial."

Andrea stood again, her mind racing, trying to compute the significance of the information. She glanced outside the room, saw two of the screws staring inside. She resumed her vigil by the door. "You're entitled to an independent post-mortem," she said, thinking aloud. Her attorney instincts told her that there must be something of significance to do with the body, that could be the only reason for the swift burial — something the police wanted to conceal. They knew an exhumation order was rare and difficult to obtain. But when she focused upon the living, bruised flesh of her client, the photographic images of the dead schoolgirl on the slab rose in front of her, and it was Andrea's turn to be confused. For she felt a bond with Earl, despite all his manifest faults, a protective, almost maternal concern for his welfare, while she grieved at the same time for the eight-year-old girl, so similar in age to Calvin when she had lost him.

"I didn't do nothing to Nicki," Earl complained. "So I ain't going to have her cut up no more on account of me."

"But, Earl—"

"No more, Miz Chambers. Let her parents bury her. Let them have that. Let them bury her."

A silence fell briefly between them. While Earl gingerly felt the bruising on his face, Andrea struggled to decide what the right thing to do was. She felt a tug towards her father's world, to the world of commercial practice, and she grasped instantly, without having to articulate it to herself, just how many problems her next decision might cause between herself and her father. But before her was a young man who had been brutalised, who had no one else in the world who would stand up for him, no one who would be prepared to disregard his faults and fight for him in court. She could not turn away.

"Earl, I'll represent you in court," she said. His eyes began to light up as she continued, "I'll take the case. And I won't let go."

"Thank you, miz."

"Don't thank me. Just tell me."

"What?"

"One thing. And most lawyers would not ask you. But I can't go on if you don't tell me. Just once." She paused, then whispered, "Did you shoot her?"

He shook his head once, left to right, but uttered no sound. She nodded in reply. It was agreed, the compact was made.

"Get me out," Earl said. "On bail tomorrow."

"It's hopeless without something. A surety, somewhere to reside, something."

"Roots Johnson will have the money," Earl said, buoyed by the confidence inspired by having a real lawyer represent him.

"Roots Johnson? How will I find this Roots Johnson?"

For the first time, Earl stood. He slid along the wall next to the door so that he was inches away from Andrea's right ear. "Calvin will know," he whispered.

The shock of her son's name made her mind swirl with terrible possibility. She grabbed his arm hard. "Calvin?" she asked. "Is that where he's gone? To find this man, Johnson?"

"You promised," Earl replied. "To help."

"Only if you tell me the truth."

"I am telling you the truth."

"So tell me, then," she said, her voice rising, beyond her control, "where to find my son."

"He's going to the Mashango sound clash."

But Andrea didn't allow him to continue. She put her hand over his mouth. "Oh, God," she said. "God, I've been so naïve." She looked frantically around the room, along the walls, quickly scanning the small square of corked ceiling, and in doing so she released Earl.

"What happen?" the Yardie asked.

"Why have they let us in here? Why have they left us alone? We're being set up, Earl. We're being bugged." She moved the chair, looked under its austere wooden seat, found nothing, saw nothing. "This conference is without prejudice. It's, er, it's . . ." She tried to recall the terminology, the form of words, the protections under the law. "It's legally privileged, it's inadmissible in a court of law."

But as hard as she searched, she saw no trace of a bug.

Hogarth heard Earl's answer as a strangely distorted mechanical sound as he sat in the visitor's control centre behind Andrea's consultation room. He stopped the covert recording equipment. The large metal spool of tape stopped turning. He hit another button, the rewind, then the play, and again Earl's static-filled voice came through the speakers.

". . . the Mashango sound clash," Earl said.

Hogarth switched off the tape, then gestured to the greying jailer that he wished to be alone. Only when he was did he speed-dial on his cellular. There was finally a click at the other end as the phone was answered. Hogarth spoke first; he knew Roots Johnson was never the first man to speak.

"You know what the Mashango did to your soldier, Johnson?" he asked the Yardie. There was no response.

"You know where to find them tonight?"

"They can't hide," Roots replied.

"But if we move quickly, we can take them all tonight."
Hogarth knew that Roots Johnson wouldn't respond to
this, that he had to amplify his plan. "My spies tell me —
that is, those spies who spy on my spies tell me — that the
Mashango want to meet me. Not just the soldiers, but the
politburo itself. I'll arrange a meet. Tonight. At this sound
clash I'm sure you know about."

"Why?" Roots asked simply.

"Because time's running out. Because Earl Whitely's got
Andrea Chambers to represent him."

"Earl won't talk no more."

"Remember, he's already talked," Hogarth said irritably.
"To Internal. About the three dons. And it's all your fault.
You recommended giving Whitely the contract."

"Three shots, three dons dead. He don't waste bullets.
And he's fired some more. The brief's son, Calvin
Patterson, came. About Whitely's bail. The boy rapped
about the three dons, too."

"How much does he know?" Hogarth asked.

"That's what I'll find out. Tonight at the sound clash,"
Roots said, hanging up immediately.

In the ballistics lab of the central London branch of the forensic science executive, Fisher and Kelsey stared at the charts on
the walls, full of pictures of deadly weapons and high-
powered ordnance, their proof marks and rifling patterns,
muzzle energy and recoil tables. It was a large work-space full
of scientific equipment and weighty firearms manuals from
around the world, with thick white-painted bars on the windows to prevent other types of gun enthusiasts from breaking in to add to their collection. On one of the laboratory
worktops there was a Bunsen burner. Fisher took out a cigarette, lit the Bunsen with his lighter, then lit the fag with the

Bunsen. Kelsey sat alone in the corner of the room, wiping his steel-rimmed glasses. Fisher puffed crudely on his cigarette and blew a couple of smoke rings.

"You can't smoke in here," Kelsey pointed out, tapping a red sign on the wall to that effect.

"And we must obey all the rules, mustn't we, Kelso?" the DS replied. He jumped up on to the worktop and perched there while he pontificated to the other officer. "You see, Kelso, ballistics is like the DNA of dangerous weapons, it's the fingerprints of firearms. And if the lab rats here do their job properly, we should be able to nail Earl Whitely to the courthouse door."

"So you're confident?"

Fisher tapped some ash on to the newly scrubbed lab floor. "Let's just say that out in the street firearms are Whitely's weapons, but in here they're ours."

Kelsey could not stand Fisher's lecturing any longer. "You're a firearms expert, then?" he asked.

"No, but I'm an expert in human nature, Kelsey. And that expertise tells me that we're going to crack this case not with witnesses but with bullshit sci-fi wizardry." Kelsey was about to reply, but thought better of it. Fisher, picking up on the fact that his colleague was avoiding an argument or even a debate, pursued him further. "What's the matter then, little Kelso?" he mocked. "Not still sulking, are we?"

Kelsey methodically replaced his glasses. "What you lot did. To Earl Whitely. It was cruel."

"It was necessary," Fisher said.

"According to who?"

Fisher paused, then moved swiftly across the lab to Kelsey, until he was right in the seated man's face. "Yeah, you're right, Kelso. 'Cos what happened to Nicki Harris wasn't cruel. And what Nicki's mum and dad're going through now? That ain't cruel neither."

"Two wrongs don't make a right," Kelsey shouted, getting to his feet.

"No, but it bloody well feels like it," Fisher shouted back.

At that moment, a forensic scientist, a woman in her early thirties, dressed in a white coat, came in.

"You've got to tell me, Doc," Fisher said. "Is it a boy or a girl?"

The woman looked at Fisher, saw the gormlessly amused look on his face, and then addressed her remark to Kelsey. "I hope your friend doesn't intend to be a policeman when he grows up," she said.

"He won't grow up," Kelsey said.

The woman took a slip of paper out of a long outer pocket. "There was sufficient clarity of rifling on your bullet to make a positive ID." She paused, looked around at the two men, certain that her next words would have a tremendous impact. "I'm afraid the bullet was fired by a Carbina. An old SP model."

There was no immediate response from Fisher, except possibly confusion. But Kelsey reacted very differently, his face twisted with shock.

"Are you sure?" he asked.

"The lands and grooves ratio. The number and twist," she said.

"What?" Fisher asked. "Doesn't it nail Whitely or something?"

"Oh, sweet Jesus," Kelsey said.

"What?" Fisher asked. "What?"

"The gun that killed Nicki Harris," Kelsey replied. "The make. It's an old police gun."

Stevie Fisher pretended to blank this revelation, but his mind was already racing, perming through the possibilities, creating fanciful scenarios, trying to find an angle, guessing where the skim might be, but all the time thinking, above all, of DCI John Hogarth.

CHAPTER FOURTEEN

The dance-hall pulsated with the thud-thud-thud of a monstrously loud bass. All around the semicircular stage hundreds of gyrating bodies surrendered themselves to the music, and the dance-floor appeared to crawl with oiled muscles and torsos, and gold chains and legs. All the time the bass assailed everyone and everything in the semi-darkness, which was more complete than the frosted city night outside, for the hall's high windows had been blacked with huge, dirty sheets and the only light came from those racks of spots that were co-ordinated with the sound system. There was a primitive feel to the hall itself, a long-abandoned church, its large stone pillars punctuating the dance-space and the broken blue-tiled floor, where once there had been pews. And all this overtaken, converted to the needs of a new religion, where people, both black and white, gave themselves to an older rhythm, and where the communion consisted of coke and crack and Es. Lucozade cans were scattered across the floor, as were chewing-gum wrappers. Free water was available to keep people hydrated as they pushed their bodies, as the narcotics pushed them, deeper and deeper into the night. And on the left-hand side of the stage, swamped by his sound system, was Calvin.

His vibes were being jammed at random intervals by a system on the other side of the stage area, operated by a frenzied man, dressed in exotic tie-dye clothes and with a bandana tied around his forehead. This man was lost in a trance, and flipped his discs and scratched them and

voiced the 'lyrix' oblivious to the hundreds of dancers, as
if he were on his own, in a black recess of his mind. Calvin
was focused too, but in an entirely different way. His mind
was paralysed with fear, for no sooner had the music
stopped than the hall was plunged into a cloud of spectral
dry ice, billowing from vents on pillars and walls, like
frozen breath in the heat and tumult.

Then between the two sound systems appeared the MC,
with a goatee and psychedelic make-up on lips and eyelids,
making him look like the Devil himself. This man had long
dreads that somehow defied gravity in all directions. The
long coils of black hair appeared to Calvin to be a nest of
snakes on the man's head.

"Nice," the MC said into a hand-held mike. "Give it up
for Mr Calvin MC."

A torrent of cheering and whooping flooded towards
the boy on the stage, intoxicating and frightening in its
intensity, making him shake the sweat from his face to try
to clear his head.

Dry ice swirled around the MC like a misty cape as he
turned to his right, away from Calvin, and hailed the other
sound system. "And big up, too," the MC screamed, "dee
Ma-shango Warr-ior."

At this incitement, there was a volley of gunfire. Bullets
shot through the air, bursts of flame exploding in the
darkness between the crumbling pillars, then they
smashed into the plaster of the roof high above the heads
of the dancers. Shards of plaster showered down from the
ceiling from this 'gunshot salute', and the people screamed
in appreciation. Calvin caught his teeth chattering and he
ground them hard together, but they were only stilled
when he felt behind his back with his left hand, and there,
tucked into his waistband, was Earl Whitely's nine-mil.

In the carpark at the rear of the hall, amid a sea of cars,
old and new but always stylish, five men with bandanas

stood around the open rear door of a customised American Jeep. Each of the black men proudly wore the telltale tropical colours of the Mashango, and they glanced back at the hall when the gunshots went off. They stood tightly around another man, a white man, who spoke in a steady, controlled voice.

"Now's the time to take Johnson," Hogarth said.

One of the Mashango, a man in his mid-twenties with a heavily scarred face, tribal scars that Hogarth realised must have been self-inflicted, turned away from the DCI and addressed his compatriots. "How we can trust this po-lice man?" he asked.

Hogarth sensed that the meeting was on the verge of going wrong, so he didn't allow anyone else to answer, saying, "You can't. But your real question should be: How can you trust each other? When the big prize, all of London, is handed to you on a plate, can you be sure you'll stick together?"

The Mashango furtively glanced around at each other, each now suspicious of the other men, for whom they had sworn to die. They each had one hand, and only one, in a jacket pocket or tucked inside the front of the coat, and Hogarth knew that meant they all were packing, that each had a finger on a trigger. Seeing the dissension spread between them, as each secretly imagined what it would be like to control the major trafficking in all of London, Hogarth knew it was time to press his point.

"I know you hate me," he said. "And you should know, I hate you. I hate all of you. I hate what you do in my city. What you stand for. What you sell. I hate your arrogance, and your greed. I even hate the stupid clothes you wear."

One of the Mashango had had enough. Seeing blood, he pulled his nine-mil on Hogarth, just out of the pocket of his leather jacket, enough for Hogarth to see it but not so that revellers rushing in and out of the hall would notice.

"Why don't you kids forget about your cap guns for a minute?" Hogarth said. "We don't want it to end in tears." He even smiled, staring deep into the man's eyes, until he was certain he had backed the youth down. The youth put the gun away. "What I was about to say," Hogarth continued, "was that I hate Roots Johnson even more than any of you. Even more than I hated the three dons. When they were alive," he added as an afterthought.

"Why?" the scarred man asked.

Hogarth paused. He gave the impression that he was assessing his loathing for Roots Johnson on the spot, tapping into unexpressed feelings. His rehearsed lines came out as perfectly spontaneous. "It's personal," he said.

"So why did you call a meet here?" the Mashango demanded.

"To offer you something. As a sign of goodwill. To begin the relationship between us correctly." He now had their interest completely, and like a master storyteller, weaving a plausible narrative out of a fantastic tale, he dropped his voice, and spoke in a confidential whisper. "There is a huge stash of product, ten keys, more perhaps, in the sound system inside. It's yours. My gift."

The five men looked at each other and their eyes lit up, one by one, like candles on a dark night, as they calculated the possibilities, almost tasted them.

"In the speakers," Hogarth continued, "right beside Calvin Patterson."

In a car parked opposite the front entrance of the hall, another black man pulled the high furred collar of his designer leather jacket up around his cheeks. With his knitted woollen ski hat, more suitable for the slopes of Gstaad, low over his forehead, it was very difficult to discern who this man was. But on the dash of the Ford Profile his soldiers had stolen just an hour previously he had an Arsenal shirt. It was Peckham's shirt, delivered to Roots just that morning, and the don carried it with him now as once the relics of saints were carried into battle against unbelievers. Roots waited in the car with the lights off. The faint strains of a classical string trio could be heard from the stereo speakers as he whispered into his mobile.

"I'm sorry," he said. "I wanted to come today. I couldn't."

"So tomorrow?" the woman's voice asked hopefully.

"I'm sorry, Katherine. Not tomorrow," Roots replied.

"So when?"

"Maybe never."

There was a pause in the conversation, and Roots wondered if he had done the right thing by calling her. But he had cancelled their business meeting, and considered it rude not to apologise. It was, in fact, Katherine who spoke next.

"Mr Johnson, forgive me for being so blunt. But I had hoped that we might have been able to do some business together. Some mutually beneficial business." There was the clink of a glass or a bottle or both down the line, and Roots imagined her there in her dated office with a bottle of Louis Roederer. Then she continued, "Yesterday, you said something."

"I said several things."

"Yes, but you said something I've been thinking about all day. You said I didn't like champagne, not really. And you were right. I don't like it. But I drink it. And I've been thinking that I drink it because I . . . I need it." The words came out in a rushed gabble, as if she had been practising what to say to him and it was almost a relief to get it out. "But at least it means that I understand one thing. And that's pain."

She paused, but Roots did not respond. It was time to respond, to give something of himself in return for this confidence, and he would have liked to, to have spoken to someone, to her, about his father, about this titanic hero of his childhood who had died in an American jail.

"I think . . . I think you're in pain," she said finally.

"I can't see you," Roots replied.

"Why not?"

"It would be dangerous for you."

"I don't care."

"You don't know."

"Yes, I do," she said. "In a way."

Just then, Lifer's enormous face filled the glass of Roots's car window. Lifer nodded once behind him, and there in the shadows the crew had assembled. They were ready. Roots nodded back.

"Tomorrow," he told Katherine. "I'll try to ring you."

"Try harder," she said as she hung up.

Roots couldn't help himself and he smiled briefly at her tenacity, but this moment of good humour died when he picked up Peckham's shirt. He folded it neatly in half, then again, then rolled it compactly so that it would fit into the large outside pocket of his leather jacket. He got out of the stolen car as another vehicle turned the corner and entered the street.

Behind the wheel of her hatchback, Andrea squinted through the gloom and towards the large building, which she hoped was finally the right hall. She had been led a merry dance for the best part of that evening, since the information that Earl Whitely had given her as to where Calvin would be performing was incorrect and no one had been in Calvin's flat when she called round. The front door had been sealed by the police and there was no sign of life inside.

She had eventually learnt that the location of that night's gig had been moved, and then moved again, to throw unwanted members of the law enforcement community off the trail, since the clash was not properly authorised by the council and was thus illegal. But news of the final location shot across the invisible underground grapevine of the Yardie and the dance scenes and was available to those in the know, those who could be trusted, but this category did not include Andrea. This fact, in itself, saddened her, for fifteen years before, when she and Calvin's father had been students at the LSE, she would have been among the excited youths rushing around after-hours London to find the latest place to be. Now it was Calvin's time, and it worried her sick. She began to grasp why her own father had stayed up with his *Daily Telegraph*, pretending to be stuck on the cryptic crossword, until she returned safely from a party. Being overly protective, protecting one's children from themselves, she decided — yes, that could be love.

She slowed down and pulled over to the kerb. Two youths, a black male and a white girl, rushed arm in arm towards the entrance of the hall one hundred yards further down the road. Andrea leaned over, stretched to reach the small handle of the passenger window, and then wound it down.

"Excuse me," she called. The youths stopped. "Is the, er, sound clash in there?"

The two youngsters cracked up. Andrea had indeed felt stupid saying it. The boy turned to his girlfriend and said in an exaggerated middle-class accent, "Heggs-cuse me, Grandma."

The kids dashed behind the parked cars and away from Andrea. She smiled uneasily to herself, even though she fully realised that the joke was on her, and scanned both sides of the road in an attempt to find a parking space, but they were full. As she drove slowly nearer and nearer to the hall, the boom-boom of the bass began to reverberate within her car, and she wondered if her son was responsible for the music. It worried her, since it must have been dangerously loud inside, and if Calvin was doing his MC bit at the turntable she thought he might be irreparably damaging his ears. How old and fusty she had become — how many times her father had shouted up to her to turn the music down in her bedroom. Andrea continued past the hall itself and the music began to fade as she turned the next corner, where there appeared to be a huge open space being used as a carpark. Finally, she found a space among the hundred-plus cars, parked chaotically in all directions on the wasteland. The ground itself was rutted and broken, and when she got out of her car she stepped in an oily puddle. Calvin Patterson, she thought to herself, you are grounded till you're thirty-five. She walked briskly with her head down towards the main road, but as she turned the corner the music suddenly stopped. It was as if the final notes hung there in the air, waiting to be topped.

Inside the entrance to the hall, Roots and his crew formed a tight circle. Without any further instruction from the don, they all pulled nightmarish black ski masks over their faces and flicked off the safeties on their guns.

"Remember Peckham," Roots said.

"No prisoners," Lifer hissed.

Outside, Andrea paused and looked around during the strange silence between the dying of the bass and the next deafening noise, the thundering of gunfire. She heard dreadful screaming from inside as she rushed to the entrance. Women screaming in terror, men screaming in pain. More gunfire, short bursts of it, punching the night air, and now people were tearing out of the hall hysterically, bursting out of the narrow entrance like water through a crack in a dam, and then hurtling off in all directions, scattering past Andrea, running into her, pushing her, a human tide fleeing the bullets as the gunfire started up again. And Andrea went in the opposite direction, driven by instinct and adrenalin, towards the gunfire, towards her son, while from the opposite side of the road a lone figure watched. Hogarth.

Andrea fought her way to the very threshold of the hall, the border between her safe world and the world into which Calvin had fallen. Terrified ravers tore past her, while a spectral fog swirled over the Gothic space, with its pillars and blacked-out windows. Gunmen in black death-masks waved their guns around like reapers in the darkness, and Andrea saw that on the tiled floor bodies were scattered, broken and bloodied, as pools of blood slowly spread from exit wounds. She screamed for her son, but her voice was lost in the chaos. She rushed across the floor, trying not to slip in the pools of blood. Then from behind her there was another shot, which seemed to explode in her ear canal, making her shiver. All the time she scanned the crowd, what was left of it, for Calvin, until someone yanked her from behind. She was hauled backwards, away from the direction in which she wanted to go, towards the stage, and huge hands twisted her painfully around. She looked up and saw a monstrous, distended ski mask, black wool stretched to its very limit across a massive pumpkin of a face. There was no hole for the mouth, but Andrea could see the crazy eyes behind two slits.

"Get the fuck out," the mask cried at her, and she could see lips moving beneath the taut wool, as if it the twenty-stone man inside were trying to eat the mask itself. The man raised a machine-pistol towards her face. "Get out," he cried. His other hand squeezed her thin arm tighter and tighter, like a vice being screwed closed on her flesh.

"I want my son," she shouted back.

The gunman's head was flung back so that his eyes

looked directly at the vaulted roof, and he laughed demonically. Andrea broke free and stepped over bodies and hauled herself on to the stage. And there she saw a lone body, a young black man slumped with his back to her. He had been shot from the other side, and she could see the exit wound, a star shape of tattered flesh in his back, which she recognised as being a shotgun exit wound.

"Calvin," she cried. "Oh, God, Calvin."

She pulled the body over and then was confused. For the youth had a bandana and a face that was not her son's. She glanced frantically around, over the mess of wires and electrical equipment, thinking that perhaps Calvin had not after all come to the gig, when she saw him. Sitting behind a speaker, with his knees under his chin, rocking himself like a child having a nightmare. She flung herself at her child and held his head close to her midriff. Then she squatted down.

"Are you hurt?" she asked, but he wasn't even looking at her, still trying to rock himself, and she wasn't even sure that he knew she was there.

She held his face in her hands and attempted to make him look at her eyes, calling out his name, then again, but when his eyes did meet hers she was terrified, for they appeared to look straight through her. She looked directly behind her, and there saw another masked figure. This man ripped off his ski mask, oblivious to mother and son, and began to spin in a maelstrom of his own. He leaned against a speaker with one arm and tried to retch, but his stomach knotted and it was a dry retch, a sickness in his soul he could not cast out.

Roots threw his mask down and for a moment, across the clouds of dry ice which still billowed across the stage, his eyes met those of the white woman cradling Calvin Patterson. Roots guessed instantly who she must be. He approached her, wiping the spittle from his mouth with the back of his leather sleeve, but she shielded her son from him.

"Leave us alone!" she shouted.

He grabbed Calvin's hand. She fought with him to have it released, and he was stunned by the coiled energy the woman possessed.

"The police," he shouted.

"We've got nothing to hide," she shouted back.

Roots knew he couldn't reason with this mother, he had to show her, to prove to her the danger to which she was about to expose her son. He padded the rear of Calvin's waistband and there he found the nine-mil they had returned to him in the lab earlier that day. He watched as Andrea's face filled with horror, but he took no pleasure in it, he had to weaken her resistance if he was to have any hope of saving her son. Outside, police sirens wailed.

"We've got to get him out!" Andrea cried.

"Here," Roots said, pointing to an open rear exit.

In the space of ten seconds, the three people were out into the iced night air. The sirens closed in fast, and Roots had listened for sirens almost all his life, so he knew there was little time. He led Calvin by one arm; Andrea supported the other.

"He's not injured," Roots tried to reassure her.

"He's just a child."

"Got a car?" he asked.

Andrea pointed to her hatchback, and they took Calvin over to it as the police arrived at the front of the hall. She opened the passenger door and Calvin, confused but coming out of his fear in the freezing air, got in automatically. Andrea turned and looked up at the striking Yardie.

"Say nothing," he said.

She looked down at his left hand, saw his long fingers curled around the gun he had removed from Calvin's

waistband. She grabbed it from him, and he didn't resist.
In an instant, he knew that his job was done and mother
and son no longer needed him. He turned and moved
behind one car, then another, so quickly, so silently, that
to Andrea he seemed simply to have disappeared into the
night. She broke out of his captivating spell when she
realised that the police sirens had now stopped, and that
officers were probably racing through the front of the hall.
She jumped into the car, tossed the gun into the well of the
rear seats and accelerated out of the wasteland. Her mind
buzzed crazily and she over-revved the engine, taking
tight turns, left and right, right and left, but always further from the hall.

"Calvin?" she cried. "Calvin, talk to me."

The boy turned, spotted the gun lying in the well
behind her, being buffeted from side to side as she drove,
and he reached for it.

"Leave it," she shouted, but it was too late. The gun was
now in his hand. She threw the car right, left, slamming on
the brakes, barely making the turn. "Where did you get
that?" He didn't reply. "Calvin, for Christ's sake. Is it Earl's
gun?"

"I want to get out," he said coldly.

"No. Did you use it?"

"I want to get *out*," he screamed at her. He partly
opened the door. Andrea glanced to her left, then back to
the front, adjusted the steering wheel, then saw her son
open the door wider, so that now she could see a strip of
pavement racing past outside. The engine was louder, the
pistons straining. Cold air rushed into the car. She had no
option and she knew it. In his mood, he was capable of
jumping out.

Andrea slowed the car. Then stopped. She sweated, terrified, rested her head on the wheel and said, "What are
we going to do?"

Calvin didn't reply. He fully opened the door. She moved to stop him stepping out, but he struggled free, and again she realised that her little boy was so much stronger than she was. The gun was still in his hand.

"I'm going to Rufus's," he said calmly, as if nothing had happened.

"No, please. Get in. I'll drive you there."

He expertly slipped the gun into the rear of his waist-band, Yardie style, then he leant into the car. "I didn't use it," he told his mother.

He closed the door quietly and turned into a dark alley. Soon, Andrea had lost sight of him, and she didn't know what to do, didn't even know what she wanted to do. As she put the car into gear again, the image of her son played slowly again and again in her mind — her teenage son with a gun. Try as she might, she found it hard to distinguish him in those moments from the gunmen in the dance-hall.

CHAPTER FIFTEEN

The next morning, Andrea stared at herself in the apparently safe, bright light of her bathroom mirror. They had added the en suite to the bedroom a year before, when Cameron had repeatedly asked her to 'get really serious', as he had euphemistically called it. Instead of giving him a direct answer, she had buried herself in a pile of catalogues from fitted furniture manufacturers and more expensive boutique designers. She had told Cameron that she would 'think about it', then she said she would need to think about it some more, then she needed to think about colour schemes and shower screens, so that after four months they no longer talked about it explicitly, even though his non-proposal of marriage remained a subtext for much of their intimate conversations.

As she stared at herself, she traced the faint black lines just below the surface of the skin beneath her eyes. Although they were just a symptom of stress and worry, it appeared as if her eyes were bruised. She splashed tepid water over her face from the sink, as if this would remove the marks. It was with a strange, distant feeling that she watched herself in the mirror take the smooth plastic bottle of mouthwash, gargle some of the vile green liquid, and then spit it out in the sink. She felt as though she were watching someone else, another woman with a teenage son in trouble, who appeared calm and quiet the morning after she had found him with a gun, a woman whose composure showed none of the turmoil that wrenched Andrea's insides, and she envied this other woman, for unlike Andrea she appeared to know what to do.

The door to the bathroom opened behind her and Cameron came in silently, putting his comforting arms around her. She suddenly felt exposed, vulnerable, and pulled her towelling bathrobe tightly around herself.

"Hey, what's the matter?" he asked.

She turned round to face him, feeling the hard, rounded sink in the small of her back. She dropped her chin on to her chest bone, and her still-wet hair fell forward across her face.

"Come on, Andy," he insisted. "Don't shut me out." He stroked her creased forehead. She closed her eyelids; the caressing did feel good. "Please," he said.

She nodded and took a breath. "Last night," she said, "when I found him, he was crying. Actually crying. With gunsmoke and this dry ice stuff all around him. And I . . . I just can't remember when I last saw my son cry. Even way back then—"

"Don't do this to yourself, darling."

She opened her eyes and looked up into his freshly shaved face. He always looked five years younger when he shaved. And his hopefulness, his youthful optimism, untouched by any real adversity in his life, had always been deeply attractive to her. She fed off it, drew strength from it, when her life in all its complexity and madness assaulted her again.

"Even way back then," she repeated, "I can't remember him crying. His mummy was leaving him and he didn't shed a tear. Not one. My little man. Cameron, I love him so much and I just know he hates me."

"Give him time."

She took his hand, squeezing it hard. "He hasn't got time. Not in that world he's living in. That's the one thing he hasn't got."

He freed himself and put a hand on each of her shoulders. "You know," he said sombrely, "sometimes to keep it together, you've got to leave it alone."

"What is that? Philosophy?"

"No. Fleetwood Mac," he laughed.

She pretended to be furious and whacked him on the chest with her fist, but Cameron had broken the spell, as he always seemed to do when she was in her darker moods. She kissed him on the cheek, which for them was a more affectionate embrace than a cursory kiss on the lips. "Actually, it's the Carpenters," she said.

"No way," he protested. "God, I was in love with Karen Carpenter and those words never passed her sublime lips. Trust me on this."

They looked at each other, both flicking mentally through the embarrassments of their record collections. Then they both said, not quite together, "The *Eagles*."

They laughed again.

"We are seriously sad children of the seventies," she said.

Cameron was about to respond when the doorbell rang downstairs. It rang again insistently and Cameron agreed to answer it. Andrea left the bathroom after him, but squatted cross-legged on the bed and attempted to run a comb through the knots of her wet hair.

"Andy," he called up from downstairs. "It's for you."

"What?" she called down, damp hair like a curtain in front of her eyes.

"I don't know. A package of some kind."

She stopped combing and sped down the stairs. The wooden, varnished steps were cold beneath her bare feet and minute grains of grit embedded themselves in her soles, causing her to question again their decision not to carpet the stairs. Cameron stood to one side in the narrow hall so that she could pass, and he had left the door slightly ajar, so that gusts of arctic air rushed into the house from outside. When she reached the oak door, she stepped on to the doorstep as the breeze pinned her wet hair against her scalp. Standing outside was a deliveryman with a massive bunch of flowers of all colours. She thanked the man and closed the door.

Cameron smiled his impish, schoolboy smile. "From me," he said.

"But why?"

"Because you had such a shitty birthday."

She cradled the precious blooms in her arms. The perfume was sharp, but pleasant in her nostrils. Then she gently laid them on the glass-top table in the hall and flung her arms around Cameron's neck. She craned her head up and kissed him hungrily, trying to lose herself once more. Their lips finally inched apart, though the tiniest film of saliva still joined them. It vanished when she spoke.

"Shitty birthday, was it? That means you didn't like my special dessert."

"I liked it," Cameron insisted. "But, you know, last night when I was waiting for you to return, I was flicking through Delia's cookbook in the kitchen. And can you believe there wasn't a recipe for chocolate soup?"

"I am totally devastated," Andrea said, pretending to be shocked.

She could now feel his warm hands inside her bathrobe, caressing her lower back, edging down towards her buttocks. She cursed herself as she felt her body beginning to chill, even though she loved him and would have relished the release of sex. He pulled back, recognising the all-too-familiar signs.

"I'm sorry," she said.

"What about?"

"That we haven't been . . . you know."

"Hey," he said gently. "You're my best friend as well as

my lover. I can cope if it's best-friend time right now."

She smiled briefly and folded herself into his arms.

"But, Andy," he whispered mischievously, "I'm going to need a good shag soon."

Andrea was about to pick up her flowers again when she spotted the phone on the glass table. She thought quickly, then decided to risk it. With Cameron still holding her, she picked up the digital cordless and speed-dialled.

"Rufus? Calvin?" she said when it was answered. Glumly, she replaced the handset into its cradle.

"What?" Cameron asked.

"They hung up on me," she said. She picked up her flowers. Gorgeous though they were, they no longer smelt so good, or at least she could not smell them. "I'd better get ready for court," she said.

"You're sure you want to defend Calvin's friend?" Cameron asked, concern creating folds of deep skin on his forehead.

"No," she replied simply.

"Then why do it?"

"I can't just tell him I love him, Cameron. I have to prove it."

"For God's sake, Andy, you haven't been in a criminal court for ten years."

She knew this all too well, but she tried to bluff and smile bravely. "I haven't been in a disco for ten years. Doesn't mean I can't dance."

Cameron stroked her matted hair. "I might take you up on that," he said. "Now, go dry your hair, counsellor."

At the same time, in Rufus's flat, Calvin replaced the receiver of his grandfather's clunky old telephone. The old man was still in his bedroom and called from behind his shut door in his croaky morning voice, "Who was it, Calvin?"

Calvin slumped back on to the battered sofa in his box-ers. "Wrong number," he shouted back. He had not made the mistake of bringing the gun into his grandfather's flat again, but had hidden it in the forlorn bushes at the foot of the block, tightly wrapped in a plastic bag. He was so exhausted after the sound clash that he would have loved to have lain in all morning, but he forced himself to his feet in the draughty flat. He, too, began to ready him-self for court.

He flicked on the black-and-white television as he pulled on his clothes, which still smelt acrid, of cordite and gunsmoke. On the box there was a brief report on the local news. They were burying Nicki Harris today.

Roots and his crew emerged on to the windswept roof of a vertiginously high tower block. It had been a night of rev-elry after the shoot-out, and Roots's soldiers were still speeding on the adrenalin rush, still exchanging war sto-ries about their role in the triumph. Each of the half-dozen men had an open bottle of champagne, grasped around the neck as one might try to strangle a chicken, and they swigged and spoke, swigged and spoke, sometimes spray-ing champagne out from their mouths as they laughed. Roots had nothing to drink.

The roof of the block was a forty-feet-square area with a head-high wall and rusting wire fencing up to ten feet to prevent jumpers. To one side was the housing for the lift machinery, something like a concrete shed rising one hun-dred feet in the air. Next to this was the smaller exit of the emergency stairs, and it was from here that the crew had emerged, the lifts not having worked in the building for months. The wind ripped across the exposed place, mak-ing the fence wires hum, while to the sides it appeared as though London lay at their feet, in miniature, manageable, so near that they only had to reach out and it would be

entirely theirs. Most of the crew were so intoxicated by
now that they could barely stand, but Lifer, with his great
bulk, showed no reaction to the pints of champagne he
had consumed. As the soldiers rough-housed, and play-
fought, taking out their guns and aiming them at one
another, pretending to shoot, pursing lips and shouting
'Boom', Lifer approached Roots. The don stood at the fence
and held the wire in each hand, staring down at the bewildering pattern of roads and railway lines, the crawling
cars, the hint of the river in the distance, while sullen
clouds were driven hard by the wind and seemed to pass
inches overhead.

"What happen?" Lifer asked.

Roots looked round at his lieutenant, who still wore his
shades. He looked at the obscenely thick golden dollar
medallion swinging from Lifer's neck, worn with as much
pride by the huge Yardie as if it were the Medal of Honor.

"All those people," Roots said, "going to work. I wonder when they'll find out about last night. If they care."

"Them won't care," Lifer said confidently. "And they
ain't just people. You see," he said, sweeping his fat hand
over the horizons of London, "they're all your subjects.
They is all our customers now. Only they don't know it
yet. But they will. They is going to know soon, no problem." He raised the bottle in his other hand and toasted
Roots. "With the Mashango gone, it's all yours."

The wind buffeted Roots, penetrating right under his
knee-length leather jacket, so that he had to fold his arms
to keep his chest warm. He shivered, and he knew that this
was the type of chill that came from within the body as
well as without.

"It's yours," Lifer repeated.

Roots carefully surveyed his crew, cavorting with guns,
celebrating the greatest achievement of their young lives,
the massacre of other Jamaican men, and he wondered

how many people they had killed between them, how many funerals they had caused, how many unidentified corpses they had consigned to morgues. Briefly, he thought of Katherine, and this surprised him, about how she had been in a different kind of pain when she had spoken with pride of her child playing in the Canadian snow, the child from whom she had been separated. All kinds of pain, he thought, all kinds of pain.

"Now we has a monopoly, we could raise prices. They all gotta come to us," Lifer said. Then he shook the dregs of the champagne out of his bottle in excitement as an even more stunning idea struck him. "Or we could lower prices. Ya, man. Lower them all. Like a kind of promotion. Get new customers. More customers, so cheap we make all the city customers. Oh, Lord, imagine that one. A sick city, only wanting our medicine. That's what we should call ourselves. The medics or some shit."

"I don't want it," Roots told him.

"Is what you say?"

"I want out, Lifer."

The huge man flung the heavy-bottomed champagne bottle over the top of the fence, and it fell in a silent parabola and smashed in the streets below. "Uh-huh. Out as in out of your fucking mind? *Out*? Of what?" he asked.

"Of the guns. The killing."

"And how you think you can get out?"

"Music," Roots said. As Lifer cursed in disdain at the mention of legitimate work, he continued, "A studio, for black music. Run by us. For ours."

"No, no, no, we got retailers screaming for product. We got the competition all gone. No, this is our time."

"Your time, maybe. Not mine. Not any more."

"You stop dealing and the turf wars start up again. We don't deal and there's going to be a hole. And someone will fill it. In blood. Someone will have to fill it." He shook the fence with one massive hand. "Out there? It's a city of addicts. They need us. They need our product. We go, they go crazy."

"I can't help that," Roots said.

Lifer was about to provide more arguments, but thought better of it. He simply asked, "Why?"

Roots said nothing. Instead, he slowly and lovingly pulled Peckham's Arsenal shirt out of his long outer pocket. It billowed in the breeze like a flag.

Lifer pawed his nine-mil from his waistband, and while he checked the clip he said, "A Yardie can't resign. It ain't no job." Satisfied that his gun was ready, he slid it back in his waistband. He went right up to Roots, and for the first time that the don could remember he took off his shades in daylight. His small, dead eyes stared up at Roots. "A Yardie, it's who you are. No matter what you want to be. It's what you are. And the only way out? That's in a box."

As the rain began to fall, Roots began to fold Peckham's shirt up again. He didn't argue with Lifer, for he knew the fundamental truth of the man's warning.

CHAPTER SIXTEEN

The hearse containing Nicki Harris's body arrived at the graveyard in the driving rain. The yellow headlights of the black vehicle shone brightly in the deteriorating light, even though it was still relatively early in the morning. The large police presence was divided into two parts — those officers, including members of the top brass in dress uniform, getting a drenching, and the beat officers there for crowd control. For Nicki's small coffin was now at the head of a long, snaking and thoroughly unwanted procession. It was the main story, the only real story, in the eyes of the media, and any idea of privacy for the family was impossible. But there was a more malign contingent, as Nicki Harris had rapidly become the icon, the rallying call, of extremist right-wing groups, who lined the route to the cemetery respectfully, armed with new weapons, with banner pictures of the eight-year-old girl, which they had copied and enlarged from newspapers and police press releases. These Union Jack-draped groups saw Nicki's death not so much as a tragedy but as a spark, as an opportunity, to demonstrate to the unbelieving country the truth of their message, that the race war was already being waged in the streets and that the casualties would mount.

When the hearse finally stopped, and the honour guard of police officers lined up with PC Harris to carry the small coffin to the grave, the solemn duty and the undoubted honour of opening the hearse back doors was given to the officer investigating Nicki's murder, DCI John Hogarth.

After the ceremony, after she had thrown a handful of wet dust on to the coffin, Dawn Harris was supported by her husband as she left her child in the ground. People around the graveside moved silently aside to allow her through, not just out of respect, it seemed to Hogarth, but to ensure that if the tragedy that had been inflicted on the Harrises was contagious, then they would not also be exposed to infection. Despite the canopy of black umbrellas, the curtains of rain had made the paths dangerously slippery, and mud had been trodden on to the paving stones by those people who had walked over other, older graves to get a better view of the circus. But to everyone's surprise, Dawn did not go meekly back to the waiting cars. She changed course. She made her way directly to Hogarth, who stood alone under a dripping oak tree. Its leafless branches reached out like black arms into the low, dirty sky and afforded Hogarth no real shelter from the storm.

Dawn now stood inches away from him, so close that he could see the drizzle of raindrops than ran down her thick lenses in haphazard fashion. She took her glasses off when she reached him, and again he was struck by the still intensity of her dark eyes. "My husband tells me you're a decent man," she said. "So, please. Tell me the truth."

A small knot of people had quickly gathered behind her, and uniformed officers struggled to keep them back.

"Do you really know who Nicki's killer is?" she asked.

"I really know," Hogarth replied.

"And he'll be punished?"

"Yes," Hogarth said.

Dawn nodded and wiped the water from her eyes. "I want to meet him," she said, her voice cracking. "I want to ask him. Why he killed my baby."

As her stare burned into him, Hogarth could feel his resolve faltering. There were people everywhere in the cemetery. He was convinced he could handle the press, members of the public, other police officers, even the top brass. But this woman, this mother, she frightened him. He knew she was dangerous, or rather, her grief would now be his opponent, and he would have to channel it, blunt it, subvert it. He assessed her carefully in the rain before him, and didn't think she was weak enough to have the grief turned upon herself. Her thirst for justice, which he understood was just a primal desire for revenge, would now be her life. He had to harness the woman's power, and he had come prepared.

"I've buried seven children," he said, "in my time as a police officer. And every single one of them has said to me what I am convinced your Nicki is saying to me right now. She doesn't want your tears, Dawn. But she does want your anger. Because anger can be love, too. When it hurts enough."

As he spoke, she looked up at him, confused, yearning for someone to tell her how to deal with the pain she felt for her daughter. It encouraged him further in his task when he saw her momentarily touch the gold crucifix around her neck.

"That bullet," he continued, "that killed your Nicki? It keeps travelling. It pierces all of us. All of us who care. Because I believe that what happened to Nicki must be — and you have to believe this, too — it must be a sign. To show us, how to choose . . . the right thing to do."

As he finished speaking, he saw that her eyes had glazed over, and that her mind was in turmoil. He had earlier doubted whether the date of the burial was the right time to make his next move, but now he saw her confusion he was certain, and he was glad that he had taken precautions. He glanced to his right, to the next tree, and beckoned another man forward. This man, with his tightly belted raincoat and cunning eyes, affected a half-smile, half-frown of sympathy when he joined them.

Hogarth took both of Dawn's hands and held them together in his own. "I want to help you, Dawn. But you must help me. I've already spoken briefly to your husband about this."

She now looked at the other man blankly, numb with emotion.

"This is Colin Stackman," Hogarth whispered to her. "He's a reporter."

Another crowd had gathered in the rain outside the high-security Magistrates' court, not far away across South London. But this crowd, awaiting the arrival of Earl Whitely, was far from silent. The police had divided it up on to opposite sides of the road. The side nearer the court complex was exclusively white, mostly young men with short haircuts, their faces distorted with anger as they screamed racial abuse across the street. On the other side was an equally familiar group of anti-fascist protesters. White and black were evenly mixed in this group, and they tended to have longer hair and were more student-like in their appearance. However, the front of their line, directly opposing the police, was manned (and it was an exclusively male contingent) by neat black men in black suits and white shirts with bow ties — black separatists, an honour guard of the Family of Islam. This side of the road chanted back anti-Nazi slogans, though they carried banners advertising for the benefit of the media several disparate on-going disputes and causes.

Suddenly, a right-winger could contain his rage no longer, and he broke through the police line. He ran into the open road between the groups, a kind of no-man's-land, and hurled a wooden placard at his enemies. Two police officers ran up to him from behind and tried to wrestle him to the ground, but they couldn't keep their balance in the driving rain, and the group of three fell to the floor, a tangle of arms and legs in struggle. This triggered a violent response from both sides. Coins and cans and placard sticks flew in opposite directions across the road, while the police line fragmented as officers on both sides took evasive action or piled into the crowd to make arrests. A police Sherpa van skidded to a stop between the lines and riot control officers in NATO helmets, with long plastic shields, jumped out with their batons drawn. It was a scene of total chaos, rain and raw hate, recrimination out of control, blood boiling, heads lost. And it was into this cauldron that Andrea forced herself to represent Earl Whitely.

She took advantage of a change in the focus of the fight, for the prison van that contained Earl had arrived and the crowd swarmed around it like corpuscles around an alien body in the bloodstream. It appeared to Andrea that the driver of the van had even slowed deliberately so that the photographs of the surrounded van and the TV shots that would be on the news could be taken. She was now about twenty yards from the van itself, but she could clearly hear the drumming on the side of the vehicle by scores of fists, and the cries of 'Black bastard' and 'Murderer' and 'Child killer'. She knew that caged inside was a teenager with cigarette burns on his scalp. Her chest ached for Earl, who would be terrified. She feared that the city had gone crazy, that all the poison and hatred in the air had swollen to such an extent that it would flood London. She had seen this fervour in the London streets when she was a student and Brixton had gone off, then Southall, and other flashpoints in other racially mixed cities in the summer of 1981. It was happening again, and instead of being buoyed along by it, as she and Calvin's father had been in the early eighties, she and her son were now somehow at the epicentre of the madness. She fought her way through the exclusively white crowd, for no other reason than they were nearer the entrance to the court. She was closer now to the front of the van as it inched its way forward towards the side entrance, when a tall, thin man almost pushed her over, and flung himself directly in the path of the van. The driver had to jam on his brakes, and the man unfurled what he carried. The crowd all around Andrea cheered furiously as the man held up for all to see a rope noose. Andrea felt sick.

She spun away and pushed with more determination towards the court doors, where a smaller gaggle of reporters awaited. When they saw her, with her sober lawyer's suit and briefcase, they rushed forward. In a flash, Andrea was surrounded, tapes were shoved in her face, flashes went off around her, and a microphone boom wafted over her head. Hand-held lights, illuminating the rain, which had eased to a drizzle, blinded Andrea so that she could not properly see the faces of the reporters who were firing the questions.

"Are you representing Nicki's killer? Has he admitted killing her? Is he a Yardie?"

Andrea kept her head down, trying to ignore it all, trying to think of something else, of anything else. Flowers, Cameron's flowers, she thought to herself, but she could not visualise them as the scrum carried her forward with her feet barely touching the ground. Then one question stunned her to a halt.

"Do you have a black son?"

She snapped her head round, squinted into the lights. "Who said that?" she cried. "Who the hell said that?"

There was a momentary silence as other hacks observed how the question had hit home. Then almost immediately there was a barrage of similar questions. "Who's the father? Is he a Yardie? Is the boy half-caste?"

Andrea was pulled and tugged as the breath was knocked out of her. How do you know? she wanted to cry.

But the answer appeared in front of her. One of the officers from the police station, the blond detective she recalled as being particularly hostile, DS Fisher, blocked the doors to the court building. He smirked, and held her eye for a fraction of a second to let her know that he was responsible for leaking the personal material. Then he opened the court doors grandly for her.

"She's a brief," he muttered to the security officers just inside the door.

Andrea dashed inside and shut the glass door quickly, but the reporters outside pressed up to the panes, mouthing questions at her that she could no longer hear. The feeding frenzy looked to her now like something out of a silent movie, but more pathetic and remote. She was under no illusions. The case was a tinderbox. She would be under the strictest scrutiny, as would her advocacy, as would her family.

As she was patted down by a woman officer, she looked around at the trappings of criminal justice that she had spent ten years attempting to put behind her: the royal coat of arms, the rampant lion and the unicorn, the court lists, the policemen in uniforms comparing notes, the thick glass counter that divided the cells from the body of the public space. The stale smell of yesterday's cigarettes still hung in the air, and the lobby was full of the detritus of those who are forced to wait with nothing to do — graffiti on walls, plastic cups under tables, the foam backing to chairs systematically pulled off. The décor had the absurd feel of an airport lounge, with low-slung modern furniture, but Andrea knew that this was a place of few arrivals, of few return tickets — the huddled masses who filled such court lobbies all over the country were more likely to be there to witness the departure of their loved ones, coming in the front door, going out the back.

She devoutly wished she could be elsewhere. On some

sunny riverbank with Rufus, perhaps, joking with the old
man about how he never caught anything; or at home, in
what Cameron called the spare bedroom, the one she regularly cleaned and dusted, in which she kept many of the
presents she had bought for Calvin over the years, which
he had never come to collect. She couldn't think of a
preferable place involving her own father, and that dis-
tressed her. But she laughed to herself when she realised
that such a place would have to involve tropical fish of
some kind, and consequently that the two older men she
admired the most, Gordon and Rufus, were both crazy
about fish. She had never looked at them in this light
before, had never made this now obvious connection, but
that was what courtrooms were all about: connections.

At the far end of the glass-fronted atrium, Andrea saw
the doors to the main courtroom, still shut, guarded by
armed police next to the metal detectors. The crowd was
now massed outside the doors of the court, and the police
were beginning to search people who sought entry into
the complex. Though she had been secretly worried that
her nerve might fail, it did not, for she thought again of
Earl, alone and frightened inside the van, surrounded by
a lynch mob, with no one to speak up for him but Andrea.

She saw a dispensing machine along the far wall and
decided to gather her composure by getting a drink. There
were many choices, hot and cold, and she opted for a hot
chocolate. She put in a fifty-pence coin, and the machine
swallowed it. She searched in her purse for another coin as
members of the public began to fill the waiting areas, but
she had used her last fifty pence. She looked around to see
if there was anyone who appeared vaguely friendly, who
might have change for a pound, and it was then that she
saw a familiar figure making his way through the front
doors of the building, holding his hands in the air to be
searched by the police. It was Calvin.

She rushed through the growing crowd and then stopped dead ten feet away from her son. She held her breath hard inside her as she watched Calvin being searched by a uniform, his hands still in the air as if he were surrendering, while the man kept asking questions indistinctly. All she could hear was her son's voice saying no in response to each enquiry. He looked at her as he was patted down and a metal detector wand was brushed over his body. It was the shameful face, with his mouth turned down at the sides, that she remembered from when he was a boy and had been caught snooping around in the fridge or had broken something in the house. After the security officer had finished with him, Calvin made his way towards her. She took his elbow immediately and led him into a corner of the lobby.

"What the hell are you doing here?" she whispered.

"Thought I better get used to these places," he replied sarcastically. "You seem to think this is where I'm ending up."

"All right. You've made your point."

He shook his head. Then he reached into his padded jacket and took something out. He offered it to her. "Now I've made my point," he said.

Andrea looked down at a small bar of plain chocolate, her favourite. Insignificant as this piece of confectionery was in the whole scheme of things, her heart soared.

"To say sorry," Calvin said. "For last night."

He could barely get the words out. But for Andrea, each word was a revelation, since she simply could not remember when he had previously apologised to her, for anything. She flung her arms around his neck and hugged him, the plain chocolate still in her hand. Calvin froze in embarrassment, standing there like a block of ice.

"People are watching," he whispered.

"Let them," she replied. "You used to let me kiss you

when I dropped you at school."

"I was six."

They broke apart, and with her heart still pounding she proudly looked him up and down. "You haven't really changed," she said.

"You have," he retorted.

"Oh, thanks."

She smiled and wiped her eyes, though there were no tears in them. "I hope you're better at flattering your girl-friends."

"I don't got no girlfriends," he said in an adult fashion. "I got me baby-mothers for my kids."

"What?" Andrea cried.

Calvin laughed, throwing his head back slightly and looking at her out of the corner of his eye as he always used to when he teased her. "Only joking."

Andrea put her hand to her chest. "Jesus, I thought my heart was going to stop."

"I don't see what the problem is. You were pregnant with me when you were twenty."

"Twenty-one," she said.

"Yeah, well, even that's only four years older than I am now."

She looked at his baby face and she could not believe it. She had met his father when she was just nineteen, and she had thought then she was so grown up. She guessed Calvin thought the same about himself now. She told herself that she should keep remembering that fact. He simply didn't see himself as her little boy. But it was all so unfair to Andrea, having been deprived of a decade of his life — could she really be faulted if her affections and attitudes towards him had been frozen for ten years? But while she thought of this, he took something else out of his pocket — a small square white envelope. He held it out.

"It's for Earl," he said.

"No bloody way." She pushed his hand away.

"They won't let me see him in the cells."

"Good," she said.

"He's my friend," he snapped.

"I don't care," she retorted, equally sharply.

He looked pained at this, his eyelids suddenly heavy, half closed. "No, you don't, do you?" he said.

Once more she realised just how fragile their relationship was, how every word was ammunition, a weapon or a shield. "Calvin, I didn't mean it like that. You know I didn't mean it like that."

"Do I?" he snapped back, precisely as she thought he would.

"Please, Calvin," she pleaded, "that's not fair. I wish you knew just how much you hurt me." The words had just slipped out, with no premeditation, and she was horrified by them. "I mean, I hope you never do. Oh, shit. Christ, I just don't know what to say any more."

It had been written over a decade that this was to be the final script for all their heated conversations, accusations and pleas, arguments that neither could win. There usually came a lull in hostilities, when the wounds were once more open, and then there was the opportunity to make a point tell.

"The chocolate," he said. "I wanted to give you the chocolate. It had nothing to do with Earl."

"I wish I could believe that."

"Me too."

She shook her head, annoyed in large part at herself — she was the adult, she should ensure that things didn't flare out of control. "We're going to have to talk about last night," she said. She looked around, ensured that no police officers were in the immediate vicinity. "About the *gun*," she whispered.

"What gun?"

"Don't treat me like an idiot, Calvin."

"Then how do you want me to treat you?"

"Like your mother," she said.

His face screwed up at this. "Christ, when will you learn? Last night, I saw nothing."

"Nonsense."

"Look, you see nothing, you hear nothing, you say nothing." He pointed out of the window. "Out there? It's not a courtroom. There are no rules. There is only the gun. And you want me to call you Mummy."

Just then a jailer appeared. "Cells are open," he shouted.

Andrea looked from her son to the cell door, then back again. She remembered how Calvin had looked when the police had dragged him in in chains in the police station, and how much she had wanted to show him she loved him, so much so that she had lost control and had slapped him when he had been disrespectful.

She knew that she could spend no more time with her son, that she had to visit her client in custody. "Wait here," she urged him. "Please."

"Tell Earl to forget Johnson," he said to her.

"You've tried to get his surety?"

"Tell Earl to forget Johnson," he repeated, as if he hadn't heard a word she had said. He offered her the letter again, and this time she took it.

By the time that Andrea had identified herself to the jailer behind the glass screen, Calvin had been swallowed by the crowd. As she waited for the outer security door to be opened, she glanced quickly at the milling people, but the faces blurred together and Calvin had gone. When the jailer checked through the peep-hole and then opened the heavy tank-metal-grey door, she realised that she was still holding Calvin's letter.

"Birthday card?" the jailer said sarcastically, looking down at the envelope.

She smiled, a tic more than a smile, and guiltily shoved the document into her coat pocket.

"Mr Whitely's got the hotel to himself this morning," the man said.

It was the same old joke, the one she had heard a thousand times before when she last practised criminal law. In a strange way it was reassuring to her to discover that this routine at least had not changed. She stepped into the airlock between the outer and inner steel door, and the jailer pulled the open one shut with a dull thud. Instantly the hubbub of the lobby disappeared and Andrea was trapped in the confined space with the large man. He slowly opened the inner door, and she saw the reception area of the cells, with its long counter on the right-hand side behind which jailers filled in paperwork and read tabloids. There was a large blackboard on a bare stone wall directly opposite her, and on either side of the blackboard doors made entirely of steel bars, behind which were the two wings of individual cells. A radio played a golden oldies station, cups of tea steamed in soft plastic mugs, there was the smell of bacon and fried bread. But when Andrea was led to the high-security cells, the banter of the dozen or so jailers ceased instantly, as if someone had switched their radio off. A dozen pairs of eyes crawled over her body, and she understood the disgust in their eyes. A woman, a white woman, representing a child killer, the black killer of a white child. On the front page of all the tabloids she could see the grainy enlargement of Nicki Harris's school photo. A much younger Nicki with her jacket and school tie, her hair in bunches. Nicki smiling gap-toothed, Nicki alive, hopeful, even if she was only hoping for simple things, like her new front tooth growing. Andrea understood their revulsion at the killing, she shared it, but she struggled to empty her mind of that emotion long enough to fight for Earl Whitely.

"I want to see my client in a conference room," she said.

The screws looked at each other, said nothing.

"I'm not seeing him in a cell," she insisted.

The oldest jailer, who was clearly in charge, turned the volume on the radio down. "Jim," was all he said, but it was sufficient for the man who had led Andrea in to turn to the right at the end of the counter and use his keys to open a conference cell.

"Thank you," Andrea said to him. He did not reply.

She entered a room with no natural light, four bricked walls, so thinly painted grey that the pattern of bricks could be discerned beneath, like a skeleton under the skin. There was a wooden table with a gap under it, where a drawer had once been. The table was stained everywhere with coffee rings, and two chairs were propped on opp site sides. Cigarettes had been stubbed out on the hard stone floor, and it was so cold that Andrea could feel the iciness rising through the leather soles of her shoes. She put her briefcase on the table, for no reason except to do something, for she knew that the jailers were watching her through the reinforced glass top half of the door. She paced around the table and then shoved her hands in her coat pocket to warm them. Her breath frosted in front of her mouth. Then, in her right-hand pocket, she felt Calvin's letter. She now had her back to the door, and she quickly took it out. On the envelope she saw her son's still-childish handwriting, in which he had scribbled the words: Earl Whitely. She could feel a sheet within the envelope, and as she explored its outline with her finge tips she decided that it was a single sheet of thin airmail paper, possibly folded in two. She guessed that it was from one of the pads of blue airmail paper Rufus used to write to his friends from the GPO who had retired home to Jamaica.

The door was flung open, and Andrea shoved the letter back in her pocket. Two large screws had Earl chained and manacled between them.

"I want to be alone with him," she said to them.

"He's dangerous," one of them replied.

"He's my client," she said.

The screws turned their heads and gazed through the open door to the older jailer, who hovered outside. He must have agreed, though she could not see it, for they began unchaining Earl.

He still wore the baseball cap. He appeared pleased to see her, and even smiled widely at her. It was, she reflected, a far warmer greeting than her son had given her. He was so eager to speak to her that he began to say something before the jailers had left the cell. She shook her head rapidly and he was immediately silent. She indicated that they should sit down, choosing the chair facing the door, so that the jailers outside could not see Earl's mouth. When they were at the table, she made a quick circling motion with her index finger, and he understood that they were probably being covertly taped.

She looked at her watch and said the time out loud, adding, "This is a legally privileged conference between Earl Whitely and his legal representative, Andrea Chambers."

"Alphonse," he whispered back. "Earl Alphonse Whitely. Do you think it matters?"

She shook her head and smiled. "How are you doing, Mr Whitely?"

"Ride here was a bit rough, ya know."

She nodded. "I saw the reception committee."

"Are they allowed to do that, Miz Chambers? Aren't I presumed innocent or some shit?"

"It's not shit, Earl. It's the most important thing you've got going for you."

"Nah," he said, leaning back in his chair and raising his voice, "you is."

She was touched by the confident way in which he said it, and she only wished that she could have been so sure of herself. Earl had a disarming smile, with perfect teeth, and mischievous eyes. She knew the type. Calvin's father had been blessed with something of the same charms at the LSE. But she didn't have time to reminisce, so she beckoned him nearer and the two of them hunched across the table, their heads inches apart. "Earl, Calvin said that you should forget Roots Johnson."

Earl cursed to himself, and put his head on the table and his arms over his baseball cap.

"Earl?" she whispered.

He looked up, defenceless. "Please, Miz Chambers. Please tell me that there is someone else out there for me."

Now she was confused. "Who do you mean?"

He licked the end of his finger and drew three letters on the table surface: I-C-U. The spittle of the first letter almost immediately began to vanish, but he rubbed the word out to be safe.

"ICU?" she whispered.

"Internal," he whispered back.

"Internal? Police Internal? Earl, what the hell is going on?"

"Is they outside?" he persisted.

"Earl, there's no one outside for you."

"Not even Calvin?"

She wondered what to say, thought guiltily about her son's letter again, but couldn't bring herself to hand it over. "Yes, Calvin's out there." She quickly wanted to change the subject. "But if Internal are involved, Earl? Jesus, that changes everything. You've got to tell me."

He leaned back again. When he spoke, it was much more loudly. "Nah, not yet." He even looked round at the jailers outside and smiled defiantly at them. "I know how it goes, Miz Chambers. Your lawyer's ethic. If I don't tell you, you can't answer no questions about it in court. I want to wait. See what them po-lice say about me."

"They're going to say that you killed Nicki Harris. What do you think they're going to say?"

"Well, that's bullshit."

"Tell me, then, why it's bullshit." She leant across the table and whispered with such intensity that it was practically a hiss. "Where were you when Nicki Harris was shot?"

Suddenly, Earl was silent again. Gone was his bravado. He sat with his hands in his lap in the wooden chair, and appeared to shrink before her eyes. He didn't even look at her when he eventually said, "All I care about is the bullet, Miz Chambers. Find out about the bullet."

She leant right in to his ear, so close that her lips were millimetres from his singed scalp. She put her hand in front of her mouth to hide her lips from the prying eyes outside. "Calvin's gun. It's your gun, isn't it?" she breathed.

"You've got to get me out. You are going to get me out, aren't you?"

There was a sharp rapping on the reinforced glass of the door. "Come on," shouted the head jailer. "Time."

"Is it your gun?" she repeated to Earl.

He looked at her like the terrified man-child he was. Then he nodded.

CHAPTER SEVENTEEN

Andrea emerged from the cell area and into the smoke-filled lobby of the court complex. It was fuller now, with a massed police presence inside the building, cordoning off the warring factions, some of whom grabbed a last hurriedly puffed cigarette before entering the courtroom. The police provided two entries into the public gallery of the courtroom in an attempt to reduce the opportunities for friction. Among the uniformed officers who searched people seeking entry were other men in plainclothes. These men took down the name and address of every entrant, frequently provoking an argument as a protester refused to comply. The sight of these men intrigued Andrea, and she tried desperately to think back to her time at the Bar, when this would have been just another day at the office. Then she suddenly remembered. The men were Special Branch. Either they were there to intimidate and deter the public, or the case had some kind of wider security aspect that had been kept from her. She tried to fit the pieces into the vague jigsaw that was being assembled in her mind. First, Earl had been in contact with the Internal Complaints Unit. Now, Special Branch were on the scene. Try as she might, she couldn't for the moment make a sensible connection.

She walked slowly through the crowd, looking for her son, but he was nowhere to be seen. She approached a tight circle of black youngsters, with their backs to the rest of the room, but Calvin was not there either. She

checked by the drinks machine, back by the cells, but he
was gone. She looked at her watch — there were still
twenty minutes until court proceedings were due to begin,
but she was behind the clock since she had to speak to the
prosecution rep before they started. She was about to
scour the room again, moving to the staircase leading to
the upper courts, when a strong hand grabbed her shoulder from behind. Her head whipped round to see DS
Stevie Fisher standing behind her.

"Looking for your son?" he said, his grin coldly affable
and thus more hostile than if he had been entirely deadpan.

"Where is he?" she asked.

"That's a good question, one I'm sure you have to ask
yourself a lot."

Two other men lurked behind Fisher, both of whom
Andrea vaguely recognised from the police station two
nights previously, one overweight man and another
younger man in glasses. She tried to push past the officer,
but he blocked her way.

"I've got to go to court," she protested.

"Not yet," Fisher replied, keeping his hand on her
shoulder.

"I'm under arrest, am I?"

"Not yet," Fisher repeated. "You see, I asked Calvin
what he gave you and, you know what, he wouldn't tell
me." Fisher partly turned his head to talk over his shoulder. "He wouldn't say, would he, DC Brigson?"

Andrea saw the fat man fumble anxiously with a
paper bag in his hands. "No, he wouldn't, DS Fisher," the
second replied.

"So perhaps you'll tell us, counsel," Fisher continued.
"You know the building is on full security alert."

Suddenly, Andrea felt as if the envelope were smoul-
dering like a fuse in her pocket. She shoved her hand
defensively into her coat, felt it there, squashed it down

further. "He gave me some chocolate," she said.

"No, after the chocolate," Fisher said wearily.

Andrea realised that they had been observing her close-ly, and it was pointless trying to bluff. "It was an enve-lope," she said.

"For Calvin's murdering friend?"

"It's legally privileged."

"Not if it concerns the planning of a crime. You *can* con-firm to us that it doesn't concern the planning of any future crime whatsoever?" Again he glanced over his shoulder. "What's that us detectives were speculating about, DC Brigson? Getting rid of the murder weapon? Wasn't that it?"

"Yes, DS Fisher," Brigson replied.

"So please tell us that it's an innocuous little epistle from one chum to another," Fisher said.

"Why don't you go and catch some criminals," Andrea retorted.

"Oh, we've caught one, Miss Chambers. In fact, we've caught two. Only we let the second out of the nick, as you well know."

In her time in the criminal salt-mines, Andrea had had at least a dozen conversations such as this with over-zealous detectives, and she had always got the better of the bantering. But this was different. She sensed that every time she responded she provoked the officers more, moti-vated them further to nail her son.

Fisher came much closer. "I've seen hundreds of kids like your Calvin," he said. "I've seen how they change. One day it's Meccano and comics, the next it's guns and crack. Because kids like that don't have parents any more, or not any that they listen to. They only have the street. It's all they listen to. So that boy you got out of our nick two days ago? He's not your son, Andrea. Somewhere along the line, he got snatched.

And this fit young criminal got put in his place. To break your heart. Goodbye little Calvin, hello broken heart. And at the end of it all, you'll wish, you'll really wish, that the bullet which killed Nicki Harris had hit your beloved son instead."

Andrea's face was flushed from the battery of words, but she tried to think clearly, to fight back. "Where is my son?"

"He left the building. He didn't like our questions," Fisher said. "I don't think he likes the police. He probably gets it from you. Come on, DC Brigson."

Fisher and the other two detectives walked past her and headed for court, while Andrea dashed to the landing on the first flight of the open stairway so that she could get a better view outside. Calvin wasn't there. She glanced at her watch. She now had fifteen minutes, but the envelope was still in her hand and she had to read the letter. She knew that there was only one place in which she could seek a moment's refuge in the court building.

When she finally closed the door to the loo cubicle behind her, she leaned back against it momentarily and closed her eyes. Her mind swam behind her eyelids with images and words and threats and warnings. Slowly she took the envelope out of her coat pocket, pinching it between her index finger and thumb. Creases ran in all directions over it now, like the lines of a Tube map, and she wished she had never accepted it from Calvin.

She held it up in front of her face, then raised it a shade higher. There was a frosted window high on the wall of the lavatory, which allowed natural light to pour in. She examined the envelope against the light, hoping to see something, enough that she would not have to open it. The outline of the blue folded paper inside was now visible as if X-rayed, but she could not make out any words. She hesitated, tapped the envelope on her pursed lips. If she opened it, she would be abusing her son's trust, violating his privacy, but more than that, he would go crazy. She just knew it. She continued to tap the letter, considering. And if he knew he couldn't trust her with this, he was less likely to trust her in the future, and he barely shared his confidences with her as it was. No, there was nothing for it. She couldn't open it. Slowly, she smoothed out the creases as best she could, then replaced the envelope in her pocket. She removed some lint from her coat lapel and breathed deeply, preparing herself for court.

Then her hand snatched the letter out of the pocket and her fingers ripped the back of the envelope open. She pulled out the blue paper, unfolded it, seeing that she was right, that it was airmail paper. She held it up so that she could read the contents, knowing that she simply could not help herself. Calvin was her son. He had written to someone charged with murder. She had to read it. She was his mother. She had to.

There indeed was Calvin's writing on the paper, but it would be a gross exaggeration to describe the note as a letter. There were only two words. And a dash. And a question mark. Andrea's mind raced. She even mouthed the words to herself, trying to fit this new piece into the slowly unfolding picture.

"Deny everything—?"

She read it again and again. "Deny everything—?" What was there to deny, and wasn't it implying that Earl should deny the truth, or why didn't it just say tell the truth? And if this was a truth that Earl could not afford to tell, what was it, how did Calvin know about it, and did it also incriminate him? All these questions and countless variations on them raced round and round in her head until suddenly she froze. There was a voice outside.

"Miss Chambers?" a woman's voice called. An elderly woman's voice, the hoarse voice of a lifelong smoker. "It's the usher, Miss Chambers. The court's convening."

"Coming," Andrea said, the note in her hand, shaking.

She waited until the footsteps of the woman had receded and then ripped the blue paper up and flushed it down the bowl. She waited to see if any of the wafer-like paper would float back to the surface, but none did. There were ten minutes until the magistrate was due in, and she had not even spoken to the other side.

After Andrea had negotiated the security checks directly outside the court doors, she stood at the very threshold of the courtroom. She paused for a second and took her coat off, draping it over her arm. She rolled her neck, tried to focus her energies, to forget the various trials of the morning. It was her old routine — close out the real world, get into the zone, think of nothing but the courtroom, imagine it, visualise performing in it, take your time, do it in your own time. When she felt she was ready, she reached forward to push open the door. But it was wrenched open. And there stood Hogarth massively in front of her, blocking out most of the courtroom behind him. He looked down at her in his penetrating way, with those still, slow eyes, not with hostility, like those other officers, but with immense concern. The curious thing, Andrea sensed, was that Hogarth's concern was for her, for her welfare. He examined her as if he were a surgeon and she was his most troublesome, most interesting patient. He stood in front of her for perhaps two seconds, but Andrea knew that it was easily long enough for him to serve notice to her that it was personal, that the contest would be between them.

Suddenly, he brushed past her, and the vista of the teeming courtroom opened before her. Andrea's heart plunged in her chest. There were one hundred people, maybe more — a bewildering array of mankind, old and young, white and black, reporters and policemen, members of the public and court staff, all chattering excitedly, all waiting for the entertainment, and she knew that the show could not begin without her. As she walked slowly through the rows packed with people, she rediscovered how it was possible to be perfectly alone in a crowded space. People started whispering and staring at her, beginning with the police ranks, becoming quiet as she passed, so that it felt to Andrea that she was slowly drawing a veil of silence over the court as she advanced.

She briefly glanced at the Bench immediately in front of her, the highest perch in the room, with a high-backed red leather chair for the magistrate. Directly above that again was the royal coat of arms with the dual mottoes: *Dieu et mon droit* and *Honi soit qui mal y pense*. God and my right, the first one said. It was, she knew, the battle-cry of Richard I at Gisors. She could feel dozens of pairs of eyes now fixed upon her, watching her every move, so she tried to concentrate on the second motto, anything to stop feeling self-conscious. *Honi soit, honi soit*, she repeated in her mind. It really meant shame to him, but the courts used it in a more fundamental sense, a darker sense, she remembered — it was the vengeful part of the law. Evil be to him who thinks evil. That was it. The motto of the Most Noble Order of the Garter. The flip-side of rights and justice: vengeance.

By now Andrea had reached the front of the court, where there was a row reserved for the advocates. She glanced to her left, where a woman she assumed to be the prosecutor was speaking in whispers to DS Fisher. A gaunt, overly made-up woman, slightly older than Andrea, she was surrounded by piles of paper and files. She had dark mascara layered on and deep red lipstick which contrasted markedly with her washed-out face. Her suit was an exquisitely tailored designer label, of the type Andrea had occasionally taken off the rack in Harrods or Harvey Nichols, and then replaced immediately when she had looked at the price tag. But the luxuriousness of the material merely accentuated to Andrea the artificial highlights and ashen roots of the woman's fake blonde hair, its plastic appearance. She chuckled to herself. God, I am such a bitch.

"Hi, I'm Marion Slavin," the woman said.

"Andrea Chambers," she replied.

"Yes, I know. DS Fisher here's been telling me all about you."

The wide-boy detective looked disdainfully at Andrea, then handed the prosecutor a report. His task done, he slipped back through the court, and Andrea made the mistake of glancing back at him so that she saw row upon row of faces riveted upon her. She felt as if she had suddenly looked down after climbing a high ladder. The rows appeared to ebb and flow back and forth, a minute shimmering under the stripped lighting. She heard some clinking from the right-hand side of the court, and she turned to see the empty dock. It was a large heavy wooden construction, something like a cattle pen. Sheets of reinforced glass had been fitted into grooves in the dock, so that the top half was a glass-and-steel cage, with just enough room between the high vertical strips of glass for an arm to reach, but not enough for someone to leap through. Andrea knew the glass would be bulletproofed. Though the dock was empty, she was haunted by an image of a young black man standing miserably and alone behind the glass — her son.

"Your punter's CRO," Marion Slavin said. She handed Andrea a pair of badly photocopied paper sheets. "He's hardly St Francis of Assisi."

Andrea scanned the papers. "Is that all on his 609?" she asked of her client's record. "Minor dishonesty? Bits of weed?"

"I know," Marion said coldly, "let's put him up for a

community action award, shall we?"

Any pretence at civility had evaporated. Andrea would get no help from the prosecutor. She had to get down to business. "Can I see the police report?"

Marion handed Andrea another sheet. It was headed Operation Trojan. "It's a summary," she said.

Andrea took it, four paragraphs of hastily scribbled handwriting, outlining the background to the case. Her eyes skimmed down the lines, but she couldn't absorb any of the detail. "How about forensics?" she asked.

For the first time there was the hint of a dent in Marion Slavin's confidence. Her eyes shot round to the back of the court, where Fisher and Hogarth had been, but the officers had gone. "Uh, tad too early," she said unconvincingly.

Andrea made a mental note of the equivocation. Her old instincts told her that the opposition was hiding something. She tried to press the issue. She moved along the row, so that she was practically touching her opponent, and now she could smell the woman's heavy, incensed perfume. "Can I look at the CPS file?" she asked.

"I'm not CPS," Marion said dismissively. It meant that she was a barrister, and it was unusual that she should already be involved in the case. She calmly turned over the report Fisher had given her. "DS Fisher tells me you were once at the Bar."

The supposedly casual comment was another deliberate blow. It was a professional put-down, the implication being that Andrea was only a mere solicitor now. But more than that, it meant that the police had somehow found out this obscure detail of her personal history.

Andrea tried her best to brush it off. "What can you tell me about the case?" she asked.

"Read the report," Marion replied, averting her gaze.

Andrea now scanned the thumbnail sketch the police

had prepared. But as she read it, she was reminded again that it wasn't just a case, it wasn't her case or Earl's, it belonged in truth to a person who could never come to court. The first line related that Nicola ('Nicki') Harris was shot and killed by a single bullet outside St Margaret's school two days previously. She hadn't reached the bottom of the page before there was a rapping at the door.

The usher was at the back of the court and shouted, "Court rise."

Andrea watched as the stipendiary magistrate entered from a door behind the Bench. She knew from the court list outside the doors that his name was Ackroyde, but more than that she did not know — she was too out of touch with current criminal gossip. The man had a permanently irritated face, it seemed to her, as if his shoes were too tight, or he constantly had a toothache, and none of this unfortunate impression was diminished by the gorgeous flower in his lapel. He sat, and pursuant to court choreography everyone sat after him. Next, the door behind the dock opened and two huge jailers brought in Earl Whitely. There was an audible intake of breath from the public benches, almost as if this were Salem and the wretched boy was a witch. He glanced across at Andrea, no more than thirty feet away, then he nodded sharply. Andrea didn't understand the message, until Earl struggled with the jailers and lifted his hands above the level of the wooden half of the dock. He was still handcuffed.

The clerk, an Asian man, was now on his feet just below the stipe. He turned to his left and Andrea's right, to face the dock. "Are you Earl Whitely?"

"Earl Alphonse Whitely," Earl said.

"Don't interrupt," the stipe barked.

"Sit down," the clerk said, then he spun round to the stipe. "Sir, the only case in your list today. Earl Alphonse Whitely."

The stipe peered at Earl through his horn-rimmed glasses, satisfied himself that it was the same young black man he had seen the previous day, then addressed the lawyers. "Is this . . . man represented today?"

Andrea got to her feet. She could feel the presence of Marion Slavin to her left, and she knew that dozens of people had their eyes glued to her back. But she surprised herself. Her breathing was calm, controlled; she was coping.

"Andrea Chambers, sir," she said. Then she looked back at the dock as the jailers forced Earl to sit between them, and her anger boiled over. "Sir, I must ask that Mr Whitely has his handcuffs removed immediately."

"Why?" the stipe asked, surprised.

"Because it's humiliating and unnecessary."

Marion Slavin shot to her feet next to her, and her heady perfume wafted over Andrea. "Sir," Marion said in a pained, deliberately perplexed voice, "I must confess some confusion. Handcuffs are standard procedure in Yardie gang-related murders."

Andrea gazed briefly into the pallid face beside her before she addressed the court. "Ms Slavin has clearly forgotten that my client is presumed innocent of any murder," she said. "Besides which, I imagine that there must be some purpose to the Authorised Firearm Officers with live ammunition stationed directly outside the doors of this courtroom."

The stipe considered a moment, touched his thin lips briefly with his black-and-gold fountain pen, then told the jailers, "Uncuff him."

Andrea sat down, a buzz racing through her body.

"Are you intending to apply for bail, Miss Chambers?" Ackroyde asked her.

Andrea rose swiftly to her feet, said yes, then subsided again.

"I imagine there are objections to bail?" Ackroyde asked Marion Slavin.

Marion smoothly, unhurriedly eased herself upwards. She smiled confidently. "Perhaps the most expeditious way to proceed is if I call the officer in charge of the case, sir," she said. Then in a louder voice, she added, "I call DCI Hogarth."

Andrea turned around in her seat to look at the doors to the court, but as if in some kind of conjuring trick Hogarth had appeared from a side door to Marion's left. In a flash, he was in the witness box on the opposite side of the court to the dock and Earl Whitely, holding the Bible high.

He looked all the while at Andrea and said in a slow, deep voice, "I swear by Almighty God that I shall truthfully answer any questions the court may ask." He put the Bible down, still looking at Andrea. "Detective Chief Inspector John Hogarth, officer in charge of the Nicola Harris murder, sir."

"Yes, thank you, DCI," Marion said admiringly. "Can you give the court the briefest of outlines of this case."

For the first time Hogarth turned away from Andrea and to his left, so that he could address Ackroyde face to face. He spoke in a cold, documentary tone, stripped of emotion as far as possible, so that each statement sounded like a cast-iron fact.

"Nicki Harris was gunned down in cold blood two afternoons ago by this man, Earl Whitely," he said. "This occurred outside St Margaret's junior school, less than two miles from this court. The accused was then seen by a member of the public running away from the direction of the incident with a gun in his hand. He was arrested and charged with the murder within hours. There are on-going enquiries."

The stipe had been making a careful note of Hogarth's words. "Yes, you don't have to prove your case to me at this stage, Officer, but I would like to hear the bases for your objections to bail."

Hogarth now stared hard at Earl, directly across the width of the courtroom. Andrea followed the gaze. Earl stared back, not flinching.

Hogarth continued, "Police intelligence confirms that Earl Whitely is a Yardie, sir. That is, an illegal immigrant from Jamaica, who is heavily involved in serious crime. It is almost certainly the case that Nicki Harris was tragically caught in the crossfire of a gang-related shoot-out between rival groups, or posses, as they are known."

Here Hogarth paused, and Andrea wondered why. Again she followed his eyes and saw that they had alighted upon the ranks of reporters, who were furiously trying to keep up with his words. He only continued speaking again when most of the journalists had looked up once more. Andrea saw that in Hogarth she was dealing with a consummate professional.

"What about his antecedents?" Ackroyde asked.

"This accused has no fixed abode in the United Kingdom," Hogarth said. "He has no known family ties. He has no known community ties — except among the ranks of drug posses. I wonder whether you could be provided with his Form 609?"

Marion Slavin handed another pair of badly photocopied sheets up to the usher, who passed them to the court clerk, who handed them to Ackroyde. Andrea cursed to herself. Earl's relatively minor record of offending was going to be one of her main points in cross-examining Hogarth, but expert operator that he was, he had stolen her thunder.

The stipe glanced at the record. "Not the worst."

Andrea again saw how Hogarth stared at Earl, and how Earl now looked back almost expectantly. It appeared to her that Earl actually expected Hogarth to agree with the stipe. But when he continued, he had cranked the intensity of his voice up a notch.

"We say that Mr Whitely's lack of convictions is a measure of how effective he is in his chosen . . . profession. It is notoriously difficult to persuade people to testify against Yardies."

Andrea shot to her feet. "I object to that comment." Hogarth looked at her with his head infinitesimally cocked to one side, telling her that she was too late. "Perhaps Mr Hogarth will understand how difficult it also is to get people to testify against the police."

"I understand," Hogarth said reasonably, before Marion could object or the stipe could reprimand Andrea.

She sat down again somewhat confused by Hogarth's concession. Why had he accepted this provocative comment from her? She glanced at the witness box again, and there was a fractional change to the line of his mouth as he became aware of her gaze. Andrea couldn't decide whether or not it was the hint of a smile. Then she became convinced. He was playing with her.

"Yes, wait there, please," Marion told him as she sat down.

It was Andrea's turn. As she stood, her eyelids opened and shut very slowly on Hogarth, like camera shutters. Even behind her eyelids she could see the retained image of the man she had to crack. She attempted to break away from Hogarth's magnetic presence, to look at her client, but Earl was fixed upon Hogarth. She looked up at the stipe, but he, too, stared at the DCI. And for his part, Hogarth stood there so cool, so calmly, as if he had been waiting for this moment ever since that first encounter in the interview room of the police station when he had slammed down the wet photographs of the dead Nicki Harris. All Andrea's plans of attack suddenly appeared useless, ineffectual. She knew they would bounce off the seemingly invincible figure in the box. She had nothing to use but her instincts, and even as she asked the first questions, she felt deep down that these were precisely the prompts that Hogarth had wanted. She was feeding him his best lines, and she didn't know how to stop it.

"My client wasn't arrested at the scene?" she asked.

"He was spotted running away from the direction of the murder. With a gun."

The lawyer part of Andrea's mind served up the information that the police didn't have the gun, but the part of her that was Calvin's mother, the part she believed was essentially Andrea Chambers, most of her, warned that she had seen Earl's gun, and in her son's hand.

"Miss Chambers?" the stipe asked. "Have you finished?"

There was total silence in the courtroom, and she knew that everyone waited upon her. Don't mention the gun, she warned herself, but then she saw Earl behind the bullet-proof glass. She had to do everything for him, because if she didn't, who would? If she pulled her punches, then what right had she to be in the courtroom at all?

"Have you found this gun?" she heard herself ask. The words had come out, even as she was debating them.

"No. But we'd like to ask your client about it."

"Hasn't he been interviewed?"

"He refused to co-operate. Even though we warned him that adverse inferences could be drawn from his silence. Inferences of guilt."

"Has a single person identified him as being present at the shooting?"

"There is only one adult witness. A teacher. She is still receiving counselling."

"I think the answer is that no one has identified him," Andrea insisted.

"I think the answer is that no one is fit enough after witnessing an eight-year-old girl being murdered." Hogarth paused, then added, "She found Nicki's body, she had the child's blood all over her when the police arrived."

Every answer was a blow to Andrea. She felt her face flushing, sweat running down her back. Her eyes blinked rapidly, her mouth was dry, her tongue felt huge and clumsy in her mouth, her thoughts were fuzzy, trite. She noticed Marion Slavin slide the report that was face down on the desk further away from her. It must be a forensic report, she guessed. Why else would the opposition be so sensitive about it? Either that or it was some intelligence information, but why would that be shared with prosecuting counsel in court? It was more likely to be forensics.

Andrea decided to wing it. Earl's record and background were a nightmare. Her only hope was to demonstrate that there simply wasn't enough evidence to hold him. "Isn't it right that the evidence against my client is purely circumstantial?"

Hogarth paused again, considered this question gravely. It was the first flicker of hope Andrea had experienced.

"Yes," he said finally.

There was a murmur behind her. But she couldn't dwell on it. She had to move in, milk the point.

"Purely circumstantial?" she asked.

"Except for one thing," Hogarth said.

"Which is?" she asked. He was silent and looked hard at Earl. "Which is, Officer?"

"A full and frank confession," he said quietly.

Andrea felt as though she had been scythed below the knees. There was chaos around the court, and the stipe shouted for silence. Andrea's hands dropped to the bench in front of her to support herself. Marion Slavin grabbed the concealed report, and Andrea saw photocopied photos of a bullet, a section of barrel rifling. It was a ballistics report.

"He confessed to me," Hogarth continued calmly, in the storm of noise. "Off the record. He wouldn't be taped. But he confessed. To all of it. A full confession. Off the record."

Earl had now rushed to the front of the dock and banged his fists so hard on the glass panels that Andrea feared they would smash. He screamed at Hogarth, "You is a liar. A blood-clot liar. I'll kill you, Hogarth. You blood-clot liar. I'll kill you."

The jailers pulled him back and he struggled with them, flailing out with his arms, though the men towered over him. Restrained, he banged his head on the glass, again and again. His forehead cracked hard against the reinforced panes. His eyes were wild, manic. Still the jailers struggled to drag him away, and still he banged his head.

"Take him down," Ackroyde shouted.

"I'll kill you, Hogarth," Earl screamed. "I'll kill you."

Andrea saw that Hogarth was standing quite still and gazing patiently at her.

CHAPTER EIGHTEEN

Earl dragged the two jailers into the conference room in the cell area, even though they tried to hold him back, or at least to slow him down, pulling on his steel handcuffs as jockeys might do on a horse's bit. Andrea waited in the cell, behind the wooden table, and heard the chaotic procession of the three men before she saw it, and then when they did burst into the room she was horrified to see the raw flesh on Earl's wrists. The metal inside of the cuffs had scraped away the teenager's top layer of skin as if someone had run a razor blade along it.

"Shut it, Whitely," the smaller, more highly strung of the jailers shouted at him.

"I'm going to kill him, I'm going to kill him," Earl screamed, hearing nothing except Hogarth's words from the witness box.

"Take off his cuffs," Andrea shouted above the din.

"No way," the larger jailer shouted back.

"For Christ's sake, his wrists are bleeding," she said.

"Stop fighting us, Whitely," the smaller one screamed at Earl.

Andrea rushed around the table and grabbed the smaller man's white shirt. Earl was flailing about, and he unknowingly kicked her hard, his foot scraping across her shin, but still she harangued the smaller screw.

"You take it off now," she demanded, right in his face.

"We'll have to lock you in with him."

"I don't care. Free him."

The highly strung man glanced at his larger colleague, who shrugged, while Earl still bucked between them. The muscles in the smaller jailer's neck stuck out like cables, and Andrea could almost see them pumping with blood as he undid the cuffs. In a flash, Earl was free, and the two men dashed out of the room, as if fleeing a crazed stallion. They slammed the door shut on Andrea as Earl exploded around the room, kicking the walls, while Andrea backed herself into a corner. The men looked in from behind the safety of the reinforced glass. Earl's T-shirt hung off him like a rag as he picked up one of the wooden chairs and hurled it against the brick wall. The legs splintered, the seat clattered on to the ground near Andrea, and she covered her head with her arms. Outside, she could see that a dozen jailers awaited a chance to teach Earl a lesson, to "restrain" him. They began to open the door.

"Keep out," she screamed at them.

Earl slammed his body against the wall opposite her, then, his fury spent, he crumbled to the ground, till he squatted with his back to the wall with his head in his hands. Andrea glanced quickly at the door. She held her hand up to keep the jailers at bay, and the room was filled with Earl's desperate, hopeless sobbing. The boy's body convulsed as if he were gripped by a terminal fever. She gingerly made her way past the wreckage of the chair, past the table, and to her client. He didn't appear even to know she was in the cell with him. She repeatedly told herself to be brave. Even though in his frenzy Earl could have flown at her at any stage, she moved closer, telling herself that this boy was Calvin's friend, was just a boy like her son. She reached his side of the room as jailers jostled each other to watch the suicidal lawyer, pressing their faces against the glass from the outside.

At first, Andrea just waited, trying to get a sense of his breathing, the rhythm of his sobs. She remembered the time she had left Calvin, when he was ten years younger than Earl was now, and Calvin had not shed a single tear. Yet here was a supposed Yardie gunman, weeping uncontrollably.

"Earl?" she whispered. There was no response; he didn't even look up. "Earl?" she repeated. "Earl, you've got to tell me. Before it's too late."

His fixed eyes now burned into her. His face shivered as he spat out the words. "What I can tell you? That make one difference."

"You've got to tell me the truth," she said, unnerved by the ferocity of his words.

"And Hogarth can tell any lie. And the court will believe him?" he shouted.

"If he's lying, you've got to give me something to fight him back with. You've got to give me the truth."

"I didn't shoot no girl," he cried. Then he shook his head and gripped his singed black hair with his fingertips. "But I can't tell you the truth."

"Why not?"

"Because they will kill me, Miz Chambers."

Andrea took his arm, felt the muscles of stone in his biceps, his triceps. "Who will kill you? The police?"

Earl's head snapped around to the door, where he saw the jailers. He sprung to his feet, dashed across the room, picked up a shattered piece of chair leg and flung it hard against the glass. The wood bounced off, but the jailers scattered. He rushed back across the room, to Andrea, who still squatted by the wall. He moved her around, so that her back was to the door, and joined her in this position. His face was right next to hers, and sweat dribbled from him on to her.

"You gotta, like, advise me," he whispered, barely audibly.

"I am here to advise you."

"No," he protested, trying to keep his voice from rising.

"Not like your client. Like your son." His eyes did not move from hers, and pleaded with her for help. "I'm down in so much trouble, Miz Chambers. I've done so many bad things."

"Earl," she said, "we never really know the right thing to do. We say we do. But we don't. Not really." She glanced back at the door; the jailers hadn't returned. They continued to squat, whispering. But now Andrea's knees began to ache. She continued, "But if I was your mother—"

"I never had a mother," he interrupted, and this confession appeared to Andrea to cause him more pain than any he had previously made. Her heart ached for him. She put her arm around his back as he said, "She dumped me at a police station. In Trench Town. I never had no family. All I had was the posse. The posse was my family, Miz Chambers. And now they want to kill me."

"But I thought it was the police," she said, confused.

"Both," Earl replied.

"And?" she said, waiting for clarification, while her mind raced through the possibilities, each more fantastic than the last, intriguing her, scaring her.

"I can't tell you no more," he said. "Or you'll be in danger."

"I don't care."

He looked at her and stood up. He spoke in a trembling voice, regarding her warmly. "But I do," he said. "You is Calvin's mother. So I do."

Andrea stood, too. She was glad to relieve the pressure on her knees. "Remember," she said to him. She made the index finger of her right hand corkscrew in the air, and he understood her warning about bugging. He nodded. "So where does that leave us?" she whispered.

"The bullet," he breathed back.

"I think they've got a ballistics report," she said.

"Then you got to get it," Earl said. "Think you can "get it?"

Andrea nodded once, but in her mind she doubtfully rattled through her options, discarding each method of finessing the report in turn.

The court reconvened ten minutes later, and excitement still pulsed through the cramped room. Andrea sat in the advocates' row at the front, her body tense, defensive, as she tried to block out the chaos around her. Reporters were on their feet chattering loudly, members of the public shouted recriminations across the aisles at the opposing faction, police officers patrolled up and down, threatening to make arrests. But in the witness box in front of her and to her left, Hogarth waited calmly; he might have been alone in the room. With a start, Andrea remembered Calvin, and she turned her head quickly to try to locate him in the crowd. She found it difficult to focus on the sea of animated faces behind her, though she was sure he was not in the room, and if he was, he was not in a prominent position.

Then she heard the rap on the door. The stipe swept in; people stood as one, then sat, all except Andrea and Hogarth. The circus began again, but without Earl.

"I want my client present," she said to Ackroyde.

"After his outburst?"

"He has a right to hear everything. I can take the court to the relevant law."

Ackroyde pondered this, took off his horn-rimmed glasses and cleaned them with a large white handkerchief. When he replaced them, he said, "He'll have to remain in handcuffs. And if he breathes a word, I'll have him taken down."

Andrea nodded without replying. She knew it was the

best she could do. The thinner jailer, who was waiting at
the cells entrance, with the door slightly ajar, nodded, and
a battery of the four largest jailers surrounded Earl as they
escorted him in. Andrea made eye contact with him, and
briefly smiled, trying to reassure him, but his face was the
hard, streetwise mask that he habitually wore in public.
Andrea glanced down and to her left at Marion Slavin,
who tucked the ballistics report into the confidential case
file. Andrea bent down to whisper to her.

"Any forensics?"

"I told you, no," Marion hissed back.

Andrea nodded as if in agreement. She straightened her
back and then focused on Hogarth. The large man
appeared to come to life when she made eye contact with
him, as if he had suddenly been connected to the mains.
His eyes were instantly brighter, as if someone had shone
a torch into them. Come on, he seemed to be saying to
Andrea, come on. She steeled herself, and fought back the
butterflies in her stomach. She tried to keep hold of one
idea, one recollection, and that was of Earl as a child,
being dumped outside a police station in Jamaica.

"What would be the first thing that you would want to
analyse in this case?" she asked Hogarth.

"You tell me," he replied. "You seem to know."

"It would be the bullet, wouldn't it? The one which
tragically killed Nicki Harris."

"If you find it," Hogarth said.

Andrea's hopes leapt at this, for she thought she saw
him purse his lips briefly once he had answered, as if he
had made a mistake. She pounced on the opportunity, her
cross-examination technique returning more strongly all
the time, as she endeavoured to corner him. "Are you seriously telling the court, DCI, that the entire resources of the
Metropolitan Police haven't found the fatal bullet?"

"Sometimes you don't."

"But did you find it," Andrea pressed, "in this case?"

Hogarth hesitated, glanced at Marion Slavin, or at least that was Andrea's impression. She tilted her head to her left, perceived the slightest shake of the prosecutor's head. She quickly tried to decode the signals. There was nothing in the police report about finding the bullet, but all her years as a lawyer told her something was wrong here. She had to probe remorselessly until she exposed it.

She settled again on Hogarth. "You see, you wouldn't need a ballistics report if you hadn't found any bullets, would you?"

"No," he said.

"I mean, what is the annual budget of the Met?"

"One billion. Two."

"It costs a lot of money to arrest the wrong people, Mr Hogarth?"

"I find that offensive," Hogarth said, as though he took this professional slight personally.

"What I find offensive, Officer, is a concerted effort to subvert the law by the people supposed to uphold it."

There was a murmur in court, one side of the room almost hissing at Andrea, the other faction muttering in agreement.

"Miss Chambers," the stipe warned, "you are playing with fire."

Andrea chose to ignore him; she kept staring at Hogarth. He needed softening up before she probed again. "Have a look at the injuries to my client, DCI. At the burns to his hairline. He was your prisoner in the police station. So have you done anything to find out about them?"

"Oh, what does he say about them now?" Hogarth asked simply.

Andrea glanced at the dock, at Earl, who appeared to show fear and hope at the same time. She wondered if she had gone too far in the heat of the moment, and she focused back on what he had told her, what had consumed his interest — the bullet.

"Why is evidence being withheld from the defence?" she asked Hogarth.

"What evidence?" he said, calmly.

Andrea leaned to her left, right over Marion Slavin, and she saw perspiration appearing through the prosecutor's foundation. She hesitated, tried to consider again whether there was any logical answer to her dilemma, for what she was about to do could destroy her case and her credibility. She decided that this was a gut thing — it was impervious to logic, it was a call based upon sheer instinct. She assessed Marion Slavin's increasing nervousness, then went for it. From the police file, Andrea snatched what she believed to be the ballistics report.

"That's confidential," Marion protested.

"Sue me," Andrea replied. She held the report up for the whole court to see. "This evidence has been withheld from the defence," she said. There was uproar in court behind her.

"Silence!" the stipe screamed at the public. Then he turned his ire on its true target, Andrea. "Do you appreciate the gravity of your allegation?"

"Perfectly," Andrea said, as calmly as she could, but her palms sweated and she felt sick with worry. She couldn't let it show. "I asked if there was any forensic evidence," she told Ackroyde, "and I was told that there was none."

The court was on a knife-edge. The tension increased as silence returned. Andrea quickly, hopefully, skimmed the ten or so stapled pages. She flipped immediately to the end, to the photocopies of the photographs she had glanced at earlier. There was a snubbed, fired bullet. There was a barrel cross-section, computer-generated, she now saw, not a photograph, to indicate how the striations on the recovered bullet could have occurred. She turned to the front, scrolled through the paragraphs of scientific widget-speak. Her eyes landed on key words, though she did not absorb them all: lands–grooves ratio, right-hand twist, class characteristics, primer, stria, microscopy, ricochet, Carbina SP, blood, skull, dented, victim, dead.

Andrea recoiled. There was a photo buried in the middle of the report of Nicki Harris's shaved head. It showed the entry wound to the girl's skull.

Just then the neurotic jailer put up his hand and addressed the stipe. "The prisoner wants to speak to his brief."

"Your client appears to want to give you some instructions," Ackroyde said, patronisingly.

Andrea did not reply, but edged her way along the front of the court to the dock on the right-hand side. She took the ballistics report with her. When she arrived at the dock, Earl leaned forward so that his mouth was right at the gap between the glass partitions. He even turned his head forty-five degrees so that more of his mouth could fit through, although she saw that this made little difference, and when he spoke, his hot breath steamed up the glass. She leaned as close to him as she could manage, and she could see his hands doubly handcuffed in front of him. A flesh-coloured bandage had been carelessly wrapped around his wrists.

"Listen, Miz Chambers," Earl said, excitedly, "you a lawyer, you know the law. Me? I'm a gunman, I know the guns."

She understood his point instantly. She turned to the end of the report, where the ballistics expert had reached his conclusion as to the nature of the gun. She showed it to Earl.

"Carbina SP," she said.

"Boom," Earl laughed, hysterically.

"What? What is it?"

He gestured her closer still with his head, and then he whispered in her ear. What she heard caused her insides to rise and then fall, as if she had jumped out of a plane at thirty thousand feet.

"Earl," she whispered, "you better be right. The shit is going to hit the fan."

"But righteous shit, Miz Chambers. Righteous shit."

Andrea stared at him, and knew that the course of both their immediate futures depended on her next questions. She walked slowly back to her place in the advocates' row, the bombshell ticking steadily within her. She glanced at the back of the court and saw the door open. The two police officers whose job it was to guard the entrance tried to push a young black man back out of court, but Calvin would not be deterred and insisted on being admitted. He said something to the officers, and they immediately turned and looked at Andrea incredulously. She wondered if Calvin had told them that she was his mother, a fact of his life that was good for gaining entry into courtrooms, if little else. As he was allowed into the public benches, she caught his eye. She smiled at him, and he tried to return the gesture, forcing the beginnings of a grin, but he was very self-conscious, for dozens of people watched them.

Andrea turned her attentions back to Hogarth, and she noticed that in the hiatus the big man had composed himself once more, as though he had frozen himself from within, so that the lines on his large face appeared like cracks or fissures to her.

Her heart beat hard within her chest, not now with fear, but with anticipation. "So my client's alleged confession just happens to have been made off the record, Officer?" she asked. It was more of a statement than a question.

"In my experience," Hogarth replied, "experienced criminals never confess on the record."

"Nor do policemen, in mine," Andrea retorted quickly.

"Miss Chambers," warned the stipe.

Andrea ignored him, and again set about Hogarth. "Are you familiar with the penalties for obstructing the course of justice?"

"As familiar as you should be with those for obstructing the police."

Andrea could hear mutterings behind her after Hogarth's veiled threat, but she knew that both Earl and her son were now watching her, and she couldn't back out. In fact, she realised with some surprise that she no longer wished to do so. For what must have appeared to have been an instant to the rest of the transfixed courtroom, she brought her eyelids together. In that intensely private moment, in the most public of arenas, Andrea acknowledged to herself that she could do this job. An advocate in the criminal courts, barrister or solicitor, it didn't matter — she could do the job.

"The ballistic analysis of the fatal bullet showed that it was fired from a Carbina SP," she said to him. The DCI fumed silently, and did not reply. "I'm sorry, Officer," Andrea chided him, "the court didn't hear your answer." Hogarth averted his fierce gaze slightly. Andrea next feigned ignorance. "You see, I don't know much about guns, Mr Hogarth, so please tell us: what type of people have in the past used Carbina SPs in the UK?"

She could see that he could not contain himself for much longer. The muscles in his face twitched. It was as if he were grinding his teeth down to avoid responding.

"Who?" Andrea repeated, raising her voice. "*Who?*" she then shouted more loudly.

In a gush, Hogarth's defences burst. "You know full well," he shouted back.

It was Andrea's moment to attack, and she knew it. "So do you, Officer. But you can't say it, can you? Can you?"

"The police," Hogarth hissed, the words sounding shredded through his clenched teeth.

People stood all around court, shouting in anger or disbelief, or to join in since everyone else was shouting. Police officers in the aisle behind Andrea had to be reinforced by reserves, who charged into court to keep the warring factions apart. Coins began to fly from one side of the room to the other, and some people ducked, while others were hit. Andrea saw a pregnant woman struck in the face and fall back to her seat clutching her eye.

"Clear the court," the stipe shouted.

The bulk of the police officers, in two lines on either side of the aisle, linked arms, while the rest began to push the crowd out of the doors. Andrea turned and looked desperately for her son, but she could not see him. She tried to push through the police line to make her way into the public area, but the officers were too strong. Then she heard her name being shouted repeatedly.

"Miz Chambers, Miz Chambers," Earl screamed in the din, as the four jailers dragged him away.

There was no one to prevent her from making her way along the front of the court, behind the police line, to the right-hand side, where the dock was located. She pressed herself against the glass at the furthest side of the dock, the area nearest to the cell entrance.

"See, I told you," Earl shouted joyously, as if the chaos were exclusively a protest about his incarceration. Missiles now rained down on the glass, coins bounced off the surface, and they caused the jailers to let go of Earl and duck. The overwrought thinner jailer fled behind the cell entrance door itself. Earl used the opportunity to press right up to where Andrea was.

"You were at the shooting, weren't you?" she demanded.

"I work for Hogarth," Earl whispered.

"What?"

"The police brought me over here. To work. As a trigger."

A coin rebounded off the glass panel and struck Andrea on the cheek. She held her arm over her head for cover. "A trigger?" she asked.

One jailer now held Earl from behind and began to drag him away, but he broke free again. He pressed his mouth to the gap in the glass, almost as if he were trying to kiss Andrea. Spittle fell from his lips as he said, "To shoot people."

Andrea squeezed her hand through the glass, and briefly took hold of his arm, just above the wrist, pitying him while being scared of this self-confessed killer all at once. He looked back plaintively, his eyes wide and still in the madness about them, and she knew that he had spoken the truth. A second later she was snatching at empty space as the jailers tore him away and Earl Whitely disappeared behind the slammed cell door.

CHAPTER NINETEEN

Roots and Katherine walked along the South Bank in the intermittently sharp sunshine that had broken through the morning's rain. Despite the early season, the sight of the sun had brought out the performers in this Bohemian part of London, and as the black man and white woman walked, they passed lone buskers and jugglers and small groups of music students trying to repay their loans by playing classical favourites.

As he walked on the wet pavements, past second-hand booksellers with large wooden trays of battered paperbacks, past news-stands awaiting the first edition of the *Standard*, Roots occasionally glanced at Katherine. When he did, he dwelt on her intelligent, steady eyes, her strong face, her long hair tied back behind her head, until he sensed the nature of the bond between them: loneliness. She wore an ankle-length camel-coloured coat with a large collar, which she turned up; she had on calf-length brown leather boots, and the heels tapped pleasantly as they walked. Roots had discarded his long leather jacket for a midnight-blue cashmere overcoat. The jacket had been covered in blood.

"I didn't think you'd call," Katherine said frankly.

"Nor did I," Roots replied, immediately making her smile.

"So why did you?" she began. "Am I allowed to know that?"

He nodded, and slowed his pace, noticing that she

slowed too, and their arms brushed together. Roots imagined that he could still smell the gunsmoke in his nostrils, and though he looked out across the Thames as it glimmered through London on a brightening day, he felt himself still lost in a cloud of dry ice.

"I read this article," he said. "In one of your Sunday papers. About Yardies. It said our life expectancy is thirty-five."

"Oh, you know the press. They exaggerate everything," she replied.

Roots stopped dead, and she stopped too. He looked sadly at her, hoping that the next words would mean something to her, so that he could hold on to the fact that one person on the planet, no matter how much of a stranger she might be, might be affected. "I don't have any friends who made it to thirty-five," he said. "And next month? I'm thirty-four."

At first her face clouded with shock, but after this he thought he sensed an interest, an intrigue, a connection between them.

"By the time I was thirty-four," she said, "I was married, then pregnant, then a mother, and the director of my own company." She paused, as if she were articulating these things out loud to herself for the first time. "And by the time I was thirty-eight, I had lost all of that."

"And your point is? 'Cos I'm hoping you have a point," Roots said.

"My point is that things can change. Quickly. I tell myself that things happen for the best, but it's difficult to believe that always, Mr Johnson." She smiled and took his elbow as they continued to walk. "Look, I feel a little silly calling you Mr J. Am I allowed to know your first name?"

"Roots."

"You were christened Roots?"

He looked at her, and didn't want to lie. "It's kind of my

street name. But I've got to tell you, Katherine, the last man to call me by my real first name ended up flying through a bar window Jamaica."

"I'll risk it," she whispered, lowering her voice as they reached a string quartet, playing their hearts out on the wet pavements.

Roots's heart wanted to burst, for the harmonies seemed to reach into him and drag up his memory of his spar, Peckham. The students playing their violins with such confidence could not have been much older than Peckham was, and Roots momentarily envied their lives as he grieved for his best friend. He whispered shyly in Katherine's ear, "It's Valentine."

She looked up at the Yardie as if this revelation merely confirmed an essential truth she had already divined about him. The music stopped, and the small crowd clapped politely. One or two people dropped coins into the black beret on the ground in front of the quartet. Roots fumbled around inside his coat pocket. Then he became embarrassed when he realised that all he had was £50 and £20 notes. He could simply have passed on, but he wanted to mark the moment for Peckham. So he discreetly removed a £20 note, folded it up as tight as he could, and dropped it in the beret, quickly ushering Katherine onward. She looked at him, amazed.

"What? They were good," he said shyly.

As they walked under one of the railway bridges, a train clattered over. She shouted at the top of her voice, though he could barely hear her, "It's a lovely name. Romantic."

Just as quickly, the train had passed and the noise faded. "Nah," he said, "it's cricket. My dad was cricket crazy. And Sonny Valentine was a West Indies legend. A bowler. But not one of those pace men. No, Valentine bowled spin. He had guile, mystery."

Her face shone with delight at the tale, and she asked, "Is your father into music, too? Or did you get it from your mother?"

Roots stared at her, as behind her a dredger slowly moved up the Thames, so low in the river it was practically shipping water. He had already decided that he did not want to bullshit her, that he would tell her the truth or would simply not answer the difficult questions, and there were so many difficult questions about Roots Valentine Johnson.

For her part, she had recognised his reticence, and tried to make light of her obviously awkward enquiry. "It's OK, Valentine." She smiled.

This simple statement was for Roots a strange, magical spell. No one had called him Valentine since he was back home, and now here he was in the centre of London two decades later, with a woman he barely knew, feeling death close in all around him. He decided to tell her what he had told no one in Britain in all that time. He felt sure she could take it.

"My father shot a DEA agent in Miami, Katherine. When he was running coke. They executed him when I was still just a kid. It broke my mother's heart." Roots Johnson would never have believed how liberating his words were. For years he had kept so many secrets tied around his chest that sometimes he felt he could no longer breathe. But now he had untied the first of them, and something clicked inside him. He began to shiver. "It's cold in your country," he said.

"You want to try Canada," she replied. As they continued on their way, she boldly took his arm, hooking hers through his elbow. He didn't object. "Why did you come here?" she asked. "To England."

Roots laughed loudly, but he instantly knew that it was one of those shrill laughs where the joke was on the man laughing. He shook his head. When he thought of it now, he could barely believe it himself. "Politics," he said.

"Politics?"

He made the fingers of his right hand into a kind of gun. "In the eighties, they called that" — he indicated his fingers — "a ballot-box back home. The party paid me ten dollars a week. To . . . canvass."

"I don't understand."

"Nor did I. But I was only sixteen, ya know. Fighting against the right. Against the CIA. Against everything. We were socialists, we liked Castro. So the CIA gave the right wing guns." He knew his voice was getting louder, as after all these years the crude injustice of the struggle once more burned in his stomach. "We were one small island against the CIA. How could we compete? Except by selling."

"Drugs?"

"Ganja at first. Then it all got crazy. And here I am. No home. No family. No politics. Nothing, Katherine. Nothing."

His breath was short, and he ached for the idealistic youth he had once been, young Valentine Johnson, who had stood with his father on the beach and imagined the palm trees dragging the night over the island from the depths of the Caribbean. The man he was now felt ashamed, for he had let that youngster down, just as, he believed, he had let down his spar, Peckham.

Katherine sensed his turmoil, and unhooked her arm carefully. Then, with her small, warm hands, she held his long, thin ebony fingers. They were ice cold.

"It's all right," she whispered.

She smiled, and he couldn't help smiling back, even though he knew that it could never be all right, at least, not for him. And he was confused as to whether he wanted to tell her this hard truth, or whether he could allow himself to enjoy her comforting, unwitting lie, just for a while. But he didn't have a chance to say anything before his mobile rang. Katherine let go of his hands, and when he took the phone out of his long pocket the spell was broken, the fleeting magic of their walk had gone. Roots put the phone hesitantly to his ear, while she remained just a foot in front of him.

"Earl's gone overboard," Hogarth said, in a voice more agitated than Roots expected. The Yardie looked down at Katherine's strong face as the policeman continued, and he felt stronger. "Johnson?" Hogarth went on. "Johnson, we've got to do something. Whitely's talking — about everything." Roots wondered what his life would be like without the game, without his business, what life would be like for a civilian; he imagined the stresses of trying to make a living on the other side of the law and it frightened him. "Johnson, are you with me?" Hogarth shouted. It was the only time Roots could remember the DCI losing it so badly. Earl was putting his life on the line. Roots only hoped that the reckless youth understood it. But when the don looked at Katherine again, as she gazed up at him with concern, he knew that he already felt freer, because now he was scared, like the millions of other civilians in the city. What he was about to do would be a watershed, perhaps the final watershed in his life. It would be more dangerous, more treacherous, than killing rival gang leaders, than pitting himself against the cream of the international law enforcement community, and the world of shadows in which he moved would talk about it, about how the supposedly great don, Roots Johnson, lost it all. But he didn't care.

Roots clicked off his mobile.

"What was it?" she asked. "Bad news?"

Roots nodded. He carefully replaced the slim cellular in his pocket, then he thought about it. The phone was a burner. It had been illegally obtained, used illegally, and

what had been a fact of his unlawful life since mobile
phones became commonplace now nauseated him.
He snatched the phone out of his pocket and took three
powerful strides towards the wall of the riverbank,
then he threw it with all his strength out over the edge.
It tumbled end over end, spinning over the small
white-topped waves, and finally plunged into the water
and disappeared.

He returned to Katherine, who looked at him in
amazement. She was too surprised by his bizarre actions
to speak.

"I hate mobiles," Roots said apologetically.

"With a vengeance," she finally said.

Roots nodded, smiled, but secretly told himself: No, not
with vengeance, please. Vengeance is the one thing I don't
want. He felt this because he knew that living a life of
vengeance was living a life catching up with bad people
who had done bad things, and then doing even worse
things to them. The night before, he had avenged Peckham's
death, and now he was ashamed. He quickly moved behind
Katherine because he knew there were tears in his eyes.

"What are you doing?" she asked, craning her neck
around to look at him behind her.

Roots pointed down the river. "A little way down the
river, there's a site," he said. "It's just a pile of bricks right
now. But one day — I really mean this, Katherine — one
day it's going to be a studio. Just a small one first up. But
I'm going to work hard, and I just know it will grow."

"It will take a lot of time and effort," she said.

"Yeah, well, I got time," he said confidently. But then
an army of doubts and questions surrounded him as he
fully grasped the magnitude of what he had done. "I
hope," he added.

They continued walking and passed the National Film
Theatre. The glassed front door was open, and just inside

trendy people with glasses of wine or bottles of designer beer adopted artistic poses in their almost exclusively black clothes.

"Race you inside," Katherine said. "I think we should celebrate your plans. Last one to the bar's got to drink the house champagne."

She began to rush towards the bar, but stopped. She had noticed that Roots was riveted where he was standing, directly under Waterloo Bridge. She followed his eyes to a newspaper stall, where the vendor was putting out the poster with the day's headline. The banner letters formed just one word: MASSACRE.

Katherine rushed up to him. He was staring at the still-tied bale of newspapers. There was a picture of the dance-hall, and around it ten smaller pictures, mugshots, of unidentified victims. The police appealed for people to come forward, at least to identify the corpses. Katherine stared into Roots's transformed face, at the shame and the revulsion and the fascination that now played there, and she knew. She felt herself unconsciously beginning to back away from him.

"Katherine, please," he said, now following her.

She turned, and now her feet moved faster, virtually running, but he was swifter, more lithe, and in a few seconds he was ahead of her. He gazed down at her frightened eyes, which suddenly hardened as he blocked her path, and she was consumed with anger. She hit him, with tight fists, again and again on the chest.

"How could you? How could you?" she cried.

"They killed my best friend."

"I don't care."

"It's finished. I'm out."

"You'll never get out," she shouted.

"I told you it would be dangerous."

"I didn't know the danger was you." She broke free of

his grip, turned, pulled her long coat tightly around herself and walked in the opposite direction to Roots's beloved studio site.

Hogarth stood in the court complex's specially designed security control room. Around him were banks of CCTV monitors and control panels for the entire hi-tech building. Fisher, Brigson and a fretting Kelsey stood around the DCI nervously as he barked out orders.

"I want the entire cell area shut down," he shouted at Fisher.

"Yes, guv," Fisher replied.

"*Now!*" Hogarth shouted, more loudly. He watched one of the screens, which showed Earl Whitely pacing around his cell in the pit of the building, talking relentlessly to himself in his excitement and fear.

Fisher dragged in one of the court security officers, an emaciated, pockmarked man, and relayed Hogarth's order. The man fiddled with switches on the panel, looking around himself worriedly.

"This is an emergency," Fisher told him.

"What emergency?" the man asked.

"There could be an armed break-out attempt."

Hogarth went to the far corner of the room, where he had a view down over the restricted carpark, now bathed in a brilliant sunshine, which bounced off the greasy windscreens of police and prison vehicles. He spoke easily, but so that the rest of the men in the room could not hear.

"It's Hogarth. Are you available for . . . work?" he said when the call was answered.

"I knew you'd want to deal with me soon enough," came the arrogant reply.

"Lifer," Hogarth explained patiently, "understand this: I don't want to deal with any of you. But Johnson's become a problem."

"Forget Johnson. He's no longer with the programme. I'm the man now, Hogarth, so show me some respect, ya know."

"I need something done. Quickly."

"Like I said, I'm the man."

Hogarth put his hand over the phone and addressed Fisher. "How long till shutdown?"

"Almost done," Fisher replied, and the security officer nodded.

Hogarth returned to Lifer. "I need you in court," he told the Yardie.

"Ten minutes," Lifer said.

Andrea and Calvin circled each other in one of the conference rooms, off the main lobby. The hallways outside teemed with people who had been cleared out of the courtroom, and there was a double line of uniformed policemen, blocking the doors of the court. Each end of the police line was flanked by armed officers. The room in which Andrea and her son argued was small and square, with cigarette butts stamped into the floor and a broken chair propped against the graffiti-daubed wall. Someone had recently spilled coffee on the carpet, and it steamed and reeked at the same time.

"What did you mean by that note?" Andrea shouted. She wore just her suit, having left her coat in the courtroom.

"Why can't I see Earl?" Calvin demanded, deliberately ignoring the question.

"We've been over this, Calvin. Only legal visits are allowed," Andrea replied.

"Then why don't you see him?"

"There's a problem with the security locks. The computer."

"Bullshit," Calvin shouted.

I know, I know, Andrea said to herself. Then she remembered her original question. "Don't change the subject. What was that note about?"

"You read it?" he shouted, his almond eyes feigning hurt at the betrayal. "I trusted you."

"No, I trusted you," Andrea said. "What the hell did that mean? Deny everything? Earl told me he was there at the shooting, Calvin."

The boy stopped suddenly, stunned by his friend's confession. His animated hands dropped to his sides.

"Yes, that's right," Andrea said. "So you'd better tell me the truth now. Were you there?"

Calvin's face screwed up as he tried to calculate Earl's angle. The gun was a police gun, Earl had admitted he was there, there was a shit-storm about to break, and Calvin could see no other option but to tell the truth.

"Were you there?" his mother repeated.

His head dropped. "No," he said quietly.

Andrea moved in swiftly, so that she could stare up into her son's eyes. Like every mother, she believed, or at least she wanted to believe, that she should be able to tell when her child was not telling the truth. "Don't lie to me, Calvin," she said.

"Yeah, call me a liar," he shouted back. "Just like those cops."

"I'm not like them."

"Aren't you?"

There was a pause, a stand-off rather than a truce. Andrea tried to take her son's hand, but he recoiled. He spun around so that he faced the high meshed window on the outer wall. When he spoke, it was quietly.

"Earl came back to the flat with that gun. He said a girl got shot."

Andrea felt paralysed inside. Every word, she knew,

would take her son away from or directly into the heart of dreadful danger. One part of her didn't want to know any more. She wanted simply to take Calvin away from the courtroom and the case, and hide him. But she also now felt a loyalty to Earl, which confused her, since the Yardie had admitted that he was a gunman used by Hogarth. "Did Earl say," she asked tentatively, "if he shot Nicki?"

Calvin turned around, seemingly furious that she even had to ask this. "Earl's my friend. He wouldn't be my friend if he did that."

"So did he say who killed Nicki Harris?"

Calvin shook his head, and raised his right hand in exasperation. "Do you want to make it worse?"

"I only want the truth," Andrea protested, she knew hollowly.

"There is no truth. Not here."

Calvin went for the door, but Andrea blocked him. She spoke quickly, painfully. This was as hard as hell for her, but she had to say it. "Last night," she said, "when I saw you in that hall, Calvin, you were this close." She held up her right hand and made a small space — an inch — between her thumb and forefinger. "You were this close to it. To death, Calvin. It was all around you. In the smoke, the masks, the guns. When I saw that body there on the stage? I thought . . . oh God, I thought it was you. My baby. And I wished, I wished so hard, that you had known the truth before you had died." Unwanted tears rolled down her face.

"What?" he asked, confused and frightened.

She shook her head, for she had lived the lie for so long that she momentarily wondered whether she was making it up.

"What truth?" Calvin asked, angry now, as if he were about to fly at her.

She crossed her arms defensively, realising she was

scared of him, actually scared of her son, and she hated herself for it, for it was unnatural and thus, she believed, it had to be her failing. "I didn't leave you," she said. "I didn't walk out on you, Calvin. I never would. Ever. Calvin, they *took* you away from me. And . . . and they were right to. I was unfit. Then. I was on the edge of breaking down. With all the pressure. The mixed races. The prejudices I never thought of. I just saw you as my son, my baby. But no one else saw it that way. Apart from Rufus. The truth is, I couldn't cope. The truth is, I went to court and I lost you."

There was silence in the room. Calvin's face froze in disbelief. As the certainties of a decade melted before his eyes, a new, more complex world rose around him.

"But I'm stronger now," Andrea said. "And I want to try. Again. If you'll let me."

"Why'd you all lie to me?" he demanded in a cold, detached voice, as though his brain still functioned, though his heart was still.

"Because the court said you should be with your father, and I wanted what was best for you. So we agreed. That it would be my fault."

"Dad wouldn't agree to such a thing."

"Listen to me. He was different then, Calvin. He believed a black child should be with the black parent."

The shock had now worked its way through his body. "I don't believe you," he said, as tears shone in his eyes.

"Don't blame him. I don't any more."

"I don't believe you," he shouted now.

"All I want is a chance," Andrea pleaded.

But Calvin shoved his mother out of the way, burst out into the court lobby and ran towards the exit.

Minutes later, Earl finally managed to calm himself sufficiently so that he could sit on the hard bed in his tiny cell. He had his head in his hands as he calculated the odds now that he had told his brief a part of the truth. It was entirely novel for him to feel good about himself, to cast off the lies that had weighed him down all through his teens; it was a high he never would have believed. He looked up when he heard the cell door begin to open, and he hoped that it would be Miss Chambers. But the world spun around one more time for Earl Whitely when he saw Lifer coming through the door. Earl rushed up to the monstrous Yardie, who put his fat finger to his lip. They hugged each other like brothers.

"We going to get you out, star," Lifer said to the ecstatic Earl.

"How?" Earl whispered.

"We bribed them jailers."

"I knew the crew would come through for me big time," Earl said.

Lifer gave Earl a small piece of metal. "This is for your handcuffs. We goin" to ambush the prison van on the way back. Roots Johnson has taken care of everyt'ing. You gotta hurt the screw riding in the back of the van. But not too much. He's been paid. Just make it look real, ya know."

"Nice," was all Earl replied, trying to contain his joy, so that he could regain his street cool.

"Keep the key in your mouth," Lifer ordered. "Between the teeth and gums. Like a deal of rock."

Earl knew the routine. It had been part of his education, part of his life — a roll of shiny foil in the mouth, containing crack. This was the world he knew, this was the world he felt comfortable in, so his emotions swung around again and he was certain, he was convinced, that the life of the gangster was the only one to lead.

Andrea followed Calvin out of the court complex and into the street, but her son had disappeared into the crowds.

Even though the sun now shone, she shivered in the cold air, as she only had her suit jacket to warm her, and the light knitted material seemed to allow jets of the icy breeze to blow directly on to her skin. However, now that she was out in the open, she decided to try to gain access to Earl and the cell area from the other side, from the official carpark.

She saw that a police van had backed itself against the metal cage in front of the rear court doors. All around her there were marked police area cars and Sherpa Transit vans, but the carpark was devoid of people, save for a driver in one of the vans. He was reading a newspaper, which he had open across the steering wheel. As she approached across the newly laid tarmac, a black, practically spongy surface, she saw the rear parallel glass doors of the security airlock open. Two detectives, Fisher and Brigson, escorted a huge man out of the building, but Andrea could not see who he was since his head was covered with a large grey blanket. Fisher opened the rear door of the van, and Brigson assisted the prisoner up, before joining the other two in the rear. At the sound of the van doors slamming, the driver neatly closed his newspaper, folded it in two, then started the engine and drove off past Andrea.

She briefly watched it pause at the junction with the main road, before it disappeared. All her concentration was now focused on gaining access to the cell area. Since the rear doors opened so freely, she knew that either the governing computer was up and running again or the whole thing had been a scam. She reached the metal cage, at the side of which was a buzzer on the brickwork of the building. She pressed it once. The cage door sprung open. Andrea looked around. She stepped inside the cage, and now was confronted by the first of the double glass doors of the airlock. She glanced around for another buzzer to press, but there was none. She turned around in confusion, and was looking at the carpark now from behind the wire mesh of the cage when the glass door began to grind open, seemingly on its own. Andrea stepped into the square box of glass, with doors to her front and back. The outer door ground shut slowly. She waited. Then waited some more. She felt as if she were in a lift, waiting for the doors to open, trying to convince herself that though they were taking unnaturally long to do so, this was no reason to panic. Still the doors did not open.

She could now see a long corridor which, she assumed, must lead to the cell block via a back route. She banged her fists on the door, but the glass was so thick that her hand barely made a sound. She looked all around her. Down at the rubber pressure pad on the floor, up at the security camera in the ceiling. She tried to force the inner doors apart, but there was no chance. Behind her, the carpark was empty, and now she felt panic beginning to work its way into her stomach, knotting it horribly, as she imagined court resuming without her.

Her fears were at once allayed, and replaced with new ones of a more sinister order, when she saw Hogarth walking down the corridor towards her. The inner doors opened. Andrea and the DCI were face to face and utterly alone.

"You've breached security," Hogarth said.

"And you've broken the law," she retorted, her relief at being freed resolving itself into anger.

"I don't know if I should arrest you," Hogarth said coldly. "Then what would young Calvin do? Though, of course, he's lived most of his life without a mother."

Andrea felt threatened by every word the large detective said, but she kept telling herself that this was Hogarth's plan, and she was determined not to allow him to succeed in intimidating her. She would have to fight back.

"Earl says he works for you," she said.

"Works?" Hogarth enquired innocently.

"Killing people."

"And Earl Whitely never lies?"

"Yes, he does," Andrea retorted. "He lies all the time. But I think he does work for you. So I really want to know: who do you work for?"

Hogarth approached, so close that she could smell the cigarette smoke hanging over his clothes like a veil. He looked intensely at her, his eyes very still. "For you, Andrea," he said. "I work for all of you. And deep down? You know it. You want it. You don't like me, but you need me. You always have."

"Who are you to judge these things?"

"A simple officer of the law. Who gathers the evidence. Who sifts it. Lives with it. While it lives with me — always. If you'd seen what I've been forced to see, then you'd know. Something's got to be done."

"By bending the rules?" she challenged him. She was very angry now and was not about to let him get away with it.

"By breaking the law," he said. "If it's necessary."

"What gives you that right?"

"It happens every day. It always has. Grow up, Andrea. Like your son has."

"Leave Calvin out of it."

"I can't," Hogarth said flatly. "But I don't want to hurt you or your son."

Andrea's mind raced with a chaos of thoughts. Was this a threat that she could use in court against him in some way? But how could she prove it? And what if he was right? Could she — dare she — take that risk? She thought of Calvin storming out of the conference room, minutes earlier, not able to bear the truth she had revealed to him, but at least she had made a start. For years all the family lies had festered. She had made a start, and that gave her the courage to stand up to Hogarth. "You don't scare me," she said.

Hogarth was absolutely still. "You know," he said, "sometimes I even scare myself."

He turned slowly, precisely, and left a shaken Andrea alone as he walked to some stairs that led up towards the lobby. She could feel the sweat trickling coldly down her back as she watched him, and she wondered what damage she had done. Slowly, she edged her way along the narrow corridor, which led to the cell area. And she suddenly recognised the jailers" counter in the reception area, even though she was now coming at it from the opposite direction. The head jailer saw her, morosely took up his keys, and then opened the metal grille that led to Earl's cell wing. Andrea walked slowly, aware of every step that she made on the hard floor, until she finally saw the black-board outside the cell with the name "Whitely" scribbled upon it in chalk.

The wicket gate, the peep-hole in the centre of the door, was open, and Andrea quickly glanced into the cell, without bending down fully to get a proper view. But she looked back at the jailer immediately in confusion. Earl was not there.

"Earl?" she called.

There was no reply.

Then she saw it. The scrap of material tied to the metal lock of the wicket gate. She touched it instinctively, and realised that it was Earl's T-shirt.

She saw him hanging there, his body resting against the inside of the door, quite still as the ligature cut fatally into his throat.

Part Two

CHAPTER ONE

The correspondence in Andrea's in-tray steadily mounted up. Though she had spent most of the week following Earl Whitely's death back in the office, her mind was torn between what she now came to see as the irrelevancies of the corporate world and the life to which she had been exposed, to which her son was being exposed daily, south of the river. Her colleagues in the office, including her father, spoke solemnly about bottom lines and deadlines, but every time such words were used, her thoughts flashed immediately back to that cell door, and her client, and Earl's body, hanging so still in that posture of death, which had met its own bottom line, its own still-unexplained deadline.

The glass wall behind her began to darken like a pair of light-sensitive glasses as the sun came out over the City. A day of whale-grey clouds scudding fast across the rooftops of the financial office blocks, with a strong wind hurrying them on, whining outside her window. The silhouette of a bird of prey, a kestrel perhaps, wheeled round and round, below Andrea's fourteenth floor, until it finally came to rest on the water tower of a neighbouring office. Siobhan had stepped out of the office to make Andrea a hot chocolate and herself a coffee, so she found herself temporarily alone in the hurly-burly of the law firm. Across her desk were splayed confidential documents relating to a hostile take-over, stamped in red across the top like official secrets.

Her computer hummed quietly on the right-hand side of her desk, the screen blank and the cursor flashing impatiently. Andrea glanced from the toolbar to the legal papers she could no longer bear to touch, and then back at the screen. She had an idea. She slid the mouse over its pad so that the cursor became a small white arrow pointing at a small square box in the centre of the toolbar with a blue globe within it. A small dialogue rectangle appeared below the arrow with the words. 'Search the web'. Andrea double-clicked. A sign-in screen appeared with her name as user name, the password box empty. She had never learned to touch-type, so she tapped the six letters of her password with the index finger of her left hand and the middle finger of her right: C-A-L-V-I-N.

The computer tower and modem whirled and churned through the digital information and the screen finally washed black, until the home page of her service provider appeared. There were suddenly so many options — channels for news and sport and entertainment — and she ran the cursor over them until she arrived at the icon she wanted. The FIND option. When she double-clicked this, a number of search engines appeared and, not having surfed the Net much in the past, she chose the search engine already designated. The dialogue box was in its default position, which would allow her to search the whole web. Her excitement grew as she homed in on her goal — the combination of the chase and the fact that she felt like a girl again, disobeying her father by lying under her sheets with a torch, reading *Anna Karenina* for the third time running, deep into the early hours. She glanced up at the glass panels on either side of the wooden door. She could see no one out in the corridor, but Siobhan had left the door slightly ajar. Before she knew exactly what she was doing, she had jumped up from her swivel chair, traversed the thick carpet, shut the door, and was back in front of her VDU typing the letters: Y-A-R-D-I-E-S. Or at least, that is what she had wanted to type, but in her excitement she twice misspelled the word. She was totally focused now, and looked at the screen intensely, too intensely, for when the modem churned again and the screen faded to black, she started back, for she glimpsed a face in the sight-saver protective screen. She tried to laugh at herself, but that made the image even more disturbing. For her nose was practically touching the glass, her head was bowed, her shoulders hunched, and her face, even allowing for the fact that it was being reflected on to glass with a black background, was strangely haunted. Here she was in the midst of a safe, thriving law firm, her father's life's work, surrounded by people who liked and admired her, and she felt utterly alone. She secretly asked herself the question she had asked time and again in the ten years between the court humiliation when she had lost Calvin and now. What am I afraid of? And she knew the answer profoundly, not in the sense that she understood it, but in that it was as much a part of her as the marrow in her bones. What am I afraid of? Myself. That was it, she knew. I am afraid of myself, of what I can do, of how I can punish myself, and believe I deserve to be punished because I have given life to a son who has seen through me and does not love me. Though the screen now began to resolve into Internet home pages that matched Andrea's search request, she put her head in her hands, and her heart ached because Calvin blamed her for Earl Whitely's death.

The door opened suddenly and her father strode into the room, favouring his right leg as he always had since a ligament injury had put paid to his squash-playing days. "Ah, excellent," he said, when he saw the legal papers strewn over the expanse of her desk. "Will you put that hostile to bed today?"

She looked blankly up at him, and inside she felt a

combination of affection and shame, because she wished that she could have been as good a parent to her child as he had been to her.

"What? What is it, darling?" he asked. Gordon was right by her desk now, and nodded knowingly. "You've got four hits," he said.

"Pardon?"

He indicated the screen. "For Yardies. The TV docu-clip looks the best," he added, squatting on the edge of the desk as he clicked the mouse on the documentary home page.

"Dad, Calvin blames me for Earl's death," she said.

"That's ridiculous," he replied. "You were trying to do the right thing. As far as I know, that's not yet a crime in this country. But you're the expert in criminal jurisprudence."

She smiled, and saluted her good fortune that she had such a father. She wondered what prevented her from telling him how warmly she felt. Gordon was transfixed by the screen. The video clip had loaded and there was a smaller box, rather like a miniature television within her computer screen. A reporter spoke into the camera as he walked through some London back streets.

"My God," Gordon said, "in my day we thought *Quatermass and the Pit* was cutting-edge technology."

Andrea put her hand over her father's on the mouse, and thrilled at feeling the now-loose skin on his hands, the wispy hairs on the back of his palm that had turned almost to silver. She clicked on Pause. The reporter froze.

"Dad, the inquest is today."

"They just adjourn it the first day, don't they?"

"I still want to go," she said.

He turned his palm upwards so that he could close his bony fingers around her hand. He shook his head, and smiled with a certain resignation. "You're like a dog with a bone," he said.

"Oh, thanks."

He added, whispering, "You're like your mother." Tears shone in the old man's eyes, and he clicked the mouse impetuously to distract his daughter from this fact.

Skin against skin, hands intertwined, they both now listened to the reporter, whose words sounded slightly distorted in his digitally reconstituted voice. ". . . has fuelled speculation of a new Yardie turf war. While so-called dons have been gunned down, there are claims and counter-claims of police corruption. The man charged with this internal investigation is Detective Superintendent Mason of the newly formed Internal Complaints Unit." The reporter turned to his left, to where a bulky, overweight man stood. "DSu Mason," the reporter continued, "how seriously do you take these allegations of police corruption?"

Andrea watched fascinated as Mason weighed the question carefully before he answered. He instinctively brushed his moustache with the back of his right hand. "Corruption is just crime," Mason said. "I take all crime seriously."

The footage now switched to a series of black-and-white photographs of murder scenes. An alley, some wasteland, a timber yard, in each of which Andrea could just make out a body that had been dumped.

Gordon clicked off the clip. "Yes, quite enough of that, thank you. Real nightmare material."

"Dad, I'm a big girl now."

"I was talking about myself," he said, causing her to laugh.

He stood up and walked slowly around the desk to gaze over the City. Andrea quickly clicked the sign-off screen and was disconnected from the Internet. She swivelled around in her chair and saw the familiar outline of her father's back.

"Darling," he said, without turning around, "I want to

warn you about something."

She stood and joined him at the glass. "I know it's dangerous," she said.

Gordon shook his head. "Not the case. I don't care about the case. I care about you."

Andrea was confused. "Now, are you speaking as my boss or my father?"

"As your friend," Gordon said, gently, then adding, "I hope." He was silent for a moment, and it appeared to Andrea that he was weighing the pros and cons of what he was about to say, as he always did. "It's not easy being a parent," he said finally. "I think we both know that now. But I think you might usefully ask yourself why as a parent you're doing certain things."

Andrea grew increasingly concerned, for her father's voice became lower and lower, as it had done years ago when he had broken the news to her about her mother's malignant growth.

"This case. Have you been doing it for Calvin or for yourself?" He held up his hand as she was about to answer. "Don't tell me. Tell yourself. Truly. But can I just say that if there is an element of trying to prove yourself in court, you don't need to. Not to me, anyway."

Andrea turned and leaned against the glass with most of her body weight. It was a strange sensation so far up, because if the glass gave way nothing would prevent her from crashing to the ground. She almost defied the window to do so. "The last time you saw me in court," she said, "they destroyed me."

"That's what barristers do to their witnesses, you should know that."

"I pleaded for my son, and they said I was an unfit mother. And I'm not unfit, not any more, Dad," she added, trying to convince herself. But that was the person who most scared her, the post-custody-battle Andrea, the damaged woman who had publicly been tarred as unfit.

Gordon turned, and saw her pain instantly. He hugged her tightly. "Andrea, we tell ourselves that we have our children's best interests at heart, but I wonder. When you told me you were pregnant, I convinced myself that I wanted you to terminate the pregnancy in your best interests. But I now know I was just thinking about my own."

"Dad?" Andrea said, alarmed at his frankness.

"Which father would want his only little girl to have a child — and I know it's an old-fashioned phrase — out of wedlock? I wasn't thinking about you, darling, I thought of myself. How many white middle-class fathers would want their daughter to have an illegitimate child by a black man — no matter how charming?"

"Dad, you are not racist."

"Aren't I? Really? I try not to be, but aren't these the facts of this society? So if you really love Calvin, if you want him back, shouldn't you drop this case, because everything to do with it is poisoned. It's done and dusted. Earl Whitely is dead. Finding the truth about how he died, it won't bring him back for Calvin. But the truth, if it wasn't suicide, will just make Calvin resentful, will make him hate this society even more. And, darling, like it or not, you and I are part of it. Andrea, you prove what really went on and do you know what will happen? You will become the messenger. And they always shoot the messenger." He hesitated after his increasingly passionate words, and tried to snap out of his sombre tone. He clapped his hands once. "Right, here endeth the first lesson."

"Dad, thanks," she said, kissing him lightly on the cheek, her mind spinning with the dozens of questions that the conversation had raised within her.

"I hope some of that made sense," he said, beginning to leave the room.

"No," she said, laughing.

"So you're not going to the inquest?"

She crossed her arms. "Objection. Counsel has asked a leading question."

"Don't go," he said, in a tone that was more of a plea than an order.

Andrea nodded as her heart told her what to do.

When Katherine opened her office door, she was confronted by Roots Johnson. She looked down at the Yardie, who had retreated five steps back down towards the pavement, and saw in a flash that the smile he attempted to sport was forced, for the rest of his features were set in a mournful cast, about which he could do nothing. He had a single long-stemmed white rose in the fingers of his left hand.

"You wouldn't return my calls," he said.

She did not reply, and the silence between them was as clear to both as the sound of the black taxis and cycle couriers speeding through the one-way street behind him.

"Please, Katherine," he said. "I need your help."

"I've been busy," she said. Then she thought about it, and to tell the whole truth added, "I've made myself busy."

From Roots's vantage point at the foot of the steps, Katherine appeared as remote and as untouchable now as had the sunburnt American and British tourists he remembered from his youth, guarded in their luxury hotels along the Jamaican beaches. For he saw no sign of hope in Katherine's sad face, with its large, glistening eyes, except for this one thing: she looked as miserable as he had felt for the last week. He tentatively raised his left hand, and the bloom of the rose bobbed slightly in her direction. He set himself a test, or rather he decided to test how things would turn out for the two of them, because he convinced himself that if she would only take the flower, then they would be together. The flower was the thing. If she would just take it from him, then despite the impasse they seemed to be in, there would be hope. He held the rose up higher, closer to her, and then instantly regretted the experiment.

"I don't want your flowers," she snapped at him.

The intonation of the words caused Roots's heart to pound harder. She didn't want his flowers, but she seemed to imply that she did want something from him, or was such an interpretation just a fabrication born of his desperate hopefulness?

"I didn't think about you," she said. "Not once. I didn't wish you would come round like this and force me to see you. I didn't wish I had had the chance to hurt you for what you've done. I didn't hate you. I didn't miss you, Valentine."

"I'm sorry," he said simply.

"I want your word," she replied.

Encouraged by these four syllables, he dared to step once, twice, three times, nearer to her. They were now no more than three feet apart. He could smell her perfume, and he ached to touch her hair, which was now shining freely around her shoulders. "About what?" he asked.

"That you really want out," she said.

"I do."

"Then do something about it," she snapped, far more coldly than before. She turned swiftly and shut the heavy door behind her.

This too must be what life is like for a civilian, Roots thought, trying to comfort himself. For he had never before had a door shut in his face by a woman. Over the years, women had schemed and networked to get close to the don, so finding himself standing alone facing a shut door was so alien and so painful that Roots wanted to cry out aloud. But at least he had made a start. She had offered him some hope. Now it was up to him — he had to begin to make the studio a reality, had to blow away his dreams and replace them with solid work. He bent down and laid the rose fastidiously at the foot of the door.

He turned and skipped down the stairs, walking more and more quickly down the street, as his mind plotted its way back into Katherine's favours.

What Roots did not see, however, was that Katherine had rushed to her office window from the hall corridor, and watched him until he turned the corner and disappeared from view. Once he had gone, she forced herself to count to ten, then she returned to the front door and opened it. She reached down, and was careful to avoid the triangular thorns that punctuated the sweep of the stem. She raised the white rose to her face and her heart swelled as she admired the simple perfection of the interlocking petals. It was as if Roots had created the flower himself. She half closed her eyes and was about to smell the fragrance of the rose, but with a strong act of will just managed to stop herself.

However, she did not know that Roots's path was not a direct one, but a circuit of the Georgian block in which her office was located, and consequently ten minutes later he once more passed her front door, albeit on the other side of the street. The Yardie's heart beat faster in his chest when he saw that the rose had gone.

Fisher and Brigson sat in an unmarked police car, parked directly opposite the coroner's court. The feeding frenzy around the death of Earl Whitely had slowly faded in the intervening week, but now that the inquest was to be opened formally, the press pack had returned. Fisher smoothed back his blond hair, and watched as the reporters and TV crews jostled for prime position around the entrance to the old redbrick Victorian coroner's court. He tried to spot the attractive redhead who had covered the story for regional news, but he couldn't concentrate.

He was forced to wind down the driver's window to let the smell of piping-hot pastry out of the car. He had already eaten. He stared at Brigson with hatred evident in his eyes, for there was little more repugnant than the smell of hot food after a full fried breakfast.

"What?" Brigson asked defensively. "It's comfort eating."

"The only crumb of comfort you give, Brigson, is to the nation's pastry-makers. Anyway, what do you need comforting for?"

Brigson took another bite, then spoke while chewing. "Kelso. I quite miss him."

"Forget Kelsey. He wasn't one of us. Not really."

"What do you think'll happen to him?" Brigson asked, genuinely concerned.

"They'll give him a couple of months to forget everything on sick leave, then transfer him behind some desk."

This prospect appeared to upset the overweight detective, and Brigson slowly wound down his own window, took a last conservative bite of the pie, and then flung the remaining half out of the car. To Brigson, it was the waste of perfectly good pastry, but it was his small gesture of mourning for Kelsey, whom he had found unobjectionable. Fisher sensed Brigson's unusually doleful expression. He attempted to change the subject.

"So what's your waist measurement now, Brigsy?" he asked jokingly.

Brigson stared out of the side window so that he didn't have to look at Fisher.

"Brigsy?" Fisher pressed.

"Fifty-eight inches," Brigson said.

Fisher now affected a burst of mock outrage. "Fifty-eight? Fifty-eight inches? Not centimetres? Jesus, Brigsy, that's nearly five foot. Christ, you're fatter round the waist than Ronnie Corbett is tall, do you realise that, you fat bastard?"

Brigson turned with great composure and said, "I believe that for a modern policeman, being fit in the mind is more important than being fit in the body."

"Nah, it's a balance, Brigsy, and you've bust the bloody scales."

A brief silence followed the bantering, in which Fisher was relieved that he had got his obese colleague back on side.

"Brigson?" he said finally.

"Yes?"

"What's it like being you?"

Brigson laughed, even though the joke was on him. This further reassured Fisher, for it wouldn't do to have squad members moping about the departure of Kelsey — it would be bad for morale, but more importantly it would be dangerous. Stevie Fisher knew of some specialist squads that had been destroyed when dissension spread through them, when officers started to question what it was they were doing. When there was dissension in a squad, he knew, dissenters felt that it was safer to speak out. That couldn't happen. Kelsey couldn't believe that he was safe. At least, that was what Hogarth had impressed upon Fisher.

For his part, Brigson missed DC Mark Kelsey, not just because he had liked the young detective, but because Kelsey had had the courage to express some of the doubts Brigson was beginning to have about the squad's operations. Brigson was not a hero, nor was he a loner by choice or inclination. In fact, he had spent the better part of his life trying to fit in, to be accepted by the pack, and his childhood and youth as an overweight person had taught him how difficult that was. He loved the force more than anything else in his life because the Met, for all the jokes about his size, had embraced him and made him feel part of something. So even though he hated what had happened to Earl Whitely, he was not about to 'blow the whistle'. But as he smiled at Stevie Fisher's last joke at his expense, Brigson thought that if Kelsey went on the record, then maybe, just maybe, he would join him.

"Can you believe it?" Fisher shouted, jabbing Brigson's stomach with his elbow. "There she is. Just like the guvnor said."

"What? That redhead?"

"Don't be a total plank, Brigsy," Fisher scolded him. "There," he said, pointing to a woman who appeared from under the flyover at the end of the road.

Brigson squinted into the sun reflecting off one hundred cars as they sped along the elevated stretch of road over the major roundabout. He put his hand over his eyes for a better view.

"The guvnor knows his women," Fisher said, rejoicing vicariously in the accuracy of Hogarth's prediction. "The guvnor knows everyone."

And then Brigson saw her, striding purposefully towards the media scrum outside the coroner's court. Andrea Chambers. He watched as Andrea was engulfed by reporters, and thought again of Mark Kelsey, and he said to himself: No matter what Fisher might say, the guvnor doesn't know me.

CHAPTER TWO

Andrea sat in the heavy silence of the dark-panelled court waiting room, a silence that was only broken outwardly by the ticking of a hexagonal clock face on the wall opposite the blinded windows. But within, her head was filled with the barrage of questions hurled at her by the reporters outside the court. Each chide, each deliberately provocative question, still resonated in her mind, though she sat quite still now in her black court suit, out of respect for her dead client.

"What did the body look like? Was it definitely suicide? Did he confess to Nicki's murder? Did he know your son?"

She was quite alone in the large half-lit room, and she sat on a hard wooden bench, identical to those propped against all four walls. There was a surgical quality, she had always found, to coroner's courts, even though they were meant to be no different to others in the jurisdiction, and she imagined that she was in a dentist's or a doctor's waiting room. The sharp smell of detergent had nothing to do with the nature of the legal inquiries that were undertaken within those walls, she realised, as she saw streaks of drying soapy water left by a mop over the large, even tiles of the floor. But she remembered the dreadful time when she had sat alone in the waiting room of the pregnancy clinic in High Holborn while she was at the LSE, and again she felt the fear that the young Andrea had felt as she waited to hear whether there was any greater significance to her late period. She didn't know then what scared her more — telling her father or telling her boyfriend, Lawrence Patterson, for there were rumours that Lawrence, who was several years older than she and who was doing a master's degree, had got another white girl pregnant when he was a fresher. He had persuaded this other girl to terminate the pregnancy, and this was something Andrea knew that she couldn't bring herself to do. It wasn't that she was anti-abortion or anything close; in fact she had marched with the pro-abortion lobby several times. But the thought that there might be life growing inside her filled her with amazement and dread, and she was determined, no matter what, to keep the baby. No one had stood by her, except for Rufus, who was still going strong in the Post Office back then, and it was Rufus who had delivered the bawling baby Calvin into the world, just as he had delivered his own son. Andrea had believed passionately that any woman had the right to choose, and she had unequivocally chosen life for her child. To the extent that she could influence it, she regarded life as sacred and non-negotiable, and she realised that this was the reason she now sat in the coroner's court for Earl Whitely.

On the lime-green walls were two signs. The first was the usual admonition not to smoke. The second was a reflection of the times, and it simply said: NO MOBILE PHONES. However, thoughts of her pregnancy and the birth made Andrea long to speak to her son, and she edged back one of the dirty blinds with her fingertips so that she could see outside. There was a phone booth on the corner right next to the court, but it was barely visible in the media scramble. Having negotiated the mêlée once, she was in no mood to have to try again. She deftly opened her briefcase and removed her mobile phone. But she felt guilty, and try as she might she could not avoid the

looming presence of the sign on the wall. Andrea had
always had a thing about rules, about not breaking them,
which she attributed to the fact that her father was a
lawyer, and a major component of her youth had been a
quest for his approval. She still hated parking on yellow
lines, even singles; she winced when she returned a video
a day late; she hated being even a pound overdrawn; she
hardly ever exceeded the speed limit, certainly not in the
city. And yet she had broken one of the biggest rules of
them all, one of the holiest taboos. She had had an illegitimate child — she hated the word — and what was more,
she had mixed the races. Now she wanted to speak to her
son, so she dialled Calvin's number anyway. As she had
half expected, there was no answer at his flat. She immediately put her back-up plan into operation and pressed
the speed dial for Rufus. There were three rings before the
old man answered.

"Hi, Rufus, it's Andrea," she said, standing at the window as she spied on the press pack through the gaps in the
blinds.

"How ya doing, darlin'?" he enquired.

"I'd be better if I could speak to Calvin."

"He stayed out all night," Rufus replied.

Andrea's heart jumped at the news. "You mean you
haven't seen him since yesterday?"

"I mean the boy stay out all night," Rufus said calmly.
"Darlin', I know it's gotta be tough on you, but you must
give that boy some space."

"Earl wasn't my fault."

"And he'll see that." Rufus paused and then laughed
heartily down the phone. "When he's about my age, that is."

Andrea was sufficiently relieved to laugh too. She sat
back down on the bench, trying to put her sorrow about
Earl Whitely out of her mind for a moment. "You know, I
was just thinking about the birth," she said.

"Oh, Lord," Rufus laughed.

"You were so calm. I was the one swearing my head off and begging for drugs."

Andrea heard a click down the phone, and she recognised the noise Rufus habitually made when he was happy. "I was proud that day, darlin'. My first grandchild. And the first thing it sees in the world is old Rufus smacking its botty. Maybe that's why the boy never talk to me."

"You should have been a midwife."

"Should?" he said, taking mock offence. "I was. Calvin. His father. Kids in the village back home. Even kids round here, in the tower block. I did that twice. I guess the only thing I deliver better than the mail is babies."

Andrea could now hear footsteps coming slowly down the corridor outside. "I've got to go," she said, putting the mouthpiece right next to her mouth. "Get him to call."

"Yes, boss," Rufus said, hanging up.

Andrea attempted to put the phone back in the side pocket of her leather briefcase, but the door flew open too quickly and she was caught struggling to fit it in the space next to her *Guardian*. It was a man who entered, dressed in a pin-striped suit, with a trim waistcoat and pince-nez glasses setting off his monk's circle of silver hair. He carried an old but fastidiously tended tan briefcase and a copy of the medical journal, the *Lancet*, under his arm. Andrea knew immediately that he had to be the pathologist. Though he spotted the incriminating cellular in her hand, he pretended not to have seen it, and positioned himself in the diametrically opposite corner of the room. He dusted the wooden bench with the journal, then sat, holding the journal at a sufficient height that Andrea could not see his face and vice versa. He tutted at something he read, lowered the journal, glowered at Andrea as if she were to blame for the provocative article, then continued reading

There was a minute or two of silence, then Andrea saw an opportunity. She coughed, for no reason other than to get his attention, and then asked a question the answer to which she knew was blindingly obvious. "Are you in the case of Whitely?"

"Hmm," the man grunted from behind his journal.

"I found the body." It surprised her that she could say 'the body' with such facility, that the words did not stick in her throat as she felt they should, but she knew this was the special mystery of court buildings — things could be said easily within them that one wouldn't dare say outside.

The pathologist lowered his journal slightly and gazed through the top of his pince-nez at her without speaking, as if to suggest: you've got me interested, but only slightly.

"I'm Andrea Chambers," she said, shuffling along to the bench on the wall which separated them. She guessed that she had hooked the man's attention since he now dropped the journal on to his lap.

"Ah, Ms Chambers," he said. "Yes, I've heard a lot about you."

This worried Andrea, and she wondered who had spoken to him. But she tried to subdue her curiosity — this was about Earl, not about her. "Isn't it just a formality today?" she asked.

"I have another inquest, a live one — or a dead one, I suppose." He laughed, but not too much, at his own *bon mot*, and his silver mop of hair bobbed accordingly. "The court juggled the dates for my convenience, et cetera. We're very busy just now. A lot of them about."

"Who?" Andrea asked.

"Dead people." The doctor laughed, this time more vigorously, and his thin, oyster-shell mouth parted a fraction. Andrea could see a row of tartar-stained teeth. But when he grasped that she had not actually joined in the mirth caused by his comic masterpiece, he resumed reading the medical journal.

"You did the autopsy, then?" Andrea asked. The man grunted, keen now to ignore her if possible. She quickly scanned her eyes up and down, from the precisely, if ridiculously, cut hair, to the royal blue monogrammed socks peeking out of his immaculately polished brogues, and decided that she would have to attack his vanity. That's what she loved about Cameron — for a man, he had surprisingly little vanity, save for his penchant for blow-drying his hair before they went out in the evenings. A pang of guilt gnawed at her, and she promised herself, silently promised Cameron, that she would pay him more attention, or at least shag the poor man before he burst. "It must have been a very difficult autopsy to do," she said. "Even for you," she added tauntingly.

She was pleased to see that the man's hard shell of self-confidence, of self-worship, had been pricked. He stared at her hard. "It was a pretty standard prison DIY, Ms Chambers." He now examined Andrea with a disdainful curl to his mouth, as if he were first setting eyes on an exhumed corpse. "As you should know, hanging's just about the most common MO for prison DIYs."

Andrea pounced on the opportunity to provoke him further. "I just don't believe my client would have killed himself."

"And what makes you so sure of that?"

Andrea tried to think of the most infuriating thing she could say, then it came to her. It was simply the truth about how she felt about Earl's death. "Instinct," she said triumphantly. "I'll trust my instincts above scientific guesswork any day."

This was not only music to his ears, it was Mozart to a male chauvinist pig-like professional. "Ah, women's instincts. That cornerstone of civilisation."

"How about lawyers' instincts?" Andrea asked. "Do you trust those?"

"I don't trust lawyers, Ms Chambers," he said, adding, "Present company excluded, of course."

At this, they both could not help smiling, and Andrea was again astonished by the totally contradictory attitude that men of this class and generation (and she did not exclude her father from the category) had towards her sex. They were sexist and chauvinist, but they would never be discourteous, especially once they believed that they had tossed their testosterone around the cave sufficiently to subdue the nearest female cave dwellers.

"Are you trying to nobble my evidence, Ms Chambers?" the doctor asked.

"Of course," Andrea replied.

"Splendid. In the finest traditions of the English law."

"Look, does it need nobbling? I mean, are you a hundred per cent sure it was suicide?"

"I'm ninety-nine per cent of the way there."

"So what's the other one per cent?"

The doctor folded up his *Lancet* and stretched as he stood. Andrea stood instinctively as well, now realising that he was actually barely taller than she was.

"The other one per cent, Miss Chambers, is life. Or death, I suppose. In all its strangeness and unpredictability. But if you have any doubts? *Voilà.*" He undid the buckle keeping his briefcase together and removed a bundle of enlarged black-and-white photos of Earl's body. Andrea steeled herself as he flicked through different shots of the ligature marks cut into the young black man's neck, and told herself that she couldn't let herself down, couldn't let Calvin's friend down.

"I've concluded hanging," the doctor said, dwelling on a photo of Earl's neck from the side. "Self-strangulation without hanging is virtually impossible. Body and mind seem to prevent it. How can you strangle yourself to death with your hands, for example? There seems to be some impulse deep inside us, even if we hate ourselves enough to try to do it, that fights for life at the last. That's why a bullet or a noose is better. One action, then it's too late."

Andrea remembered the darkest days, those just after the court had taken Calvin away from her, when everything in her life had appeared broken, and she could not bear her own company. But even then, during the blackest nights, she had never thought about killing herself. The despair she had felt was so complete that she could not then even imagine life without it, and still she had not contemplated suicide. Using this grief as a tentative yardstick, she simply did not believe that Earl would have killed himself.

"OK," she said, "could someone have strangled him and then hung him on the door?"

"No. Ligature strangulation leaves horizontal marks. Your client — sorry, ex-client — had rising ligatures consistent with hanging. See?" He pointed casually at the deep grooves cut into the side of Earl's neck, and Andrea thought of how much even a paper cut hurt. She wondered what poor Earl had gone through in those tormented moments when he knew he was going to die. Then she had another idea.

"What if someone had strangled him from above? From a bench? There was a bed thing at the end of the cell."

The doctor fanned through the photos again, and his eyes narrowed as he considered this possibility. He shook his head. "That someone would have to be monstrously strong, who could literally lift him off the ground with his bare hands. And it would have to be someone who knew him. Who tricked him somehow, got behind him, that kind of carry-on."

This scenario, unusual though it might be, gave Andrea fresh hope. Finally she had a scientific theory consistent with the post-mortem facts and consistent with Earl being murdered. "May I?" she asked, as she took the bundle of photographs. She wanted to ask the doctor more, to firm up the analysis, but at that moment the large wooden door to the waiting room opened.

A court usher, a wizened woman in a black cotton gown, with striking, almost gypsy features and tanned leathery skin, entered. "Doctor? This gentleman would like to see you. In private." The usher opened the door fully and Andrea saw Hogarth standing outside.

The two men walked out into the dark corridor and Hogarth muttered something to the pathologist that made him turn into the room and stare suspiciously at Andrea. He swept back into the room, snatched the bundle of photographs from her, then walked down the corridor towards the court, the metal caps on his heels clicking as he went. The usher followed him, so that Andrea was left alone with Hogarth. The DCI slowly shut the door, turning the smooth round brass handle twice to ensure that they were locked in. He said nothing at first, walking over to the window, where the media could be seen through the blinds. Andrea was behind him now, and she looked at the door. It would have been easy for her to have opened it, to have slipped out, but her mind burned with the images of Earl's body, and she wanted to demonstrate to Hogarth that she would not be intimidated by him.

"Why are you here?" he said. He turned around, and the slatted light covered him in strips of light and shadow.

"Earl was my client."

Hogarth listened, absorbed. She could practically hear his mind ticking over as he made his computations. "You're not wanted here, Andrea."

"I thought it was a free country," she said.

"Sometimes," he said blankly. "This inquest is the last rites. Not just for Earl. But for the case."

"I'm not giving up," she replied.

"You haven't got a client, so you haven't got a case," he said.

"I'll find one."

Hogarth shook his head, pursed his dry lips, and she couldn't believe it when she saw his brow knit in concern. "Who could be your client? Earl didn't have a family." He paused, adding, "But you have. Perhaps you will not believe me, but I am concerned about them. About you."

Andrea wanted to get closer, to see if the last words were cant and hypocrisy, and though one part of her was aware that Hogarth had a magnetic quality, she did not want for the moment to resist it. It reminded her of watching a fan, as the blades spin round in a blur, and there is that inexplicable desire to put your fingers closer and closer to it, to see how far you dare go. She stepped right up to him. "Earl said he worked for you," she told him.

"How are you going to prove that?" he asked, staring down at her. "Earl's dead."

"I'm not," she replied. She could smell the cigarette smoke that clung to his clothes, an ether that always hung around him. "So I keep asking myself, why would the police hire a Yardie gunman? Even hypothetically. Off the record. Just between you and me in this closed room."

She could see that Hogarth was intrigued by some part of her, by the way she openly challenged him, perhaps, or was it the same emotion that runs through boxers' minds when the final bell rings, and they hug each other after having spent twelve rounds trying to flatten each other? Andrea now saw the cross-examination in the Magistrates' court the previous week as just the first round in their contest, and she believed that Hogarth saw it in an identical light.

"You think you're doing the right thing," she said. "Well, convince me. If you do," she added, allowing the words to hang alluringly in the air, just long enough to sharpen his curiosity, "if you do, it all ends here."

"Why?" he asked.

She tried to guess what was going on in his mind. What was it this man thought about Earl Whitely, about Yardies? She tried to get into his character, to imagine that she was within the huge frame of the detective opposite her, that she could now see with his eyes, that she now looked down at this woman who had impugned him in a court of law. "Because," she said, "I don't like drugs dealers. In fact, I hate them. I think they are as good as murderers, the murderers of all the children who die of drugs."

Something sparked behind Hogarth's eyes, and she could almost hear it as the connection between them was forged. "So you know Earl dealt drugs to children?"

Andrea was shocked. She had been told that Earl was dealing, but it sickened her to think who his clients might have been. One part of her told her that this fact was enough to make her drop the case, but it was overcome by the stubborn streak in her, the one that had got her arrested in the Brixton riots a decade and a half previously, the side of her that despised the abuse of power. "I don't want to defend that," she said, "but he was just a kid."

"Nicki Harris was just a kid," Hogarth shouted, losing his composure for the first time.

His eyelids slowly closed like stage curtains coming down at the end of an act, and he rubbed them repeatedly. Andrea could see the tracery of veins in the lids, and his eyeballs rolling fractionally behind them. When he opened his eyes once more, he reached into his jacket, and Andrea instinctively backed off, as if he were about to draw a .45. Instead, he removed a well-worn black wallet. He held the wallet open for Andrea to see. There on one side was his warrant card behind a clear vinyl covering, but on the other was a photograph of a young girl, sitting under a Christmas tree with a red paper crown on her head.

"She's beautiful," Andrea said, aching inside as she couldn't help thinking of all the Christmases she and her son had missed. The girl in the photograph was being held from behind by this same man who now towered above Andrea. The Hogarth of the picture hugged his daughter tightly as if he would lose her for ever if he were to let go. Andrea could see the similarity in the eyes of the serious little girl and the detective, and when she looked at Hogarth again, for a moment he didn't appear quite so threatening. "She looks like you," Andrea told him. Then she glanced from photo to man and back, correcting herself. "You look like her." She couldn't believe it, she was even smiling, and Hogarth briefly smiled back, but the upward turn of the mouth was just the fleeting ripple of a small pebble in a dark, still pond.

"If anyone pushed drugs to Abby," he said quietly, "I'd kill them."

"That's as a father," Andrea said. "Any parent would understand that. But as a policeman? You can't take the law into your own hands." This last sentence, she knew, had lost his attention, for he flipped the wallet shut. She cursed herself for trotting out the trite cliché, for Hogarth must have heard it one thousand times.

"Earl was someone's son, Chief Inspector," Andrea told him. "Someone, somewhere." This drew a blank from the big man. "Earl didn't deserve to die," she protested. "Not if this is a civilised country."

Now Hogarth sprang back to life, his former control returning as he shoved the wallet back in his jacket with enough disdain to indicate that it had been a mistake to reveal this small part of himself to her. "Remind me," he lectured Andrea, "what is so civilised about a country with a legal system geared to protecting the guilty?"

"And the innocent."

"In my job you don't see too many of those."

She got the impression that Hogarth was on the verge of opening up to her, that this man carried an immense burden on a journey whose conclusion was uncertain. And in a way she didn't yet fully understand, she believed that she was now a fellow traveller, and that gave her the right to question the whole enterprise. "Earl was guilty, so someone had Earl killed?" she asked.

"The autopsy said suicide," Hogarth said.

"No, the autopsy said a ninety-nine per cent certainty of suicide." She braced herself, but was convinced that she should push him further. "That leaves one per cent. And I think, Chief Inspector, that one per cent . . . is you."

Hogarth grabbed her arm powerfully, and Andrea felt his steely fingers press right through her flesh and directly to the bone. He spoke with gritted teeth and lips bared to the gum. "If it wasn't Nicki Harris who died," he demanded, "but Calvin, what type of man would you want hunting your child's killer? How far would you want that man to go?"

Andrea was about to object, to refute him, but she hesitated. Her arm ached, but she didn't struggle. It was as if Hogarth wanted, even needed, her to feel how strongly he felt.

"The letter of the law?" he continued. "That's fine so long as it's someone else's child who's dead." He tightened his grip, and she badly wanted to cry out, but she did not as he added, "I once was where you are now, Andrea. I hope you will accept that. I accepted the rules. I placed my trust, my life, in them. And they made me. What I am now." The power finally drained from his fingers and he freed her arm.

Andrea saw the misery and pain in his lost face. If she could, she would have reached out to it. "It's not too late," she said. "To go back."

He shook his head. "You and me, Andrea. All the way,"
he replied.

And both of them knew it.

Minutes later Hogarth and Andrea stood in consecutive
rows in the antiquated, cavernous courtroom, with the gas
candelabra hanging from the ceiling and walls of dark
wooden panels. Andrea did not turn around, but she
could feel the detective's presence towering over her,
and the formalities of the brief court proceedings that
followed were unreal to her. Still intoxicated by the
encounter with Hogarth, she imagined that the seemingly
distant, echoing proceedings constituted the opening
chorus of a drama comprised of two players, neither of
them entirely good or bad.

"This inquest into the death of Earl Alphonse Whitely
is adjourned for further enquiries," concluded the coroner,
an incongruously young man in the ancient surroundings.

"Court rise," the usher cried.

Everyone stood, and in the dream-like trance the
suffocatingly hot room had created, Andrea wandered
out until she suddenly found herself in the throng of
reporters outside the courtroom. She made no comment to
the questions that were fired at her from all sides,
because the secret determination she felt to pursue the
case was not capable of soundbite comment. She
hardly even blinked as photographers scuttled backwards
in front of her and fired flashbulb after flashbulb of
blue light at her face. The voices and questions merged
into the distant hum of the traffic speeding across the flyover, and Andrea thought again of the party she had given
Calvin on his fifth birthday, of how she had wanted to cry
when she had burnt his birthday cake, and how he had
hugged her and had pretended that he hated cakes
anyway. Where was that generous part of her son? she

wondered. Had the custody battle extinguished it for ever?

She had now made her way out of the media scrum and the photographers had either got their shots of her or had given up. But then she spotted something across the road. It was nothing much — a face barely glimpsed in the melting crowd of onlookers opposite. A man's face she believed she had seen before, even though she could not place it. She stopped momentarily on her side of the road, while the crowd streamed past opposite like a river. There he was again, and now she was convinced she had seen him before, with his enlarged, almost comic yellow eyes. He looked back at her. There was the briefest moment when something passed between them, a mutual recognition as their eyes met and then dwelt upon each other, before he spun on his heels and shuffled quickly towards the fence by the railway sidings. Andrea debated with herself as to whether she should pursue him, because although common sense told her not to follow a man alone into an unknown area, her head told her with equal conviction that this was the man in the next police cell to Earl's on the night that Nicki Harris was shot.

Lost now in a blue haze of excitement and apprehension, Andrea stepped out into the road without taking her eyes off her target. Her eardrums were immediately pounded by a car's horn as a black Porsche, an old-model 911, skidded to a halt inches from her, and the young man inside screamed at her, though she could hear none of his words through the tinted windscreen.

She held up her hand in token apology and as she reached the traffic island in the centre of the road she paused to allow a brown UPS delivery van to race up to the roundabout in the opposite direction. When she looked again towards the railway fence, the man had disappeared from view. There was the black arch of a disused railway bridge, and she supposed he must have passed through it.

She quickened her pace on the other side of the road, walking as fast as she dared without actually breaking into a run. She reached the mouth of the arch, saw nothing of the man, craned her neck this way and that, with no success. She felt self-conscious now, as the crowds had thinned to the extent that she was alone, and although she could hear the low rumble of activity all around her she could see no one. She hesitated a fraction more, weighing on one side of the scale the folly of entering the increasingly derelict area alone, and on the other her need to track down her only lead on Earl Whitely's death. Looking all around, she went under the railway arch.

The black, cavernous area was in fact a series of arches supporting a freight line, each numbered with a small, black rectangle of metal — 1272, 1273 — but where the sequence began and where it would end she could not guess. Foetid water dripped slowly through cracks in the slimy black brickwork, and she became aware of crunching underfoot, seeing, when she brought herself to look down, piles of pigeon droppings, mounds of it. Her stomach turned, and more so when she breathed deeply, for there was the high, rank smell of something rotting, a dead cat or dog, she imagined. She glanced behind her. The entrance through which she had ventured was already little more than a semicircle of light behind her. Still she advanced. Now she heard pigeons, not cooing but cawing at each other over territory. The rumbling grew louder, then louder still, until Andrea was deafened as a train thundered above her. She covered her head as dust and rubble and she couldn't bear to think what else rained down upon her, and it seemed to her that the very bricks shook themselves apart with the din. She saw another semicircle of light, this time in front of her, and she ran towards it, slipping but managing to right herself before she collided with the filthy walls. She ran in the all-consuming din, as metal wheels ground against metal rails, like a huge hand scratched down a massive black-board, accelerating all the time, as if she were trying to catch up with the train above her, until finally she burst out into the cool sunlight beyond the final arch.

Open air had never felt so good to Andrea in her life, as she lifted her face into the breeze and allowed it to wash over her. She bent over double and coughed out the stench from the arches, and in the relief of the moment she forgot her purpose. So when she stood up straight, she was shocked to see the emaciated man four feet in front of her. There was a jagged piece of wooden fencing clutched men-acingly in his right hand, a stake post rotting and now broken, with the nails still in it. He wore denims with a white-painted skull and the fading name of a rock band on his back.

"What do you want from me?" he shouted at Andrea in a thick Scottish accent, Edinburgh rather than Glasgow, as the goods train rattled into the distance above them.

"Please," she gasped, holding up her hands in a conciliatory gesture. "I just want to talk."

"You just don't get it, do you? Who you're dealing with."

"I saw you. In the cells," she said as calmly as she could.

"I don't mean me. I mean *them*." With that he lifted the wood, now with both hands, and hurled it inches past Andrea and into the tunnel.

She glanced around the wasteland, and realised that she was mad, that anything could happen to her down here and no one would know. But there was no way out, the area being cordoned off by high fencing, except back through the arches. She began to edge backwards, and the man, seeing this, approached her.

When he was just inches from her, he shouted, "I am not a grass! I am not a fucking grass!"

His eyes had the same emptiness she remembered from

the police cells on that first night, and when she glimpsed the black, dead veins on his wrist, she realised that he must be strung out.

"I'll tell you what you want to know," he said, now contradicting his earlier statement, "but you've got to pay me."

"No," Andrea said firmly. She desperately tried to recall how she had dealt with her junkie clients when she was at the Bar, how they had often tried to guilt-trip her, how they would say anything for money for another fix. Her instinct told her to stand up to the man. It wasn't him talking, but the poison in his veins.

"Look, I could fucking break your skull on those bricks and take all your fucking money."

"No," she said equally firmly, but her resolve was shrivelling within.

The man clasped his hands to his head of sweat-drenched hair, as if he were about to rip out each strand. "Just a tenner and I'll tell you what I know about that black fellah."

Andrea edged further into the tunnel as the junkie stood in the sunlight, withdrawing from drugs before her eyes. When she was a sufficient distance from him, fifteen feet, twenty, she half turned and began to walk more quickly.

"Please," he pleaded. He sobbed, the agonies running through his bloodstream, the pain such that he seized up and fell to his knees.

Andrea saw her opportunity to run, to escape, but she stood still. She glanced at the safe end of the tunnel, then back at the man. She couldn't bring herself to abandon him. He was on his hands and knees when she reached him, coughing his guts out.

"They're crawling over my face," he said. "The fucking ants."

She stared hard and of course saw no such thing, but

was appalled and at the same time intrigued. She watched
the man beating his face with his hands, and for a moment
she wanted to know what it was like to feel this, or better
still (and to her horror) she wanted to see ants actually
crawling over the wretched junkie's face, into his nose and
mouth. She cast around inside herself for an explanation
for her sudden preoccupation with the morbid, and at first
thought that it must have come from seeing the pictures of
Earl Whitely's body. Or was it a rebellion of her imagination, which for the best part of a decade she had trained
and leashed in a comfortable middle-class professional
existence? Finally, she decided that it was to do with
Calvin, for these were undoubtedly the sights that confronted her son in his life on the streets of South London.

"Is it heroin?" she asked.

He nodded.

"Do you have a prescription? Methadone?"

He squatted on to his haunches as the fit passed and
wiped his mouth roughly. "I sell it. Buy myself the real
stuff. Please, just a tenner. I'm dying here."

Andrea was torn between what she knew she should do
and the plight of the wretched man in front of her. His
eyes dripped with tears, though he did not seem aware
that he was crying, and his entire body shook with the
tremor that now gripped him. She tried to imagine him as
she used to try to imagine her very worst clients, as someone's son. She grieved for his mother, then scolded herself
harshly for being so sanctimonious. What right had she?
But here was another human being who was suffering, and
she believed that nothing gave her the right either to deny
his pain, to walk away from it, or to judge it. How could
one type of suffering be deemed less worthy than another,
and on what moral scale? She then defied every principle
she had in dealing with such people. She gave him a £10
note. In doing so, she knew perfectly well that relieving

his pain today would guarantee that it returned more strongly tomorrow.

The junkie's eyes lit up at the sight of the crisp new note, and she felt sick at herself. "What they did to that black fellah," he said, pocketing the note, "that was outta order."

"So that's why you came to the inquest?"

He shook his head. "Meant to have met my handler."

Andrea realised what he meant. He was a police informant after all.

"DS Fisher," he said. "Know him?"

Andrea nodded.

The man stood and trembled with anticipation at the coming high. "There was this new copper. A young one. He didn't seem to like what happened to Earl."

"What was his name?" she asked.

The man shrugged. "I'd never seen him down the nick before." He did up the shiny metal buttons on the front of his denim jacket and moved past Andrea.

"Look," she said, "can I get you a tea or something instead?"

"Tea and smack?" The man laughed. "What is it? Fucking Christmas?"

He went further into the tunnel and Andrea called after him, "The young officer, would you recognise him again?"

The man continued to walk, more confidently now, a strut, and said without turning around, "I don't know what you're talking about. I don't even know who you are."

She waited until she had seen the small silhouette of the shadow-man pass out of the other end of the tunnel, and all the while she calculated the best route to Hogarth's police station.

CHAPTER THREE

Roots Johnson had a tape measure in his hand as he walked around the broken buildings of the derelict site. His laptop was perched on one of the tottering walls, and every now and then he returned to the computer to enter a new dimension into the database. The graphics software he had purchased in Tottenham Court Road after seeing Katherine was a formidable tool, and as each measurement was logged in, the shape of his studio began to materialise on the screen in rotating 3-D.

Stamping around the filthy site, even though he was systematically ruining his Calvin Klein super-soft classic-fit jeans, filled his heart with hope, not of an uncertain future, but simply of seeing Katherine smile. He yearned to see her again, to smell her hair, and he debated with himself whether to ask her if she had accepted the white rose. He decided against it. Every thought in his mind, whether it concerned winding up his 'runnings' or creating a blueprint for the studio, now had a focus, an imperative, and though his various tasks ran in different directions, underlying them all, like the rails that linked them, was Katherine. Roots couldn't believe it. He had been touched. He had allowed himself to be touched, and by this white woman whom he had never even kissed. It was the most unexpected occurrence in his life, this meeting of minds in the city; it was an epiphany, a revelation to him, which beckoned the Yardie to another life, whose currency was not killing.

As he rotated the built-in mouse on the computer key-board, he heard the boom of a ghetto-blaster, a truly mon-strous one, fast approaching. He quickly finished the plan and then marvelled for a moment as his personal office in his studio complex took off on the screen and spun before his eyes. By this time, Lifer had clanked his way into view, with the blaster on his right shoulder, carried like a bag of coal, and a sports bag in his left hand. The gold dollar sign swung from the huge Yardie's neck, and the rat's-tail of twisted hair straggled over the folds of fat at his neck. He flung the bag into the middle of what used to be some kind of classroom.

"You wanna count it?" he asked Roots.

Roots clicked the mouse on the Save icon on the laptop. "I trust you, Lifer," he replied.

The other man cocked his head sarcastically, away from the blaster, so that his wraparound shades were now at forty-five degrees to the rubbled ground. "That mek me wanna cry, ya know," he said. He sat on the wall further along from the computer, and rested his music box on his fat thighs. "What happen?"

"I was just thinking about Peckham," Roots said.

There was a pause in which Lifer switched the music off and Roots unfurled his tape measure, holding it against another wall. Lifer grasped the cue, and took the other end with evident relief — anything to avoid having to talk about emotions. He held the tape against the bricks of a half-demolished wall.

"Higher," Roots said. "Get the tape level, ya know."

Lifer did so, asking as casually as he could, "So you is serious about getting out of business?"

Roots did not answer. He noted the measurement, flicked the tape so that it jumped out of Lifer's fingers and recoiled quickly into its plastic casing. "Where are the others, huh?" he asked.

Lifer banged his forehead with his palm in an exaggerated fashion. "Me gone forgot to call them."

"I said we all of us had to meet," Roots said.

"I know, Don, but I been busy sorting out some runnings, and boom, it's gone."

Roots clicked the mouse on Save again, then hit the Intelligent Off button, to save the nickel batteries. Meanwhile, Lifer looked admiringly at the bulging sports bag.

"You got to hold tight, Don," he said. "Yessir, in that dem bag is a whole heap of money. And I'm telling you now, with that much green, we can play in the majors. And I ain't talking about London or Europe, I'm talking the world league now."

Roots leaned against the wall, against his wall, crumbled as it might be, and crossed his arms. "Give it up, Lifer."

The huge man paced around incongruously within the relics of the classroom, as if he could not utter any further words if his legs weren't working. "There's this consignment a lickle bird tell me about. Top-grade stuff. Colombian. Don, this is driven snow, this is snow before it hits the shitty earth. This C is almost pure. Now with your brains and my rep as an enforcer, this cartel gone lay a couple of key of this mer-chan-dise on us."

"For what?" Roots asked.

"For a deposit." Lifer paused, rolled his head, cracking some muscle in his neck. "For what's in that bag."

Roots watched the other man with disgust, but the revulsion was not aimed at Lifer, or at all the Lifers who populated the posses and cartels. Roots felt disgust at himself. He imagined himself as a younger man with the same lascivious delight at the prospect of his first cocaine kilogram deal, and he contrasted this with the youth who was prepared to take a gun to fight for what he believed to be politically right.

Lifer latched on to Roots's hesitations, and approached him. His large padded jacket was undone, and Roots understood what that meant. "I gotta tell you," Lifer said, "people, they is getting nervous about you. They is saying to me on the street, on your streets, that if Roots Johnson go straight, that really means he is going straight to court. Into witness protection. QE. And they ask me: Lifer, is the don cut a deal with the police now or what?"

Roots still had his arms crossed, but his palms were sweating as he watched the jacket swinging around Lifer's body. He glanced left, right, wondered if he could tumble backwards over the wall if necessary.

"That's what they is thinking," Lifer added.

"And what about you, Lifer?" Roots asked.

"I'm behind you."

Roots paused. He knew his next words would raise the stakes, that they would possibly send the volatile Lifer over the edge. But he didn't care. "And you, Lifer, what are you doing behind me?"

Lifer 'kissed his teeth', a form of cussing, clenching his teeth hard and making a clicking sound with a sharp intake of breath.

"Like I said," Roots continued, "we better part."

He stepped towards the bag that was between them, thinking: You're going to go for your gun, come on, you know you want to go for your gun. And as he bent down to pick up the bag, Lifer stamped on it with his hoof-like foot.

"I want my cut first," he hissed.

Roots stared at the larger man, but could only see his own eyes in the mirrored shades. As he looked at himself, he saw something he had never seen previously in the mirror: fear. He wondered if Lifer saw this, too, even though Lifer would never have guessed that Roots was now scared not for his own life but for what he had to lose — the chance to redeem himself.

"How much cut you want?" he asked.

Lifer's fist flashed towards the rear of his jacket, then returned with a gleaming gun in it. Then he did exactly the same with his left hand, so that two nine-mils now pointed at Roots's eyes. Roots looked at the two black tunnels, inches from his face.

"I want one hundred pro-cent," Lifer hissed.

"No," Roots said.

Lifer stepped forward one pace, over the bag. The gun barrels rested on Roots's face, one on each cheek.

"I will shoot," he said. "I ain't joking."

"You never is joking, Lifer," Roots replied. He pressed forward with his neck muscles, right against the barrels, so that the tips would be imprinted on his flesh. Lifer's hands gave an inch, then more, and Roots was able to reach his foot out and stamp it on the sports bag.

"Don't mek me kill you," Lifer shouted.

"No one can make you do anything," Roots said quietly.

Sweat burst out on Lifer's face, globules of it that hung on his greasy skin and did not move, and then his head dropped a couple of inches as he heard the clicks behind him. Roots saw the other Yardies in the crew behind Lifer, with guns aimed at the big man's head.

"You're never going to make it, Lifer," Roots said. He watched fascinated as the huge man's forehead creased in calculation, and then saw the muscles of the face slacken. Lifer lowered the guns, then let them slip out of his hands and past his outstretched fingers. There were two clunks as the metal of the nine-mils hit the rubble.

He looked hard at Roots. "You knew?" he asked.

Roots nodded.

Lifer spoke with desperation, not born, it appeared to Roots, from fear, but from an undiminished conviction that he knew what was right. "I'm telling you right now," he said, "you don't deal product? Someone else's goin" to. You can't fight it. It's the way it is. Down here on the street. This ain't no debating chamber. This is life, Johnson. And now the three dons are dead there is going to be a vacuum, and that vacuum will suck the scum of the earth into this city. So we can't let that happen. I can't. Not while it's there for the taking. Not when I can take it." He glanced behind him, looked at Roots out of the corner of his eye, then gambled. He kicked his two guns across the ground to Roots's feet. "So you gotta do it. You gotta kill me."

Roots saw his other men aim more carefully at Lifer. They moved left and right so that Roots would not be in the direct line of fire. He thought of Katherine's reaction to the newspaper story of the Mashango massacre, of how she flew at him with her fists and beat his chest. If he was true to her, to himself, in his oath to change, then he had to start here. He raised his hand towards his crew.

"I ain't going to kill you, Lifer. But I want you to tell people that Roots Johnson ain't no trafficker no more. He's retired. And now his business is music."

"Hear what," Lifer said, "ain't no one gonna believe that Stevie Wonder act."

"They might. If I let you live. When you deserve to die."

Lifer shook his head. He even laughed, though what prompted his laughter Roots could not decide. Was it scorn at what he perceived as Roots's weakness or just joy at his devilish good fortune, pulling a gun on the don and walking out alive? "I don't wanna bullshit you none," Lifer said, "but if you don't deal, then I will. But you think you wanna change? Forget it. People like us don't get a second chance. People like us don't get a first."

"Lifer, you're always going on about slave mentality. But more than anything I ever heard, that is slave talk. I don't want what people give me. I don't want no one to give me a chance. I'm going to take my chance. Myself."

Lifer stroked the thick gold dollar medallion around his neck. Roots could see that he felt stronger, he was back to his arrogant self, and he obviously thought he had triumphed over Roots, so he was going to push it.

"Anyhow I walk out of here without a bullet in my head," he said, "then you gotta know. It will be war between us."

"It always was," Roots said.

Lifer began a deep, dirty laugh, which resonated through his fat frame.

"Is what now?" Roots said angrily.

"I was just thinking, you is a hard man, Roots Johnson. Bwoy, there was two guns in your face and you did not even sweat none." Lifer let the praise hang in the air a moment, then added, "Not like that English."

Roots ground his teeth in fury, realising what Lifer was saying.

"You know what they is saying on the street?" Lifer continued. "They say that English bwoy died like a pussy. He begged for his life on his hands and knees, before they cut them off."

Roots picked up the nearer of Lifer's nine-mils and jabbed it against his temple. He knocked the Yardie's sunglasses off his head with the tip of the gun, then pressed it into his head. Lifer's pig-small eyes squinted in the light and his face trembled. "Scared now, Lifer?" Roots screamed. "Are you scared now?" Sweat ran in rivulets down Lifer's puffed cheeks. As Roots's mind filled with nightmares of Peckham's dismembering, he jabbed the gun harder so that Lifer's head buckled with the force. Lifer nodded, biting his trembling lip. Roots itched to kill this man, and with startling clarity he knew again one of the essential truths of his life: that certain men simply did not deserve to live, and Lifer was one of those men, as had been the corrupt police officer he had killed when he was just twelve, the man who had raped his ten-year-old cousin. He pressed the gun harder into Lifer's skull, his finger curled around the smooth, cool trigger, and he thought of Peckham, and the box that had been delivered, and the Arsenal shirt, and Lifer's taunts.

"Do it, do it, do it, man," Lifer screamed.

Roots imagined his finger closing around the trigger, the clap of thunder as the bullet exploded. He felt the recoil working up his arm, through his shoulder as the fat Yardie's life withered.

But he could not do it.

Roots pushed Lifer over the bag so that the huge man tumbled on to the rubble. A cloud of dust and debris billowed around his body. "Give him his music," Roots said, indicating the ghetto-blaster, "then get him out of here."

As Lifer was led away, Roots went back to his computer. He touched one of the keys, and the 3-D studio spun as a white-lined skeleton on a blue-wash background. I let him live for you, Katherine, he thought. I let him live for you. He would never tell her this fact to her face, but the mercy he had shown changed his heart, and made him, he then believed, a weaker man. He took out his new mobile phone. In the plastic cover of his computer he had stashed a piece torn from the *Standard*'s front page, upon which a number had been scribbled. It was the name of a financier he was once told he could trust.

"I want to speak to Mr Ellis," he said calmly, even though his heart still pounded from the confrontation with Lifer.

"Speaking," came back a pukka voice.

"Jerry Vasquez gave me your number," Roots said.

There was a pause down the line. "I'm sorry, I know of no one by the name of Vasquez."

Roots understood the code. The financier was worried

in case Roots was a plant and the call was being bugged. It
was the kind of conversation he had had a thousand times
over the years, a dialogue loaded with hinted-at meanings,
and here he was, a veteran, making a beginner's error. He
wondered whether he was just thrown by the heat of the
conflict with Lifer, or whether there was a more fundamental process at work, a draining of the survival skills he
had for so long taken for granted.

"My fault," Roots said.

"Yes."

"I have some business."

"What kind of business?"

"Lucrative business."

"Ah, my kind of business," Ellis replied.

"When can I see you?"

"This afternoon?"

"Yes," Roots said simply. Then he added, "Johnson."

"I know," the financier replied.

Hogarth met his 'tame' reporter, Colin Stackman, outside
the coroner's court, and the two of them went in Hogarth's
car to Nicki Harris's house. During the journey, Stackman
chattered effusively about how much money the two of
them could make for an exclusive from Nicki's parents,
and Hogarth did not entirely ignore him, but he treated
Stackman's greed-driven rantings in the same way that one
might treat Muzak in a supermarket. He heard them, but
he did not listen; he was aware of them without caring.
What John Hogarth did care about, and deeply, was the
effect his encounter with Andrea Chambers in the coroner's court had had upon him.

As he and Stackman passed through the maze of South
London streets, Hogarth was troubled by the fact that he
had shown more of himself to Andrea in that one conversation than he had given to his wife in the previous

month. He tried to divine the cause of the unease the woman had aroused in him. It wasn't a purely physical thing, though he did find Andrea attractive. It was, he decided, her wilfulness. As he was standing in the witness box in the Magistrates' court the previous week, even though she attempted to expose him as a corrupt man in the most public glare, he did not want the contest to end. Some of the answers he gave, he now realised, were thinly disguised invitations to her to take the battle one stage further, to burn one more bridge, to drive the two of them still nearer the conclusion. What he wanted was release, whether in victory or defeat; he wanted release from the demons that had laid siege to his soul since the shooting.

It was Stackman who rang the doorbell to the two-bedroom semi, and Dawn Harris answered, her hair still wet and smelling of shampoo, her eyes wide with surprise. She looked lost, the way people who are extremely short-sighted appear without their glasses.

"I'm sorry if we're a little early," Stackman said.

Dawn looked blankly from Stackman to Hogarth, who stood two feet behind him.

"We could always come back later," Hogarth said. "If it's not convenient."

Dawn was about to reply when her husband ran down the stairs, shouting, "Nonsense, guv."

Harris pushed past his wife to welcome his two guests. As he did so, the cheap blue blazer he wore caught on the brake handle of a child's bike, which was propped against the radiator by the front door. Hogarth looked at the small yellow saddle, the round blue bell with the name 'Nicki' Tippexed on it. When he looked up, he realised that Dawn was watching him.

"You'd better come in," she said.

Hogarth nodded, and edged past Nicki's bike, being as careful as he could not to touch it, even with his coat. The

hall was warm with the aroma of baking, and Hogarth
smelled freshly ground coffee beans. The sitting-room curtains were still drawn, and the room had a sepulchral feel.
There was, he knew, something more than grieving here,
there was despair. Dawn settled into an armchair, without
saying anything further, while Harris bounced backwards
and forwards, showing his guests to the sofa, while he
began to draw the curtains. Hogarth noticed how Dawn
held her hands in front of her eyes, shielding them from
the light.

"Leave them closed if you like," Hogarth told Harris,
who obeyed straight away.

"Good thinking," Stackman said. "Don't want any tele-
photos through the window, do we? You see, Peter?" he
said, addressing Harris, whilst at the same time totally
ignoring Nicki's mother, "didn't I tell you that the DCI
knew how to run things?"

Harris agreed, and stood in the middle of the room,
foolishly. Everyone else was seated. Now feeling awkward
in the ensuing silence, he announced, "I've had Dawn bake
a cake."

"Lovely." Stackman smiled. His face was reptilian, all
bumps and hollows.

Hogarth eyed Dawn, and he saw her contempt towards
her husband's fawning. Their daughter is dead, he thought,
and the fool has his wife bake a cake. He remembered how
that particular morning, just before he had to set off for the
inquest, he and his wife had acted out their increasingly fre-
quent marital row. He had confiscated her tranquillisers,
and she had sulked in bed. He had told her that she didn't
need chemicals, and then she had completely thrown him
with this reply: "You don't treat me like a human being."
The phrase had worried him all day. You don't treat me like
a human being. He had stood there with the bottle of pills
in his hand, and thought that perhaps he was wrong to

deprive her of them. After all, he knew from being present as dozens of corpses were cut open on the pathologist's slab that scientifically everyone was little more than bare bone, water and chemicals. He had seen all too often how chemicals could prolong life and ease pain, but could also poison and kill. He wondered now, as he sat in what had once been Nicki Harris's home, into which category his wife's use of tranquillisers fell. He had initially been angry at her that morning for capitulating so easily to her addiction. But the more he thought about it, the angrier he became with himself for driving her to that small bottle. He had withdrawn from her systematically over the years as he became more and more convinced that he carried home with him each night the contagions of the city, and what had first been an act designed to protect her, had now become set into hard habit. What had happened, Hogarth realised, was that bit by bit, tablet by tablet, she had become immune to him, and he to her. That morning, for the first time in their relationship, he threw the bottle of pills back on the bed.

Harris now fidgeted around for cups and saucers in the walk-through kitchen. The kettle was boiling. "How did the inquest go, guv?" he called, getting out some plates for the cake.

Hogarth found it difficult to pull his gaze away from the accusing eyes of the girl.

"Guv?" Harris repeated.

But before he could reply, Dawn, who was sitting across the coffee table from Hogarth, directly below her daughter's photographs, cut in. "I don't understand how you can be winding down the investigation," she said.

"We're not winding it down," Hogarth defended himself, but without conviction. Nicki's eyes bore into him from a dozen angles, and his migraine grew worse and worse. "We've just run out of leads."

Dawn reached for the coffee table, where her ashtray-like

glasses lay. She put them on, better to see the DCI, but she said nothing about his explanation.

In the tense silence, Stackman piped up, "After all, Dawn, Earl Whitely is dead."

"But there were other men involved in the shooting. The teacher, Mrs Jeffries, she said three men."

"She couldn't describe them," Hogarth said.

"Post-traumatic shock," Stackman added knowingly, as if he had had personal tutorials with Sigmund Freud himself. He took a small notepad from inside his jacket and scribbled a few words.

"You must have some clue, Mr Hogarth," Dawn persisted. "You must have some idea who they are."

At this, Harris hurried into the room, with a tray. "Cherry cake," he said.

Hogarth used the opportunity to make a temporary escape. "May I?" he asked Harris, indicating the kitchen. "Just some water."

"I'll get it, guv," Harris obliged.

But Hogarth got to his feet anyway, and the junior man knew not to interfere. Hogarth entered the tiny space, and turned the cold water full on in the dull chrome sink. There was a splash as the jet of water struck metal, like a hard rain drumming on a corrugated roof, and this aggravated the pain in his head. He dowsed his face with water, then straightened his back so that the cold trickles ran down the grooves of his cheeks and curled around his chin. He had a view out on the back garden, a postage stamp of overgrown green lawn, little more, with high white-painted fences on three sides, comprised of broad horizontal wooden planks he could just see between. Hogarth's eyes wandered vaguely over the area as he tried to focus on the pain in his head, to find it, and then by force of will to squeeze it into nothing. But he did not succeed. To his surprise, he caught himself groaning, "Oh,

God." He had seen Nicki's old swing rusting and over-
turned in the grass. He remembered his daughter Abby,
and even though he tried to think of something else, of
anything else, he now wondered if the two girls might
have got on together. He saw Nicki Harris now, in the
postage-stamp garden alone, on the swing with no one to
push her, working the seat backwards and forwards over
and over again with her tiny legs, with white socks pulled
neatly up to her calves and shining red shoes. And then he
recalled how she had fallen on the tarmac outside the
school after the shooting, with blood slowly seeping from
her head, and he wanted to wound himself.

Just as suddenly he broke out of this disturbing spell
when he heard Stackman's jarring voice from the next
room, selling his deal to Nicki's parents. "Dawn, I know
you and your husband have been considering my paper's
proposal very carefully."

"It must be an exclusive deal?" Harris interjected, as if
he were negotiating the best price for insurance cover for
his Ford Escort.

"I'm afraid so," Stackman said more quietly.

Hogarth hadn't realised that the water running into the
sink was splashing on to his trousers. He looked down and
saw dozens of small black patches of dampness, which
reminded him of blood spatter patterns after a stabbing.
That was how blood often looked on clothes, just a black,
damp stain. He reached into his trouser pocket and
removed a thin plastic-and-foil sheet, which contained
twelve paracetamol tablets. He tossed two tablets into his
mouth and then made a cup with both his hands and
scooped ice-cold water past his lips to wash them down.
One of the tablets got stuck in his throat and he had to
dry-swallow it down. It left a trail of bitter chemicals all
the way down his throat and into his stomach.

"But without wanting to sound insensitive," Stackman

lectured Dawn, "any news story, no matter how tragic, only has a limited shelf-life."

"Shelf-life?" Dawn cried, aghast. "Life? My Nicki's dead."

"And we want to . . . compensate you, to make you more comfortable in any way we can, for the pain of reliving these memories. Nicki's story is waiting to be told, Dawn."

Harris whispered, "We owe it to Nicki."

Hogarth now turned and stood in the knocked-through archway between the two rooms. He saw Dawn cast such a look of venom and detestation at the man to whom she was lawfully bound that he knew then that Dawn Harris would not be a weapon in his cause, but a weakness.

"We'd better go," he said. "This is wrong."

Harris started to his feet, seeing a fat cheque disappearing out of reach. "No, guv," he protested. "We've discussed it. We want to go with Mr Stackman's offer."

Stackman sat there smugly. He undoubtedly thinks I'm just trying some reverse psychology to close the deal, Hogarth said to himself. And this angered the detective, because when he inspected Dawn's face again, he knew that she would not just be obstructive, she would be positively dangerous.

"Wouldn't a newspaper story prejudice legal proceedings?" Dawn asked, her question directed to none of the three men in particular.

Harris stepped nearer his wife, bent over her, looked down at her as she sat in her armchair below the mantelpiece with the photographs of her dead daughter. "Dawn," he said, "there aren't going to be any more legal proceedings. There are no more suspects, are there, guv?" He didn't wait for Hogarth to reply. "Look, if anyone could have found them, the guvnor could have. We've been on telly. Done the appeal. There are just no more clues. So, please, Dawn." Now Hogarth watched him kneeling down beside her armchair, and his knee cracked. Hogarth wondered whether this was how the venal, greedy man had proposed to her. "Please, Dawn," Harris continued, "we've got to do this. For Nicki."

During this desperate entreaty, Hogarth saw that Stackman had silently slid some consent forms out of his briefcase onto the sofa, and removed a cheque book from the inside pocket of his jacket. Dawn stood, brushed past her husband, stepped over Stackman's legs by the coffee table, and stood face to face with Hogarth.

"The bullet," she said neutrally. "It came from a police gun. That's what that woman said in court."

Harris was on his feet too, desperate behind her. "Oh, Jesus, Dawn. That bloody Chambers woman was just stirring it."

"The rifling showed it was a Carbina SP," Dawn said precisely, still staring at Hogarth.

"It's just a type of gun the police have used," Harris shouted. "And criminals can get. Second-hand. We been through this one hundred—"

"I want to hear it from him," Dawn said, gazing up at Hogarth.

He was aware of the thump-thump of his migraine as the inside of his head became a percussion instrument, and he felt his eyes stretching tight like drum skins.

"Will you find these men?" Dawn asked him.

He paused, considered quickly how he should answer her, not wanting to lie in that house. "I wish I could give you hope," he said, meaning every word.

Dawn nodded slowly. "I'm sorry," she finally said. "I don't believe you."

"Dawn," her husband cried.

Dawn turned and addressed the others. "I don't believe any of you any more." Then she walked out of the room, closing the door gently so that the paper-thin walls would not shake and disturb the tightly packed pictures of her daughter.

CHAPTER FOUR

Andrea stood outside the police station to which, a week earlier, she had raced through the night to rescue her son. Outside the front door a bracket had been fixed into the reinforced concrete that constituted the wall, and she hesitated and looked up at the blue lamp sporting the words Metropolitan Police. Even in the height of her rebellious student days, when her head swirled with the Marxist ideological certainties of Calvin's father, the iron laws of history, the class struggle, even then she had never actually been anti-police. She had protested against police brutality and corruption in Brixton and elsewhere, but that was decidedly not the same thing. It was not the uniform she objected to, but the abuse of the power of the uniform. She felt as though she were about to return to the enemy's camp.

She spotted a noticeboard next to the door, and behind its glass front she saw a poster. It had a pristine white background and heavy blue type. It was the Met's 'Statement of Common Purpose and Values'. Her eyes skipped over the first paragraph, relating how the sworn purpose of the Metropolitan Police was to uphold the law fairly and firmly, to prevent crime, and to bring to justice those who broke the law. As she read the high-minded, even noble, sentiments, cloaked as they were in user-friendly market-speak, she could not help thinking of Hogarth, and their encounter in the coroner's court. She marvelled again at the fact that he had shown her the photo of his daughter, and she thought of the pain in his eyes. She tried to recall his words, how he had sought to justify breaking the law for a higher end, and when she did, she saw the mission statement of the Met not as a coherent creed, but as a series of competing goals. If Hogarth was right, bringing offenders to justice was not the same as upholding the law.

Andrea spied people moving within the police station through the smoky glass doors. She entered. There was a young woman police constable, stocky, but with a gentle face, arguing with a heavy, drunken man, who leaned over the front desk, trying to chat her up.

"You've got a producer," she told him. "So you've got to produce all your driving documents."

"But I've lost my licence, love," he slurred.

"Did you tell that to the officers who searched your car?"

"I wish it had been you. I would've let you search everything," he said, leaning closer still.

"Yes, madam?" the woman officer asked Andrea.

"I want to see Sergeant Miah, please," Andrea replied.

A shadow of confusion passed over the officer's face. "He's a custody sergeant. Can I ask what it's about?"

"It's a private matter," Andrea said, trying to speak as nonchalantly as she could. But she could see that she had not succeeded, for the WPC eyed her suspiciously.

"What's your name again?" the woman asked.

"Andrea Chambers."

The WPC then moved to the office behind the front desk and whispered to someone there.

In this interlude, the drunken man, with his belly hanging over his loosely belted checked trousers as if he were pregnant, turned his attention to Andrea. Every time he spoke, she felt as though a whisky bottle had been opened under her nose, obliging her to inhale the sharp fumes.

"Are you a copper, too?" the man asked her. "Or are you undercover? I'd like to go under the covers with you."

Andrea looked at the pathetic specimen in front of her, and dearly wished that she could summon the same reserves of patience she had so recently witnessed in the WPC. Instead, she smiled sweetly and said, "Sod off." She moved as far away from the disgusting man as the cramped enquiry area allowed, crossed her arms and waited, arching her back and stretching it so that just her shoulders touched the wall. The WPC returned and, pointedly ignoring Andrea, flicked through the open register of traffic producers on the front desk. The man appeared relieved that he could speak to a markedly less threatening woman. Finally, Miah edged his way through the door that led into the station. He seemed paler than Andrea remembered him. The amber lustre to his skin she recalled from that first night had now vanished, and she saw a sallow, miserable man, with his neat black moustache and side-parted black hair.

"What do you want?" he said coldly to her. The earlier friendliness had disappeared, too.

"I just need some information," Andrea said quietly, trying to control her unease, while all the time a voice inside her was telling her that she had made a mistake.

Before Miah could reply, two suited detectives, Fisher and Brigson, emerged through the door. Fisher lifted up the counter, so that he was on the same side as Andrea. He did not speak but eyed her disdainfully.

"Information?" Miah said. "You lawyers. I can't believe you. I showed you nothing but courtesy when you came to my station. And what do you do? You go into court. Make all sorts of wild allegations. About this station, about these officers, about my prisoner. And then you come back, and expect me to help you?"

Andrea saw Fisher sneering down at her, but he said

nothing. Brigson, with a crumb or two around the edges of his mouth, was also silent, but he appeared embarrassed by the confrontation. The drunken man grinned with joy, clearly believing Andrea deserved the dressing-down.

"I was just doing my job," she said.

"Your client Earl Whitely killed himself," Miah said. "That's the only information you need."

Andrea became incensed by the casual way in which Earl's death had been dismissed. She decided that she had been right earlier — this was the enemy's camp.

"End of story," Fisher said.

Andrea turned defiantly to him. "That depends on whose story you choose to believe, DS Fisher." She wanted to let him know that she remembered his name.

"And you choose to believe a gunman who dealt drugs to kids and hanged himself from the wicket gate," Fisher snapped back.

Andrea fervently wished that she could have found a stunning riposte to his comment, but she was too aware of all the people staring at her, and of the suffocatingly small size of the area. "I want to see the station duty states," she said to Miah.

"Why?" he replied.

"To see which officers were on duty the night Nicki Harris was killed by a bullet from a police gun," she said, deliberately, provocatively. One part of herself begged her to calm the situation, while the rest of her advised her, however unwisely: Fuck them.

Fisher began to protest. "Anyone could use a Carbina."

But Miah raised his hand and Fisher did not continue. "The duty states are privileged," Miah said in an officious voice.

"Then I want to see Earl Whitely's custody record. You've got to keep them twelve months under the Code. But I can quote you chapter and verse if you like."

She noticed Fisher glancing quickly from Miah to Brigson, then back to Miah. Miah, however, remained calm.

"The Codes of Practice apply to all prisoners," he said, pausing long enough to underline his next point, "who happen to be alive. That's not something we could accuse your ex-client of. Now, you'd better leave. Before we charge you with wasting police time. I'll quote you chapter and verse on that if you like."

Fisher stepped across to the glass outer door, delighted, and held it open in an exaggerated manner, with a sweep of his arm, as if he were a courtier laying his cape over a puddle of mud for a lady.

As Andrea passed him, he whispered to her, "How's Calvin?"

Andrea parked her car in the carpark behind the block of flats and then rushed up the stairs to Calvin's door on the first floor. She was surprised to see the door ajar, and a rake-thin white man in his mid-twenties with a cigarette hanging out of the side of his mouth carrying out a speaker.

"Calvin?" she called.

The man, who wore a hooded denim jacket, said, "He's inside."

Andrea burst through the door and saw her son squatting against the wall, where there was a long extension lead, sufficient for half a dozen plugs. He wore baggy black trousers and a skin-tight white T-shirt. He pulled out the plugs one by one, coiling the freed wires with great care. "Hi," he said, glancing up, before he returned to his task.

The flat was in a worse mess than usual, with plates of half-eaten food on the floor and dirty shirts strewn across chairs. She stepped over a pizza box and kissed him lightly on the head. He didn't respond. "What's going on?" she asked.

"Nothing," he said. He had pulled out the last plug, but pretended to be preoccupied with the cables so as to avoid her gaze.

The man returned. "The deck, too?" he asked.

Calvin nodded uneasily, glancing over at his mother. Andrea waited until the man had picked up the mixing deck and left them alone.

"I don't want you doing another sound clash," she told him.

"You can't stop me," Calvin replied, but it wasn't said with the hostility Andrea had expected — the teenage tantrum reply, looking for an argument. It was cooler. More certain. You just can't stop me and you know it, her son seemed to be saying to her.

"I can advise you, then," Andrea said, trying another angle.

Calvin looked at her now, evenly, without emotion, and that brought his words home to her with far greater impact. "Like you advised Earl?" he said.

The comment drained from Andrea any will she still had to engage her son further in a debate. It was, she decided, pointless. With Earl's death, the fragile thread with which she had hoped to tie herself to Calvin had been broken. On the small corner table, she saw an opened packet of cigarettes, a three-quarters-empty bottle of vodka, and she grieved because she knew that she could do nothing about any of it.

"I'd better go," she said.

Calvin nodded, and she was sure that he was upset too. She cursed herself that the most consoling aspect of her visit was that her son was pained by their relationship too.

"Were you at Rufus's this morning?" she asked.

"Yes," he said.

"I rang."

"I know."

She felt her lips pursing as she had confirmed to her what she already knew: he had hung up when he had heard her voice. She walked to the door. "Be careful, son," she said softly.

"You too," he replied. He even smiled momentarily, and that lacerated her heart even more. She passed the white man on the balcony. He allowed the remains of his cigarette to fall from his mouth as she approached, and stamped it out, barely breaking stride.

Calvin had not moved by the time the man returned to the flat.

"Teacher or something?" he asked.

"Something," Calvin said distractedly, still smarting from the encounter. Then he recovered his street cool sufficiently to ask, "You got, you know, the other . . . stuff?"

The man paused. With a grandiose gesture he took a small box, the size of a cigarette packet, out of his denim jacket. Calvin took it, and handed over some notes, wound into a tight roll.

"Nine-mil, wasn't it?" the man asked.

But Calvin didn't reply as, fascinated, he tapped ammunition for Earl's gun into the palm of his hand. Feeling the cool shells against his skin, he thought about his mother and the pain this would cause her. He didn't want to hate her, but he didn't see how he could avoid it for long when he hated every single aspect of his life, and she had given that life to him.

Andrea drove slowly back to the law firm, taking care with her lane changes, constantly checking her mirror, indicating in plenty of time, doing everything to be the perfect driver, and at the same time castigating herself for being the very opposite of perfection as a mother. As she approached London Bridge from the south, her radio was on in the background on the twenty-four-hour news channel, but she paid it scant attention, as she was engaged in the most acrimonious litigation of her life, and the most oft repeated — Andrea versus Andrea. She took in little of the sun rebounding off the sheets of glass in the office blocks north of the Thames, of HMS *Belfast* squatting with its gun barrels plugged off Southwark; she didn't even see that Tower Bridge shimmered in the blue distance, with its arms raised to allow a cutter through. All this she missed, for in her mind she was yet again in that courtroom of her own construction, at once in the dock and the witness box, where she was both prosecutor and accused. It was a tribunal to which the jury rarely seemed to return, and if they did, it was invariably with a guilty verdict, because while she had always been prepared to accept the innocence of her clients in the teeth of truly overwhelming evidence, she had always considered herself guilty in some aspect or other of her relationships, as a daughter, or as a mother, and she made this judgment on herself based upon the most flimsy of material. Now she saw Calvin's distance from her as an exile caused entirely by herself. If he does not love me, she decided, it is because I am not worthy of love. And, the sentence of the tribunal continued, if I am not worthy of his love, then I am not worthy of my own.

Such was the ferocity of her own indictment that she missed the beginning of the breaking news story on the radio. But a connection was being made on a subconscious level, and as more and more information filtered in, Andrea flicked the left indicator, and amid two lanes of northbound cars hooting from behind, she stopped almost exactly in the centre of one of London's busiest bridges. She turned the volume control, and listened to the reporter, while the hatchback's engine idled.

". . . mounting controversy surrounding the Nicki Harris case. A short time ago, Nicki's mother, Dawn

Harris, summoned reporters to her home when she made this statement."

Andrea stared out over the highway of water, stretching away from her to the east and west as far as her eye could see, and she felt the agreeable vibrations of the car transmitted through the pedals and the soles of her shoes. The voice she next heard, Dawn's voice, was more controlled than that of the grieving mother she recalled from last week's television appeal. It appeared to Andrea that finally Dawn was speaking from her own script.

"Over the last few days," Dawn said, her words filling the car, "I've met with the police officers conducting the investigation into my daughter Nicki's death. And . . . and I'm not satisfied with the way the police have conducted their inquiry."

At this, Andrea heard an outburst of questioning, and her heart went out to this other mother, for she herself had so recently been in the eye of the media storm, and had experienced how each publicly asked question felt like the lash of a whip.

"Dawn, are you going to sue? What does your husband think? Is he resigning from the force?"

"This is a decision I've taken on my own," Dawn said.

There were other less distinct questions in the tumult, and Andrea continued to empathise with the ordeal Dawn Harris was now enduring. She remembered how they had asked her if it was true that her son was black, and who the father was, and whether her child associated with murderers.

Dawn spoke more loudly now, until the reporters were silenced. On the bridge, cars continued to pass, and the drivers looked across at her, mouthing angry, silent words at the queue she had caused behind her, but still she listened.

"I've been told that there are currently no more leads,"

Dawn said. "I mean, no further leads about the identity of
the other men present when my daughter was killed. But I
cannot — I will not accept this. We live in a city of ten million. Someone knows something. And I'm asking them to
come forward. So today I'm putting up a reward for any
information from any source — I don't care — that leads
to the arrest of the men who killed my Nicki. The reward
is five thousand pounds. I know it's not very much. But it's
all the savings I've got. And I've refused a much larger
offer from a national newspaper for Nicki's story. The
truth is I don't want my daughter's story told in a paper. I
want justice for her in a court."

Andrea then heard what sounded like a door slamming,
and another flurry of questions. She imagined the small
woman with thick glasses, with the strong, earnest face,
turning quickly on her heels and entering what was once
her daughter's home. She switched off the radio. In her
rear-view she saw a police motorcyclist racing across the
bridge towards her. She raised her left hand in apology,
without turning around, and put the car into first gear.

It took her less than fifteen minutes to negotiate the
"ring of steel" anti-terrorist defences around the City.
Then she worked her way around the one-way systems
until she could drive into the underground carpark
beneath the law firm. She made her way into the lift on
autopilot, for Dawn Harris's staggering announcement
played over and over in her mind. The truth was that
Andrea was not simply impressed by Dawn's heroic
actions. As she had learned to do over the darker years, she
turned the issue on herself. She struggled to decide
whether she would have had such unalloyed courage if it
was Calvin who had been killed. Her first instinct, of
course, was that she would have done precisely the same
as Nicki's mother, but then another part of her objected.
How is it, then, this dissenting faction seemed to say, that

when your son was taken away from you, you failed to appeal? Where does that rank in the canon of heroic motherhood, counsellor? And against this withering accusation, Andrea repeated again and again in her mind like a mantra: I loved my son, I loved my son, I loved my son.

The lift bell rang once, and the doors opened on to the firm's main floor. Andrea rushed towards the nearest conference room, where she would find a television screen. The room she entered had a long, smooth mahogany table, capable of seating twenty people, and at the far end of the book-lined room there was a video and digital television stack, used for international video conferences and for Test match cricket coverage in the summer. Her father, who was still on the waiting list for MCC membership, tolerated this one aberration from the work-efficient ethos. Andrea quickly found the remote and zapped the television on. She surfed the channels quickly, finding no report of Dawn's announcement until she reached the cable channels. And there on satellite news was Dawn. It was odd to be seeing now that which only minutes before she had so vividly imagined. The street in which the Harrises lived was drab, and on first inspection Dawn did not appear to be the heroic, battling mother of Andrea's imagination, but a frightened, timid suburban housewife with an army of scavengers on her doorstep. Andrea nodded to herself when the news editor cut to an establishing shot further back, from the top of a news van perhaps, which showed the chaos in the road, with newspaper and television crews clogging up the entrance to the mosque opposite. Andrea knew exactly where the South London mosque was, having represented a Pakistani youth who had defended himself from a racial attack with a lock-knife. This had been years ago when 'Paki-bashing' was a prevalent pastime in the area, and everyone who was not white or 'nigger' was a Paki. Sergeant Miah, she thought, would have been so considered, even though he was Indian. It didn't matter.

She propped herself against the table as Dawn began her speech on television. But then the door behind her opened. When she tore her eyes away from Dawn's face, she saw that her father had entered the room. She looked at him, thought briefly about the summer cricket, and smiled. "Dad," she said, indicating the screen.

He nodded. "Siobhan told me. Amazing." He joined her now, but instead of watching to one side he stood directly in front of her.

"Dad," she said again, hitting the volume.

Gordon Chambers carefully removed the remote from his daughter's hand and pressed the red button. The whole system — video, television, cable — fizzed with static electricity as it died. It was then that Andrea realised that, unusually for him, her father had not returned her smile. She gazed up at him expectantly, and he did not disappoint her. "We've got to talk," he said.

"We talked earlier," she replied.

Now he looked down, sheepish, his eyelids half closing. "But I didn't tell you what I really wanted to say."

"Now you've got me worried," she said.

He put his hands on each of her shoulders, a firm grip, a no-nonsense one. This was not tenderness but affection, the hard kind, the kind that hurts. "Darling, I'm only telling you this because I have to. Because you're about to be faced with a choice, and you're about to do something, I can just see it, that will change everything."

Andrea tried to laugh this off, nervous as she saw his face flush crimson, and his forehead pucker to such an extent that even the top of his nose was creased. "A man has come to see you," Gordon said.

"What man?"

"A policeman."

Andrea's mind raced into half a dozen dead ends, and every time she backed out she saw the shadow of Hogarth.

"He's in my office now," Gordon said, "and to be frank, having heard about Dawn Harris, I'm not surprised he's here."

Andrea began to move past her father, in an attempt to end the unbearable suspense that hampered her very breathing. Gordon held her firmly in place. "Dad, what's his name?" she asked, half hoping, half fearing, that her father was about to utter the name Hogarth.

"Miah, I think. An Indian chap."

Andrea's thoughts spun again, now in ever-increasing circles, as she tried to reconcile Miah's hostility to her with his visit to the law firm.

"Andrea, you don't have to go," Gordon said, maintaining his grip. "You might think you have to, but you don't. He's got some information for you. About the case. And I know you think you want it. But I want to give you an option. If you want I'll go and see him and courteously, politely" — he paused — "charmingly, if I can manage it, send him away and tell him never to contact my family again."

"Dad, dad, dad," she cried.

"I know you'll go. I know you better than you do yourself."

"Why?"

"Because, my dear, you're precisely like your mother." With this, the strength appeared to be drawn from him, and he moved out of her way and sat in one of the finely chiselled French period-effect chairs around the conference table. Andrea's path was now clear, but she found herself nailed to the spot. She held out her hand and he raised his arm. She saw how it quivered, and she realised that her father was no longer the hero of her childhood, but an old man.

"I was engaged to someone else before your mother," he said in a weak, distant voice, which seemed exhausted as it reached back forty years.

Now she had to sit. "What?" she whispered.

Gordon smiled briefly. "You didn't know that, did you, princess? She was a sort of distant relation of the clan Chambers, really. A kissing cousin of a kissing cousin, from the rich half of the family, i.e. not ours. And there were only three months to the wedding day when I met your mother at this legal ball. She was walking out, as we used to call it, with someone else as well. It was the most inconvenient thing in the world, and perhaps that was what made it so exciting. But the days went by and the preparations were being cast in stone, and your mother and I were hopelessly in love. I just didn't know what to do, when your mother decided the matter." He slowly shook his head, as if he still could not believe what he was about to say, even after all the intervening years. "She went to see the other woman. She confronted her. Your mother said, 'You may marry him, you may have his ring, but I shall have his heart.' And to prove it, she showed one of my more . . . effusive letters to her."

Andrea was shocked into silence. Her image of her mother, hitherto that of a quiet, cool person, simply could not accommodate her father's words. But he pressed on.

"You probably don't remember, darling, but when you were young, right up until you were five, I think, we always had to open your birthday and Christmas cards, because the other . . . party used to send you messages saying your mother is this, your mother is that. And then they stopped, when everyone in the family knew that your mother had that first shadow on that mammogram. Do you remember how stoically she accepted it?"

Andrea, of course, had the quiet suffering of her mother

indelibly etched into her memory. Even at the end, even when it was truly desperate, her mother had been the calmest person in the family.

"Your mother believed that it was a judgment on her. But she never regretted what she had done. She never showed any remorse. She knew what she had wanted, and she had accepted that if this was the price, she would not complain about its payment."

Hot tears filled Andrea's eyes, and more so when she saw them matched in those of her father. "Darling," he said, "that is your flesh. You are what your mother was."

"No," Andrea cried back.

"When you were pregnant with Calvin," Gordon insisted, "and everyone else was against you, you would not be swayed, not for one second."

"I wanted a child, Dad," she sobbed, "because I'd lost Mum. Didn't any of you see that? It wasn't an accident, it wasn't bad luck. I wanted a baby."

Tears now ran freely down her father's face, and he wiped them away with the back of his suit sleeve. They left a shiny smear on the dark pin-stripe. "Andrea, I thought if you had a child, I would lose my girl. And I'd be all alone in the world."

"You idiot." She smiled through the tears, and hugged him, and wished that these things had been said fifteen years earlier. Then she realised that they could not have been, for like anything that is alive and true they had to grow and take their unique shape.

Both father and daughter wiped their eyes. They stood up.

"Let me go to him," Gordon offered.

Andrea shook her head.

They walked into the open-plan area, to the rest of the office appearing as the most senior and the most junior partner in consultation, but Andrea was again that teenage girl she hated to think of, comforting and being comforted by her father.

When they reached the tank in the middle, he whispered to her, "You lost a mother, and I gained a fish tank."

"I kept telling you to get a dog. A cat, at least."

Gordon shook his head. He put his right palm flat against the slightly misted exterior of the tank, down which droplets of condensation dripped. Fish glided past, unworried, accustomed to legal loiterers. "I still get a bit upset when one of them dies," he said. "But I always just buy a new one, and after a while, you forget." He winked at his daughter. "Not quite the same with *homo sapiens*, methinks." He gripped her hand once more. "Be quick, then. Some of us actually work in our offices, you know."

She smiled, turned, and headed for Sergeant Miah.

As she walked along the corridor to her father's end office, she realised how rarely, even before the onset of the illness, her mother had smiled. She had been a content rather than an outwardly happy person, if such a distinction could be made, in the sense that she had been satisfied with the content of her life. Andrea had always believed that her mother was reserved, that she lacked passion, as she expended most of her energies in a furious assault on nature in her Kentish country garden. Living in the country was the only subject she could remember her parents crossing swords about. Gordon hated the commuting but he had endured it, so that his wife could garden. Andrea began to see her mother not as a passionless woman, but as one who was passion-spent, one who had used up life's allocation in one bewildering act of ardour, in which she had won the only man on the planet she wanted.

She paused at the threshold of her father's office and considered his offer one final time. She knew that if she put her hand on the brass handle and turned it she would be committed to a headlong pursuit of Hogarth, that she would have to discover the truth about Earl Whitely's death and Nicki Harris's shooting no matter what the cost. Her father was not twenty yards away in the open-plan area, and it would take just a flexing of the neck muscles to turn, a little air from the lungs to activate the vocal cords, and she would be spared the storm of trouble that lay ahead.

Her fingers quivered over the polished brass.

Then they gripped its cool, round surface.

And she knew that she was, without question, her mother's daughter.

She opened the door and was blinded by the sunlight that flooded directly into the office. The sun had burst around a cloud and the light-sensitive glass had not caught up. Sergeant Miah sat patiently, self-contained, his thighs a few inches apart, one palm resting on each. Once more the gentleman, he stood as she entered the room.

"Miss Chambers, I'm sorry," he said. "The station. It was an act."

"I know," Andrea replied. "My father says—"

"You must give me your solemn oath that you will not subpoena this witness. Nor can you name him to the press."

Andrea nodded. "Who is he?"

"DC Mark Kelsey. Like me, he's disgusted with what happened to your client. But unlike me, he was in the cell block when it happened."

"Will he speak to me?"

Miah nodded. "He will. His wife won't."

"How do you know?" Andrea asked.

Miah handed her Earl Whitely's custody record. There was an address scribbled in red Biro across it. "Because she's my daughter," the sergeant said, as a sad, fearful look broke over his face. It appeared to concentrate his intensity and passion, and his words cut into Andrea. She was under no illusion that this was the most difficult thing the Indian officer had done in his life. "I did mean one thing I said in the station," he continued. "About wasting police time. Don't waste mine." Then he dropped his voice and his words were coated in venom. "Get the bastards."

CHAPTER FIVE

Roots paused outside the black glass frontage of the City building, criss-crossed with metal stanchions, like a three-dimensional game of noughts and crosses. The financial house's façade reflected the world darkly. Roots thought this was appropriate, since he had heard that some of the deals that went on within the Square Mile were the shadows that inexorably followed his type of dealings on the street — laundering money, washing it, cleansing soiled corporations. He wore a simple but stylish suit, one taken from the rack of such designer garments in the lab. It was a three-button black single-breasted, with turn-ups on the trousers and lightly padded shoulders, not that Roots needed these. He had chosen a white Oxford shirt, thinking that the button-down collar would give him a more businesslike appearance. It was the finishing touch which gave him the biggest problem: the tie. In the end he went for a Zegna, a dark creation of swirls on a jet-black background. Now, as he gathered himself before entering the bank, he tugged at the tie around his neck. It felt like a noose.

The revolving door led into a large glass atrium, through which the sunlight poured. Two huge palm trees, and they were trees not plants, stood guard on either side of the façade, and a marbled expanse of floor swept its way to a burled walnut reception desk, carved ingeniously into an undulating wave, the colour of glowing embers. Two glass lifts shot up and down through glass tubes in the atrium roof, carrying executives as if on magic carpets outside the fabric of the building. Roots had never been in such a building in his life. And although he could face down a loaded gun, this place made him nervous. He could feel his hands becoming clammy as they gripped his business plan. This is my passport, he kept trying to reassure himself, this plan is my justification for being here. This affords me the right to mix with these people. He was seized with doubts, trying to think back to the moments before he had printed off his business files, as he wondered if he had spell-checked the document. In truth he must have checked the spelling a dozen times. But now, in this alien world, he couldn't be sure.

Behind the desk, a woman receptionist sat with headphones clamped over her head and a mouthpiece, little more than a ribbon of shiny metal, through which she communicated with the dozens of flashing lights on her console. A thick-set security guard stood over her, in a brown uniform. He too had a button-down collar, but his fat neck bulged over it everywhere. He looked ridiculous. Roots now wished he had been natural. He had never worn such a shirt before; why had he started now? He reached the desk.

"I have a meeting with Mr Ellis," he said.

For an instant, the receptionist broke off her conversation and stared with wide, surprised eyes at him. He realised that she was staring at his short Yardie fade haircut, about which he could do nothing. It was so normal in his world, it was the style most men wore, but now Roots imagined that he might just as well have carved into his hair the word 'criminal'.

"Name?" the security guard asked.

"Johnson," Roots replied. Then he paused as the man wrote it down on a tear-off slip. "Valentine Johnson."

The woman meanwhile scanned a list on the desk in

front of her, and whispered something Roots could not hear to the guard.

"You're not on the list," the sceptical guard told him.

"It was a last-minute arrangement," Roots said. He told himself to calm down. He knew that in his world no one in their right mind would ever dare to look at the don so sneeringly, no one would dream of keeping him waiting like this. But if this was how black people were treated in what Roots considered the 'respectable white world', then he had to get used to it. He was buying his freedom. As the receptionist fingered one of the touch-sensitive buttons in front of her and whispered into her mouthpiece, Roots questioned what he was in fact doing. Buying his freedom? He imagined himself now as a child on that windy beach in his childhood Jamaica, with the swirling branches of the palm trees, the arms of his ancestors, above him. They had never bought their freedom from slavery. They had fought for it. From the mountains, from the dense uplands where they cut down the British army soldiers and the slavers. He wondered now if they would curse him. But there are many ways to fight, he consoled himself, and this fight he was about to begin without a gun would be as treacherous as any his family had experienced through the generations.

"Wait here, please," the receptionist told him. She nodded to the guard, and the man tore the strip of paper from the visitors' register, folded it in half, and slipped it into a plastic sleeve with a clip. It was now Roots's security pass. As he attached it to his suit jacket, Roots lost himself in a memory of the time when he had walked right through the interior of Jamaica. He was barefooted most of the way as his makeshift shoes had fallen apart soon after he had set off from Trench Town during the night. He walked north-east and up into the Blue Mountains, but he became restless and wanted to see it all, to see this island to which his family had been brought in chains by the British. He spent the next days travelling the spine of the country in a forced march, avoiding the main road, cutting between Chapeltown and Spanish Town, north of May Pen, around Mandeville, until he reached Black River and the sea again. As he stood at the south-west corner of the island, the boy listened to the old men, and he marvelled that only four hundred miles of the Caribbean now separated him from the coast of Honduras and Nicaragua and the magical names of the Yucatan, Escarcega, Chetumal, Ticul, the land of the Aztecs. The boy stayed in Black River, living on his wits, helping out the fishermen for a few dollars, until it was safe to return to Kingston. He had killed that corrupt policeman. And now he was to lose the name of his parents and gain the name of the streets. Valentine became Roots, and he now saw that the journey he had begun in Trench Town did not end at that Caribbean beach, but had continued all the way to this London bank and from here, he hoped, to Katherine.

Lost in these memories, Roots Johnson did not know precisely how long he had been standing at reception, but now the nearer of the two glass lifts opened and a man stepped out. He marched over towards Roots with his hand extended.

"Mr Johnson? I'm Simon Ellis," he said, shaking his hand. Ellis had short red hair and, though he was in his early thirties, a paunch that was exaggerated by the paisley braces he wore under his open suit jacket. Roots noticed that his small hands were weak and cold, with polished nails, though the manicure could not conceal the white speckles of vitamin deficiency. He indicated the lift. "Please, come up."

"Thank you," Roots replied.

While they were in the lift, Ellis asked, "Does anyone know you're coming?" Roots shook his head. "Excellent, truly excellent. I really want to hear your plans."

"I've written a business plan," Roots said, offering his cherished document.

"Why don't we just chat about it first?" Ellis said, as energetically as before. As the lift shot up into the air, and London spread beneath him, Roots was already beginning to have his doubts about the man.

Ellis whisked him through the lobby on the ninth floor, then along a corridor and into his art deco office, with massive reproductions of Klimt studies of women, draped in fantastic shimmering clothes or naked on beds, barely concealed beneath sheets. He had a massive semi-circular desk, covered with an array of executive toys and strange objets d'art that appeared to Roots to be piles of wax from a dripping candle. He noticed Roots's fascination with the artwork.

"Young experimental artist. I'm, like, her backer," he said. "Weird stuff. But a cracking girl, really." When he saw that Roots was not responding, he leaned back in his leather bucket chair and put his arms awkwardly behind his neck. "Now, you wanted to talk to me about money."

"Music," Roots said, crossing his legs as he sat in an armless chair opposite him.

Ellis's face dropped. He leaned forward, put his hands on the desk as if he were praying, and addressed Roots like a child. "Well, you have to understand that not only is music not our field of interest, but it is inherently a rather problematic area of business."

"It's very lucrative," Roots said, unfazed.

"It's very risky."

"I'll take the risk."

"With our money."

"And mine," Roots said. He considered his situation, the building, being in this rarefied corner of the city, and above all he considered Katherine's words, the pain in her face as she realised that he had been responsible for the

Mashango massacre. There was nothing for it; he decided
to expose himself a little further. "I'm prepared to deposit
a very significant amount of . . . collateral. As a sign of
good faith."

"That's what I'm interested in," Ellis said. "Good faith."
His voice was still jocular, but his eyes had become fixed
and serious, like those of a cat looking out of a window at
a bird. "Just how significant is your collateral?"

Roots leaned forward in the chair, took out the Mont
Blanc pen he had bought with a bundle of £50 notes in
Harrods for just such an occasion, and wrote on a yellow
Post-it from the pile on Ellis's desk. He wrote '$870'. Then
he added a 'k' after the numbers. He looked up at the financier and saw, as he had expected, a change in the man's
face, as if finally someone had opened the window and the
cat now had direct access to the bird.

"Well, this puts a rather different complexion on
things," Ellis said.

"I want you to match and double it," Roots said calmly.

Ellis's eyes were still fixed on the figures. "Where are
the funds invested, if I may ask?"

"Cash," Roots said.

Ellis burst out laughing, and his right hand rested
instinctively on his rounded stomach. "It's all money, Mr
Johnson. You must have a big bed to put it under."

Roots was now certain that he was being patronised by
the other man, but he needed to do business with him,
he needed to wash his money. "It's in cash accounts,
mainly," he said. "In the British Virgin Islands. You have
facilities to—"

"Of course. Look, give me your plan, leave your ideas
with me, and I'll go through the numbers with our rocket
scientists."

"I want to deal just with you," Roots said. It wasn't that
he trusted Ellis, for he certainly did not, but he had

already divined the nature of the man. He knew that Ellis could be his; for a retainer, a secret handshake, Ellis would do anything for him. And he consoled himself further with the thought that if it wasn't the usual transaction with a high-street bank manager, this deal was no more questionable than hundreds of others that were being transacted in the same Square Mile that week. It would be his last illicit act, his signing off, and when the studio was up and running, he would be cut free from his old life for ever.

"And I want to deal exclusively with you, Mr Johnson," Ellis replied. "But I make the deals. The backroom boys, they look at the maths. And believe me, they really are rocket scientists. Well, one of them is. Worked for NASA, till one day he turned up higher than the space shuttle in orbit."

Be careful of this man, Roots told himself, he is reckless. How is it supposed to impress me that his analyst was dismissed for drug abuse? He wished there was another way of laundering his cash and then obtaining the rest of the money for the studio, but he was realistic enough to know that there was none. No respectable bank in Britain would accept $870,000 cash from a Yardie as collateral. In truth, he would not do so himself.

"I believe in speaking frankly, Mr Ellis," Roots said. "I need to know. Are you interested?"

Ellis hesitated, stood, broke off a small piece of wax from one of the artworks on his desk. "I'm very interested," he said.

Minutes later, when Roots was out on the street once more, now without his business plan, he found an access alley between two buildings. He momentarily stepped into the narrow space between the opposing walls and clenched his fists. "Ya man," he shouted. He took out his mobile and dialled. When it was answered, he said,

"Katherine? It's Valentine. I've started." His chest swelled with joy as he began to see a way out of the wrong turns he had made ever since that day in Kingston when he had first killed a man; turn after turn after turn, one after another, leading him away from his mother, from his home, and away, he now realised, from himself. He was coming back.

It did not take him long to get a cab across the city to Katherine's office. He was barely past the street door when she slammed it closed behind him, and the two melted into one another. They smothered each other in wet, desperate kisses, since this was what they had both hungered for, and what the two of them needed — these two lonely people, finally connecting in the city. Katherine pulled off his tie, and he ran his fingers through her hair till they rested in the space at the back of her neck, with his palm touching her warm skin and the back of his hand covered in her fragrant hair. They kissed again, overbalancing, rolling along the wall, trying to take off each other's clothes, his groin against her stomach, her breasts against his lower chest, and he marvelled as their hands locked together and the fingers meshed, a tapestry of black then white, black then white.

Simon Ellis was losing his patience on the phone. He still sat behind his semicircular desk, with the phone propped between his ear and his right shoulder, his head tilted to lock it into place.

"I've already told your colleague," he said. "Black. Johnson. Valentine Johnson." He screwed up Roots's business plan and tossed it into the basketball-hoop bin. "Come on, Officer. I gave you Vasquez, now I'm giving you this Johnson."

"Congratulations, Ellis," the voice replied. "Now, you'll only spend four hundred years in the slammer."

*   *   *

As the afternoon light began markedly to fade, Andrea
arrived at a crescent of mock-Alpine homes. They were
badly copied Swiss cottages, not in Swiss Cottage but in
South London, surrounded on one side by the overland
railway track, and on the other by a brewery with columns
of steam standing in the air above two tall chimneys. The
air, she noticed immediately as she got out of her car, was
rich and malty, while in the background there was the
tick-tick-tick of the railway lines as distant, unseen trains
approached or departed, appearing to tap out a Morse
code to announce their movements. She looked once more
at the custody record, and the sergeant's red Biro
scribblings, and was sure that she had found the correct
street. The Kelsey home was on the right-hand side of the
crescent, nearer the railway, and had a steep driveway up
from the road, upon which an old-model Citroën was
parked. She walked up the drive and pressed the bell. In
the unreal atmosphere of brown wood and brick house
fronts, window boxes and wide, low, cantilevered roofs,
like tiled tents, she practically expected to hear yodelling
as she buzzed. But it was an entirely ordinary tinny ring,
and soon she heard footsteps approaching the front door
from the other side. It opened fractionally, and an attractive young Asian woman peeped out through the crack.

"Mrs Kelsey?" Andrea asked.

"Yes?" the woman asked, confused. She had a slightly
chubby face, which added to rather than detracted from
her looks.

"I'm Andrea Chambers."

She had barely finished giving her name when the door
was slammed to. But it was a predominantly glass door and
she could see the distorted image of the woman holding
her head behind it.

"I need to speak to your husband," she called.

"Go away. Mark's got nothing to say." There was no

trace of her ethnic roots in the young woman's voice, unlike the rich cadences in her father's.

"Please, Mrs Kelsey."

"Leave us," the woman cried, banging the glass from the inside, as if to chase away the evil that Andrea had brought upon the house.

Andrea then heard a man's voice behind her. "What's going on?"

She turned and saw a man she did not recognise at all from the police station. Kelsey had not shaved for a couple of days. His hair was matted and greasy and there were dark smudges under his eyes. He carried some kind of metal canister in one hand, and a small chocolate orange in the other.

"DC Kelsey?" Andrea asked.

But before he could reply, the front door was opened again and his wife flew out, wearing her baggy pink tracksuit trousers and Sloppy Joe fleece top. "Send her away, Mark," she cried to her husband. "Send her away."

Kelsey tried to smile, though he was visibly shaken by his wife's desperate entreaties. He kissed her lightly on the forehead. "Don't worry, Gita," he whispered. He gave her the chocolate orange, which was the trigger for her to burst into a fearful stream of tears as she buried her head in his chest. He put his free arm around her shoulder and began to usher her inside. "You'd better come through," he mouthed to Andrea, although his wife could plainly hear the invitation.

On the way through the house, Gita Kelsey turned into her sanctuary, the kitchen, which Andrea briefly spied before this door too was closed in her face. The kitchen was small but immaculately clean, and full of baskets of lemons and limes and oranges, and this citrus aroma finally blotted out the pervading smell of the brewery opposite. Andrea glimpsed baby-feeding bottles. Then Kelsey opened the rear door and let her out into the garden. Just as the front driveway had led steeply up to the door, now the well-tended lawn led as steeply down to the high railway fence at the bottom of the garden. The crescent's Swiss cottages were in fact at the top of small rise. Kelsey stood over a bonfire at the bottom, behind a brush hedge.

"All this rain," he said. "Wood's too wet." He slowly unscrewed the top of the canister and poured some liquid on to the pile of singed firewood. Andrea now saw from the writing on its side that the canister contained lighter fuel. "Can you pass me that sack, please, Miss Chambers?" he said.

On the grass beneath a dead tree, Andrea saw a black bin-liner. It was wet at the top. "It's heavy," she said.

When she passed it to him, Kelsey reached inside and took out documents, dog-eared books, a framed certificate. Andrea saw that it was the flotsam of his once-flourishing police career. He was burning it all.

"Have you resigned?" she asked.

"I'm actually on sick," he replied.

"Will you resign?"

"They'll probably sack me first."

"On what charge?"

"They'll find something," Kelsey said. "They always do." He looked at her with eyes that were still defiant, those of a man who had not given up.

"I'm sorry," she said.

"So am I. I loved the job." He came to his Hendon passing-out photograph. It had been framed in a thick, white mock-stone surround. He tried to break it over his knee, but it was too solid. He dropped it on the ground and stamped down on it with his boot.

"You know why I'm here," Andrea said, once he had tossed the broken frame on to the burning pile. Acrid jets of chemical flames lapped around the celluloid, and it curled up on itself, then disappeared. "I want you to help me find out what happened."

"Why?"

"Because it's the right thing to do."

Kelsey laughed, shook his head slowly. "I haven't heard talk like that since I left uniform. They don't talk like that in CID."

"Hogarth does," Andrea said, wondering what the man who had confronted her that day had made of this young fresh-faced officer before her now. She imagined that he would have liked Kelsey, would have admired his openness, his simplicity.

"Hogarth's different," Kelsey replied.

"How?"

"He's more dangerous."

The fire crackled and Kelsey squatted down very close to it, so that the flames glowed on his face. Andrea imagined that at any moment his hair would be set alight. She remembered the baby's feeding bottles she had glimpsed in the kitchen, and she felt a pang of guilt at imposing upon this young family. "You've got a child?" she asked.

"Two. Four and eighteen months."

"Then I'm going to give you a choice. I promise I won't force you to come to court. I won't even harass you to speak to me."

Kelsey stood up. His eyes were narrow, and he spoke fearlessly. "But that's why I've got to do it. Gita doesn't understand. But I'm doing it *because* of my kids, not in spite of them, Miss Chambers. And seeing you in court, knowing how we . . . they . . . how we pressurised you using your son, I think you understand, too."

Andrea wanted to reach out and touch the man, for she had finally found a soul mate, who was lost like her in the limbo between duty and family. She wanted to grab him and shake the solution to her dilemma out of him, to ask him whether they were doing the right thing, and why, and what they would achieve, and what it would do to them if they failed.

"I saw Dawn Harris's announcement," Kelsey said. "I'm glad. In a way. Brave woman."

"So are there any more clues?"

Kelsey picked up a stick and prodded the burning pile. "I tell you what I know. But what I know, I don't understand. Or I don't believe. Or no one else will believe."

"Try me," Andrea said.

She waited for Kelsey to speak, but he was distracted by a shadow in the kitchen window behind them. She glanced over and saw that Gita Kelsey was watching them with unrelenting horror.

Roots awoke suddenly, sweating. For an instant he did not know where he was, and the cloak of often-repeated nightmares refused to lift from his eyes: here he was face to face with the Jamaican cop, and as the man fell dead, he had Lifer's face, then Hogarth's, then Roots's own. He turned over swiftly in the strange bed, and when he saw a naked woman sleeping next to him, the usual glut of self-loathing rose in his throat. It was dark now. A circle of purple sky through a dormer window reminded him that he was in a studio flat above Katherine's office. The room had been painted a cool eggshell blue, and all over the ceiling, in a glorious chaos, dozens of tiny stars shone. When Roots inspected them more closely, he saw that the stars had not been painted on, but were tiny spots of artificial light set into the roof. The effect was magnificent. He was also aware of a bottle of champagne next to the bed, but it pleased him that they had been so entirely absorbed in one another that they had not even opened it, and now there was a small damp circle on the beige carpet where the condensation had run down the bottle.

"Valentine?" Katherine whispered, sensing his stirring.

She turned her head a fraction, and he saw her hair spread like a glorious fan on the pillow around her. It thrilled his heart to hear his real name, and this filled him with even greater disgust for himself, and for all the other casual, passionless, loveless one-night stands he had engaged in throughout his life. How many times over the years, he wondered, had he woken up in an alien bed, next to a woman who no doubt had some of the same redeeming qualities as Katherine but who did not even know his real name.

"Valentine," she said, now turning over to fold her body into his, "what's the matter?"

He smiled and said, "Nothing."

He stroked her hair, wondered at it as he allowed it to play through his fingers. As she moved the sheets, there was the heady, unmistakable smell of sex in the air, and he knew that he could do it again. But he didn't dare tell her what he was thinking, not because he didn't ache to, but simply because he didn't dare ruin the fragile mystery of this strange attic room, and the wordless intimacy of the previous couple of hours. He was firmly convinced that the mention of guns and drugs and killings in this place would cause this moment to dissolve, and he would find himself back at the end of Lifer's guns as they pressed into his cheeks. For Roots was committing one of the biggest sins of the professional trafficker: he was thinking of the future. And he wondered whether, by thinking of this frightening expanse of time, as it spread out indistinctly before him, he was at last confirming to himself that he was truly getting out. Yardies, he knew, didn't think of the future. Of course, they dreamt of future wealth, and future gold, and future guns, but that all happened in a nebulous time, a kind of extended present. And Roots knew perfectly well the reason why these gunmen from Jamaica lived lives of consummate bravado. He knew why he had: because at the time he had picked up his first gun, at the time he did his first deal, someone, somewhere, had fired a bullet, what they would laughingly call "my bullet" when they were drunk or sated with blood after a shoot-out. "My bullet no find me today, star." But Roots had seen enough of the broken and bleeding bodies of his island folk to know that "his bullet', all their bullets, had begun their inexorable journeys to their helpless targets. Every day over the preceding two decades, he now realised, with every deal, his bullet completed another stage, perhaps only a few inches but usually more, of its journey to its final resting spot. He looked at the circle that was the window above them, and he lay back on Katherine's pillow as she kissed him on the neck. He imagined that there were two out-of-control locomotives speeding through the night on the same track, set on a course of dreadful collision. He shivered, and a cold sweat broke out on his forehead, so different from the beads of perspiration he had dripped when his black body had laid over hers.

"Valentine?" she asked, her voice full of childish enquiry, almost playful.

"Yes, darlin'?" He stared at her with half-closed eyes, and could just make out the web of his long eyelashes.

"What a couple of specimens we are."

He wanted to say: I want you to stop the train, I want you to get me off. But although she might have understood his anguish, he felt he had not yet earned the right to burden her life with it. Instead, he asked, "Did you pick my flower up that time?"

Her face creased with embarrassment, and a smile curled her lips. "Uh, no," she said.

"You lie," he pretended to shout in patois.

"Well, did you spy on me, then?"

"No," he said with deliberate exaggeration, protesting

his innocence too much.

"You lie, too, Yard Man," she shouted back, in a perfect imitation of him.

They laughed and rolled over and over on the bed, trying to tickle each other. She was stronger than he had anticipated, and worked her clever fingers under his left armpit so that he laughed so much he needed to cry. Finally, he managed to grab her offending hand. He squeezed it tightly and held it firmly to his chest.

"Hey, you'll break it," she said.

Roots Johnson pressed it still more firmly against his breast. "No," he said, "you will."

They kissed breathlessly, until an image so filled Roots's mind that he could think of nothing else. He broke away and lay on his back, looking up at the ceiling.

"So what do you want to do tonight?" she asked, stroking the short, wiry curls on his chest.

"I've got to go," he replied.

"Look, I don't want this to get too intense either. But I do think we should eat." She smiled.

Roots shook his head. "I want to stay, but I've got to go." And the thought that plagued him was of the sound clash that night, and of a young boy standing with the same reckless indifference to life that had become his shield, his weapon and his weakness. He thought of young Calvin Patterson, and Earl Whitely's gun in the boy's waistband, and a bullet, unseen by Calvin, speeding through the dry ice and smoke of the dance-hall towards the boy's head.

CHAPTER SIX

When Roots Johnson arrived at the dance-hall, he heard
Calvin already checking out some of his lyrics and dubs.
Roots still wore his black business suit, though he had the
jacket slung over his shoulder, had left the tie at
Katherine's, and had rolled up the sleeves of the white
Oxford shirt. Though he had journeyed from Katherine's
central London studio flat down through the more familiar haunts of South London, his mind still lingered in her
room, with the stars and the cool blue walls. He wondered
for a moment what his life might have been like if he had
met her a decade before, before the business had really got
crazy, before cocaine became crack, when he still looked
back to his days in Jamaica, rather than forward to his
death on this foreign, colder island. All his life had been
spent on one of these two islands, and he estimated that
this happenstance of geography must have had some effect
upon him. He told himself that it would, in truth, have
been useless meeting Katherine even one year before this.
He had been, was forced to be, self-contained, had surrounded himself with his own unapproachable waters, had
wanted to be alone on his private island. Until now. It was
the beauty of the twin process which fascinated him: as he
daily became more aware of death closing in all around
him, he reached out for life. He reached out for Katherine.
And if the depths of his heart told him that he could not
save himself, he longed to save another person. In the way
he had not saved young Peckham.

Roots stopped at the rear of the hall, a public sports hall that had been hired for the clash, and watched Calvin going through his paces on the stage ten yards in front of him. He could see the boy's back, hunched over the mixing deck, as he rapped out his words. The more Roots listened, the more concerned he became, because Calvin's lyrics were now dark and wild, true gangsta rap, fêting the blood on the streets, soldiers fallen in battle. It was not a protest against the culture, it was not commentary, it was a homage to gun law. Roots realised that he was listening to the boy's obituary.

He waited until two of the stewards, who were laying a rough fibre covering on the smooth, polished wooden floor, had momentarily gone out front to collect the next roll of covering. This was Roots's moment. He advanced steadily, but not hastily, while all the time Calvin laid bass rhythms under sampled melodies. Still Roots approached, checking one last time that the two were alone, then he pounced on Calvin from behind, snatched Earl's gun from the rear of his waistband, put his right arm around the boy's throat and the gun to his cheek. Still the music played.

"That easy," Roots shouted into Calvin's ear.

The boy couldn't see his assailant and bucked, trying to twist his shoulders without success. Just as suddenly as he had attacked, Roots let the boy go. Calvin spun around, hatred now in his eyes.

"We need to talk some," Roots said.

Calvin reached out to the deck; his fingers knew the spot without him having to look. He turned all the channels of the amplifier right to the top. The infernal, distorted noise pounded in Roots's head; he felt as though his eardrums were being tightened to their very limits. Calvin stood looking defiantly at him, and the Yardie knew that the boy was even nearer to death than he had first suspected. Roots held out the gun. Calvin grabbed it back. There was a moment then when Roots wondered if the boy's fury was sufficient for him to use it. The two stewards ran back into the hall without the covering, drawn by the thumping noise. One of them shouted from the other end of the hall, but his words were swallowed by the din from the speakers. Calvin slipped the gun back into his waistband, then pulled one of the plug sockets below the deck. The music died, and Roots grabbed his arm roughly, dragging him through the back doors and out into the service carpark of the sports complex. The boy struggled on the way out, and Roots's jacket fell to the floor. It became covered in dust and grit. He didn't care.

"You can't do no clash tonight," he said, immediately they were outside.

"It's what I do," the boy hissed back.

"It'll be the last thing you do."

Calvin kissed his teeth, Yardie style, dismissive, disrespectful. Roots pushed him against the outer wall. Calvin lunged towards the bigger man, but Roots shoved him back again.

"You better listen to me good, Calvin Patterson. 'Cos you're going to be hit tonight. By associates of the Mashango. They think you set them up in the last clash."

"I never," Calvin protested, sounding like a schoolboy.

"Tell them. When they spray your system with Uzis, huh?"

"I ain't scared," Calvin shouted.

"I never said you was, my brethren."

The muscles across the boy's face were pulled taut by the confusion of thoughts racing through him. "I ain't afraid to die," he said.

"Any fool can die," Roots told him. "But you man enough to live? Without a gun, little man?"

"I heard about your spar, Peckham. He didn't have no gun when they killed him."

It grieved Roots deeply that on the street now Peckham's memory was just a cautionary tale, to warn young men never to be without their guns. At Calvin's words, the wound inside him that was the loss of his young friend bled again. He suddenly felt weaker, and he leaned against the wall next to Calvin.

"I was only trying to help you," he said.

"Then tell me who killed Earl."

"What do you know?"

"I hear rumours."

"You don't want to hear the truth," Roots said.

Calvin stared unblinkingly at the former don, and the boy's eyes said unmistakably: Yes, I do. Roots tried to gauge just how driven Calvin was about this. He knew that the boy would finally find out anyway. He decided that if he told him now, perhaps he could persuade him to relent.

"The man who's been bragging about killing Earl," Roots said, "he's got a lot of enemies."

"Now he's got one more," Calvin replied. "Who is he?"

"He can't keep running from them. They'll get him."

"Who *is* he?" the boy shouted.

Roots's head dropped, and he tried to think of a way out, but could come up with none. He finally said, "Lifer."

Calvin's forehead crinkled as he digested the information. "I've heard his rep."

"He's earned it."

Calvin now removed the nine-mil from his waistband. He cradled it in his right hand, feeling the pleasing weight of the weapon. "I'll take my chances," he said.

"And what about your mother?" Roots asked.

"She don't care," Calvin said, distractedly, a stock response, as he checked the clip of bullets.

Roots wanted to slap the boy, to slap him so hard that he

cried, for the Yardie had never properly appreciated his mother until she was dead. He wanted to say to Calvin, if only the boy could have understood, that he would gladly now bend down in front of his mother and beg her forgiveness for everything he had done after she died. Instead, he said, "What will it do to her? If you take a bullet? Have you thought of that, big man?" He grabbed the boy's right wrist and squeezed bone and flesh hard so that the boy's grip on the gun weakened. "OK, you want Lifer. Then think smart. You better call off the clash tonight, or you'll never live to get a shot at him."

Roots was relieved when he saw the logic of this wash over Calvin's face. The gun drooped in the boy's hand and the barrel pointed to the floor. Roots knew that he had achieved all he could with the boy, and now it was up to others. He let go of Calvin's wrist, picked his jacket up off the floor, and began to leave. From inside the sports hall, he could hear the echoing shouts of the workmen as they adjusted the floor covering, and he hoped that their efforts would now be in vain, that Calvin would not do the sound clash. As he was about to leave the carpark, he turned.

"Calvin? Your mother? I've seen her," he said. Then he added, "She cares."

"I know," Calvin replied.

Andrea waited until the last of the reporters had abandoned their vigil outside Dawn Harris's home. She waited patiently in her car, sipping at cold Styrofoam cups of coffee, parked in the next street, from where she could see both the mosque and Dawn's front door. Every half-hour or so, she drove around the area, trekking aimlessly through the maze of streets, just killing time, until she once more parked at her observation point. She began to realise just how boring and draining police surveillance work must be.

When it got dark, she was provided with better cover. As she sat in the gloom in the driver's seat, she tried to think about anything except what her father had relayed to her about her mother. She felt as though by telling her about the other engagement he had dug up the very roots of her family life. It was different now — the frictions between her parents had another, deeper cause, and most of all she felt entirely different about herself. Her flesh was capable of such things. It frightened her. She paused to consider how many mother–daughter relationships would have been strong enough to allow the telling of such a thing, and then she realised that the truth was that she knew precious little about her parents. Who they really were, what they really felt about things. These were the people who had brought her into the world, and what did she in fact know about them? But she did not linger upon this, because she immediately wondered if Calvin felt the same way about her. He probably considered her a stranger, too, and this fact upset her more than anything Gordon Chambers had said about her own mother.

Fifteen minutes after the last of the press contingent had retreated to studios, offices or hostelries, Andrea decided that it was her moment to confront Dawn Harris. But no sooner had she got out of her car than a cab raced past her on the road and parked outside the house. It hooted once. Andrea saw the curtains in a top front room move, and the lights go out upstairs. She was now alongside the mosque, on the opposite side of the road to the house. A large man flopped his right arm out of the driver's window of the cab, tapping the paintwork as he waited. She could see that he had a thick forearm, as thick as one of her own thighs, covered in tattoos and finished off at the wrist by a chain-link silver bracelet. Andrea had a moment of startling clarity as she crossed the road near the taxi, noting that the cabbie was watching her in his rear-view. She seemed to float above herself so that she looked down at the lone woman in the middle of a South London road at night, between a mosque and the front door of the mother of a murdered girl. And she asked herself harshly: What are you doing in this place? What can you possibly achieve? She was armed now with such information as Kelsey had been able to impart, but she could just have easily passed it all on to another, more experienced trial lawyer, as her father had suggested. The answer was that she wanted to punish the people responsible for Earl's death, and she wanted to help Dawn Harris find the truth about Nicki. She wanted both these things, but above all she knew that she wanted to take on Hogarth. To go head to head with him, to beat the truth out of him, not because he was a bad man, but because he was in pain, and in a way she did not yet fully understand, the agony she felt inside was inextricably linked with his. She wanted to put Hogarth out of his misery, she wanted to prove to herself that she could do it, because if she could, then she knew that she had recovered from the previous decade, and then she could begin to love herself. She knew that while she still held herself in contempt, she would never win back Calvin's affection.

By the time she reached the front door, Dawn Harris had already opened it, and had stepped out with a patch-work overnight bag in her hand. She was startled when she first saw Andrea's silhouette on the driveway, and then her surprise turned to anger as their eyes met and she realised who this other woman actually was. She put down the bag and double-locked her front door.

"Mrs Harris?" Andrea said. There was no reply. Dawn's back was still turned. Andrea tried again when the woman faced her. "Dawn, please. I want to help."

Dawn picked up her bag, adjusted her thick glasses, and lowered her head as she walked towards and then past Andrea. Andrea tentatively put out an arm, but Dawn simply brushed past, her head still set as if she were charging an invisible target ahead of her. Andrea turned as she approached the taxi.

"Earl Whitely didn't kill Nicki," she called after her.

Dawn paused for a fraction as the words sank in, then she walked even more determinedly towards the cab. Andrea ran after her. She stood between Dawn and the passenger's nearside door.

"Dawn, I think I know who was responsible for Nicki's death," she whispered.

Dawn's eyes were frightening in the half-light of the streetlamps as they filled with disgust for Andrea. She dropped her bag and slapped Andrea. Hard. Just once.

"You all right, love?" the cabbie called out. It was clear he was talking to Dawn.

Andrea was forced back against the cold metal door of the cab, only inches away from the other woman, as Dawn raised her hand again. Andrea braced herself for the stinging impact of the blow on her face. She tried to keep her eyes open but could not, and with her eyelids shut she desperately whispered, "I want to get them, Dawn."

She felt the blow in her mind a dozen times — on her left cheek, then her right, then her right again. But no actual blow fell. When she opened her eyes, Nicki's mother stood in front of her with her overnight bag once more in her hand.

"Who?" she asked.

"It's a long story," Andrea began.

"Who?"

"They allowed Earl Whitely in illegally."

"*Who?*"

"Dawn, I'll tell you, but you've got to listen to all of it."

Andrea glanced nervously at the cabbie as she heard the driver's door open and heavy footsteps behind her on the other side of the vehicle. He rounded the back of the cab and approached the two women.

"Go away!" Dawn screamed at him.

"But I've been waiting."

"Go away!" she shouted even more loudly.

Andrea reached into her pocket, pulled out a £5 note. Gave it to the man. He snatched it from her, then swore to himself as he left. He slammed his door, over-revved the engine, and accelerated off. The two women were now alone as the night wind raced between the row of Victorian semis and the modern tower of the mosque. Andrea expected a barrage of questions from the other woman, but Dawn Harris was silent, though she breathed heavily and her shoulders heaved.

"Earl Whitely worked for them. He was going to expose them. They had to kill him," Andrea told her.

Tears rolled down Dawn Harris's face, past the bottom of her glasses and slowly on down her cheeks. When she finally spoke, it was in barely more than a whisper. "Who killed my Nicki?" she said.

Two weeks later, on a blindingly bright morning, with high, fast clouds and the crisp blue sky of the first days of spring, Andrea stood alone outside police headquarters. The commendation ceremony had ended, and officers, some in dress uniform, others in suits with their families, milled around outside the building. Hogarth was with his wife, Karen, and his daughter. A photographer crouched before them on the steps, trying to capture the family group. Hogarth and Karen stood next to each other, with Abby nestling between her parents. Andrea recognised the girl from the photograph Hogarth had shown her in the coroner's court, but Abby was, of course, much larger now.

"Another one, DCI?" the photographer ventured. "And this time smile? It's not a mugshot, you know."

Andrea shouldered her way through the effusive

crowd, but when she reached Hogarth's family she could not bring herself to intrude.

"Hold me in this one, Daddy." Abby smiled up at her father.

"In a moment," Hogarth said, noticing Andrea. "Hold Mummy's hand."

He moved towards Andrea slowly, turning his back on his wife and daughter. He looks far more tired, she thought. He even looks older, as if his life-clock were racing forward uncontrollably. People stood all around the two of them, but they might just as well have been alone.

"I thought you'd be here sooner," he said.

"It takes time. Legal formalities."

He nodded, and she didn't need to say more — they both knew about legal red tape. By now his wife had come over, confused at his departure.

"It's all right, Karen," he said.

"John?" she asked, worried by the look on his face.

"Take Abby home."

"What's going on?"

"It's all right," he said again.

Karen Hogarth now looked Andrea up and down suspiciously, and Andrea wondered if she recognised her from the tabloid coverage.

Hogarth now addressed her. "You realise there's no turning back from this?"

"For either of us," she replied.

He nodded. "Have you thought," he said, "we both pretend to be doing the right thing. And really, we're serving ourselves. We're accomplices, you and I, Andrea."

With such force of will as she could muster, she tried to ignore his last cutting comment, even though his words were accurate and telling. She removed a folded document from her pocket and handed it to him. For a moment, she and Hogarth were separated only by the length of legal paper in their hands, mere inches between their fingers. She said, "John Hogarth, this is a writ and summons accusing you of assault and battery and causing the unlawful killing of Nicki Harris."

Abby ran up and held her father's leg, looking up at Andrea, smiled widely, on what she believed to be a happy day. Andrea remembered with an aching heart when Calvin was that small and used to dash around beneath her feet at home, and when she used to carry him up to bed when he had fallen asleep downstairs, and the warm, safe smell that surrounded him whenever he slept deeply, and she recalled her most fervent hope for him: that he would have a life not only as good as hers, but infinitely better in any way she could make it. And she wondered if serving the writ would reinforce or damage that hope.

CHAPTER SEVEN

After she had served the writ, Andrea began her preparations for her onslaught against Hogarth in an almost physical way. She realised over the next couple of days, as she spent hour after hour trying to digest the Rules and Orders of the Supreme Court, precedents, and books on civil trial procedure, that it was not just her mind which she needed to strengthen. Her body was weak, too. The words on the page blurred and danced before her eyes. She woke each day with a dull ache at the back of her head, just above the neck, and by the time she had made her way from Hammersmith to the City office, the pain had circled her head and throbbed relentlessly on either side of her temple. When she sat in the firm's law library, hour after hour, through hastily grabbed sandwiches, or at the computer screen reading on-line law reports, her back ached, and it felt as if the vertebrae themselves had all concertinaed one into the other. After two days of solid, but not wholly productive, work, she decided that she had to tend to her body as well.

She agreed with her father that she would spend every other day actually in the office, and would keep abreast of her commercial clients as best she could. In this respect, Siobhan was invaluable, and now that Andrea had insisted that the firm promote her from articled clerk to assistant solicitor she rose to the added responsibility. It amused her that her ambitious, feisty assistant relished helping out with the corporate work, but kept angling to get a piece of the unlawful killing action against Hogarth.

During the days when she did her research and preparation from home, it became Andrea's practice to force herself out of the house at least once. She knew that if she did not enforce this discipline she could go for a week without actually leaving the house during daylight hours. So began her daily run. She did press-ups, too, for the first time in her life, as part of the warming-up routine, though she found that it aggravated her back if she did them properly, so she allowed herself one small compromise and knelt down, then placed her palms on the ground, pivoting from the knee and not the tips of the toes.

She tended to hit the roads around Brackenbury Village during the break she allowed herself for lunch, and after the first week she became mortally bored with doing laps around the rows of Victorian houses in the immediate area and began to venture further afield as her stamina grew. By the middle of the second week she had progressed as far as Chiswick, and although this was not even two miles to the west, she felt as though she were discovering a strange new world, full of leafy lanes and more expensive family homes. As she pounded along the old road west out of London, she thought again about Hogarth and his daughter, and when she remembered young Abby's eyes as she held her father's leg, she felt a pang of guilt. She knew that if she were successful in unmasking Hogarth, Abby would surely suffer from the scandal. There would be tension and perhaps acrimony at home, there would inevitably be a media frenzy, perhaps Abby's friends would tease or bully her at school. All this, Andrea knew, would not have happened if she had not served a writ upon her father. These thoughts were then complicated by her recollection of the first time she had encountered Hogarth as he slammed the still-wet black-and-white photos of Nicki Harris on the interview table in front of

Calvin. Dawn had suffered, too. Calvin had been caught up in the mess. The ripples of the shooting outside St Margaret's school had touched so many of their lives.

Andrea increased her pace, not particularly worried that rain had started to fall, driving herself faster and faster, hoping that in the dryness of her throat and the screaming of her lungs for oxygen she could dispel all these conflicting thoughts. Then, as the low gunmetal clouds burst above her, a dreadful stitch chewed into her side. It was so vicious that she had to stop. The rain poured down on to her face in slanting sheets. She was two miles from home and in pain. She looked around for shelter, but there were only private homes along this stretch of the road, save for two buildings. One was a Tudor-fronted public house, the type once used for horse-drawn coaches entering the fringes of London after a long journey from the West Country. She had no money, she was dripping wet, and she hated entering bars alone. So she ventured into the second building.

It was dark inside the church. The building straddled the apex of three roads like a huge beached ship, and was low and wide, made of Queen Anne red brick. But there were no electric lights on inside; the only illumination came from a bank of candles in a small chapel to the right of the aisle, and from the window arches. Most of the glass in the south and west walls was comprised of stained-glass narratives, whose tranquil, terrible beauty surprised Andrea with their magenta and azure pictures of winged angels and saints and sinners. She looked around, but saw that the church was empty. She sat down on the nearest wooden pew and nursed her stitch with her fingers. Her track suit was soaking and her socks squelched in her trainers. She arched her back and tossed her head back, marvelling at the fine wooden trellis-work of the roof. She had not been brought up religiously, though her mother occasionally used to go off to church alone, and she had never had any religious instruction, like many of her C of E friends in Kent. To her, religion was this rather noble thing that other people did, like recycling waste paper, or walking the Pennine Way. It did not touch her life. And this church was a Catholic church. She had never set foot on Catholic ground in her life.

As her breathing began to normalise into a deep, steady rhythm, the pain in her side began to recede. She closed her eyes and tried to slow her breathing further, and now a flush of hot sweat burst through her skin and she basked in the afterglow of exercise. Slowly, she became aware that she had synchronised her breathing pattern with a steady ticking behind her. When she looked at the back wall of the church, she thought she would see a clock, but instead there was a wooden box against the wall. Knowing that Catholics, unlike most of the serious criminals with whom she had once had professional contact, were apt to confess, she imagined the box to be the confessional. But she realised that this conclusion must be wrong, as two long thin stays reached from the top of the box right up to the roof. She got to her feet and squelched a dozen paces towards the back of the church until she stood in the multicoloured pool of light the west window cast upon the tiled floor. The steady ticking grew louder, and she saw through the window that there was indeed a clock, but it was on the outside of the building. Towards the top of the west arch, the stained glass gave way to plain glass, and she could make out the black-and-gold face of the church clock, protruding on two wrought-iron arms from the exterior wall. There was a brass plaque on the wooden housing in front of her, and she now saw that within the box the timing mechanism rocked backwards and forwards, conveying its unchanging rhythm up the stays and to the hands of the clock.

Andrea read the plaque. It spoke of the clock being dedicated to two sons of the parish in the mid-nineteenth century, of how these two brothers had fallen in the Crimean War, one in 1854 at the Battle of Inkerman, his brother a year later in the siege of Sebastopol. It spoke about how the young men had 'fallen gloriously', and it was those words which troubled Andrea. She wondered whether their parents really believed that, that their children had fallen gloriously; she wondered whether they believed it, not in the public glare of a memorial service or in a church, but in their bedroom, at night, or on those inevitable mornings when they awoke with a start, realising that their sons were not home, and would never come home again. She wondered whether these parents felt any differently about the loss of their children than Dawn Harris now felt about the loss of Nicki, because in the brief meetings she had held with Dawn she had realised that Dawn didn't want revenge, or retribution, or compensation, or even justice. All Dawn wanted was to say goodbye to her daughter. As the two stays moved in time, up a few inches and then down, giving life to the clock face, she told herself that the sacrifices she was makingto win back her son, and the risks that the case against Hogarth would inevitably entail, were nothing. In any event, she reassured herself, a civil action was even more slow-moving than a criminal trial. Now writs had been served and the creaking legal dinosaur had been prodded, it could be months until anything of moment happened.

Soon, Andrea became aware of a man approaching from the far end of the church. Her instinct was to step out of the partially open door to her right and back into the road, but when she saw the pleasant, smiling face of the priest, she no longer felt awkward. She had never associated a church with smiling.

"I'm tempted to ask if you're seeking shelter from the

storm," he said, grinning.

Andrea smiled back, and looked down at her trainers. "I'm sorry for the puddle."

"Not to worry," he said.

"It's a lovely church," she told him, as if he didn't know it already.

"Not a bad office," he said.

She saw that he had a young, puppyish face, with chubby cheeks and bright, eager eyes. It made her feel old. A priest younger than she was.

"Are you new to the parish?" he asked. "I don't think we've met before."

Andrea pointed out of the door, where the weather had not changed. "Rain. I was running. Sorry."

"There's no need to apologise. How far are you going?"

Andrea glanced to her left, up at the stained glass, then further up to the clock face on the outside wall. "I'm not sure," she replied.

That afternoon, after she had a shower, she sat in her kitchen with a steaming cup of hot chocolate. She wore her towelling bathrobe, and her hair was in a towel. Then the front doorbell rang. Andrea picked up the eighteenth-century law report she had downloaded from the on-line law library and continued reading it as she went to the door, holding her cup in the other hand. A small gust of wind crept through the door as it opened, cooling and drying the droplets of water clinging to her legs. Siobhan stood outside, her face pale and strained.

"Just because I'm skiving, it doesn't mean you can bunk off too," Andrea said to her assistant.

"I rang at lunch," Siobhan said, entering as Andrea opened the door more widely.

"I was out jogging."

"I left a message."

"I dashed for the shower. I was soaking." Then she paused, the concern on the other woman's face worrying her. "Siobhan? What's the matter?"

Siobhan shook her head, incredulously.

"What's happened?" Andrea pressed, more anxious by the second.

"It's Hogarth."

"What about Hogarth?"

"He's had the case listed in court."

"Nonsense," Andrea said, "it's only two weeks."

Siobhan held up a fax that had come through from the High Court. "Day after tomorrow. Andy, he's striking out your case."

The next twenty-four hours were the most legally intensive in Andrea's life. First, she buried herself in the law books to try to divine what Hogarth's tactics would be. It did not take her long to find out, and the answer chilled her because it spoke of the man's unshakable confidence. Under an Order of the Royal Supreme Court, Hogarth was able to apply for the writ against him to be struck out, dismissed, if the court could be persuaded that Andrea's allegations were without any proper evidential basis, that they were improperly founded in law or in fact, that they were vexatious and frivolous and scandalous. Andrea saw with great clarity that Hogarth was not simply going to defend himself. He was about to attack her. He was contending that Andrea's legal work was so factually misconceived, so weak, so futile and worthless, that it was an abuse of the process of the court. He intended to humiliate her in public. And all this in precisely the same courts of law in which, a decade earlier, she had lost her son.

By the afternoon before the hearing, the legal arguments were going round and round in her mind. This in itself was not an unusual phenomenon for an advocate. But in those distant days when she had been at the Bar, she had usually been involved in another case the day before a trial started, and if she had had an 'early bath', just a morning's hearing, she would join other counsel waiting on the cab-rank in one of the habitual watering holes of the profession. In such places, moderately good wine would be drunk in immoderate quantities and the usual collection of legal war stories would be told, all with the purpose of dulling the anticipation, nerves and anxieties induced by the impending case. There was a pervasive ethos at the criminal Bar, one she now saw was repugnant and dangerous, which said that the better the advocate in court, the less preparation they appeared to do before the case. Oh, I'm doing just another blagging, as armed robberies were called; just another murder, probably carve it down to manslaughter by diminished; yes, got another rape, but the victim probably won't show — my punter said she was a bit dodgy anyway.

Although Andrea had never actually seen her cases in that light, she had never openly challenged this ruling ideology, and soon her cases merged the one into the other. What, she now wondered, would that woman in her twenties have made of the Nicki Harris case? Would it have been just another, albeit pretty diverting, case? Now, as she paced around her Hammersmith house, the magnitude of her case against Hogarth blotted out everything else in her life. It was not only the most important event she could think of, it was the only event. As she rehearsed her arguments again, this time in front of the mirror, something the received wisdom of the profession warned against, she found that she began to lose her train of thought. Words became confused, key points were forgotten, her posture and pitch suffered as she scrabbled about mentally. She kept glancing at the clock. There were still almost eighteen hours to go, an unbearable expanse of nerve-racking time, since she couldn't even conceive that she might actually get any sleep. Becoming increasingly desperate about her performance, Andrea took a long look at herself in the smoky hall mirror. She decided to take a bold step, and went to see the one person in the world who had the invariable knack of calming her down.

Rufus snipped away at Andrea's hair as she sat on one of his wooden high-backed chairs. She had one of his bed-sheets around her shoulders, and he had positioned the chair next to the sofa so that she had a view out of the high, grime-covered window as he worked away behind her. Suddenly, the snip-snip of the scissors came to an end.

Although she could not see what he had done, she trusted him now as she had done since she had first met the man nearly twenty years previously. He had known her since she was barely more than a girl, and he still treated her like that hopeful teenager of the early eighties. While she hated being treated as a kid by her father, she loved it with Rufus. She didn't even attempt to understand this contradiction.

"Don't know why you need a cut anyway, darlin'," he said. "You'll be wearing your wig tomorrow."

She shook her head.

"Don't move now," he said, pretending to admonish her.

"I'm a solicitor now, remember? We don't wear wigs."

"Just as well you come to the Rufus Patterson Studio, then," he laughed, glancing proudly around his clean but meagre flat, piled with fishing tackle.

"Thanks," she said. "I'm sure the hair's great."

"I ain't finished yet." He snipped one more time flamboyantly, raising his old scissors above her head with a flourish. "Now I finished," he said. He held up his shaving mirror in front of her.

Although it was a tad shorter than she would

have wished, a bit too much like Purdy from the *New Avengers*, Andrea beamed up at the old man. "Hey, I actually look OK."

He shook his head gravely. "No, sir. You actually look beautiful. Darlin', if I was only one hundred years younger and I still had me back, and you hadn't had me a grandson . . ."

"Rufus," she said, getting up, careful to keep the cut hair within the sheets. "You are an old rogue."

"That's my job, ya know," he said.

"God, and this didn't cost me seventy-five quid."

"No, but it costs you a kiss, daughter."

She unwrapped the sheet, lay it on the floor, then kissed and hugged him. She loved it when he called her 'daughter'. Rufus always called things as they were. He had called his wife 'wife' while she was alive, his son 'son', and Andrea 'daughter'. Only for Calvin did he break the rule, since he usually called his grandson 'son'. She wondered if that was just a natural thing, or if in some way the old man looked to Calvin to fill the gap left by his real son, Calvin's father, who rarely saw or even spoke to Rufus.

"You is shaking, darlin'," he said. "You coming down with something? I give you one of my toddies, fix you up soon time."

Andrea compressed her lips, shook her head, as the impending horrors of the next day flooded through her. "Rufus, I'm scared."

"Everyone get scared some time."

"How about scared to death?"

The old man shook his head slowly. "Ain't nothing in the whole world should scare a man that much. 'Cept one thing." He paused, and before Andrea could ask him more, he said, "I remember when I first saw me wife at that church dance back home. I thought, That sister look fine to me. And I know you won't believe this" — a mischievous glint came into his eye — "but I used to be a bit of a ladies' man back then, ya know. So I started across the dance-floor and say, 'Woman, you better be saving them dancing shoes for me.' I held out my hand and she put her little fingers in mine." Andrea saw the old man's eyes cloud with the distant memories, and such was the passion of his words she could almost hear the swell of the band. "Darlin'," Rufus said, "when we danced, and I felt her bare shoulders against me, I was scared right to death. I was so scared I thought my heart had stopped. And I thought, I can't lose this woman. I can't be without her. And I wasn't." He had tears in his eyes, even though he smiled.

Andrea hugged him. She remembered the funeral so well, how Rufus had mentioned the same incident.

"Want me to come to court with you tomorrow?" he asked.

"Would you?" Andrea replied, delighted.

"No problem. That judge dare give my daughter a hard time, old Rufus be up there on his hind legs cussing him out, ya know. Ain't no one going to touch my family."

Andrea's heart thrilled at the words. She had never even been married to Rufus's son, her skin was of a different colour, their daily worlds were so inconceivably far apart, and yet he considered himself inextricably linked to her.

"You is as good family as I got," he added.

Andrea hoped that Calvin would one day feel precisely the same affection for her as she now felt for Rufus. "Have you seen him much?" she asked.

"I go round every morning. But that bwoy, he sleep all day, he's out all night. I think some old vampire gone bit the boy. I'll go round his flat later, cook him up some proper food."

"He doesn't deserve you," Andrea said.

"He my grandchild."

"Still—"

"Ain't that it about families? It ain't just what we deserve."

An hour later, Andrea rang the tinny bell at the Kelseys' front door. She waited, looking at the absurd Swiss cottages in the crescent around her, until finally Kelsey opened the front door, a copy of *New Scientist* in his hands. He appeared to have recovered something of his former self. He was clean-shaven, with a bright, healthy glow to his face, and his dark hair neatly combed. He wore smart casual clothes, and with his intelligent eyes behind the steel-rimmed glasses he had a kind of preppy look, like an MBA student who had popped out of a business school tutorial.

"How's it going?" she asked.

"Oh, OK," he said.

"You're looking very well."

"Bit of distance from it all and all that."

She became aware that he had jammed himself between the open door and the jamb, and had not invited her in. "Did you get the message?" she asked. "Gita said she'd pass it on."

"So it's true, then?"

She nodded. "Hogarth's applying to strike me out tomorrow." Through the mottled glass of the door, Andrea could see another figure standing in the background, one she assumed to be his wife. She moved slightly to her left. She could just see some suitcases lined up in the hall between Kelsey and his wife.

He noticed. "Gita and the kids," he said. "It's best if they stay with family during this."

From behind him, his wife hissed, "You don't have to explain to her." She came to the door and opened it further, so that husband and wife stood side by side.

Andrea gave Kelsey a slip of paper with the listing. "Royal Courts," she said. "Ten thirty."

"He'll be there," Gita said bitterly.

"I'm sorry about this," Andrea replied.

Kelsey's wife stared back at her. "No you're not," she said.

Andrea turned to go, unwilling to impose further on the unhappy couple. But as she walked back down the steep driveway, past the old Citroën, Kelsey called after her.

"Is Hogarth going to beat you?" he asked.

She turned, and realised that this would be how onlookers would perceive the case the next day, a contest between two people, not a quest for truth or justice, but simply this: her versus him. It was now difficult for her to see it in any other light herself.

"He won't win," she said. "Not if you're there."

Kelsey nodded, and she wished it could be as simple as that.

She was now within hours of putting herself on the line in court, and though she tried to still her mind as she got into her car, the legal arguments began to spin once more. By the time she had reached the main road and the hatchback began to grind forward through the rush-hour traffic, she was lost deep in the mire of point and counterpoint. So total was her absorption in the arguments that she failed to notice the car that followed her steadily, always keeping two vehicles between her and it.

CHAPTER EIGHT

The light was beginning to fade by the time Roots and Katherine arrived at the derelict site, and on the other side of the Thames, the north bank, reflections of the street-lamps along riverside walkways appeared as strings of pearls on the surface of the water, and danced to and fro with the swell. He parked the white Golf outside what had once been a small brown hut that had stood guard at the entrance to the complex, and then rushed around to the passenger's door to open it for Katherine.

She laughed at his act of exaggerated, old-fashioned courtesy. "I'm not an old woman," she said.

"But you are a lady," Roots replied.

Gone was his leather jacket, and he wore a knee-length coat of dark cashmere, as dark as the waters now appeared at the end of the site. It did not have buttons down the front but was double-breasted, with a thick woollen tie-up belt. The overall effect was of a type of Cossack coat, far heavier than most people would have worn in early spring, but Roots felt he needed it. For the Yardie this had been the coldest winter he could remember out of the number of cold winters he had endured on this foreign shore. When he was a boy, and had wandered the island in that time of hiding after the first killing, he had heard old men talking of such things, and these men were considered to be wise in their rural communities. Roots had always thought that they spoke foolishness, because the country wisdom was that men chilled from the inside when they knew they were going to die. Yet Roots had never in his life felt so alive. And here at the site of his future studio, with Katherine, holding the preliminary architectural blueprints he had commissioned, he felt as he had in his youth. Then, as now, he had done a dreadful, frightening, courageous thing. Then he had killed a corrupt man, who richly deserved to die, for in the Yardie's moral universe there were some men who had forfeited the right to live. Now he had avenged the death of his spar Peckham, he had cut out the heart of the Mashango in one raid, and had told both Hogarth and Lifer that he was out. So why, he wondered, was he constantly cold?

For her part, Katherine wore a simple waist-length suede jacket, and a pale blue neck scarf. Her hair was down around her shoulders, and Roots marvelled as a whisper of breeze came in off the river and shook the longer strands.

As they reached the broken wall at the front of the building, he turned to her, no longer able to contain his joy. "You see?" he said excitedly. "Didn't I tell you? All it needs is a little work and . . ." He paused, anxious to see the same enthusiasm he felt on her face. He spoke in a deeper patois. "Lickle work, then dis bwoy on his way, honey."

Katherine's lips smiled and her head nodded, but his heart dropped when he saw what was in her eyes. For he realised that she saw just a pile of broken bricks.

"Yes, uh-huh," she said. "It's just so much work."

"I ain't scared of hard work, Katherine." He never abbreviated her name or called her anything but Katherine unless it was a more intimate term of endearment. "I never have been scared of hard work. But this work is honest. Can you understand what that means to me? For the first time in my life, I can do something I can be proud of. I can sleep at night and not worry if the police come or a rival come or any other person come to get me. And OK, it means rolling up my sleeves and getting dirty. I can do dirty." He bent down in front of her, even though it made his expensive coat run along the ground, and rubbed his hands in the rubble. "And I'm gonna mek you dirty, too, Miss Music Executive." He held up his hands right in front of her face, so that the chalky, dust-crusted palms were just an inch from her nose. Katherine shrieked with pretend horror and tried to duck, but Roots was quicker, and as she tried to burrow under his arm his fingers found their target and streaked her face. When she straightened up to face him, he laughed uncontrollably — she looked like an Indian brave.

For an instant she was angry, then a more devious, more determined look washed over her, and she squatted down, rubbed her hands in the dust, and stared up at him with a maniacal grin. "You're dead, Yard Man. Where's that coat?"

Roots began to back away towards the depleted shell of the building, pretending to be scared. "Whoa, sister. This here is cashmere, ya know."

"Was cashmere," she said crazily, laughing. She cornered him against a broken-down wall. Their fine clothes were covered in dust, but neither cared.

"What am I going to do with you?" she said, leaning against him.

"You already done it."

"What?"

He paused as he flicked away a few stray hairs from her face. "Saved me."

The frivolity seeped out of her face as it set in a more concerned gaze. "Saved you?" He did not reply. "Valentine?"

"Saved me a piece of your fine white ass," he said, bursting out into laughter, grabbing her buttocks and drawing her between his thighs, so that her groin rubbed against his. They set about each other with desperate, open-mouthed, uncontrolled kissing. But then Roots suddenly froze. His face creased as his instincts honed in on a sound that was not right.

"What's the matter?" she asked.

Roots wasn't sure what it was, but he didn't like the low rumbling that lay just below the hum of the city, like a subtle bass riff below a strong melody.

"We gotta go," he said.

"Why?"

"I want to see the rest."

He took her hand firmly, no longer the gentleman as his street antennae reverberated with impending disaster. They had made it halfway back towards the Golf when Roots saw the first car. As it skidded round the block of warehousing opposite, the tyres screeched and the car lunged sideways, then it shot towards them. Another car tore around the other corner of the warehouse, also hurtling towards Roots and Katherine. Men hung out of the passenger windows with a nightmarish collection of Macs and assault rifles, Lifer with an Uzi.

"Oh, Jesus," Katherine cried, but he pushed her to the ground and dived on top of her. He rolled her behind one of the half-demolished walls as bullets smashed into the bricks above and behind them, creating secondary ricochets of stone particles, which showered over Roots as he held his head down on her face to shield her the best he could. The noise of the bullets and the screaming engines burst in his head, and the drive-by seemed to him to go on for ever as he squeezed his eyes shut against the sparks of dust, and gritted his teeth so that he wouldn't scream. Then, suddenly, it was silent again. The cars had gone. The air was still, and Roots heard a frightened gull high overhead, cawing. He rolled off Katherine, and the two sat in the rubble behind the wall. He was utterly miserable. For he knew that the skin of invulnerability that had protected him all his life had been peeled away entirely. He had thought for the first time that he was about to die. Even though he had lost count of the gun battles and shoot-outs in which he had walked through a storm of bullets untouched, he had been convinced that he was going to die right there in the rubble by the Thames. And he said to himself that if Katherine had been killed, he would have wanted to die as well. He wondered if she felt the same way, though he strongly doubted it.

But Katherine was so petrified she could hardly speak. He checked her body quickly, ensuring she was not hit.

"W-why?" she stuttered. Her hair was a cloud of dust around her head, and a tear made its way down her cheek, turning the dust and dirt into a kind of mudpack behind it.

"A man wants me to leave," Roots said.

"Then why don't you go?"

"Because I'm not running." He helped her up. Then in a flash his rage at Lifer ripped through his body and he picked up a shattered piece of brick and hurled it back towards the body of the building. It smashed into the jagged remnants of a windowpane, the shards that hung from the top of the frame like icicles. "I've been on the run all my life. From the police, the law, this gang, that posse." He grabbed her with great force, shaking her, even though she was not the object of his fury. "And I ain't running no more. No more, Katherine. I'm not leaving this city. Not till I decide I want to. I'm not leaving this country." He paused, then added, "And I'm not leaving you."

He could see from her face that she was shocked and terrified and touched all at the same time. "Valentine," she cried. "What are we going to do?"

Roots said, "Tell me about Canada."

Andrea took a half-remembered short cut through the

sprawling estate near Kelsey's home in the hope of avoiding the log-jam of traffic in the roads around the South Circular. She drove through block after concrete block in a desolate, hostile urban nowhere, with anonymous tower blocks, identically constructed, on either side of the road, and for street after street. Despite the fact that thousands of people had been crammed into these human warehouses, there was hardly a sign of life out on the streets. No children played in the fenced playing areas, token stretches of green lay neglected, overrun, and were used for illegal dumping of black refuse sacks, and thin access roads snaked off around the blocks with hardly a car in sight.

She made good progress through the practically empty roads, thinking that perhaps the occupants of the blocks didn't have cars, or didn't have cars that had not been vandalised, or simply had no need to drive anywhere. She noticed concrete walkways between the blocks, human flyovers, from one building with its mushrooming satellite dishes to the next. There were even shops in elevated arcades, with takeaways and mini-markets and off-licences with metal grilles, so that, she imagined, it would be entirely feasible to live your life without descending to ground level for days or weeks on end, without walking on or alongside grass or greenery. The idea chilled her and she accelerated to get out of this lost part of London as quickly as she could.

She did not notice the car behind her until it began to flash its lights as she negotiated yet another roundabout. She glanced nervously in the mirror. Then there was the short burst of a police siren, and she saw that the car was a marked area car. She pulled to a halt next to a patch of wasteland, with head-high weeds that were grey and brown. The buildings appeared to have retreated on both sides of the road at this point, to the extent that the nearest tower block was a quarter of a mile away. Two uniformed police officers, a red-faced man and a thin, stick-like woman, approached her. Andrea wound down the window as the male came to the offside. She had left the engine idling, and when she reached for the ignition keys she cursed herself, for she realised that she had been driving without her lights on. It was now dusk. One hundred doubts and questions raced through her mind at the sight of the dark serge uniform filling her window. She couldn't remember if she had renewed the insurance; she was not even sure now when it was up for renewal. What about the tax disc? She glanced across at it, but from inside the car could not see the date of expiry. But how could the police have spotted it if they had approached her from behind? The MoT, she thought. God, that must be it. The Korean hatchback, beloved to her, was an engineering relic of an age without ABS and air bags.

The PC squatted down to look through her window. "Switch it off," he growled.

Andrea turned off the ignition. She tried to smile. "I'm sorry. I must have forgotten to put on my lights."

"Registration. Licence," he said coldly, though his face dripped with sweat.

Andrea glanced at the glove compartment, but she knew instinctively that her documents were at home. It was so easy to break into the hatchback, and there was no alarm, so it was foolish to leave anything in the car, and she simply couldn't remember to take her documents back and forth with her. She was about to explain this to the sullen man when she noticed the WPC in the side mirror. The woman was snooping around the rear of the car.

"I've left my documents at home," Andrea said, trying to get a better view of what the WPC was doing.

The PC placed his leather-gloved hand on the mirror, deliberately obscuring her view. "Get out," he ordered.

Andrea got out, stood defensively against the car door,

and looked up with silent apprehension at the ruddy man. "If I was going a bit too fast, can't I pay a spot fine or something?" she asked.

There was a scraping sound from the rear of the car and Andrea tried to crane her neck to see past the constable, but again he blocked her view.

"What's she doing?" she asked.

"Is this your car exclusively?" the PC asked.

"Yes," Andrea replied distractedly, "but what's she—"

"So no one else has custody or control of it?"

"Yes. I mean no." Andrea stepped left, then right, just a few inches, but the man held up his hand, so that the large black glove hovered inches from her face. "Why is she doing that?"

The scraping sound ended and the WPC joined them at the front of the car.

"We won't have to do her for speeding," she said.

"Thank you," Andrea said, relieved. She immediately realised that her relief was misplaced, for the WPC nodded fractionally at the PC.

"Can you tell me what this is?" she asked Andrea.

She led Andrea to the back of the vehicle, and with every step Andrea's heart thumped harder in her chest. She expected the worst, but still froze with shock when she saw that the rear hatch was slightly open. Just inside was a clear plastic bag. And in the bag was a powder. A brown powder. The PC's body now loomed over her, and she could feel his clammy breath in the cooling air. It wafted in small puffs around her ears as he spoke behind her.

"Does it look remotely like heroin to you?" he asked.

Andrea spun around and was confronted by his implacable façade. The words spilled over from her mind into her mouth as she felt herself losing her grip. "It's not mine. It's not mine," she said.

"Your clients ever come up with that pathetic defence?" he sneered.

And then she realised. She glanced to the patrol car and saw that the number plate at the front had been unscrewed. She glanced around the darkening urban wilderness. There was no other soul in sight, and no one, she imagined, to hear her if she screamed, though in the near distance row upon row of lights from flats up in the tower blocks shimmered at her uselessly. The PC pushed her back against the rear of the car, and she felt his surprisingly bony fingers through the leather gloves, like padded claws. He prodded her on the chest just below the neck.

"This is Hogarth, isn't it?" she asked as defiantly as she could.

"Shut the *fuck* up," the PC shouted. He spat the words at her, and his forehead crumpled with anger so that his hairline moved closer to his eyebrows. "A ten-year stretch," he said. "It's that easy. This time it's sugar. Next time? Well, work it out for yourself." He raised the rear hatch so that it jabbed into Andrea's back painfully, and then he threw a shiny piece of paper on to the sugar bag. The WPC stared remorselessly at her as this was going on, and she lingered after the PC had returned to their vehicle so that Andrea expected another verbal onslaught. But the WPC said nothing. She just stared and smiled grimly as she turned, showing even, perfectly polished teeth. Andrea did not know what to do, and just stood there glued to the spot as they drove away in that infuriatingly slow fashion in which police cars drive through the city streets. By the time the car had disappeared, she was unsure whether they were rogue cops, Hogarth's creatures, or in fact police officers at all. She turned and hesitated over the piece of paper. In the deep recesses of her brain a voice told her that it might be evidence. But evidence of what? The man wore gloves; it would have been wiped for prints. And who would believe her anyway? She lunged for the photo and turned it over. And there on the shiny paper her son's face stared up at her. It was Calvin's arrest photo. From the police station. Only it had been tampered with. A crude marker pen had been used to draw concentric red circles around her son's head. Like a target.

Andrea pulled the plastic bag out of the boot and flung it to the ground. Though one part of her told her to preserve the evidence, the other part, the human part, couldn't bear to have her private space contaminated for a second longer. She stamped on the bag again and again so that the brown granules spilled out in all directions and the sole of her foot crunched them into the tarmac. She turned, her mind spinning with images of Calvin, and got into the car. She tried to ring him on her mobile, but there was no response from his flat. She started the engine and accelerated off, wheeling back around the roundabout, headed for his flat. She tried ringing Rufus's flat as she drove with blinding speed through the maze of streets, her headlights on. The vision of the outside world that appeared through the oblong of windscreen appeared to her no more real than that in a video game. She tried Rufus again when she got to the main road, but there was still no answer. But she trawled up the recollection that the old man had said that he was going round to Calvin's to cook. She flashed other cars and was flashed back as she weaved in and out of the lanes on the dual carriageway, flooring the pedal to close the distance between her car and her son. She lost track of time as she steered with one hand and manipulated the mobile with the other, and before she knew it she had to hit the brakes, stop and reverse, as she had actually gone past the entrance to the carpark to Calvin's block. She ran up to the first balcony, and rang his bell repeatedly. She despaired that there were no lights on and lifted the letter-box, but could hear no noises from inside.

"Calvin? Rufus?" she called. She called their names over and over, but there was no response. She rested her head against the cold reinforced glass of the window next to the door, and tried to clear her confused mind. Should she wait, look for Calvin, or call someone? But there was no one else she could think of calling. The truth, she realised, was that she simply did not understand her son's world. She didn't have a clue about it. It was foreign to her and she to it. She was a stranger, an outsider who was not wanted. And now she found herself between this other world and her own, the world of the majority, the world of institutions and unchallenged assumptions, the world of those who believed they were on the 'right' side of the law, for whom the police were their street soldiers and were on the side of the angels.

She reached into her jacket and pulled out the square pad of yellow Post-Its. She wrote a message on the first, then posted it through the box. Then she thought that with all the junk mail that plagued every part of London the note might get lost. She wrote another, and wondered where to put it. A breeze was getting up, and she feared that if she stuck it to the door it might blow away. Or some idle kid might rip it off for the sake of doing so. But she decided to cover all the options, and stuck the second to the door just above the keyhole, and then wrote a third note, folded it in two, and jammed it into the mouth of the letterbox. She could think of nothing else to do. But as she was about to leave, she turned and looked at the yellow note stuck to the door. It said, 'Phone home urgently. Mum.' She took her mobile phone out of her other pocket, rang Hammersmith and got the answerphone. Using the appropriate security code, she accessed the control options and then pressed 9 to divert all home calls to her mobile.

But when she read the Post-It again, her hand reached intuitively for her plastic pen. The word 'home' jarred. Where Andrea lived was not Calvin's home. She even wondered at that moment whether the house she shared with Cameron in Hammersmith was her home either. But worse than that, the word 'Mum' seemed to her to be false and trite — simply wrong. She couldn't think when Calvin had last called her that; he never seemed to use any name when addressing her. It was always 'you'. She had given birth to him, but that was about it now. The tough first seven years of his life, which she so treasured, were clearly of no import to the boy now. He had jettisoned them, and consequently her too. She looked at the pen in her hand with horror. She wasn't going to do it. She wasn't going to change a single word. He was still her son, and no matter how tenuous their connection now, that gave her the right to be considered his mother. She headed back to the car.

She drove slowly back across the river to Hammersmith, crossing at Putney Bridge and then crawling up the Fulham Palace Road. Now she was glad of the heavy traffic, for she had the phone on constantly, speed-dialling Calvin's flat, allowing five rings, speed-dialling Rufus's, allowing five more rings, then five seconds for a diverted call, then trying Calvin's again. She became so accustomed to the sequence of buttons that she never really knew which of the two numbers she was dialling, but each time the phone began ringing at the other end she prayed for it to be picked up.

By the time she parked directly outside her home, she was so worn out with stress and anxiety that she forgot that she had her house keys with her. Seeing the lights on downstairs, she pressed the doorbell. There were heavy footsteps as Cameron trudged to the front door, and he opened it, wearing an Aran jumper. He had a thick granary-bread cheese sandwich in his hand. When he looked at her, she saw his face drop as he registered her worry. For Andrea, it was just like looking in a mirror. She looked like shit.

"Andy?" he asked.

She bit her bottom lip and closed her eyes as she fought back the tears, then folded into him. He held the sandwich high above her head.

"I can't do it," she whispered, feeling the fine beads of wool against her lips as she spoke.

"What?" he asked somewhere above her. "The case?"

She didn't want to move, not for at least ten minutes if she had her way. She wanted to stay right there with this man who loved her unquestioningly. She wanted to smell his comforting jumper, and feel his chest rising and falling as he breathed. But almost immediately her mobile rang. She snatched it out of her coat pocket.

"Calvin?"

"It's Rufus, darlin'," came the old man's voice.

"Is Calvin with you?"

"No, I'm in his flat. No sign of the boy. What is this note?"

"Jesus, Rufus, we've got to find him."

"What happen now?"

"They threatened me. They've threatened Calvin." She glanced up at Cameron as she gripped the phone so tightly that the flesh in her hand turned white. He watched her in turn, astonished at what he heard. She stared at him as she spoke down the phone to Rufus, and even though Cameron began to pester her with a dozen whispered questions, she attempted to concentrate on Rufus.

"Who?" Rufus asked.

"The police," Andrea said. She felt embarrassed in front of Cameron, as if he were going to suspect that she had gone insane.

"You hurt?" Rufus asked.

"No, but—"

"The boy will be fine. He went to charge up my electric key," Rufus said. "It's so far to go. He volunteer to do it, 'cos his friend lives round the corner there on the high road."

"Do you know where?" When Rufus did not reply immediately, Andrea said, "Can you wait in the flat for him?"

"I'm cooking up jerk chicken. He take too long, I'll eat it."

"They might just be bluffing."

"No point risking it."

"No, but what do we do?"

"You know in boxing when you is most vulnerable? When you're running. We stay put, they won't do nothing."

"Call when he gets there, please?"

Rufus agreed before she hung up. Andrea slowly lowered the phone, and Cameron stood in front of her, amazed and rather foolish with the cheese sandwich in his hand.

"You're sure it's the police?" he said.

She shook her head as she began trembling. All she could see was Calvin walking blithely down the high road and a police van screaming up alongside him, unseen men dragging him into the back. She slowly took the mugshot of Calvin out of her inside pocket. Cameron's face changed as he inspected the red rings of the target.

"Anyone could have drawn that," he said.

"Like the police."

He put the sandwich on the table. "What did they do?"

Andrea took off her coat, then led him into the kitchen, and she told him as she turned on the cold water tap, allowed it to run and then splashed her face with the ice-cold water. They sat at the large rough wooden table and he held her hand. She felt his fingers, so warm, and his grip so sure. She kept wanting to drive back round to Calvin's flat, but Cameron told her that there was no point given the heavy traffic, that it was better to wait until Rufus called. She couldn't keep still. She began pacing around the kitchen, round and round the table, as Cameron sat, often with his head bowed, trying to find some sense, some truth that he recognised in the mess. The mobile lay silently in the middle of the kitchen table, and she glanced at it every few seconds, willing it to ring, or imagining that it was in fact ringing. But there was no further news. Finally, she could bear it no longer and she dialled Calvin's number. She started in fear.

"It's engaged," she said.

"He's probably calling Rufus," Cameron replied.

"Why would he do that?"

"Because he's going to be late?" he suggested.

Andrea shook her head. She knew Calvin well enough to know that this was unlikely. "He never rings when he's late." She tried to redial, but got the same engaged tone. She switched off the mobile completely, then turned it back on and redialled Calvin's number as deliberately as her growing sense of dread would allow. Her breath was held hard in her chest as she waited. The line clicked. Then there was the same engaged tone. Now she was fearful. She held the line for a minute. Then tried again. Still engaged.

"Oh, God," she cried with sudden realisation. "What if it's not engaged?"

"What?" he asked, standing and joining her by the sink, as the dark shapes of the houses behind loomed in a dozen different colours, a filtering of lights through curtains.

It was all becoming frighteningly clear in Andrea's mind, and as people who are recounting a nightmare can do with startling clarity, so she related her theory to Cameron.

"It's off the hook," she said.

"Then the line would be dead, wouldn't it?" he argued,

if only to try to keep her calm.

But Andrea was now beyond this, and was not inclined or able to argue verbally. She rushed back into the hall, to the table where Cameron's business line, the phone-fax, was situated. She took the cream-coloured receiver off the cradle and then dropped it, so that it landed with a thud on the floor and the extension cord twisted and writhed like a worm on a hook above it. She began dialling the number. Even before she completed it there was a recorded woman's voice coming out of the receiver on the ground. "Please replace the handset and try again. Please replace the handset and try again." After two repetitions, the loud warning signal started blaring out of the receiver, bleeping on and off, on and off. Instinctively Cameron went to replace it.

"Leave it," Andrea commanded, so fiercely that he did not resist. She dialled his number on her mobile, then listened eagerly and heard the engaged tone. She handed the mobile to Cameron.

"All right," he said, still listening. "But what are you saying happened?"

Andrea rushed back into the kitchen and grabbed her coat. She took out her car keys and began heading for the front door. She snatched a replacement mobile battery from the charger under the stairs, but Cameron stood in her way. She saw that he had replaced the handset in the hall.

"Come on, Andy, think," he said, holding her.

She speed-dialled Calvin's flat. Then held the mobile, exuding the engaged tone, in his face.

"OK, OK," he said, "but what're you going to do?"

"Go round there."

"It'll take you an hour."

"Think of anything better?"

But Cameron didn't have a chance to reply. They turned around, startled, as the business line rang once, then clicked over to fax mode. There was an assortment of electronic whines and then the shiny roll of paper started to unspool.

"Must be the Paris account," Cameron said unconvincingly.

An inch of heavy type could be seen, just the tops of letters. It was clear that it was a newspaper front page. A date ran along above the tabloid name.

Andrea looked at Cameron quizzically. "It's tomorrow's date," she said.

He shook his head, not knowing what to make of it either.

Inch by agonising inch, the banner headline was revealed.

NICKI'S — MUM — & — THE — POLICE-HATE — BRIEF.

An exclusive exposé by Colin Stackman.

At the end of the first page, there was a slight pause in the transmission. The fax growled internally while Cameron tore off the shiny paper.

"Andy," he said, "we've got to think clearly about this."

But Andrea saw the events of the day with perfect clarity. She saw all the twists and turns, orchestrated by a monstrous hand, that of DCI John Hogarth. The second page began to appear, and Andrea's eyes scanned the words. She couldn't take it all in, but certain key words caught her eye.

POSH POLICE-HATER — ARRESTED DURING BRIXTON RIOTS — HALF-CASTE ILLEGITIMATE SON — NERVOUS BREAKDOWN — UNFIT MOTHER.

Cameron seethed, and his eyes filled with a rage she had never seen before. "I'm going to find that shit Stackman," he said, "and I'm going to fucking kill him."

But to Andrea it appeared as if the eye of the storm had suddenly settled over her, even though she was about to be exposed naked to the world, even though the most cruel invective about her would be published in one of the nation's biggest newspapers.

"Why?" she asked.

"Why?" he cried. "It's slander. It's . . . it's worse. It's bloody lies."

"It's true," she said, moving to rip off the second sheet, even as he tried to stop her. "I am all those things."

"Andy?" he shouted at her, and now he was frightened. "What the hell is going on?"

"I'm telling the truth about Hogarth. He's telling the truth about me."

"No," he said, screwing the first sheet up in his hand.

She started to rip the second sheet off the fax, but he blocked her, then pressed the buttons on the machine, hammering the controls to try to stop the transmission. Slowly, evenly, the paper continued to roll out.

"I want to read it," she cried.

"No," he shouted at her.

He grabbed the fax paper at the same time she did, and it ripped. She tore at the part that protruded from his hand.

"I want it, Cameron," she shouted at him. "Give me the fucking fax."

They struggled in the hall, and suddenly there was a huge crash at the hall window beside the door. Shattered glass flew everywhere as a brick tumbled along the wooden floor, snagging the varnish, until it rolled to a halt.

Andrea ran forward and opened the door with such force that Cameron could no longer stop her. She just glimpsed a customised car as it accelerated down the street away from her front door. She ran out into the cold air and into the street, screaming after it, "You bastards." A vice closed on her chest, constricting her breathing, and she bent double in pain. She fell to her knees, fighting for breath, in the middle of the residential street. Cameron came out and held her gently, careful not to restrict her ability to take in oxygen. Neighbours glanced through curtains opposite; some lights went on, others off. But no one came out to help. This was Hammersmith, this was London, and no one wanted to know.

When she could stand again, Cameron ushered her back inside. He picked up the receiver of the phone-fax, ignored the final page of the tabloid report curling out of the machine, and began to dial: 9–9—

Andrea lurched towards him and grabbed the receiver. She whispered hoarsely, "What are you doing?" She gripped the receiver as if it were a club or a hammer.

"Calling the police," he replied.

"Which police?"

"They're not all like Hogarth."

"How can you tell?" she cried. "They don't wear badges saying 'I'm not corrupt.' It's inside them. A cancer you can't see."

She leaned against the wall and felt the strength draining out of her, so that she slid downwards until she squatted against the wall with her knees practically up to her chin. There was a pause while Cameron went over to the brick. He kicked at it in frustration before he returned to Andrea. He knelt before her, and Andrea saw that he was scared, too. Both of them were silent, their eyes closed, their foreheads resting one against the other, until Andrea's mobile rang. She saw that, after the brick had crashed through the glass, she had dropped the cellular on the strip of carpet that ran from the front door. They looked at each other as the phone kept ringing, a threatening sound now in the silence of the hall. Andrea took the lead. With trembling fingers, she reached for the phone and clicked it on.

"Mum?" she heard.

"Calvin?" For a fraction of a second a pulse of joy ran through her: he had called her 'Mum'. But then she realised almost instantaneously that this fact was not good — quite the reverse.

"Mum, my flat," Calvin continued. "It's burning."

Andrea said nothing in the next few seconds, though she wanted to say one hundred things, while Calvin confirmed the darkest of her apprehensions.

"Gramps," he said desperately, "he was inside."

CHAPTER NINE

Flames climbed into the night sky as Andrea arrived with Cameron at Calvin's flat. There were two fire engines on site, and they aimed hoses into the gaping holes at the front of the building where the window and door had once been. Uniformed police officers stood around, moving on gawpers. As soon as she got out of the car, Andrea was struck by the acrid, toxic smell of burning plastic and synthetics, and the stinging in her eyes. Calvin ran across as soon as he saw her, and Andrea's heart soared with relief. He looked unhurt. His clothes were blackened all over, as if he had rolled around in the ashes of a bonfire, but as far as she could see he was unharmed.

"They've taken him in an ambulance," he shouted at her frantically, referring to Rufus.

"Is he hurt?" she asked. There were sirens now, but in the confusion and chaos she could not be sure if they were ambulance, fire brigade or police, nor whether they were leaving or approaching.

Calvin stood in front of her, breathless, bent over, his hands on his knees, shaking his head. "They don't know how he is."

She moved to hold her son, but he shrugged her off.

"He's here," he said, looking up at her with wide, fearful eyes.

"Who?" she asked.

"Let's go to the hospital?" Cameron suggested in a low

voice, feeling uneasy about intervening between mother and son.

But Andrea now scoured the site with her eyes, looking at the emergency services not as rescuers but accomplices. The firemen were in their protective clothing, so it was easy to dismiss them. She also discounted the uniformed police. And then she saw a gaggle of men in suits. Around the police cars. She began to move towards it.

"Andy?" Cameron said, concerned.

But she did not stop, marching directly towards the police line. She saw detectives messing around, joking to one another as they watched the flames. She saw DS Stevie Fisher pretend to warm his hands by holding up his palms and stretching his fingers at the fire, and there was a burst of laughter from the half-dozen detectives. But as she got within twenty yards of the group, Hogarth came across to confront her. When she reached him, the orange glow from the heat of the fire and the tongues of flame were mutely reflected on his face.

"You did this?" she cried at him.

He was now within touching distance. "You did."

She raised her hand and was about to hit him, but he did not flinch. Not an inch. Her head spun and her teeth ground into each other with fury as she imagined Rufus in the burning flat, as she remembered the brick, the sound of the shattering glass around her front door, the words on the fax. Unfit mother. Half-caste child. As each of these horrors clouded her mind, she wanted more desperately to assault, to set about the man she instinctively knew was responsible for it all. But she could not hit him, because another force, a more elemental one deep inside her, invisibly seized her hand and held it back.

"You see?" Hogarth said. "How much it hurts? That's how much I hurt. For this country."

"Why are you doing this?" she cried.

"To protect us. From what drugs are doing to us." He towered above her, and though she told herself not to be scared, she had seen what he was capable of. "What will it take," he said, "to make you understand the damage you're doing by pursuing me?" He was so close that she heard every syllable, despite the sirens and the shouts of warning from the fire crews and the crackling of the fire and the vehicles rushing to and fro. "Only you," Hogarth whispered to her, "only you, Andrea, can make this stop."

She looked up at his unwavering eyes, deep set and concerned, and she tried not to believe that it was genuine concern for her. "You'll leave us alone?" she asked.

"It's what I want," he replied.

She felt a hand on her shoulder, and when she turned around she saw Calvin fearlessly looking at Hogarth. He put his arm around his mother and said quietly, "We've got to go."

Cameron took over the driving on the way from Calvin's flat to the hospital. The journey took no more than ten minutes, and though Andrea directed them, and engaged in the three-way conversation as she sat in the front passenger seat and Calvin shuffled around in the rear, her mind was stranded in a distant, lonely place. It was a location she recognised at once as the place where she had made the decision years before not to appeal the loss of Calvin's custody. As the car shot through the almost empty South London streets, she was aware of snatches of dialogue: Calvin saying that Rufus had managed to smile briefly at him even as they took the old man away on a stretcher; Cameron speaking on the phone to their friends Peter and Pippa, who were arranging for the house to be made secure; Calvin relating how the detectives cheered among themselves like schoolboys whenever there was a small explosion within the flat, as a light bulb or an electrical gadget blew up. But all the while she thought about

Hogarth's offer, or, to be more precise, his ultimatum. He
had shifted the responsibility on to her. He had given her
the choice. He had empowered her. She could now protect
her family, she could ensure that the onslaught would
stop. All she had to do was to withdraw from Dawn
Harris's case. When they arrived at the hospital and
rushed to Casualty in search of Rufus, she saw the case
against Hogarth in a different light. It was, she now
realised, ultimately futile. Even if she succeeded, what
would be achieved? Nicki Harris would not be returned
to her mother, Andrea's own family would be further
jeopardised, and even if they did destroy Hogarth, how
did she know that there were not a dozen other men
eager to fill his shoes? She recalled, too, in this self-
interrogation, that Hogarth claimed an overriding right to
bend the rules as he did. He claimed to do it to protect
lives, innocent lives, the lives of those vulnerable to drugs.
As Andrea stood at the end of Rufus's bed, as she saw her
son's grandfather lying there with an oxygen mask over
his face, fighting for breath, she was assailed on all sides
by the most debilitating doubts.

When the nurse insisted that the three of them wait
outside in the corridor, Cameron made an excuse to leave
mother and son together. He said he wanted to check in
with Peter about arranging a glazier for the window, and
Andrea appreciated his tact. She needed to speak to Calvin
alone. While Calvin went off to get some drinks, the doctor, an absurdly genial young man, gave her the latest
prognosis on Rufus. Calvin returned a few minutes later.
He handed Andrea a plastic cup.

"Hot chocolate," he said.

It warmed her that he had remembered what she preferred, even in these dreadful circumstances. She took a
sip, but though it was pleasant to wrap her fingers around
the warm plastic, the liquid inside was too hot to drink.

"What did the doctor say?" Calvin asked.

"They want to keep him in overnight. They're worried about the amount of smoke he inhaled."

She could see her son's hand shaking as he struggled to hold on to his cup of frothing black coffee.

"It's my fault," he said.

Her heart ached as she witnessed him tearing himself apart inside. His clothes were soiled and ashen, in stark contrast to the antiseptic cleanliness of the long, echoing corridor. His face was sooty, and Andrea knew what she had to do. She carefully placed her cup on a low, narrow metal table next to the plastic benches along the corridor wall, took a tissue from her coat pocket, wet it with her tongue, and then began to wipe some of the grime from her son's face.

"It's not your fault," she whispered, trying to calm the boy down.

Calvin stared down into his coffee cup. "He was cooking for me."

"Son, it was a warning. To me. To drop the case against Hogarth."

Calvin shook his head, then stopped, and she continued to wipe away the smears of ash and smoke on his cheeks. "You wouldn't have known about the case if I hadn't been arrested."

"That's not the point."

"Then what is?"

"The point is that now we're all involved and the case starts tomorrow."

Calvin looked at her with his plaintive eyes. They were not accusing now, but confused, bewildered by the events that had overtaken him. It was the way she remembered him responding after the custody battle. He had done the same thing then. He had internalised it all, his pain and loss. He had blamed himself for his parents" split, as he now blamed himself for the fact that his grandfather lay in a hospital bed poisoned by toxic fumes.

"I don't want you involved," he said to Andrea. "Not if you could get hurt, Mum."

"I don't care what happens to me."

He paused, then his lips twitched as if he were about to smile, but he just said, "I care."

He put his coffee down on the table right next to her cup, then he hugged her.

Andrea sat with Rufus through the night until she was advised that there was nothing more to be done until morning. It was now the early hours, and Cameron agreed to take Calvin back to Hammersmith in a cab. But Andrea had another task.

When she pulled up outside Dawn Harris's house, she was surprised to see the lights still on downstairs. It was after 4 a.m. The street around the mosque was empty and silent, and the other houses in Dawn's row were in darkness. But as she walked up the short driveway and stood outside the front door, she could hear clanking and banging from within. She went to ring the bell, but then hesitated. On the drive from the hospital, she had talked herself into what she was about to do, then talked herself out of it again. It appeared to her, somewhat bizarrely, that Hogarth had now been joined by Calvin on one side of the argument, and that all that remained in the scales on the other side, the side that advocated going on with the case, was her stubbornness. When, she now wondered, did stubbornness become foolhardiness? She rang the bell.

She saw a shadow at the far end of the hallway, and then there were quick, padded steps as the shadow approached the door. She heard the security chain being slipped on.

"Dawn," she whispered, "it's Andrea."

There was a pause, then the door opened a fraction. Dawn's bespectacled eyes peered out into the night.

"Do you know the time?" she asked.

Andrea nodded. She noticed a smudge across Dawn's face, a white dusting of powder, like flour. Then, as Dawn took off the chain and opened the door more widely, the warm, comforting smell of baking wafted out at her.

"I couldn't sleep either," Dawn said, indicating the kitchen. She wore a white apron tied in a double knot around her waist. It was covered in flour and chocolate splatters. She held on to the handlebars of her daughter's bike, which was still propped against the radiator in her hallway, and Andrea now saw sugar granules at the side of her mouth and above her top lip.

But Andrea was so disgusted with herself over what she was about to do that she couldn't look into Dawn's face for much longer. Her head dropped. But then she wondered how she would have felt if some lawyer, someone she had trusted with a case concerning Calvin, were to visit her in these circumstances. She looked up, moved a step nearer. Lightly took Dawn's wrist.

"Dawn, I can't do the case," she said, hating herself even as she said it.

Dawn's head started back a fraction in shock, then her round, strong face digested the news. "It's a little late to tell me now. We're in court in six hours."

"I know," Andrea said. "I'm sorry. I'll get an adjournment."

Dawn fiddled with the brakes of Nicki's bike. With her flour-crusted hands, she squeezed the metal bar of the handle, then released it, squeezed and released as she thought aloud. "No, I'll do it myself," she said.

"You can't," Andrea protested. "You wouldn't stand a chance." Her words now gushed out, but they were hollow and unconvincing and full of her heartfelt shame. "Don't you see? It's all been a mistake. And it's my fault. I persuaded you to go after Hogarth."

"You said we could win."

"I was wrong," Andrea confessed wretchedly.

"All I want is a chance, to find out the truth about what happened to my Nicki. To find out what the police are doing. Or aren't. I didn't think we had an earthly. But you persuaded me."

Each of her sentences cut into Andrea, making her feel a fraud. "They've threatened me," Andrea said. "I don't care about that. But they've threatened my family, Dawn. My son."

"And they've killed my daughter," Dawn shouted, and she attempted to slam the door. But Andrea lunged into the gap, trapping her shoulder painfully between the edge of the door and the frame. Dawn let go of the door and retreated two paces. It swung open, and Andrea found herself in the hall. Dawn removed her glasses. She wiped her eyes with the back of her flour-covered hand, but Andrea could not see if there were any tears there. The cool air of the early spring night gusted over them from one side, and the smell of baking from the kitchen came from the other.

"The truth is still the truth, isn't it?" Dawn said finally.

"Yes," Andrea replied.

"I mean, that doesn't change because they can frighten us, Andrea."

Andrea was silent. There was no need to reply, as she felt the same.

"You came to my home," Dawn continued, "right here, and asked me to trust you. And I did trust you. Do you know why?" Andrea stared back, and was silent, but this time because she simply did not know the answer. Dawn continued, "I had to trust you because now Nicki's dead,

I've got no one else to trust. Look, I'm not educated like you. I don't understand the courts. The law. But if they try to frighten us off, isn't it more important to make a stand?"

Andrea wanted to reply, to agree with Dawn in theory, to tell her about the manifold differences between the principle and practice of the law, between what it claimed for itself and what it in fact ended up doing. But she saw that to say this would be cruel, would deprive Dawn of the residue of hope in a heart torn by the death of her daughter. She was not prepared to do this.

"So one way or another," Dawn continued, "I'm going to make a stand. For my Nicki." Suddenly she was overcome with fatigue, and her face contorted as she fought back a yawn. "It's gone four," she said. "I'm too tired to persuade you. It's up to you."

She moved a pace towards the door, and Andrea reciprocated by stepping out into the night. Dawn quietly closed the door behind her.

Andrea didn't pass a single car on the short drive to Nicki's school. She parked opposite the main gates, switched off the engine and crossed the road. There was now an impromptu memorial to Nicki outside the school. Flowers were piled in bunches one on top of the other, most of them still in their see-through plastic and paper wrappings. It wasn't the blooms that were important, it was the fact that they had been bought for Nicki in their hundreds, by friends and strangers alike. Children had drawn cards and threaded them into the fencing. A blue balloon filled with helium was tied to the top of the fence and wafted backwards and forwards in the breeze. Andrea peered through the fence and saw a sign on the brickwork of the main school building. On either side of the sign were large French windows, newly painted white, each divided into six smaller squares in a grid. In each of the squares, the children had made and hung a paper angel,

with a podgy white body, a round melon head, and silver
foil wings. They had been stuck to the inside of the window with Blutac. They gazed down into the classrooms of
Nicki's former schoolmates, so Andrea could see none of
their faces. One of them, which was stuck to the top of the
left-hand window, had come adrift at one wing, so that it
hung precariously askance and pointed inadvertently to
the sign on the wall outside. Andrea now looked at this. It
said: CHARITY CAKE DRIVE. SAT 3 P.M.

She winced with guilt as she realised why Dawn must
have been baking. She compared her withdrawal from the
case with Dawn Harris's response to Nicki's death.
Here was a bereaved mother, on the eve of going to
court in the highest-profile case in the land, making cakes
for her daughter's school. This thought, more even
than the dozens of self-incriminations that had laid
siege to her mind, now humiliated, embarrassed and
shamed her. She saw the various pieces of play apparatus
in a fenced area further within the school grounds —
slides and roundabouts, hopscotch squares painted on
the tarmac. She tried to remember an occasion, any
occasion, when she was a girl herself and had played
hopscotch. She could remember none. But the laughter
and screams of children now echoed in her mind as
she recalled that final birthday party with Calvin and
his friends, captured forever in the photograph in her
office desk. We never dare to think, she told herself,
when such photos are taken, that they may be the last
ones, that these joyous moments frozen on celluloid may never be repeated, that they are not the next instal-
ment in the album but the end of the collection. And
she knew with absolute certainty that she would have
treasured someone, anyone, who had stood by her side in
those turbulent months, someone who could have
convinced her not to give up and could have helped her

fight on in court. She realised that she was just that person as far as Dawn Harris was concerned, and it was simply not in her nature to flinch from her responsibility.

Andrea slowly returned to her car and put the key in the ignition. She turned it and felt the engine shudder into life. But she could not drive away. She found that she had not let go of the key, and she turned the engine off again. She sat there and took a deep breath. As the blue balloon swayed above the fence opposite, she remembered how she had been haunted for a decade by her humiliation at the custody hearing, how she had wished one thousand times that she had appealed the decision, even though her lawyers, experts in the field of family law, had advised that her chances were negligible. Slowly, she found that she began to provide answers to her own questions, to deal with her doubts about the case by ignoring them. So what if there were other men to replace Hogarth? They would not even be needed while Hogarth remained untouched and untouchable, so that was surely the first thing to address. She had to destroy Hogarth no matter what the cost, or rather despite the additional cost, as a high price had already been paid. Nicki Harris was dead. Andrea embraced that unbowed side of her which had always wanted to press on, the reckless, irreverent, true side of her which had stood on the streets of Brixton in protest, the side that longed for the truth even if she could not always understand why. It was the side of Andrea Chambers which had defied all advice and opinion and had conceived her child outside the safety of a marriage, with a man outside her culture, and had never regretted the sea change her son's birth had caused in her life. This was the part of her that did what was headstrong, impulsive, passionate and unconventional. It was the part of her, she now realised, that belonged uniquely to her mother.

She sat in the driver's seat of her hatchback and found a few scraps of junk mail in the door pockets. She took out her pen and began scribbling, faster and faster, crossing out some legal arguments, underlining others, cross-referencing from one crumpled sheet of paper to another, as her mind flooded with ideas about how to nail DCI John Hogarth in court.

CHAPTER TEN

The day started brightly outside the Royal Courts of Justice in the Strand. High speckled cloud drifted slowly down towards the Thames estuary and the Channel, while to the west, just a slate smudge on the horizon, a solid bank of low cumulus, squatted sullenly, biding its time before it engulfed the city.

Andrea paused on the traffic island halfway across the four-lane thoroughfare. To her left she could see the rear of the Royal Air Force church on an island of its own in the traffic. To her right was Temple Bar, one of the ancient limits of the City of London, with its gryphon and shield. But it was directly ahead of her, on the north side of the Strand and Fleet Street, that the real action lay. Almost the entire railed area outside the main archway of the Royal Courts was obscured by the gathered media. Cameramen jostled each other for better vantage points, photographers took light readings, and on the small patch of greenery behind the church, a television camera was already set up and a reporter practised a piece to camera. Uniformed police officers tried to keep the mêlée under control, but more media personnel arrived all the time, adding to the chaos and the strain and the arguments. Members of the public were herded behind police crowd control barriers. On the left of the court archway were civil liberties demonstrators, the old peace protesters with something new to shout about. As Andrea began to cross the zebra, she heard them shouting about her case. On the right-hand side of the Gothic archway was the more threatening group, with their anti-immigration banners: KEEP BRITAIN WHITE — END IMMIGRATION — START REPATRIATION. What this had to do with the death of Dawn Harris's daughter Andrea found it hard to fathom. But when she actually reached the far pavement, her brief-bag weighed down with legal papers, she saw just how personal the attack on her would be. A dozen of the hard-core right-wing contingent had pasted the front page of Colin Stackman's tabloid article to pieces of card. As Andrea passed the crowd, trying to focus on the law, the evidence she would call, the fact that this woman before them was the 'police-hate brief' herself swept through the crowd like wind through a field. Suddenly, she was taunted and shouted at. She saw something flying at her, and she ducked as a copy of the tabloid began its trajectory, rolled tight like a missile, then unfurled as it passed her and fanned out on the pavement. Two young women in leather jackets pointed directly at her and screamed, "Race traitor, race traitor." Andrea forced herself not to rise to the bait, but she fumed when she heard men chanting monkey noises, and someone shouting "Here's her son" as a doll with a black face was thrown at her. "She likes it black," a large unshaven man with gold ear studs shouted. Men around him laughed.

Andrea put down her brief-bag. She was only feet away from the entrance to the court building now, but she desperately wanted to challenge this man, to go over and let him know how proud of her son she was. She wanted to hit the smug, racist thug in the face. She was not a violent person, but she felt violent anger now, and her eyes misted with rage. But she kept telling herself that she should save it for the court. It might hurt now, but she had to use the fury, redirect it once she was in the courtroom, right at Hogarth. Flashbulbs exploded all around her in even greater numbers, and she gazed behind her to see why.

And there, getting out of a cab on the jagged lines by the zebra crossing, was Dawn Harris. Journalists crowded around the cab door and surrounded her. A stream of repetitious questions was unleashed at Nicki's mother.

"Are you accusing Hogarth of murder? How far does the cover-up go? What does your husband think? What would Nicki think?"

Andrea fought her way through the pack, to find Dawn upset and intimidated in the centre of the crowd. When Dawn saw her face, there was the same despair in her eyes as she had seen earlier that morning. But now she looked directly at her and smiled, and Dawn grasped her decision without the need for words. A renewed sense of hope suffused her face. As flashbulbs went off all around them, their fingers touched briefly, and the two mothers walked in silence into the Royal Courts of Justice.

Once they had passed into the shadow of the Gothic archway, they went up some stone steps and then through a pair of swing doors. It became darker as they entered the main hallway of the court complex. Ahead of them stretched the high vaulted roof, and the expanse of long, relatively narrow tiled floor space leading up to steps at the other end and the rear entrance to the court building. On either side of the hall were the stone staircases that led up to the courtrooms themselves. The walls were made of a cold, dull grey stone, and the overall effect was of a second-order medieval cathedral with courtrooms and cells where there should be chapels and altars.

Andrea and Dawn waited in the queue to go through the security checks.

"Do you know who the judge is?" Dawn asked her.

"Yesterday the court told Siobhan it was Mr Justice Anwar Singh."

"Is that good or bad?"

Andrea smiled reassuringly. "It's about the best we

could have hoped for. He's a new appointee. Liberal. Keen on the individual freedoms."

"That's good, is it?"

"It's a bloody miracle," Andrea said.

It was now their turn to pass through the security checks. Their bags were put through the X-ray machine, while they were made to step through the square frame of the metal detector. Andrea stepped through quickly and the machine was silent, but when Dawn followed her the sensor buzzed. A woman security guard with a bored, washed-out face approached and made her return to the public side of the detector.

"Coins? Keys?" she asked. Dawn shook her head. "Well, you must have something to set it off," the woman insisted.

Andrea now stepped back through the arch and, in doing so, she set the machine off herself.

"Stay on the other side," the woman shouted at her.

"Is there a problem?" she asked.

"I haven't got anything," Dawn explained.

The woman asked a colleague for a hand-held detector. But before the guard could check her, Andrea spotted it. Around her neck was a large silver locket, just visible above the buttons at the top of her pink shirt. Dawn saw where Andrea was looking and brought the locket out, and when she did so it fell open. On either side of the silver heart was a small picture of Nicki. The first of Nicki as a baby, the second of her in her school uniform.

Andrea put her hand in the small of Dawn's back. "It's all right," she whispered.

The woman brushed the wand over the locket and sure enough it set off the sensor. "Put it on the X-ray belt, then walk through again," she said.

Tears welled in Dawn's eyes. She looked up at Andrea for help. "Andy," she whispered, "I haven't taken it off."

Andrea understood immediately. She went to the guard and began to explain the significance of the locket to Nicki's mother, but just then there was a flurry of noise from out in the street. The swing doors flew open and a group of swiftly moving people, like an army on the march, burst into the court building. Andrea realised immediately that it was Hogarth's legal team. At the front were lowly barrister's junior clerks, pushing two-wheel trolleys, which had files and books of precedents stacked upon them. The books were held in place with wide straps of canvas, with buckles at the top. Next came a phalanx of lawyers, solicitors, articled clerks, and paralegals carrying the briefcases of senior partners, and beyond them three barristers with their black gowns swirling behind them like smoke. Andrea saw Marion Slavin walk in with Hogarth. Her eyes met Hogarth's for an instant, and he stared at her confidently as if to say: Are you ready to give in? She summoned all the fury she had felt when the crowd outside had abused her about Calvin, and forced herself to smile at him. His craggy face darkened, and she knew that he knew what she had decided. He now realised that he had a contest on his hands.

One of the junior clerks muttered something to another of the security guards, and he opened a side gate bypassing the security system. He waved Hogarth and his team through the gate like a porter welcoming an important guest into a five-star hotel. When they had gone, Andrea saw that Dawn had become anxious once more. She took off her thick glasses, as if she didn't want to see Hogarth's team swan along the hallway beyond security. The woman guard set about her again.

"Right," the guard said, "your locket."

As Dawn was compelled to remove the small tokens of her deceased daughter, Andrea whispered to her, "We've still got the judge."

They finally negotiated security, and walked through
the imposing marbled hall. The area resonated with a hundred different voices, as people milled around the 'Lists',
the glass cases listing the names of the dozens of courts
and the judges who had been assigned to them. Andrea
tried to be strong for Dawn, but she found it increasingly
difficult. Apart from the House of Lords, which sat in
Westminster, this was the top of the legal tree: the Lord
Chief Justice, the Master of the Rolls, the Court of Appeal,
the Red Judges of the High Court. They were all here.
The brightest, most ferocious legal brains in the country,
and she felt that they lay in wait all around her. Finally,
she confirmed that the case of Harris vs Hogarth was to be
in Court 2. She checked the plan and saw that it was on
the right-hand side of the building. She moved past
the steps leading to the left which she had been forced
to walk down a decade before. She felt again the
crushing pain that coursed through her drained body as
the judgment of the court rang in her ears. As they now
climbed the steps to Court 2 Andrea wanted Dawn to
know that she was not alone.

"I went to the school," she told her quietly. "There
were so many flowers."

Dawn appeared not to have heard. "They're selling
cakes tomorrow," she said.

"I saw."

"To raise money for the legal fund."

"I keep telling you," Andrea said. "I don't want
any fees."

Dawn stopped just before the top of the steps. She took
Andrea's hand firmly. "Nicki needs a lawyer, Andrea. Not
a friend."

Andrea nodded and understood. When they reached
the top of the stairs, they turned left along a narrow corridor. There was precious little natural light here, and it felt

to Andrea as if they were venturing deeper and deeper into a vast network of catacombs. As she and Dawn walked past the first then the second court, they kept going, until turning left again she saw that a crowd was already milling outside Court 2. The Hogarth team surrounded the entrance. Along both sides of the corridor stood both uniformed police officers and other men in suits, whom Andrea presumed to be detectives. The two mothers had to walk between them, a hostile gauntlet of men, some with truncheons, others, nearer the courtroom itself, with guns. Andrea passed DS Fisher and his overweight associate. Marion Slavin stood directly outside court, her wig low over her forehead, dark make-up like war paint on her otherwise sallow face. Finally, Andrea and Dawn reached the courtroom. On the grey wall next to the doors a slip of white paper was tacked to a small board. It rippled in the chill air that blew down the corridor as Andrea read the printed listing. Siobhan's information was confirmed.

COURT 2. ANWAR SINGH J. 10.30 A.M. HARRIS VERSUS HOGARTH.

She began to believe that they had a chance. Then the court door creaked open and an elderly court clerk stepped out, a legal dinosaur with a bald walnut head and a ripped gown. As Marion Slavin slid smoothly past him he pulled off the old court listing and replaced it with another. The new one was handwritten. Andrea saw that the ink was still wet.

"Oh, Jesus," she said.

"What's up?" Dawn asked.

Andrea looked down at her, trying to be brave, even as she feared the worst. "They've switched the judge," she said. She read the new court listing.

COURT 2. STEPHEN MALVERNE J. 10.30 A.M. HARRIS VERSUS HOGARTH.

She glanced at the ranks of officers further along the corridor. Not one of them moved, or reacted. It was as if they already knew.

"Can they do that?" Dawn said.

"They just have," Andrea replied.

The old clerk looked Andrea up and down. "You in Harris and Hogarth?" He didn't wait for her reply and she realised why. Just beyond the glass door, she could see a seat and on it a neatly folded copy of the derogatory tabloid. "Judge wants twenty mins to read the papers." With that, the man returned into the court vestibule, and picked up his newspaper.

Andrea put down her briefcase. She was going to leave it inside the courtroom, but then she thought better of it. She now knew that there was nowhere safe, nothing that could not be touched or tampered with.

Dawn touched the slip of paper, and her finger smudged the name of the new judge. "What's this Malverne like?"

"Don't ask," Andrea said. When she saw Dawn's reaction she regretted having been so curt. She could feel herself getting back into character as a trial advocate. It was almost as if she were drawing the essence of advocacy, the tough skin, the ability to think in adversity, from the walls of the old court building. Dawn depended on her, and Andrea knew it. She had to take charge.

"Come on," she said. She took Dawn's arm and ushered her further along the corridor, in the opposite direction to the police.

"What are you doing?" Dawn asked, confused.

"Going to work," Andrea said, her mind moving into overdrive.

"What?"

They now reached another stairwell, and Andrea led the way down, taking the steps as fast as she could. "Look, nothing happens in this case by accident," she said, her mind calculating the odds. "They've switched the judge. No," she corrected herself, "Hogarth's switched the judge."

"How do you know?"

"Who was the only person not outside Court 2?" she asked rhetorically, as if addressing a jury.

The women now reached the level of the hallway. At the Strand end, there was an increase in noise as the security guards slowly let the impatient crowds of public and press through. They were going to turn the courtroom into a circus ring, Andrea knew. But she steeled herself to be ready for it. She had to use the press, she had to address the crowd as well as the tribunal of law, she had to find a way to use this public platform, an arena that a few weeks before had appalled and frightened her. She led Dawn across the floor of the hall and over to the left wing. This was the part of the building that she feared the most, the part that had haunted her in the aftermath of losing Calvin. She checked the court floor plan on the listings board.

"So why have they switched the judge?" Dawn asked, trying to keep up.

"Anwar Singh is a liberal," Andrea replied. She pointed to another staircase and set off again. "Down here."

"And Malverne?" Dawn asked.

"And he's not," Andrea said. She vaguely recollected that Malverne had been in the news within the previous twelve months. He had made some disparaging comment about a woman complainant in a rape case, or something like that. She couldn't be sure for the moment, but she was certain that Malverne was bad news. She had to find a way to combat him. "In here," she said, holding open another set of doors.

Dawn peered into the dark interior of the room, at the

lines and lines of bookshelves. "You need another book?"

"A special book," Andrea said, closing the library doors.

The room was wide but not very deep, and Andrea imagined that above her bewigged barristers rushed to and fro holding red-taped briefs. It felt to her as if they were journeying into the bowels of the building. It seemed that the library had been temporarily relocated, since many books were still in boxes, piled precariously against the right-hand wall. Two desks had been set up, one for the librarian and one for private study. Each had a brass 'Home Office' reading lamp, with an adjustable shade of green glass. There was a mouldy smell, the smell of damp carpets. Andrea approached the librarian, who sat behind the desk on the left-hand side of the room. The woman was younger than Andrea but wore a cardigan of green cashmere, draped precisely across her shoulders, a single string of pearls, and had the pinched face of a hen pecking at some corn. A young male barrister stood in front of her, intimidated.

"I've already told you once," the librarian snapped, "the Sewerage Statutory Regulations are at the end of Aisle four."

"But I'm afraid I can't find them." The young man twirled his wig nervously in his left hand.

"You do know how to use a law library, I suppose?" the woman replied haughtily.

Andrea hovered on the edge of this encounter, aware of the ebbing time. She couldn't wait any longer. "I'm sorry, but could you help me?"

"I'm dealing with another query," the librarian said.

"I know," Andrea replied. "And I'm sorry to interrupt. But I've got no time."

"Learned counsel never have any time," the woman replied, having another stab at the hapless pupil at the same time. "If learned counsel bothered to prepare their authorities properly then they wouldn't always be in such a hurry."

Andrea simply couldn't afford to engage in an argument on this. "Please. Just tell me. If you've got a copy of *Who's Who*."

"I'm dealing with counsel," the librarian persisted.

Andrea turned to the young man. "You don't mind, do you?" she asked. He shook his head, relieved that someone else was incurring the wrath of the fearsome guardian of the law books.

The librarian said nothing. She turned to a box next to her desk and took out a couple of reference books with exaggerated care. She dusted the second one, a concise *Dictionary of Legal Terms*. "I can't find it, I'm afraid," the woman said without looking up at Andrea.

Andrea gazed into the box and saw the familiar red spine. "But it's there," she protested.

"That's an old edition. If you go across the road to the Inns of Court libraries, you'll find—"

"This'll do," Andrea said, reaching into the sacred box and removing the thick volume.

The librarian huffed, but Andrea tried to ignore her. She took the book, turned and saw Dawn Harris's bemused face behind her. "Bear with me on this," she whispered. She put the book on the second desk, turned on the reading light and began to flip through.

"Right, here we are," she said. "J, K, L, M. Malverne, Mr Justice." Dawn crouched over the table from the other side, and glanced up at Andrea, her thick glasses illuminated like two green ashtrays. "Mr Justice Malverne," Andrea read. "Eton, Oxford, surprise, surprise. Judge of the High Court. President of . . ." She broke off and looked at Dawn with the satisfaction of someone who has just had a flash of inspiration and solved a thorny clue in a cryptic crossword. "President of the Police Benevolent Fund. VP

of the Police Widows Foundation. The Police Shooting
Club. The Police . . . I think," Andrea concluded, "he is
quite into the police."

The librarian pointed her beak-like nose towards
Andrea and told her to be quiet.

"So what can we do?" Dawn whispered.

"Maybe one thing," Andrea said. "But it's risky."
She looked at her watch. "Come on. Kelsey should be here
by now."

When they climbed back up to ground-floor level, the
entire hallway was packed with protesters from the two
sides of the argument. Members of the public pushed or
heckled, police officers threatened to evict them all, there
were scuffles and taunts.

There was no sign of Kelsey. As they navigated their
way through the crowd a second time, Dawn said, unconvinced, "Maybe he's just lost."

Andrea stopped, then sat on one of the stone benches
cut into the wall on the right-hand side of the hall. She
dipped into her brief-bag and removed her mobile phone.
"Stand in front of me," she said.

"Why?"

"You're not supposed to use mobiles in here. Not
today."

With Dawn standing guard, she dialled Kelsey's home
number. She looked at the phone puzzled, then dialled
again.

"Nothing," she said.

"Perhaps he's on his way, then."

"The line's dead," Andrea said, trying not to let her
trepidation affect her voice.

"He's our only witness," Dawn said desperately.

"I know, I know," Andrea said, dropping the cellular
back in her bag. "There's got to be a simple explanation."
There were dozens of simple explanations, and they all

bore the unmistakable stamp of Hogarth.

Dawn pulled at her sleeve. Andrea realised that the usher was now standing at the top of the staircase, shouting, "All parties in Harris and Hogarth to Court two." He caught sight of Andrea sitting at the foot of the stairs in the hall, but did not bother to address her personally. He just repeated, "All parties in Harris and Hogarth to Court two."

Andrea could see that Dawn was trying not to panic.

"All parties to Court two," the usher shouted. "Judge is coming in."

"Any ideas?" Dawn asked as calmly as she could, given her trembling voice.

Andrea nodded. "I'm thinking." The images that swirled before her eyes were not positive, encouraging ones, but visions of defeat.

CHAPTER ELEVEN

The courtroom, although Victorian, evoked an earlier, starker era, of 'bloody assizes', and senior judges touring the country dispensing justice and orders of execution. The front half of the courtroom was panelled in dark wood, but towards the public benches at the rear the walls were bare stone, not smooth and worked, but granular, like the rustication outside medieval Florentine palaces. As Andrea entered, she found banks of dark, hard wooden benches, from the back of the court where they were at their highest, toppling down to the well of the court, the low point of the room. On either side were fifteen-foot-high bookcases stuffed with the case reports of the laws of the land. At the front of the lowest bench were seats now reserved for the mass of press and the law reporters, the only people in the room who were able to stretch out their legs. The front row was designated for Silks, for QCs. The next row back was for 'junior' counsel. This was where Andrea had practised a decade previously, and was the row into which Marion Slavin now effortlessly slipped.

As Andrea slowly took out her legal texts and blue notebooks, she glanced up at large Gothic pendant lights of heavy wrought-iron hanging down from the high ceiling of the court some fifty feet above. There were long, narrow windows of leaded glass, through which precious little natural light penetrated the body of the courtroom. Across the well of the court was the clerk's desk below the judge's bench, the highest point of the court. A high-backed leather chair had been placed in the centre of the Bench, and there were two doors, one on either side of the chair, in the back wall. There were thick royal blue curtains, which could conceal these doors if necessary, but the judge's personal clerk now tied back the curtain on the right hand side. Above the court, was the royal coat of arms, the lion and the unicorn, and the two French injunctions: *Honi soit qui mal y pense*; *Dieu et mon droit*. Andrea had entered one of the innermost sanctums of the law.

She told Dawn to sit to her right, so that she was separated from Hogarth by Andrea. As she endeavoured to get her notes, and thus her mind, into some kind of order, she was constantly aware of Hogarth's gaze, watching her with his heavy, deep-set eyes — never saying anything, just watching. Such was the crush behind her that the court had arranged for members of the public to cram into the side aisles, and chairs were brought in from outside the courtroom. Every crevice filled up with curious, angry, expectant people, many of them police officers in uniform, others, like Fisher and Brigson, there to represent the CID. There were high-ranking Met officers in dress uniforms, and Andrea felt as though she were totally surrounded by the forces of law and order.

Then, in the row ahead of her, Marion's black gown swirled and she moved to her right, momentarily obscuring Andrea's view of the front of the court. She turned to face her. "Why don't you drop it now?" she said.

Andrea shook her head.

"So you're ready to go ahead right now?" she asked, as if she knew perfectly well.

"I need some time," Andrea said. "I haven't got any witnesses."

"You should have thought about that before you went after Hogarth," Marion said. She glanced at the huge detective, but he sat impassively.

"I mean," Andrea stressed, "I haven't got any witnesses at court at the minute."

Marion laughed arrogantly and loudly. It seemed as though her crusted face would crack. "It's the same thing," she said.

Just then there was a knock at the very front of the courtroom and the clerk to the court shouted, "Court rise."

All around Andrea people got to their feet. Conversations were cut off. People moving backwards or forwards in the aisles froze in their places. All was silence and stillness until Mr Justice Malverne entered theatrically. If the packed public arena had been the venue of a heavyweight title fight instead of a court case, Malverne would have entered with flashing lights and ominous music. But as Andrea stood and watched, there was no sound except his slow, heavy feet on the Bench above the court and the ticking of an old clock high on the wall to her right. Malverne's robes of office, his blood-red gown, his bell-bottomed white wig, the ermine cuffs, all set off his imposing face with its bramble-like eyebrows and long sideburns curling forward towards his large, loose-lipped mouth.

The judge solemnly bowed to the court, and then sat slowly, so that his personal clerk could push the high-backed chair further under him. All around Andrea, people followed suit. Andrea was the last person standing, since she realised to her horror that she had not put on her solicitor's gown. She grabbed it out of her bag, sending her mobile phone tumbling on to the seat next to Dawn, and pulled it on. She couldn't stop herself glancing up at the judge. Malverne affected not to notice but eyed her with evident disgust.

The court clerk sitting below the Bench stood. He turned to the judge. "The only case in your list today, My Lord. Harris versus Hogarth."

Malverne grunted morosely. His overgrown eyebrows appeared to loom right out into the court. "Are the parties ready to proceed?" he growled.

Marion stood. "Yes, My Lord," she said sweetly, bowing gratefully as Malverne grunted his approval.

The court was deadly silent as Andrea rose. In her own head, she could hear her pained breathing, and the piston of her pounding heart. All around her were Hogarth's massed legal experts. There were piles of law books, turrets of case files, a posse of senior policemen and experienced barristers and solicitors. She had ranged against her some of the most creative, ingenious lawyers in the country, and Hogarth was backed by the largest police force in Europe, with an annual turnover of nearly £2 billion. She glanced down at Dawn, who sat alongside the aisle, intimidated and overwhelmed by the awful majesty of the law. Dawn fingered the locket around her neck. That was all Andrea needed. It gave her confidence, and a reason to dare. She thought about the children's tribute to Nicki Harris outside the school, the paper angels in the windows, and she heard once more the laughter of children at play, of that birthday party so long ago. She decided to opt for the highest-risk strategy. She half closed her eyes in an attempt to eliminate the crowded aisles to her left and right from her peripheral vision, raised her chin slightly so that she could stare directly at Malverne, tightened her stomach muscles, and felt the devastation that Dawn Harris felt but could not articulate in public.

"Before we proceed with Mr Hogarth's application to strike out our case," she said confidently to Malverne, "I have a preliminary application."

Marion Slavin shot to her feet, indignant. "I've had no prior notice of this," she hissed.

"Nor I," the judge added in a pained voice.

"And I had no notice that there would be a change of judge," Andrea riposted defiantly. "I have been given no reason why Mr Justice Anwar Singh has been substituted at the last minute."

Malverne leaned forward and clamped his large fin-like hands together. "If my brother judge is ill, it's not a matter for you, Miss . . . Miss . . ." He glanced down at a slip on the Bench next to him, looking for Andrea's name, while all around her she saw opponents itching to hold up a copy of the tabloid. "Miss Chambers," he said finally.

"It is a matter of the gravest concern to me," Andrea replied instantly.

"Why?"

"Because Mr Justice Anwar Singh was the appropriate tribunal to hear this case. And . . ." She paused. She wanted the words to hang in the air, wanted the next words to have as much force as she could muster. They were not to be aimed at the judge so much as to the public and the press. "And you're not," she said. "My application is that you should disqualify yourself."

There was an ominous murmur around the court, but Malverne did not reply at first. His lips parted as he appeared to gulp down a lungful of air. His cheeks visibly reddened. Other lawyers around Andrea winced and sat back as far as they could in their seats, or tilted their heads to one side so that they disappeared behind the turrets of files. Andrea stood alone in court with one intention. Not to tame this judge, but to incense him. She had to provoke a storm. She had to buy time to find Kelsey or it would all be over.

"I submit you disqualify yourself for bias," she added.

Finally, Malverne could contain himself no longer. His face shone with a clammy sweat in the artificial lights, but his words were cold. "Miss Chambers, you are

stretching the very definitions of impudence and professional misconduct."

"With great respect," Andrea replied in a flash, her
voice offering no respect at all, "I am trying to ensure that
not only will justice be done, but that justice will be seen
to be done."

"*Don't* presume to patronise me," Malverne shouted.

"This is a case alleging police misconduct of the most
grievous sort. I submit to the court," she said, in fact making her submission to the press contingent, who scribbled
down her every word eagerly, "I submit that it is simply
not right, that it flies in the face of fairness, for the judge
of law and fact to be so closely linked to one of the parties
in the litigation."

"Linked?" Malverne shouted. "I'm not linked to
anything."

"But you are not a stranger to the police. To police charities. And our case will be that the only thing that can save
DCI John Hogarth from the weight of the law is that: wilful charity to the police."

There was chaos in court as people agreed or disagreed,
argued or discussed Andrea's revelation. She glanced
around at the increasingly restless crowd and felt that her
strategy was beginning to work. If some of these people
were incensed, then Malverne had to know that the public would be incensed by press reports of his background.
But it was a matter of a judge's discretion whether or not
he chose to disqualify himself. If Malverne declined, it
would be virtually impossible to appeal the decision. She
had to take him out now.

"I could cite all the police charities with which
you are closely linked," Andrea said. "They are
conveniently set out in *Who's Who*." Several journalists
rushed out of court in search of precisely that.
"Has Your Lordship seen a copy?"

"Miss Chambers," Malverne raged, "you are playing with fire."

"No," Andrea replied. "I'm not playing. At all. Now I can cite the propositions of law that dictate that you should disqualify yourself, but I imagine that the court is perfectly well familiar with them."

"*Nemo judex*?" Malverne recited, enunciating the Latin perfectly.

"*In causa sua*," Andrea added. Then she translated for those members of the tabloid press without a classical education. "No one shall be a judge in his own cause."

"I think I learned that on my first day studying law, Miss Chambers," Malverne scoffed. "But you patently appear to have forgotten that I am a judge of the High Court. I have no cause. Except the advancement of justice on behalf of Her Majesty, which I was endeavouring to fulfil before you made this scandalous submission to me. Scandalous is a word with which you should be abundantly familiar, since according to your opponents, it allegedly infects your entire litigation. Now, on the papers before me—"

"Which you've had for almost a full twenty minutes," Andrea interrupted.

"Which I have read sufficiently to grasp that those acting for DCI Hogarth seek to strike out your cause of action as being fatally flawed and an abuse of the process of this honourable court. That is the essence of the scandal, is that right, Miss Slavin?"

Marion nodded. "Yes, My Lord."

"Very well," Malverne said with satisfaction. "Firstly, I reject entirely Miss Chambers's submission that I should disqualify myself."

"Then I seek an adjournment pending an appeal of your ruling," Andrea said, trying to think of anything that would delay the case.

"This is a matter of my discretion," Malverne said, "which is rarely open to scrutiny on appeal, as you should know," he added.

"I do know," she replied. "But this is a classic case of appealable discretion."

She knew that this would stretch Malverne to his very limit, and she was not wrong in her assessment. It seemed to her that as he leaned forward over the Bench, he would have preferred to have jumped down from his place and battered her into the ground for her extreme discourtesy.

"You dare to contend, in my court, that my discretion is—"

"Yes," Andrea persevered, trying to hold on to her resolve, trying to think of her son, of Nicki Harris. "I say this is a *perverse* exercise of discretion. Legally speaking."

Instead of replying immediately, or even attempting to silence the crowds, Malverne picked up his pen and wrote slowly, almost painfully, holding it like a surgeon's scalpel. Little by little the public murmurings died away. Andrea stood there, trying to think back to her time at the Bar, trying to get a handle on what Malverne was doing. She glanced down at Dawn, who sat shell-shocked at the hostility and venom flying backwards and forwards between the judge and her lawyer. She briefly smiled, and Dawn tried to smile back.

Finally, Malverne finished. "I've made a careful note of what you have said about me, Miss Chambers. We shall revisit your conduct when I have disposed of the current proceedings."

"I understand," Andrea said, trying not to sound affected by the judge's threats.

"Now," he said, "I should like to know what evidence the plaintiff in this action can call before me today to substantiate the allegations against DCI Hogarth."

The ball had been batted back to Andrea, and all eyes

now studied her again. As she tried to think of a way to put Kelsey's non-attendance in a less damaging light, her veneer of self-belief began to wear thin. She imagined the walls to the courtroom closing in on her and her chest tightened. She recalled how in a similar courtroom on the opposite side of the main hallway she had stood in the witness box as Lawrence's counsel had fired salvo after hurtful salvo at her. Her own barrister had said beforehand that his intention was not to intervene, to demonstrate to the judge that Andrea could take any invective that the opposition could hurl at her, and prematurely she had agreed. So she languished as the opposition put to her every misdemeanour imaginable. Hadn't she dropped Calvin down half a dozen stairs once? No, he was climbing them, she had tried to stop him. Wasn't she stopped by the police and breathalysed for drink-driving with Calvin in the car? No, she had been drinking with her friends, but she was under the limit. Had she ever smacked Calvin? Lost her temper with him? Broken down weeping when he had cried night after night? Had she taught him anything about black history? Didn't she know absolutely nothing of value about black culture? Wasn't she taking tranquillisers? Under prescription? Wasn't she addicted? Could she cope? Wasn't she an unfit mother? These questions and the painful echoes of many, many others now assailed her, and the strength of mind that she had struggled so hard to find deep within herself began to falter.

"I have no witnesses at court," Andrea told Malverne, "but I have a sworn affidavit from DC Mark Kelsey, formerly one of DCI Hogarth's subordinates."

Hogarth, several feet to her left, turned around to look at the back of the court. He met Fisher's eyes, and Fisher nodded.

"I want live evidence," Malverne said. "I want to hear from witnesses on oath. You are accusing a decorated senior police officer of causing the unlawful death by assault and battery of the very young girl whose murder he was investigating. Is that right?"

"Yes," Andrea replied.

"So how do you intend to prove it?"

"I shall need some time," Andrea said.

"But you've had time. And now you haven't got any more time. The reputation of one of the most respected officers in the whole of the metropolis, and by implication the repute of the organisation he graces, is at stake. Either you convince me that your case has some basis in evidence, or I will strike out your case."

Andrea glanced down at Dawn, and she saw tears rolling down the woman's face. "Sitting next to me," Andrea said, "is the plaintiff in this action, Dawn Harris. Mrs Harris's eight-year-old daughter, Nicki, was gunned down outside her junior school even as her mother was getting ready to collect her. My client is married to a serving officer in the Metropolitan Police and they have separated in the most acrimonious fashion as a result of these events. She has believed in the police all her life. The force has provided the family with a home and with food on the table. It has been their lives. So can we — even for a moment — begin to imagine the courage and conviction that Dawn Harris required to serve a writ on someone with John Hogarth's reputation? Someone her husband admired. Someone she admired. What feat of resolve must it have taken for her to cut herself off from friends and family to bring this case to court? And all the time, she knew that these proceedings will not — cannot — bring her daughter back. Nothing can. So all she asks of this court, all she asks of Your Lordship, is to give her a proper opportunity to have the truth told. To find out how Nicki Harris died. To find out why she had to bury her own daughter. And to do that, we're going to need a little time. Dawn Harris will have the rest of her life to speculate about what happened, but she has just this one chance to find out the truth."

When Andrea stopped speaking, there was total silence in court.

The judge glanced at the clock. "You have one hour," he said. He rose from the Bench. As he stormed out, Hogarth shuffled two paces to his right.

"You'll never find him," he whispered to Andrea with cold, sad eyes.

"How do you know?" she replied.

"Because he doesn't want to be found."

He joined the rest of his legal team as they filtered out of court. Dawn wiped the tears from her flushed cheeks. "Thank you," she said to Andrea.

Andrea took her hand, remembering how just a few hours earlier that morning they had been covered in flour. "It's not the end, Dawn," she told her.

"You've tried everything," Dawn said.

"Except one thing," Andrea replied, thinking how she would put her last hope into action. "One thing," she repeated.

CHAPTER TWELVE

Roots Johnson woke up to what he believed in his half-sleep was the sound of the surf rolling on to the Jamaican beaches around Black River. He marvelled at the changes in the colour of the water as it receded from his view on the beach: the yellowing, sandy, bubbling water ebbing after a wave had broken, the bottle green of the water near the shore, then the black water that ran over the coral reef a few cricket-pitch lengths out, and finally the sky blue of the distant seas, all the way to the coast of Central America. He had swum out to the reef the day after he had arrived from Kingston. The coral was so treacherous that there were the skeletal remains of two wrecks impaled on its razor-sharp spine. Young Valentine Johnson stood on the coral bed as the tide began to retreat, no longer on the island of Jamaica, now on a tiny island of his own, apart from everyone else. Suddenly, there was splashing in the water around him, fins in the water, circling him, and the twelve-year-old believed that he had been surrounded by sharks. Only when the dolphins began to leap out of the water playfully did the boy relax. Even though he was barely out of childhood, young Valentine was sober enough to know that the appearance of the dolphins was not a sign. He had killed an evil man and then he had been circled by dolphins, but in the mind of the streetwise youth, the events were entirely without portent. But when he thought about the horrific sight of the Kingston police-man bleeding to a lonely death in a festering back-street gutter, with rats crawling over him even before he was actually dead, Valentine told himself that he would never die like that.

"Hey," Katherine said, her hair dripping as she came out of the shower. "Is anybody home?"

Roots found himself lying in her studio bedroom, naked, with the duvet barely covering his muscular body. Above him, the stars of light in the ceiling had gone out, and the eggshell-blue walls appeared darker than he remembered from the night before. Perhaps, he thought, it was like a man coming into a house after being out in the blinding sun, finding everything dark while his pupils remained small black points in his eyes. For Roots had believed himself to be back near that Black River beach, a twelve-year-old boy standing on the coral and gazing at the sea under the Caribbean sun.

Katherine towelled her long hair dry. She had a larger towel wrapped around her body, but nonetheless Roots had a good view of her thighs. He smiled, catching himself staring at her shapely legs, then looked away. She glanced up.

"Why can't we stay at your place?" she asked.

"You wouldn't like the décor," he said.

She climbed on to the bed, and crawled over to him, the towel beginning to come away from her still-dripping body. She let her lips hover enticingly inches from his. He smiled and kissed her delicately on the cheek. She sat on him, her legs apart, her groin and his separated only by the thin cream sheet. He rubbed her cheek with the back of his hand.

"Seconds?" she whispered.

He smiled, but said nothing. She rolled off him.

"It's OK," she said. "It's just disappointing to find out, that's all."

"What?"

She smiled wickedly. "That it's not true what they say about black men."

"Sister," Roots replied, "there ain't nothing true what they say about black men."

There was a silence between them, and Roots put his hands behind his head on the pillow, but that made him feel even more self-conscious and awkward.

"You're nervous?" she finally asked.

"No," he replied.

She turned and rubbed his chest. "Liar."

"Yeah, OK, guilty. I'm nervous, ya know."

"Valentine," she said, "everyone gets nervous going to see the bank manager."

"Yeah, but they haven't got as much riding on it as me."

She picked up her towel again. "Haven't they?" she said. She watched him as he tried to close his eyes and recapture the good feelings from his Caribbean daydreams. It didn't work.

"I can hear your mind," she said. "Click-click-click, like a computer downloading. I've never known a man who's so noisy when he's silent."

He laughed at the thought, opened his eyes and rolled over towards her. He had hoped to join in the banter, to make some perceptive but amusing comment about her, some small observation regarding something he had noted in their short time together. But when he looked at her lying on the bed, he instantly remembered her prostrate behind the wall of the derelict site after the attack by Lifer and his crew. He couldn't mess about.

"What?" she said.

"I'm just figuring out what to do, what to do about Lifer," he said. "It ain't just business now. It's personal."

"I know what to do about it," Katherine replied. He saw that her face had lost its playfulness, and that she now spoke with total conviction. "What you do," she said to

Roots, no longer touching him, "what you do about Lifer
is nothing. Nothing at all."

In Roots's world sitting back and allowing a man to
fuck with your life or your business was not an option.
"Yo, Katherine," he said, "always stop me, too, when I
make suggestions about your records."

There was a fierce intensity in her eyes, a burning
desire to convince him of her point of view. "No, no," she
persisted. "Look, you told me that Lifer had enemies. Well,
leave him to them. You've only got to deal with Lifer if you
stay here. And you don't have to. You can go — with me.
To a new country. To a new start, Valentine. Where we
don't have to be who we were in the past."

"Where?" he asked, becoming infected with her growing sense of hope.

Katherine nodded towards a large framed photograph
above the bed. His heart swelled as his eyes drank in the
vast horizon in the picture, the flatland with crystalline
rivulets, the scattering of wet trees on the snowline, the
mountains rising from the earth, in row upon jagged row.

"Canada," she whispered.

Roots yearned with his entire heart for this safe,
untouched place.

Katherine now held his cheeks in both her hands. Her
eyes burned into his, and he wished that he could believe
every word she said, that if she believed it enough, then it
would come true. "We can do it," she told him, "we can do
anything we want."

"But what about my music?"

"Build a studio there."

"And leave London to Lifer?"

"Leave him to his enemies." She got up from the bed,
draping the sheet around her like a toga, and went to a
chest of drawers under the high dormer window. Roots
looked up through the glass at the purple-black storm

clouds that were now slowly climbing over London. The sun disappeared suddenly, and he reached over to the bedside table and flicked on the tortoiseshell lamp. The umbrella shade gave off greens and reds and blues and yellows. When she returned, she silently handed him an envelope. It was a white A3-size envelope with Katherine's name printed on the front. The flap at the back was open. He noticed now an anxious look in her eyes as she watched him, and he knew that she wanted to see his first reaction to its contents. He had no idea what it could be. He fingered it briefly, then reached in and pulled out two folds of shiny paper.

Roots glanced up at her, astonished. He had told himself not to react, to remain placid, not to hurt her if he could help it, but now he could not mask his surprise. "Katherine?" he asked.

"They are returns," she said. "It's better that way. They're less suspicious."

Roots looked down again at the tickets from Heathrow to Toronto. One was in Katherine's name, the other was made out to John Valentine.

"I figured you'd be able to obtain a passport in that name," she said. "Let's just get over there, then we can decide."

Roots was torn.

"Well, do say something," she said, standing above him.

Roots got up from the bed. He went right up to her, smelled the soapy cleanliness of her body, and put his arms around her neck. "I don't know what to say," he said.

"Say you'll come."

"I can't promise it. Not now. And I ain't going to lie and pretend. You deserve better than that."

She broke free angrily, and burst out crying. "You liar, you liar," she sobbed. "I don't deserve better. I deserve just this. A 'not now' bullshit answer."

He tried to touch her, but she hit his hand away. She dashed over to the wicker bin that stood next to the chest of drawers, snatched an empty champagne bottle out of it, held it by its neck, and brandished it in the air like a club.

"This is why," she cried. "This is why, Valentine."

When he saw her pain, how she tormented herself about her drinking, he had to let her know that the problem was not to do with her, but with himself. He braved the bottle and grabbed her.

"It ain't that, baby," he said.

"I disgust you," she wept.

"No, no, honey. I disgust myself." He let her go and found the carved wooden chair in the corner over which he had flung his clothes. He reached deep inside his coat pocket and pulled out a gun. "No matter what I try to be, Katherine, this is what I am."

"Oh, Valentine," she cried.

Roots looked down at the weapon he had carried since Lifer's attempt on their lives. "I hate what I have become, Katherine, but I know it *is* what I am. And one way or another I'm going to have to sort this t'ing with Lifer."

"And that's more important than me?"

Roots's head felt as if it would explode. He sat on the bed with the nine-mil in his hand, resting on his thigh. She sat next to him.

"What are we going to do?" she asked.

"You go to Canada. I'll join you when I've . . . finished up here. I'm seeing the bank today and—"

"You won't come," she said, holding the hand with the gun above the wrist, showing that she was not scared of it. "I don't want to be apart from you."

He was about to say the same, began to say it as lovers do, when she put her free hand to his lips. "Valentine, I *don't* want to be apart from you again." And now her words carried a charge that he had never heard from her before. She was building up to something, some further, devastating point, but so inexperienced was he in the field of emotional warfare that he could not see what it was. He could see the moment he met another dealer, a grass from another posse, a bent cop, just what turned in their black hearts, but now here he was touching a woman he loved and he was helpless to know what was coming.

He waited, knowing that the logic of the moment indicated that she should speak next. There was a break in the clouds overhead, infinitesimal, as if someone had shone a momentous spotlight into the room, then the black base of the storm clouds filled the dormer once more. He was aware of his breathing, of the fact that she seemed to hold her breath. He felt her fingers tremble as she touched him.

"Valentine," she said, "I'm going to give up drinking." Then she added, "I'm going to have to."

She hesitated long enough for Roots to become nervous. Then she said, "I think I'm pregnant."

Roots's mind swirled in confusion, but she simply bit her lip and nodded, her eyes wet with the earlier tears.

Andrea's car screeched to a halt right opposite Hogarth's police station. There was a yellow line on the road, and it would be a serious breach of security to abandon a car outside a police station, but she simply did not have any time. The clock was ticking and Mr Justice Malverne intended to strike out her case within the hour. She had thought about calling the station in advance, had picked up her mobile and then put it down three times, but ultimately she had decided against doing so, for she didn't want to give any advance warning of her arrival. Instead, she had phoned Calvin, who had just returned from the hospital to Rufus's flat. He was busy getting it ready for the arrival of his grandfather. Rufus was about to be discharged.

Andrea ran up the rough stone steps that led from street

level to the station entrance, upon which she and Rufus
had first encountered DS Stevie Fisher on the night Calvin
had been arrested, on the night Nicki Harris had been
killed. She had entered the station then with immense trepidation, but now she rushed in consumed with rage. She
burst through the doors, breathless, and stopped at the
desk. There was no one there. She shouted until a surly
young officer with prominent dark eyes came out.

"I want to see Sergeant Miah," she gasped.

"Oh yeah? Why?" the young man asked insolently,
looking her up and down, his top lip curled.

"Look, I don't have time to explain."

"Then you won't see him, will you?"

Andrea banged the desktop. "For God's sake."

"Let's calm down before we get arrested, shall we?" the
officer sneered.

"Look," Andrea continued, "if he's not on duty, tell me.
But if he's here I've got to see him."

"Your name?"

Andrea hesitated, looked down, and in that moment
the policeman worked out who she was. He was lifting the
counter when Miah appeared.

"It's all right, Paul," the Asian sergeant said, then he
turned to Andrea. "Outside."

It was getting darker as the storm front reached this part
of London south of the river. Andrea and Miah stood on the
station steps.

"You realise they'll all be watching us?" he said.

"I don't give a damn," Andrea replied. "Where the hell
is Kelsey?"

"You have to ask that?" Miah shouted back. "After all
that happened to you last night? Think what they'd do to
one of their own."

"The case collapses without Kelsey. He promised me
he'd be there."

"And you promised me you wouldn't compel him to testify."

Andrea looked at the sergeant's precisely combed hair, at his pristine uniform, in a different light. "You're one of them, aren't you?" she shouted.

"I came to you," Miah replied.

"You've infiltrated our case to ruin it."

"I tried to help you."

"Then where's Kelsey?"

"Where he belongs. With his family. With my grand-children."

"There is no case without him."

"And they have no life if he goes to court."

Andrea's eyes misted with fury, her body trembled with rage as she recalled the suitcases in the hallway of Kelsey's home. But his actions did not tally with the sin-cere man she had met, the man who had slowly burnt his relics of life in the force one by one before her eyes. "I don't believe Kelsey is a coward," she said.

Now the sergeant screamed at her. "Who the hell do you think you are?"

"Nicki Harris's lawyer," Andrea screamed back.

Several officers, uniformed and plainclothed, gathered at the station door and looked out at the two of them. The sergeant took Andrea's elbow and marched her down the steps to street level.

He looked back over his shoulder. "Look, I can help you," he whispered. "Mark's told me everything."

"So?" Andrea asked, confused.

"So I can say that I saw it all. I was in the station that night. The duty states will prove that."

One part of Andrea saw in these words the faintest flicker of hope for the case, but another part of her was appalled. "You're prepared to lie?" she asked. "To perjure yourself?"

"Now you're speaking like a lawyer. This isn't about the law any more, is it?"

"You'll commit perjury to prove my case?"

"To protect my family," Miah said resolutely. His eyes were clouded with the wretchedness of his position and his head shook slightly, as if he had to force the words out of himself. "I can stop your case being derailed. For today. For now. While you go off and find other evidence against Hogarth. So that he won't just win — like he always does."

Andrea felt sick with temptation. She so wanted a lifeline, but she wondered if she could live with herself if she grasped this one.

"Come on, Andrea," Miah said. "It is the truth. It's just another person telling it."

With the pounding of her heart, with each individual heartbeat, Andrea felt the clock ticking down to Hogarth's victory. "Don't you see?" she pleaded with the Asian man. "If I call perjured evidence, then Hogarth will have won anyway. Whatever the verdict."

"And that's what Nicki Harris deserves, is it? To have Hogarth walk away unpunished?"

Andrea shook her head. "I don't know, I don't know," she cried. "But I do know that it would defile her further to call lies in her name." She knew that there were no circumstances in which she would use Hogarth's methods, so that left her with one final chance. She fixed her eyes on the sergeant with all the passion she could muster. "You told me that you joined the police to do some good," she said, speaking quickly. "And I look at you, Sergeant, and I see someone who can still do that. So, please. Just tell me where Kelsey is."

She saw that the sergeant had finally grasped that his next decision would either end the case or give her one final shred of hope. His resolution to protect his family was weakening, and she knew she had to strike again.

"Nicki's mother is sitting in the Royal Courts of Justice in tears," she said. "All she's got is me. And all I've got is Kelsey. But unless you tell me where he is, I've got nothing. She's got nothing."

She became aware that the police officers had come out of the station entrance and were now only feet away. The sergeant looked at them, looked at her. His face was contorted with the agony of indecision. The officers began to come down the steps. The sergeant grabbed her hand.

"Commercial Road," he whispered.

He gave her the number and she squeezed his hand hard with relief.

"God help me," he breathed. Then, "Be careful," he said, "they'll follow you."

Andrea raced back to her car and shot away from the station, seeing in her rear-view that the sergeant was engulfed by his angry colleagues. She sped through the streets, overtaking daringly, outside and inside. She crossed the river and headed east from the City. She peered at the infrequently marked street numbers on the boards above the shops. As she negotiated the increasingly heavy traffic, she saw silks of every conceivable colour draped in the windows, almond-coloured mannequins like a troop of oriental dancers frozen in the middle of their alluring routine. She saw fruit and vegetable importers with their produce piled high on tables in front of their shops — green mangoes, coconuts, plantain, chillis, both red and green, hanging in huge bunches from hooks above the doors. And then finally she saw it. A shop piled high with huge grapefruits, waxy green limes, brilliant oranges. To the fury of the queue of drivers behind her, she pulled her car to the kerb, left the hazard lights flashing, then ran into the shop. She looked at her watch. There was barely twenty minutes until the court sat again. The air was sharp with the smell of the fruit, but there were no customers in the shop, nor

any staff. A round metal stool stood at a counter at the far
end where a portable television was propped on an old,
battered metallic-grey video. The television was tuned to
the Asian cable channel. In the grainy picture, she saw
three men sitting in a far-off studio arguing vehemently in
a language she did not understand. She called out, but
there was no response. But when she did so again, a small
elderly man in a tight brown suit with a blue woollen
jumper under the jacket came out. He wore glasses, and the
stubble on his face shone like silver. He smiled toothlessly.

"I'm looking for Mark Kelsey," she said.

"There is no Kelsey," he replied, still smiling.

"DC Mark Kelsey," Andrea said. "Sergeant Miah gave
me the address."

"There is no Kelsey," the man repeated, though now the
smile had vanished.

Andrea saw the blinking eye of the digital clock on the
video machine. It clicked over one more minute and she
began to lose control. She spotted a side door behind the
counter.

"Kelsey?" she shouted. When she met with no
response, she made to go around the counter to try the
door. The elderly man stood in her way, and though she
towered over him, he stood his ground.

"Now you go," he shouted.

"*Kelsey*," Andrea cried out.

"I call the police," the man warned, now beginning to
manhandle her back towards the door.

Andrea was about to shout out again when DC Mark
Kelsey appeared from the side door. The elderly man let go
of her and his head drooped. Andrea made towards Kelsey,
but he just raised his hand. The only sound came from
Kelsey's wife, Gita, who now emerged from the back room,
weeping as she held one child in her arms while the other
clung desperately to her leg. Gita Kelsey stared at Andrea

with condemnation, and at that precise moment Andrea felt that she deserved every bit of it.

Kelsey said his goodbyes, kissed his children, then joined Andrea in her car. Within minutes, she found herself caught in the traffic around St Paul's and blasted repeatedly on her horn and flashed her lights. She had her mobile propped in the crook of her neck. It gave off a constantly engaged tone.

"Jesus, I can't get through to the court," she said frantically.

"We'll be there in five minutes," he said, with the unhurried tone of a man not anxious to rush to his own execution.

"We haven't got five minutes," Andrea said.

The court was back in full session. Dawn Harris sat alone. Mr Justice Malverne leaned forward and propped himself on his ermine-cuffed arms.

"Well, Mrs Harris," he said, "we've given your counsel five minutes more. And I feel in the absence of your advocate that it's only fair that I give you the opportunity to say anything you wish. Is there anything?" His tone was surprisingly compassionate.

Dawn shook her head, and sat numbly.

"Miss Slavin?" Malverne said.

On cue, Marion Slavin stood, pulled her gown around her shoulders, and said, "The submission on behalf of DCI Hogarth is that these scandalous proceedings should be struck out forthwith as an abuse of the process of the court."

"I suppose," Malverne said, "that if this were a horse race, you'd be claiming a walk-over, Miss Slavin?"

Marion nodded, and extended the metaphor. "These proceedings should be put out of their misery," she said. "You have my skeleton argument. Can I proceed with my second point first?"

Malverne shook his head. "I don't need to trouble you."

Marion took her seat and grinned at Hogarth. But the DCI glanced at Dawn uneasily.

The judge now adopted his most reasonable tone as he read from the notebook propped on the Bench. "In this case, the defendant, DCI John Hogarth, seeks to strike out a cause of action essentially alleging unlawful killing. I shall outline the germane facts in considerable detail later in my judgment, but I wish to summarise the bare bones of my conclusions at the outset. This court had insisted, in its wide-ranging discretion in these matters, and due to the uncommon gravity of the allegations, that a proper foundation in live evidence should be laid before the tribunal if the plaintiff should wish to proceed. This the plaintiff — or should I say," he said, nodding in an entirely token fashion to Dawn, "this the plaintiff's legal adviser has abjectly failed to do. Consequently, even taking into account everything being proffered on behalf of Mrs Harris, and I include, *inter alia*, affidavits, arguments and written pleadings, I am driven to the firm view that this court has no alternative but to stop this case."

There was a mutter around the court. But when Malverne looked up, he saw that it was not a reaction of appreciation or dissent at his judgment, but astonishment from the mass of humanity gathered before him, whether case-hardened lawyers, streetwise policemen, or members of the public. And the cause of the astonishment was Andrea. Standing at the door of the court with DC Mark Kelsey next to her.

CHAPTER THIRTEEN

Andrea had asked the question twice without success. She gazed across the well of the court from her position in the third row, over the bobbing heads of journalists seated at the front of the court, and then across at Kelsey. He stood in the witness box, and seemed like a fugitive suddenly caught in the dragon lights of his pursuers. She glanced briefly at Hogarth, who now sat with his arms crossed tightly across his barrel chest. On the seat next to him she noticed a thin strip of foil-backed plastic. It must have fallen out of his pocket without him noticing. It was only when he quickly picked it up that she realised it was paracetamol.

She had led Kelsey quickly through the formalities of his evidence — his name, rank, postings. But he had seized up when she turned to the subject of Hogarth. Twice she had asked him about his attitude to Hogarth, and twice he had stood there in silence. It troubled her that he appeared not just unwilling to respond but, on a more fundamental level, incapable of answering.

"Mr Kelsey, please," Andrea said. "The court is waiting." Still no reply. She lowered her voice and said, "I know how difficult this must be."

At this, Marion Slavin shot to her feet precisely as Andrea had anticipated.

"My Lord," she snapped, "that is an utterly unnecessary comment."

Malverne nodded gravely. "I will ignore the comment,"

he said.

Andrea used all her strength of mind not to look at the judge. She stared hard at Kelsey, saying, "But you can't ignore it, can you? You know how difficult it is, don't you?"

"I object to this," Marion shouted. "It's irrelevant."

"Why?" Kelsey finally said.

Andrea's shoulders dropped a fraction, releasing the tension. She leaned forward, bending marginally closer to Kelsey, trying to show him that she was on his side, that she would not abandon him. "Tell us what it's like," she said. "Tell the court how difficult it is to go on the record against a senior officer."

"Any officer," Kelsey corrected.

"Any officer," Andrea said in sympathy.

Kelsey shuffled forward as far as he could within the confines of the box. "I looked up to him. We all did. The DCI was a legend within the force."

"And did your view change?" Andrea asked. Kelsey nodded. She repeated the question, adding, "You must speak aloud for the record."

"Yes, it changed," he said quietly.

"How do you regard him now?"

Kelsey paused. "I don't regard him," he said, thinking about it, feeling it. "He regards me."

There was a murmur around the court.

But Kelsey continued, "Every time I close my eyes I see him. Watching me."

Marion Slavin was on her feet voicing her objection, but Andrea spoke on above her. "Why did you stop looking up to DCI Hogarth?"

"Because of what he did to Earl Whitely."

Andrea found herself being drawn into the vortex of emotions around the court, but she fought to think like an advocate, to direct the proceedings as best she could. "Earl

Whitely was charged with the murder of Nicki Harris," she said, for those in court without a detailed knowledge of the case. "What did DCI Hogarth do to him, and when?"

"On the night Nicki Harris was shot," Kelsey said.

Andrea itched to have Kelsey tell it all, all in one burst. She wanted to know more about the man who had threatened her family. She glanced at Hogarth and he held her stare, his eyes defiant, seeming to say to her: Is this the best you can do? What have I done to you? How little you can do to me. She knew as she stared at Hogarth, with a witness about to expose him to the world, that she wanted it to impact on him as much as seeing Rufus in a hospital bed had wounded her. She wanted to hurt him.

"Yes," she said, coolly, "on the night my client's daughter was killed, what did DCI Hogarth do to Earl Whitely?"

Kelsey's face flushed crimson. "He had him assaulted." He then turned to Hogarth for the first time and, when he spoke, his voice was that of a pupil to a teacher, a son to a father, a parishioner to a priest. "How could you do it, sir?" he asked, his voice perplexed.

All eyes darted towards Hogarth. Andrea was amazed by the detective's composure. To all the world it was as if Kelsey had praised him, had expressed his heart-felt admiration for his senior officer. But Andrea could see from her vantage point that Hogarth fiddled nervously with the painkillers in his pocket. Slowly, she was getting to him.

"DCI Hogarth was supposed to be investigating the murder of Nicki Harris. Why did he need to assault Earl Whitely?"

"To silence him," Kelsey replied.

"About what?"

Kelsey hesitated, thought, suddenly felt unsure about himself, and said in a broken voice, "I was, er, told—"

Marion Slavin rocketed her objection. "This is blatant hearsay, as Miss Chambers should know."

Andrea scoured her mind for a reply. She dropped her head slightly, knowing that in the old days she would have shot off a riposte without thinking. But she was still not up to full speed.

"It is hearsay," the judge agreed.

Suddenly, a connection was made in Andrea's mind between this courtroom and a dusty legal text read grudgingly years before, when she was pregnant with Calvin and her back hurt as she sat in the law libraries, and she had to buy shoes a size bigger. "It's not hearsay," she protested, "not if the statement forms part of the furtherance of a conspiracy to commit a crime. Then it's *prima facie* admissible, as Miss Slavin should know."

Marion Slavin subsided, stung by Andrea's riposte. For his part, the judge could see no way round it. She was allowed to continue.

"What were you told?" she asked Kelsey.

"To keep quiet," he replied. "About what I had seen in the cell block. About the fact that Hogarth said Whitely was his informer. He wasn't meant to inform on the DCI. Whitely worked for Hogarth."

There was a breathless silence in court. Everything and everyone hung on Andrea's next question. The clock ticked. Dawn fingered her locket. Andrea saw that Kelsey was eyeing the Bible on the clerk's table in front of him.

"What work did Earl Whitely do for DCI Hogarth?" she asked, thinking back to Earl's frantic words to her in the Magistrates' court, moments before his death, how he spoke about being a 'trigger'. Kelsey did not respond at first. "What work?" she repeated.

"I . . . I don't know," he said. "I mean, I'm not sure. Oh, God, I don't want to lie. There were so many rumours."

Andrea inspected him, wondering if he had been got at. She decided to try another tack.

"I don't want you to lie," she said firmly. "Just tell us

what you know."

Kelsey no longer looked at her. His head was bowed and his fingers drummed on the front of the witness box. "The next day," he said, "ICU came to the station."

"ICU being the Internal Complaints Unit," Andrea explained.

"Everyone guessed then. Earl had been previously arrested on other charges. Then he was arrested on the Nicki Harris. Then ICU turn up."

Marion rose to her feet. "This is speculation," she said.

"OK," Andrea said, "let's deal with facts. Why had Earl Whitely been arrested?"

Kelsey felt more confident again, relating what he was sure about. "Earl had been seen with a gun shortly after the shooting. He was arrested because we believed he was present."

"Where had DCI Hogarth been at the time of Nicki Harris's shooting?" Andrea asked.

"He was out. On the street."

"When did he reappear at the station?"

"After she was dead," Kelsey answered quickly, then realised what he had said. He glanced at Dawn. "I'm sorry. After Nicki was hit."

It occurred to Andrea that she had conducted the entire examination of the witness without notes. For the moment, she couldn't think of anything else she could actually ask Kelsey without proper legal objection. She flicked her blue notebook open on the bench in front of her. When she did so, she realised that she had completely forgotten one of the most telling points in her favour. So excited was she that she wanted to shout out the question, but she reined her eagerness in. Slowly, she closed the notebook and cleared her throat. "Have you any experience of firearms?" she asked.

"I have a pink card. I'm an authorised firearms officer."

"It is an undisputed fact that the bullet that killed Nicki Harris came from a Carbina SP." Andrea paused again, watching the bobbing heads of the journalists as they scribbled down the detail. When they looked up again, she said, "What in your expert opinion was the most common use of the Carbina SP?"

Kelsey spoke very quietly. "It was a police gun," he said.

There was a buzz around the courtroom as Andrea sat down. Dawn took her hand lightly, and Andrea realised that hers was drenched in sweat. Then Dawn moved further along the row as a young man pushed in next to her. Andrea smiled when she saw Calvin, but was then immediately concerned. She leaned forward across Dawn. "How's Rufus?" she whispered.

"Not so good," Calvin whispered back, his face grey with worry. "They're keeping him in. He wants to see you."

Andrea glanced at the court clock as Marion Slavin got to her feet. "It's almost lunch," Andrea said.

"You've got to go now," Calvin said, then he broke off when he saw that Hogarth was watching them the way a boxer stares down at an opponent he's already knocked to the canvas.

Andrea thought about asking the judge to adjourn early, but Marion Slavin turned around and began her cross-examination of Kelsey.

"Are you still a serving police officer?" she asked.

"I'm still in the force," he replied diffidently.

Marion cocked her head in an attempt at some amateur dramatics, pretending that the answer was a complete surprise to her. "Oh, so you're on full active service?"

Andrea could see Kelsey's fingers began to fidget. It was just about the worst moment of any case, having your witnesses cross-examined, seeing them disembowelled before your eyes. As she watched her opponent, she decided that Marion Slavin was the type of forensic surgeon who wouldn't use anaesthetic.

Kelsey was still mumbling his reply. "I . . . I'm on indefinite sick leave," he said, as if it were his fault.

"But why?" Marion said, raising her voice, looking around the courtroom like a street vendor offering up a once-in-a-lifetime bargain. She waited. The expectation lay heavily in the air, until she cut it with her next salvo. "I'm not a medical expert, Mr Kelsey, but you don't look particularly sick to me. You're not at death's door, are you?" Kelsey looked back at her sullenly, and Andrea gritted her teeth, urging him to fight back. But it was Marion who spoke next. "So why are you on sick leave?" she demanded.

Kelsey was silent, and his silence appeared to everyone, including Andrea, to be a final, guilty capitulation.

"Isn't the truth that you have every reason in the world to lie about DCI Hogarth?"

"No," Kelsey said feebly. He looked helplessly at Andrea, asking her to throw in the towel, but she couldn't stop the onslaught, and her guts churned as she realised that Marion Slavin must have obtained some truly devastating ammunition.

"Isn't the truth," Marion continued, "that you are currently suspended from active duty pending . . ." She paused, picked up a thick file of papers, read from them. "Pending an investigation by ICU yourself?"

Kelsey stared in shame at the floor. Andrea was aware of the court doors opening to her left, and two men walking in. Given the press of people, she could not see who they were, but Kelsey could.

"Haven't you been reported to ICU for receiving corrupt payments?" Marion barked at Kelsey. "From a criminal group, a so-called Yardie posse called the Mashango."

Andrea saw Kelsey's eyes water and his hands curl into fists as the usually placid, contemplative young man was gripped by hatred and shame.

"You were reported to Detective Superintendent Mason and Detective Sergeant Woodbridge from ICU, weren't you?" Marion pressed.

Andrea saw the two men step out of the crowd and stand in the left-hand aisle along the bench from Hogarth. She recognised the smaller man, the one in the moustache, from the computer video clip she had downloaded in her office with her father. For the moment, she couldn't remember what he had said.

"You took a bribe," Marion continued.

"I had no choice," Kelsey shouted.

"So you admit receiving corrupt payments?"

"No, I—"

"You're guilty, Mr Kelsey," Marion Slavin shouted, dropping any pretence at courtesy. "You're guilty."

Kelsey pointed to the man along the wall. "He forced me to take it."

The man stepped forward and Andrea saw DS Stevie Fisher.

But Marion Slavin had tasted blood, and couldn't be stopped. "Did you report this wicked officer for forcing you to take five hundred pounds?"

"No," Kelsey protested, "but—"

"But nothing," Marion snapped. "DS Fisher isn't under investigation, is he?" Kelsey didn't reply. "Is he?" Marion shouted.

"No," Kelsey moaned.

"And tell the court. Who made the official complaint against you? Who signed the forms? Who exposed your corruption?"

"It wasn't like that," Kelsey cried. "I didn't want to take the money."

"Who reported you?" Marion shouted, slamming down the file.

"He did," Kelsey replied.

"Who?"

"Hogarth. DCI Hogarth." There was chaos around the court as people shouted and argued, while in the box Kelsey argued with himself. "I didn't have a choice, I didn't have a choice," he continued to cry. "I want to go. I want to go, Miss Chambers," he pleaded to Andrea with lost, wild eyes. "I don't want to be here."

Marion Slavin sat down deftly. Hogarth, for his part, stared across at Andrea and nodded slightly.

"Silence," the judge shouted. "I will have silence."

The court clerk leapt to his feet and shouted "Silence" over the judge's words. Gradually, the court hushed. There was an ominous tension in the room as Andrea climbed slowly to her feet, knowing how her case had just been torpedoed.

"Do you have any more witnesses?" Malverne asked.

Andrea shook her head.

"I will hear final arguments after the short adjournment," Malverne said. He was about to rise when he paused and addressed Andrea solemnly. "I have to tell you, Miss Chambers, that unless you persuade me otherwise, I'm minded to strike out your case."

To this, Andrea did not reply. To this, she knew, there was no reply.

The court clerk shouted, "Court rise," and Malverne wandered out, relish written all over his features in anticipation of his afternoon's work.

Andrea took Dawn's shoulder. "There's got to be something else," she said.

Dawn shook herself free. "I'm sorry," she replied. "I just want to be alone."

Andrea glanced to her left and saw Hogarth waiting at the

other end of the row. "You were magnificent," he whispered.

As the old usher jangled the keys to the court, eager to get his subsidised lunch, Hogarth whispered something to him and he left the courtroom. Andrea remained inside with Calvin and Hogarth. She tried to ignore the detective, opened her files, flicked through her notebooks frantically, and continued doing so even when Calvin lightly put his arm around her.

"There's got to be something," she said.

"Come on," he whispered.

"Just something I've missed," she said, picking up the blue notebook and fanning through the pages far too fast to absorb any of her detailed notes.

Calvin snatched the notebook out of her hand. "Mum," he said. It was enough to stop her, and when she looked up, Calvin was inches away, trying to control his rage as he stared out Hogarth. The detective closed in.

"You know what we've done?" he asked Andrea.

"Leave her alone," Calvin shouted.

Hogarth continued undaunted. "We've both stuck our hands into a scorpion's nest." He paused until she stared up at him and he was certain of her full attention. "I think we both know who got stung first." With that, he turned and began to walk out, but he stopped at the end of the row when Calvin shouted at him.

"Where's Lifer?" the boy demanded.

Hogarth stood there in his immaculately fitted dark grey suit. Andrea could see only his back and his huge shoulders, heaving slightly.

"I'll find him, Hogarth," Calvin said.

Andrea stood and took Calvin's arm. She looked at him quizzically. "What?"

"Rufus saw him," the boy cried, "firing my flat." Then he directed his venom at Hogarth. "He almost killed my grandfather."

Hogarth turned. "That was careless, then." He took Calvin in with his sincere, pained expression. "But if Lifer threw the bottle, who really lit the fuse? Ask your mother that." He didn't wait for a response.

Andrea took Calvin by the shoulders. "What are you saying?" she asked anxiously, but her real question was: What are you going to do now?

"Rufus described this man. I know him," Calvin replied. "He worked for Roots Johnson. He must work for Hogarth now."

Andrea glanced at the court clock. "Oh, Jesus, I'll never have time to see Rufus in hospital and get back in an hour."

"But the case is over," Calvin said in confusion. "I heard that judge say it."

"I've got to argue it isn't," she said distractedly, even as her mind trawled through the wreckage of the morning's proceedings for some scrap of hope.

"But how?"

More and more desperate measures occurred to her as her imagination spiralled out of control.

"How?" Calvin repeated.

"What if . . . what if I subpoenaed Hogarth himself?"

"Mum, you're crazy."

"No," she said, trying to convince herself at the same time. "Hogarth wants to go into the box. I just know it. He wants to go in there and preach."

Calvin grabbed her hand hard. "Christ, haven't you seen enough? It's over. These courts? They don't work. Not for ordinary people. They didn't work for Earl. They didn't work for Nicki Harris. And they didn't work for us, Mum."

"Us?" Andrea said.

"In these courts, wasn't it?" Calvin continued. "All them years ago. They said we don't belong together. You and me. I'm black and you're white. And the court said that don't work. Well, I say fuck the courts. I say it's them that don't work. So we got to find ourselves something else that does."

Andrea's mind was full of dread now, because she could see in his eyes the madness in her son's heart. But suddenly Calvin became calm. It was as if, standing in that courtroom, he had come to a judgment of his own, and this terrified Andrea even more.

"I'm going after this Lifer," Calvin said with perfect poise.

"No," Andrea begged him, "Calvin, please."

"Mum, I might not find him, but I've got to try. He tried to kill Rufus."

"There's got to be another way," she cried.

"You tell me, then."

Andrea was silent. She didn't want to lie to her son, for they both knew that for them the courts and the forces of law and order had not worked. She could perhaps have argued for forgiveness, for letting what had happened to Rufus pass. But in the agony of the moment she could not find any forgiveness in her heart. She found that the Hogarth case had left her bereft of those qualities that had sustained her in the dark times: hope, and forgiveness, and mercy, and a belief in the final vindication of the truth.

The only argument she could think of was a completely selfish one. "You want me to lose the case and lose you as well?" she asked Calvin. He was silent, absorbing her words like a boxer riding the blows, rocking with them, only to advance again more determined. He put his cheek against his mother's.

"Please, baby," she begged him. She held on to him tightly.

"You can't stop me," he whispered.

CHAPTER FOURTEEN

Roots looked at himself in the mirror as he knotted his tie. He could see Katherine's reflection in the background. He remembered how awkward he had felt with the tie around his neck the last time he went to the bank. He worked his long fingers into the knot, loosened it, then pulled the tie from his shirt collar. The moment it slipped down to the floor, he felt more natural. He undid the silver top button of his black Versace shirt, convulsed by a torrent of contradictory emotions. How could it possibly be that he, a man who had surrounded himself with death all his life, had now created the flickerings of life deep inside the woman he loved?

"I don't understand how it could have happened," Katherine moaned from the bed.

"We've been through this," Roots said. He smoothed down his shirt and joined her.

"I was told I couldn't conceive any more."

"You was told wrong."

Katherine put her head in her hands, so that a curtain of her fine hair fell in front of her face. She wept bitter tears at their predicament. He attempted to put his arm around her, but she broke away.

"We can't live here," she shouted.

"We haven't even tried."

She rushed to the dressing table, picked up the gun, waved it aimlessly. "I can't live with this."

Roots sprung up from the bed, unsure if he'd put the

safety catch on, worried by the reckless way she handled it. He took her hand, took the gun, slipped it into his waistband.

"I don't want it in here," Katherine cried.

"I'll take it out. I promise. I'll never bring one into your place again."

"You can't take them out, Valentine," she said. She held him, her grip developing into a hug. She rested her head on his chest and he put his chin on the top of her head. "They're always here," she said. She leaned back, looked at him with sad eyes, and then ran a finger across his breast. "In here," she said.

Roots stared back at her and understood that the sadness she felt was not for herself but for him. He wiped away one of her hot tears with his finger. The droplet curled around his ebony skin. In that moment, he saw the reflection of the photograph of Canada in the mirror on the dresser.

"It's as clean as it looks?" he asked her.

"Some places," she said, "you don't see people for days."

Roots allowed himself five seconds to consider this, to yearn for it, as he felt her body folded against his. But he knew it was getting late. "Katherine," he said, "when I get back, we're going to have a new life."

She shook her head slowly, but also seemed to nod. Then she went to the bedside table, opened the second of the three drawers and took something out. She returned to him and offered what was in her hand. "I want you to take this," she said, handing over a large, flat, glimmering coin.

Roots felt her press the cold metal into the palm of his hand.

"It's a silver dollar," she said. "From Canada. For you. For luck." She smiled as he pretended to bite it with his perfect teeth.

"It's not fake," she said. "But I don't think it's worth very much."

Roots looked at her. "Yes it is," he said.

He gathered his things and they made their way down the back staircase, past her locked office door, to the street.

"Will you come to see me after your meeting?" she asked defensively.

Roots didn't reply. Instead, he smiled, then gently touched the smooth curve at the bottom of her stomach. And he knew what he most fervently wished. He wanted her news to be true, he wanted her to be pregnant, he wanted there to be a mysterious part of Roots Johnson safe within her, and a child arriving into the world in recompense for the loss of Peckham and Nicki Harris. He kissed her on the cheek and jogged down the steps.

"Can you get some milk?" she said. "I'm dying for a cup of Earl Grey." She ran down the steps and he met her halfway. They kissed passionately as the clouds in the London sky rolled and darkened above them.

When they stopped, Roots asked, "What was that for?"

"So that you don't forget the milk," Katherine said.

He smiled, turned, and began to walk down the street. Katherine watched him until he had turned the corner, but now that he had gone she suddenly started to shiver. She went inside slowly and closed the door.

With Calvin gone, Andrea sat alone in the grand hall of the Royal Courts of Justice, waiting until the clock ticked around to the start of the afternoon session. She thought briefly about chasing after her son, but she knew he was right. She couldn't stop him. The case was in tatters, Calvin had gone, Rufus was in hospital, and Dawn Harris was nowhere to be seen. She had been vilified in the national press, and Hogarth was on the verge of perhaps his greatest triumph. Miserable and alone, Andrea took out her mobile, tried to ring Cameron at the office, but his personal line was engaged. She considered going across the Strand to one of the half-dozen sandwich bars on the south side, waiting in a snaking queue behind barrister's clerks and counsel in their winged collars and bands, while the Italian staff with their hygienic plastic gloves created hot ciabatta wonders. But she felt sick to the pit of her stomach. She stared across the floor, trying to lose herself in the tessellation of tiles, and saw a pair of familiar feet stepping slowly, deliberately, across the floor towards her. She felt at that moment too tired to get up and leave as Hogarth approached. She sat and waited until he stood over her in the vast, echoing hall.

"Everyone's watching you," he said to her.

She looked up. In her case-battered state, as she gazed at the crowds, they did all appear to be watching her. Across the hall, she made out the two ICU officers who had stepped forward in court to confront the hapless Kelsey as Marion Slavin cross-examined him. She particularly noticed the smaller of the men, not the redhead, but the one with the moustache. She racked her brains to recall what he had said in the video clip, but still she could not bring it to mind.

Hogarth sat on the bench next to her. "Everyone's judging you," he said. "Not me." He came closer still, so that she could feel his cold breath on the side of her face.

But now his self-assurance, his over-confidence, repelled her.

"When will you realise," Hogarth said, "I am not your enemy?"

Andrea's throat filled with bile as she recalled the pictures of Nicki on the slab, the pictures Hogarth had slammed down in front of her son. She recalled Rufus lying with an oxygen mask in a hospital bed, and cursed the fact that she could not at this very moment be right next to him, holding his fragile hand. "How's the headache?" she said.

Instinctively, the big man reached to check the pills in his pocket.

"You kill people," she whispered to him. "Have them killed."

"And you don't?" She was about to reply when he added, "Look what happened to Earl Whitely. He might still have been alive if you hadn't persuaded him to go on the record. And your son's grandfather? Who really put him into that hospital bed?"

At this moment, Marion Slavin approached them. She had her brief with her, holding the ring binder in two hands, with her wig balanced on top. "We have a proposal," she said. "We will not ask for costs against you."

Hogarth stood too. "Nor will we charge you with criminal libel."

Andrea felt the fight seeping back into her. There was no reason for them to make concessions now. The case was over. That was what everyone in that courtroom thought. If they wanted to forge some kind of deal, it meant that there was a downside for them somewhere. She stood up, fidgeted in her briefcase, tried to buy some time to think. There had to be a vulnerable spot — something, somewhere she had missed.

"Dawn Harris could litigate again," Hogarth said. "In the future."

Marion said, "You can save yourself from the harsher consequences of your ill-advised actions if you get a written undertaking from Dawn Harris. An estoppel of future legal action." She balanced the brief in one hand and with the other she pulled out a single sheet of paper full of neat paragraphs of fountain-pen writing. "Here's a draft order," she said. "You have one chance to take the deal. No negotiation. No discussion. It's all or nothing now."

They left her alone with the draft order in her hand.
She knew that it provided her with the opportunity to
inure herself from further attack. She knew that Hogarth's
threat was not an empty one, that if another court found
that she had acted maliciously against him in pursuing the
legal action then she could be sent to prison. All she would
have to do was to get Dawn to sign the paper. She looked
down. There had to be something they were now worried
about, but all she could see in the morning's proceedings
was devastation. Her case, Dawn's case, had been demolished. But as she stared at the uneven row of dots that
Marion Slavin had made at the bottom of the order to mark
the spot for their signatures, she knew that she could not
bring herself to ask Dawn to sign it. She began to breathe
more quickly as she told herself that she had tried to do
the right thing, she had believed in what she was doing,
she was trying to right a wrong. And if that meant she had
to defend her actions, that she was to be held personally to
account in front of another tribunal, in front of a jury,
then she would take up the challenge, she would go on the
record, she would defend herself no matter what the cost.

She screwed up the draft order and steeled herself to
argue again on behalf of Nicki Harris. As she stood, she
noticed that the shorter of the ICU officers had lingered
across the hall. Their eyes met fleetingly, even though
their view of each other was interrupted by the dozens of
people rushing backwards and forwards between them.
Mason glanced nervously to his left, and she followed his
eyes. He was watching the red-headed ICU officer leave the
front entrance of the court complex. He looked back at
Andrea, and now she recalled the gist of what he had said
on the video clip. Her head pounded as she made her way
across the hall, wondering if she had at last found
Hogarth's weakness.

As he saw her approaching him, he shook his head

quickly, abruptly. People passed in front of her as she moved, so that her view of Mason was like that of someone across a crowded club with a stroboscope on, for after each glimpse he was in a fractionally altered position. But his warning was sufficient for her to grasp that she should keep her distance from him. Woodbridge, the tall redhead, paused at the end of the hall and called after him, and Mason raised his hand, indicating that he was coming. Andrea spun around and proceeded in the opposite direction. She saw that she had left Hogarth's offer, the draft order, as a screwed-up ball of paper on a bench on the far wall. When she returned there, she moved as nonchalantly as she could so that she was able to watch Mason out of the corner of her eye. He waited until Woodbridge had left before he made his way down one of the dark stone stairwells into the pit of the building. Andrea now dashed across the floor, bumping into a tall, bewigged barrister who glowered at her, even though in truth he had not been looking where he was going. She skipped past a court shorthand writer, carrying her cumbersome typing device in front of her, then rushed down a stairwell parallel to Mason's, remembering that there was a corridor linking the rooms at the bottom of the building.

The corridor below hall level was dark. The footsteps of hurrying people marching on the tiled hall above resounded down the stairs, but died out gradually as Andrea moved further along the long, narrow passage. She saw Mason standing there, racked with indecision. He stared hard at Andrea as she strode up to him and turned away, then back. He wore a dark blue blazer and grey slacks, and as she drew up to him he yanked the rugby club tie he wore away from his throat.

"I saw that documentary," Andrea said.

"So?" he replied.

"You said corruption was a crime. Like any other. And that means police corruption is a crime. Like any other."

"That was for the cameras," he said, breathlessly, wiping his moustache. "It was just crap for the camera."

"I don't believe you," Andrea said. Mason turned to go, but she took his thick forearm. She stood up to him, forcing him to face her, to face himself. "I don't believe you now. I did believe you then."

When he spoke, his words were the rapid, desperate ones of a man on the edge, someone losing control, knowing it, feeling himself unspool even as he spoke. "Trouble is, Miss Chambers," he sneered, "you believe anyone. You believed that lying shit Earl Whitely."

"Didn't you?" Andrea said. "Didn't ICU? Why was ICU meeting him the night Nicki Harris was shot?"

"Because our job is to pick up and examine any disgusting insect that crawls out from under any stone. Who do you think knows about police corruption? Other corrupt bastards. And that was Earl Whitely, wasn't it?"

"Did Earl contact you personally?" Andrea asked.

"No fucking comment," Mason shouted. He wiped his bald sweating head. His eyes twitched.

"You've got to fucking comment," Andrea shouted back.

"Why? So I can ruin myself like you?"

"Why are you down here, then?"

"Because, Miss Chambers, I hate John Hogarth."

"Help me, then," she said.

"I won't testify," he said.

"You've got to speak about what you know."

"I'll tell you, but that's it."

"Don't tell me, tell the court," she shouted at him. "If you hate Hogarth, then tell the court."

Mason shook his head. "I'm sorry, but not all of us have your courage."

"So you're scared of Hogarth?"

Now Mason grabbed her. "I'm scared of myself," he cried. "Of what I'll do if what Hogarth's got on me comes out. Jesus Christ, I've got a wife and kids. I won't sacrifice my family."

"But you will sacrifice Nicki Harris?" Andrea said.

Mason did up his tie, buttoned his jacket, took out a double-sized white handkerchief and wiped his sweating face. When he lowered the white cotton from his face, he licked his dry lips once, then nodded at Andrea and began to speak.

Minutes later, she rushed into Court 2 as the parties slowly began to gather. Marion stood in the second row, on the left of the court, with Hogarth standing in the aisle next to her.

"OK?" Marion asked.

"Fine," Andrea replied. Dawn, who had already resumed her seat at the end of the third row, looked up at Andrea in bemusement.

Marion turned to the court clerk at the front of the court. "We've settled the case," she said to the clerk.

"Nothing's settled," Andrea said.

"What?" Marion turned in astonishment.

"We've got another witness."

"We've had no notice of this," Marion said. "Who is it?"

"Why don't you ask DCI Hogarth?" Andrea said.

Hogarth's mouth curled with anger and he thundered out of the courtroom with Marion Slavin in his wake. Andrea squatted down in the aisle next to Dawn.

"Hogarth's made us an offer," she whispered to the other woman. "Actually, he's made me an offer. If you agree to drop the case, to concede and undertake never to go after him again, then he'll let me go."

"Go?" Dawn asked.

"He's threatened to charge me with criminal libel."

"Can he do that?" she asked, peering with large, worried eyes through her thick glasses.

"Who's going to stop him?" Andrea said.

"So what do you want me to do?" she asked.

Andrea stood, her knees aching, and said, "I want you to give me one more chance, Dawn. I've got one more witness."

"But look what he did to Kelsey."

Andrea nodded. Dawn had expressed precisely the same fear that had plagued her when Mason told her what he knew. But she operated now on instinct, not on reason, and her guts told her to press on. "Look," she said, "I think they're scared. They must be, or why else do they want to deal? Why make us an offer?" Then she added, "Unless Hogarth's actually a really nice bloke and has got my welfare in mind."

She smiled at this and Dawn smiled, too.

"I'll do what you want," Dawn said.

"When I came to your house this morning, I didn't think we could win. And now? I'm still not sure. In fact, it's likely that we will still lose. But you know what? It annoys the hell out of me that they think we'll just roll over and stop fighting. We might not find out what happened to Nicki, but let's keep trying."

Dawn nodded, and Andrea turned to the court clerk. "Tell Mr Justice Malverne that we're going on," she said.

Calvin found out from one of the front-line West Indian takeouts that there was a blues party in a row of condemned houses that bordered Rufus's estate. He wanted to find the exact location, since he had been told by two different dealers that Lifer was partying big time after his exploits of the previous night.

He retrieved Earl's gun from the carrier bag in which he

had buried it under an apple tree in one corner of the communal park. It was pretty safe there, he knew — no one went to that park to play or take the air; it was a dealers' pitch, the equivalent of a corner store, and it only really came alive at dusk.

When he stood outside the blues house, he checked once more that the nine-mil was securely held in the back of his waistband. His hand trembled. But now the boy shook not with fear but with rage over what Lifer had done to his grandfather. He took a deep breath at the foot of the stairs to the tenement. He briefly closed his eyes and saw his mother standing there in that bullshit courtroom, weeping. He could feel now how good it was to kiss her, and that heavily bolted compartment of his mind in which he kept the troublesome memories of his early childhood now crept ajar just a fraction. He knew the truth now of what Rufus had told him repeatedly over the last ten years, that his mother was a good woman, and this strengthened him in his resolve to finish matters with Lifer. If his mother had done nothing wrong, why were the police and the forces of law enforcement tormenting her? What kind system was that? No one would touch Hogarth, he knew, and since Lifer was protected by Hogarth, no one would touch Lifer. Although Andrea had begged him not to pursue the Yardie, he hoped that she would one day understand that he did it for her as well as Rufus. He was trying to show his mother that he was no longer her little boy; yes, he loved her, he always would, but now he was grown, now he was a man, and now he would protect her. But even as the boy talked tough to himself, childish tears wet his eyes. The monster bass of the system inside thudded in his mind, and he knew that if he didn't make a move now, his courage would vanish. He glanced up, feeling the first spot of rain, then marched up the stairs.

The windows on either side of the door had no glass, or

rather the glass had long since been smashed by street kids, marking out their patch by systematically trashing it. Now wooden boards had been hammered into place with nails, so that the entire lair would be blacked out.

He banged on the door. There was no response. But this did not surprise him, for he knew perfectly well the calibre of the people who would be within. He banged again, and again and again, banging his fist raw, as he thought about Rufus trapped in the flames of his burning flat.

Finally, he heard the bolts being undone. A young white woman with a ring in her right eyelid, from which hung a small crucifix, opened the steel door just a few inches. Smoke wafted out as she looked up at him with eyes that registered nothing, washed-out eyes with dilated irises. To Calvin it appeared that she was blind, even though he knew that it was just the drugs that had drawn a veil between her and the world.

"Ya, man, I want in the party," he said in his patois.

The woman appeared to stare at someone beyond him, and spoke to this shadow person behind Calvin with such conviction that he even glanced over his shoulder to check who was there.

"There's no party," she said, laughing uncontrollably.

Calvin took out a roll of notes, which he had tied together with an elastic band. "Sure there is," he said.

Without looking at him, the woman took the wad and opened the door. He stepped in, coughing on the heavy ganja in the air.

Inside this place, Calvin knew, there would be no day and no night. The party would pass artificial boundaries of time, and the people inside would reach for new parts of themselves. He looked fearfully at bodies scattered around him on the floor, freaking out, tripping, OD'ing, crying, riding away on chemical cocktails, dancing till their legs gave way. The scene scared him, and it was fear of a kind that was afforded no protection by a gun. The music pumped heavy liquid rhythm into the virtual darkness, and smoke swirled and eddied over the prostrate bodies. He bent down, asking people whether they knew Lifer, but no one replied. Someone threw an empty can at him, but it missed. A woman on a mattress grabbed his ankle, and he tried to shake himself free, but she held on with a clawed grip and sharp nails, and he could feel with horror that her nails were beginning to cut into his skin.

He looked down at the woman, so pale it was impossible in the murk to tell if she was black or white.

"Help me, help me," she cried, thrashing her head from side to side on the soaking mattress, and in the din of the music her words were just a distant echo.

He ripped her hand off his leg and then saw that she had been chained to the bed, that thick links of metal wrapped round her naked body held her torso fast, and that hanging out of her other arm was an empty syringe.

She screamed at Calvin with such terror that her eyes rolled back in her head, screamed at him as if he were responsible for her captivity, and he did not know what to do, but he wished that his mother were with him. He squatted on the floor, ran his hands through he knew not what kind of slime and dirt around the mattress to determine how the chains had been locked into place. Suddenly, the woman's body went slack. And it was then that he felt the two gun barrels, one on either side of the back of his neck. His eyes squinted round to see Lifer towering over him with smoke billowing around his monstrous shaved head. The woman began screaming on the mattress again, and Lifer screamed more loudly back at her, while holding the guns tight to Calvin's flesh. He holstered one of his guns in his heavy leather jacket, then reached down and took Earl's nine-mil from the back of Calvin's waistband.

CHAPTER FIFTEEN

Mason stood in the witness box. The public had been allowed to jam into every available space in the courtroom, and they waited either in groups or singly, craning their heads for a better view. Mason's moustache drooped miserably around his top lip, and the portly superintendent gripped the front of the witness box as if he himself were in the dock.

Andrea had asked him the standard introductory questions, and he had replied with curt, non-committal answers, giving the minimum away, answering simply yes or no if he could. He was a practised police witness. She wondered for a moment what Hogarth would be like if she could force him into the box. He sat there along the row from her now, and though he moved not an inch, she could virtually hear the pounding in his head. He sat with his body taut, his arms and his legs crossed tightly, but he stared at Mason with neither hatred nor threat in his eyes. What Andrea believed she saw more than anything was confusion. Confusion, she guessed, at the fact that the private laws of his moral universe were being proved worthless before his eyes.

"As part of the ICU," she said to the witness, "who are your principal subjects of inquiry?"

"Police officers," Mason replied with the same brevity as before.

"Police officers who have done what?"

Mason paused, looked down, undid one button of

his navy blazer. "Anything police officers are not supposed to do."

There was a murmur around the courtroom, which Andrea translated easily: Is this man her witness or what? He was not forthcoming, he was positively surly, what in American courts they would describe as non-responsive. Andrea felt keenly the confines of her situation — Hogarth's immense presence on her left, Dawn Harris anxiously on her right, Malverne glowering ahead, Marion Slavin in the next row, eager to pounce, the nation's press two rows further ahead, and the public everywhere else. She could feel herself sweating now, cool, slow drips down her back, and she knew that she was getting nowhere with Mason. She decided to confront him head on.

"Detective Superintendent Mason," she asked in a harsher tone, "do you even want to be here?"

Mason laughed. "Funny you should ask that."

"Do you?" Andrea persisted with greater vehemence.

"No," he replied.

She rode the wave of excited reaction in court, pressed further. "But are you prepared to testify about everything you know?" she asked. Mason was silent. He looked down, wiped his moustache instinctively. "You've sworn on the Bible to tell the whole truth, Mr Mason," Andrea told him. "Can you be worthy of that oath?"

Mason's face reddened. Finally, he looked up, still troubled. "What do you want to know?"

"Did you know Earl Whitely?"

"No one really knew Earl Whitely," Mason replied. "Was that his real name? We didn't know. He had so many aliases, so many known addresses. He collected passports like other people collected stamps. He moved in and out of this country like a ghost. No one could catch him or stop him or track him. He could make a head shot with a nine-millimetre Browning into a car travelling at thirty miles per hour."

It was to Andrea as if she were hearing about another black youth, not the tearful one she had hugged in a cell the morning he died. The Earl she remembered had smiled at her with relief in his heart and had decided to tell the truth at last. And then he had died.

"Earl could make shots that police marksmen couldn't make. He was a killing phenomenon," Mason said.

"And how old was he?" Andrea asked, in a strange attempt to defend her deceased client.

"Seventeen," Mason said.

There was a gasp of incredulity around the room. But Andrea knew she had to press on. Finally, Mason was beginning to open up. "How did you come into contact with Earl?" she asked.

"He was arrested on trafficking offences. He asked to see us."

"Why?"

"He wanted to deal. He wanted a walk."

Andrea glanced around quickly. She needed to ensure that everyone was keeping up. If she could create enough of a stir in court, then maybe Malverne might be pressurised into giving her case a chance. "What do you mean by a walk?" she asked.

"He wanted his freedom. He wanted us to arrange for the most serious trafficking charges to be dropped in exchange for certain information. We were to debrief him fully on the night that Nicki Harris was shot."

Andrea was about to ask the next obvious and crucial question when Hogarth leaned forward and whispered intensely to Marion Slavin. She tried to focus, tried not to be distracted.

"What was the nature of the information?" she asked.

At this, Marion sprang to her feet. "I object. This is *prima facie* hearsay. This is inadmissible evidence."

"No," Andrea protested. "The defence wants it to be

inadmissible evidence. But it goes to the question of DCI Hogarth's motive. Evidence of motive is always admissible, as Miss Slavin should know."

"But motive for what?" Marion said scornfully.

"For killing Earl Whitely," Andrea said with a calmness that surprised her.

The court surged with noise, and the judge shouted until again there was silence.

"What was the information?" Andrea asked. When Mason hesitated, looking over at Marion Slavin, she added, "You may answer, Superintendent, unless Miss Slavin can think of any legitimate objection."

"Whitely said he was working for a senior officer." Mason took out his handkerchief. "A detective," he said. "Who was corrupt."

Andrea felt stronger now. She turned her head slowly towards Hogarth, realising that she wanted to see his reaction as she asked the next question. When she heard Mason's answer, she would watch him just as he had watched her and her son in that police interview room as they stared with horror at the wet photographs of the dead Nicki Harris. She began to grasp with increasing clarity that she had mined down to a ruthless strain in herself, one that was a dark reflection of Hogarth himself, and that thought both excited her in a way she did not understand and also made her shudder.

"Who was the officer?" she asked Mason.

Hogarth stared back at her, and she sensed a look in his eyes, an unspeakable warmth that was not reflected in his mouth or anywhere else in his face. His eyes shone. But why? She wondered if he knew and savoured something about Mason, some devastating humiliation to come. But that didn't feel right to her. What she sensed was that Hogarth was saying to her: See? You and me, Andrea. We're the same. She glanced up at Mason, who had

not answered her simple question. He wiped his head with
his handkerchief.

"Who?" Andrea asked.

Mason shook his head.

"Who was this officer?" she demanded again.

Mason stared hard into her eyes. "Whitely didn't say,"
he replied.

Andrea felt the answer as if Mason had slapped her
in the face. Suddenly, the noise of the crowd and the
impact of the question made the courtroom blur in front
of her. She felt her chest twinge, tighten, but she fought
it back with such force of will as she had left. She had
to find a way to push her own witness, and without a
clear plan she fired off questions, any questions,
questions that she hoped would wound him, sting him
into further revelation.

"Why did you not want to be here today?" she asked.
Mason stuffed his handkerchief roughly into his pocket.
"Why were you reluctant?" she continued. "What
stopped you from coming forward for so long?"

"Who," Mason replied.

Andrea picked up the clue. "Who stopped you?"

"The person who blackmailed me," Mason said, and he
appeared to be goading himself onward. "The person who
treated me like shit. Who hung me from a hook. Who
made me feel ashamed — of who I am." For the first time,
he dared to stare at Hogarth. He was on the very edge of
hysteria. "I'm not afraid of you, John," he shouted across
the court, his eyes welling. "Not any more. Not any more,
Hogarth." He broke down.

Andrea indicated to the usher that he should get some
water for the witness, and the old court attendant grum-
bled his way over to the decanter on the clerk's desk and
poured out a glass. He handed it to Mason, who appeared
shocked and frightened by his own display of emotion.

"What did DCI Hogarth blackmail you about?" Andrea asked. "Professional or private matters?"

"Private," Mason said quietly.

"And why did he blackmail you — as far as you understood it."

"Because I was investigating claims that Earl Whitely worked illegally for Hogarth."

There were now louder, more uncontrolled murmurings from all points of the courtroom.

"I will have silence," Malverne shouted.

"What work did Earl Whitely claim to do for Hogarth?" Andrea asked.

"Contracts," Mason replied.

"What kind of contracts?" she asked, the questions coming quickly now. "You've come this far, Mr Mason. Now tell the court, what kind of contracts?"

Mason paused, stared again at Hogarth, then said, "Killing contracts."

"On whom?" Andrea asked.

"Yardie leaders. Three dons."

Andrea remembered now with great vividness the footage of the broken bodies in the alleys and scrubs of the video clip. "Name them all," she commanded.

"Nathan Matthews," Mason said. "The Apostle Posse."

"Alive or dead?" she asked.

"Dead."

"Next?"

"Bigga Wayans, the Rebels."

"Alive or dead?"

"Dead."

"Next?" Andrea asked.

"Innocent St Pierre, ex-Spooners."

"Is Mr St Pierre alive?" she asked.

"They're all dead," Mason said. "They were all Hogarth's targets and they are all dead. The evidence pointed to Earl Whitely having killed all of them. On order."

"Whose order?" Andrea asked, even as she recoiled internally at the thought of her son associating with Earl, with this killer, whose tears she had wiped away, whose gun she had seen in her son's hand. "Whose order?" she asked more quietly now.

"Hogarth's," Mason said.

Andrea gazed hard at Hogarth as she sat down, and he looked back with a mixture of grudging admiration in his eyes and defiance in the firm set of his mouth. Their eyes locked for what felt to Andrea to be a dangerously long time, given the close scrutiny both of them were under, but then he snapped his head around, looked away, and with a tug of Marion Slavin's gown, he pulled his counsel to him for an urgent consultation. Andrea divined something of the shocking impact of his words from the astonishment in Marion's eyes. It was her turn to cross-examine Mason, and Andrea knew that Hogarth's case would be fatally damaged if she did not now rip the burly superintendent into pathetic pieces. He had to be destroyed. She also knew, of course, that Hogarth had a formidable arsenal of ammunition to fire at the trapped Mason. There was the personal scandal that could crush the man, and no doubt would ruin his family. But there had to be more. There had to be something else, something worse, she decided, as she watched the horror in Marion's face. She knew that Mason had been reluctant in coming forward, reluctant in telling her anything in the pit of the court building; he had even been reluctant after he had decided to go into the witness box. Her imagination soared as she thought of the degradations that Hogarth would inevitably wreak upon him. She saw how Marion and Hogarth were arguing, no doubt as the barrister reminded him of the bounds of propriety in a court of law. But she saw Hogarth's insistence triumph over his counsel's objections, and finally Marion gave up. She nodded her wigged head. She pursed her lips and turned to face the witness, who feverishly waited in the box. Andrea took up her pen in a token attempt to make a note of the cross-examination, but she knew she could not write. This case had gone beyond notes and details. It was propelled now by the raw emotion that charged the room, that intoxicated the crowd, that was the invisible link between Andrea and Hogarth himself.

Marion cleared her throat. "I am instructed by DCI Hogarth," she said coldly, "that I have . . ." She hesitated, her face still twisted in disbelief. "That I have no questions whatsoever for this witness."

Even as she heard the great roars circling around the courtroom at the revelation, and even though her mind fired a dozen questions at her, Andrea found herself battling to her feet, breathing quickly, while the blood raced in her head.

"So the defence accepts this evidence?" she shouted above the noise.

Marion turned swiftly to her right and contemptuously stared at Andrea.

The noise of the crowd still filled Andrea's head, but she continued to shout above the din, "If you don't challenge it, you must accept it."

The judge shouted for silence. The court clerk shouted more loudly still, while Andrea and Marion were on their feet shouting point and counter-point over the chaos. Slowly, a tense order was restored.

Andrea was determined to force the issue. The last thing she wanted to do was to goad the opposition into attacking Mason, but she sensed that the end of the case was near.

"They must challenge the evidence or accept it," she insisted, her voice poised, unwavering, though her guts somersaulted inside her.

"We will not challenge it in cross-examination," Marion said.

"Then you must accept it," Andrea persisted.

"No," Marion said, "we do neither."

For a moment, Andrea was confused, but slowly, as she saw Hogarth move, as she watched him palm a pill into his mouth and dry-swallow it, she realised the awful truth.

"We will explain it," Marion said. "We ask for a short adjournment and then we will call DCI John Hogarth to testify."

CHAPTER SIXTEEN

Lifer's customised BMW rolled slowly into what was once the forecourt of the derelict site. No one rode with him in the front of the car, but once he had parked it, and then glanced around to ensure there were no prying eyes, he sauntered to the boot. He opened it with relish, because there, arms and ankles trussed and mouth gagged, was Calvin. The boy bled slightly from the gash in his head where Lifer had struck him with Earl Whitely's gun. With his huge arms, the Yardie hauled Calvin out of the boot like a bag of shopping, then he dumped the boy on to the rubble. There were slightly larger droplets of rain falling now, and from his point of view at Lifer's booted feet, Calvin saw the raindrops racing through the last few centimetres of their fall until they landed around his face, his gagged mouth, his bleeding scalp, the drops then making wet pits in the layer of dust.

Lifer's wraparound shades turned robotically to left and right as he surveyed the scene. Once he was satisfied that all was clear, he dragged the boy by the feet into the broken shell of the first building. Calvin struggled and twisted his frame as best he could. He craned his neck so that his cheeks would not get ripped by the sharper stones and fragments of concrete on the floor, and tried to think of anything other than how he was going to die. He knew that his youth had been wasted, eaten up by the anger that he felt not towards the world but towards himself.

Lifer propped him on a broken chair. With his arms tied

behind his back and his ankles trussed together, the boy
found it difficult to balance. Lifer took out a gun, not
Earl's gun, from behind his back, but then, to Calvin's horror, from his boot, he removed a serrated knife. Now he
circled Calvin slowly in an awful ritual. Calvin could see
that he wanted to do something, to hurt the boy, to make
the first cut, but he also wanted to savour it, to do it slowly. Now he was behind Calvin. The boy tried desperately
to look round, but then decided that he didn't want to see.
Suddenly, he felt a huge forearm around his neck, squeezing his windpipe, and in Lifer's right hand, now up against
Calvin's left cheek, was the razor edge of the knife, the
very tip touching the bottom of Calvin's long eyelashes.
Short though he was of breath, Calvin dared not move, for
the tip appeared to him like a needle pointed right into the
centre of his eye.

"Ya, man," Lifer whispered, "I seen them, ya know.
Cutting out the eyes, then eating them. The first eye is
best. Imagine, homeboy. Seeing me eating your eye."

Now Calvin could control himself no longer. He bucked
with fear, but he couldn't be sick, he knew it, because he
was gagged so tightly he would surely choke to death.

Lifer was delighted with the response, but his cruelty
was already demanding more extreme pleasures. He
dropped the gun to the floor. Calvin wondered how he
could get it. He heard it fall, but Lifer's hand now clamped
itself on the top of the boy's head, holding it absolutely
still, like metal rivets in his skull, while he cut away the
gag with his other hand. Lifer wanted more. He wanted to
hear the horror. If only I could get the gun, Calvin thought
to himself, if some merciful hand would just give me one
shot to kill myself now, I would do it, without question, I
would eat the end of the barrel and I would pull. I am not
a coward. But nor am I a brave person. I just want to end
this. The gag fell from his mouth. He parted his jaws and

coughed up violently. He thought he was being sick but nothing came up. Lifer laughed loudly.

"Come on, pussy," the Yardie said. "Cry for me."

But now there was a change inside Calvin. He made a solemn, non-negotiable pact with himself that no matter what Lifer did to his body, he would not, not once, comply with a single thing this tormentor ordered. Just by a small fraction, he began to ease free of the shackles of his fear, tried to hold on to the part of himself that the crazed Yardie simply could not touch, and that part was not corporal. His body, he knew, was beyond help, but that was not the end of the matter. It wasn't dying that was important. It was how he died. And a pulse within him, a will, a stubborn streak that came from he knew not where, now filled him with renewed strength, and he understood the simple explanation: he already believed his body to be dead.

"Cry, pussy," Lifer taunted, running the blunt edge of the knife along Calvin's face, under his left eye, across the bridge of his nose, down into the well on the other side, then under the right eye. When Calvin remained silent, he shouted, "Cry, pussy."

"Fuck you," Calvin shouted back. "Fuck you, you botti man." Lifer lifted the knife swiftly in the air, and it hovered above Calvin's eyes like a bird of prey waiting to swoop. But Calvin wanted to provoke him, to force him to end it. "I heard them stories about you," he taunted, forcing the muscles in his face to laugh despite the horror around him. "I heard you like to party with lickle boys. So that why you bring me here, man? To have us a party?"

The knife plunged as Lifer cried out maniacally, the blade swooping down past Calvin's right eye. He waited for the searing of flesh, but there was none. Lifer had buried the knife in the broken back-rest of the chair. He let it go in disgust and the knife gyrated there, impaled an inch from Calvin's body. Terrified though Calvin was, he felt a slight charge of pride. He had almost made Lifer do what he wanted. The boy scrolled through his imagination again, desperate to find another button to press, something that would send Lifer over the edge.

"I thought you was going to kill me," he said quietly. "Is what happen, star?"

"Ya, man, you is going to die," Lifer shouted back, a shower of spittle spraying from his mouth. "But you is going to hurt first." The Yardie paced back and forth in front of the chair. He picked up the gun, held the cool metal to his own head, trying to think how best to make the boy suffer.

"So you taking orders from the po-lice, now?" Calvin taunted him.

"I ain't taking orders from no one."

"No? Word on the street is that you is Hogarth's house nigger."

The fearsome man lunged forward, pushing the barrel of the gun into the side of Calvin's right eye socket, pressing the eyelid shut over the iris. The boy breathed hard, in and out, in and out, and begged his mother's forgiveness for what he was about to do. He could feel his heart in his chest, fluttering wildly.

With his voice hoarse through fear, he shouted, "First, you was Roots Johnson's house nigger, now you is John Hogarth's house nigger. Man, I is big surprised they don't buy you an apron."

Lifer clubbed Calvin in the stomach with the butt of the gun. The boy doubled over so that his forehead was practically on his knees.

"They don't use me," Lifer shouted, more to himself now than to the boy. "I use them."

"Yeah? What've you got to show for it, house boy?" Calvin said, his body still folded in two on the chair.

He waited for the blow. For a shot, or worse, for the incision of the serrated blade. But nothing happened. He now winced every time he breathed. It was as though Lifer had punctured him, causing him to whistle as he breathed in and out. He guessed that the Yardie had cracked one of his ribs. When he looked up, however, he saw that a change had come over the man's face.

"The motherfucker's gone left the money here," Lifer said to himself. When he repeated the phrase, more slowly, like an incantation, he laughed out loud. He started around the shell of the ruins, lifting up huge planks with his immense strength. He tossed them aside, pawed at the piles of brick and rubble underneath. He picked up a crooked length of black metal, then he started smashing the rotting timbers of the floor with it. When he pulled one piece of flooring away, he jumped down into the void between the planks, and for a moment Calvin lost sight of him. But like a whale rising out of a grey sea, he rose from the void further along the wall, and now he was covered with cobwebs and dirt. He jumped up to the level of the floor, ran back to Calvin, then tied the gag once more. The material tasted strongly of the chalky rubble. He took a length of chord from the inner pocket of his black leather jacket and attached Calvin's ankle tightly to the chair, then kicked the boy to the ground. Calvin felt a trickle of warm blood in his eye. Lifer took the length of twisted metal then speared it through the gap in the back-rest of the chair and through the rotting floorboards. Calvin was staked to the ground.

Lifer rushed out to his BMW, and for a few seconds the boy was alone. More blood ran into his eye, causing him to see through a thin red film. He tried to clear his mind, to think. What was happening? Lifer wanted to kill him, he was definitely going to kill him, but he had delayed the act. There could be only one explanation: the money he now sought would give him more pleasure at this moment than causing the boy pain. Each of Calvin's breaths cut into him now. He blinked hard twice, to clear his eyes, his mind. A Yardie like Lifer lived awash with money. So this money had to be special. It had to be a huge amount. And it clearly belonged to someone else. Hogarth, perhaps. Or Roots Johnson. Lifer didn't just want to take the money. He wanted to steal it from someone he hated. As Lifer returned with a flashlight, Calvin's heart sank. The Yardie's search for money had put off the boy's death, and in the extra moments of unexpected life he realised that he was now beginning to plot and calculate again not how to die, but how to live, and hopes, cruel hopes that would be virtually impossible to fulfil, again gripped his thoughts.

Roots Johnson stood outside the black reflective glass of the City investment bank. He wore a white Armani shirt but without a tie, and though he looked more like the old Roots Johnson than he had on his previous appointment, he felt so very different. He walked through the high glass atrium, past the massive palms, thinking not of Roots Johnson, the father to be, but rather of his own father, whom he had so admired as a boy, and especially as a youth, after his execution in Miami. He was hailed by everyone in the posse, including young Valentine, as a martyr to the cause. With a sad heart, he realised that he had lost the last vestiges of this admiration, and now he saw his father as most of the rest of the world had seen him, as a foolish, reckless man. But he did not love him one jot less for this. In fact, Roots now loved him more, because his father had really been a child in a world of dangerous men, and had lost his life needlessly because of it. He wondered, as he reached the reception desk, whether he would ever tell his child about its grandfather — not the easy stuff about how he loved cricket, but the real things, the things that mattered, about how he had left his wife and his son to traffic the most lethal narcotics on the planet, how he had killed an officer of the law, and had then been executed by the law. Who deserved to know this secret history that Roots was compelled to carry around with him in his breast? He knew that he didn't wish to pass on the stain.

The woman receptionist, who previously had eyed him with such suspicion, now greeted him with a wide, manu-factured smile. Roots nodded back politely. But even as he fingered Katherine's silver dollar in his trouser pocket, turning it over and over in his fingers, his street radar was beginning to buzz.

"Mr Ellis will be down to meet you in a moment," the receptionist beamed. "Would you mind waiting?"

"I'm easy," Roots said in a low voice.

He noticed two men in dark suits standing on the other side of the atrium. They appeared to be talking intently to one another. Roots affected to look away, but continued watching them out of the corner of his eye. They were no longer speaking now, but whispering asides to each other. He glanced around at the door. It was about thirty feet away. The men were closer to it than he was. That could be a problem. He caressed the silver dollar, and prayed for all the luck that he knew, in truth, he did not deserve, but which he profoundly believed Katherine did. At that moment, Simon Ellis emerged from a side door behind the reception desk. Roots glanced to his right, to the glass lifts in which they had ascended to Ellis's office on the last occasion. Now there was a sign on the floor in front of the two glass tubes through which the lifts moved up and down. The sign said that the lifts were out of order. It could, he knew, be true. But it was another pebble in the scales. Roots suddenly turned to the two suited men and caught them staring at him. He smiled at them and they made a stab at grinning back. Roots was almost there. He just had to test Ellis.

The banker wore the same red-buttoned braces as before, the same chubby baby face, and the same broad smile of greeting. "Ah, Mr Johnson. Sorry to keep you."

"No problem," Roots replied. "Everyone's been very friendly, ya know."

Ellis glanced at the receptionist quickly, and a shadow of anger flitted across his face. She tried to maintain her painful grin, but now the muscles in her face began to twitch with the strain. Roots extended his hand towards Ellis and they shook, giving Roots the opportunity to gauge the coldness of the sweat on the other man's palm.

"So you've considered my proposal?" he asked.

"Oh, yes," Ellis replied. "Very carefully."

Roots followed his glance and saw that he had made eye contact with the two men.

"So you think my . . . film studio is a runner?" he asked quickly.

"Oh, yes," Ellis said. He broke out into a false laugh. "We can't seem to stop it running."

Now Roots was certain of his judgment. It was a trap.

"Shall we?" Ellis said, indicating some service doors to one side of the lifts.

"Not your office?" Roots asked.

"We've a new conference room, uh, at the back," Ellis said, as if he were trying to remember his lines.

"You're sweating," Roots said, but he began to follow Ellis to the rear of the atrium. Years of experience on the street had taught him that the best way to get out of a trap was to play along with it as long as you dared.

"It's the air-conditioning," Ellis replied.

"That's meant to keep you cool," Roots said. Ellis opened the service door, giving Roots a glance, as if he now realised that Roots had worked out what was up.

Roots regretted his last comment. It was too sarcastic, too easy a jibe. The sort of taunt he would have made without hesitation on the street, when he had some back-up. But here he was in an alien world and he had no protection.

The corridor behind the door was dirty, and housed a cleaner's trolley and a huge floor-polishing machine. Roots scanned the trolley for some kind of weapon. He had left the gun in the Golf parked outside. Looking again at Ellis, Roots hesitated at the entrance to the corridor.

"We're redecorating," Ellis said.

Roots saw one of the two men whisper from the side of his mouth. He was probably giving a running commentary into a wire. This had to be a police job. The black reflective glass of the façade was, of course, just a huge one-way mirror, allowing those inside to see out, so that when Roots glanced at an access road across the street, he saw a suited man, obviously a detective, whispering into a hand-held. These guys were clowns. His hopes soared at the thought. Perhaps he did have a chance. But he had to think fast. At that moment he saw a group of businessmen, looking like Japanese clients of the bank, coming through the revolving door. He had his plan.

He asked, "Can I go to the bathroom?"

Ellis pointed through the service door. "Through here."

"That's OK," Roots said. "I'll go to the one by the lifts."

"No, really," Ellis said. "It's better here."

"Thank you," Roots replied as courteously as he could. "But if you're decorating . . ." With that he turned and walked directly back towards the lift behind him. He smiled at the two men and they tried to smile back. He saw that the group of Japanese were between the revolving door and the reception desk. He picked one of a few hopeless options: the bluff. His instincts told him that it was his best chance. He marched right up to the two men, but when he was equidistant between them and the Japanese, he made a huge show of pulling something from the inside pocket of his jacket. In that same instant he squatted down and pointed it at the men. The speed of his movement shocked them. One backed off, slipping over. The other covered his face. Roots rolled over, the copy of his business plan in his hand.

The cop on the floor shouted, "Armed police. Freeze."

The businessmen scattered. The receptionist screamed. Roots lost sight of Ellis, and imagined that the banker was hiding behind the floor polisher. He scrambled to his feet and ran for his life, his blood gushing noisily in his head, all the while trying to keep his mind clear.

"Armed police," came the cry from behind him. "Stop or I'll shoot."

Roots was among the businessmen. He calculated that the police wouldn't shoot now. It was too risky. They couldn't see him clearly. But nor could he clearly see them, and that worried him. There was a gap of ten feet to the door. Open ground. They would have a clear shot at him. But what could he do? He experienced now something that he recalled happening to him only once before in his life. The sensation of time speeding up, events hurtling before his eyes, while all the while his thoughts slowed down, and amid the chaos and panic and screaming voices there was the sudden feeling that he was a detached observer, watching himself do things that he somehow could not control. It was the same as when he had killed that first man, that bloody struggle in the back streets of his youth, when the young Valentine had pulled a knife and the cop had pulled a gun, and the shots tore at his eardrums, and his stomach turned at the sight of the man's spilling guts as the boy twisted the gun back on to its owner. It all happened so quickly, but he lived it in his mind so slowly. Now he saw the policeman who had fallen over in the atrium fumble as he pulled out his gun, lying on the ground, on his back, screaming out repeatedly, "Stop or I'll shoot, stop or I'll shoot." The other shuffled across to his right, his snub-nosed revolver in two hands, held right out in front of him, jerking left, right, up, down, past civilian targets, trying, Roots knew, to get a clear shot, a head shot, or at least to target his chest. Take him out. Roots spied the revolving door. Would it be a glass coffin or a slowly turning shield? It was the only way out, the next step in his journey from that bloody Kingston back alley. He had to go.

He dived across the floor. It was pleasingly smooth, recently polished, and he slid into the gaping mouth between two panes of the revolving door. His ears were hammered by the report of a gunshot, echoing around the glass. He had known men who had been shot and had not known it till later, until after their blood was stilled and the shooting had stopped. If a bullet passed through flesh — pure flesh, no bone or heavy muscle — sometimes you could not feel it. And now Roots Johnson felt nothing, except the cold and the dampness of the glass door against his cheek, as he languished in the bank's entrance. Another shot ripped through the air. There was a ricochet, and the façade of the building itself cracked, splintered, and crashed down in curtains of glass, as if it were raining shards around the rough trunks of the huge palm trees. Roots pumped with his legs, squatting in the door, turning it more quickly, and suddenly he was out in the street again. The clouds were beginning to burst high above, and as he lurched to his feet and weaved in and out of the City crowds, the slate-bottomed storm front let rip, and rain poured down in weighty torrents, making the pavement slippery under his pounding feet and the towering office blocks mere phantoms.

The officer with the two-way suddenly appeared from the crowd and tried to rugby-tackle Roots, but the Yardie fended him off. His lungs cried out for oxygen, but he drove himself onward, glancing behind, seeing the other cops falling through the revolving door, stumbling on to the pavement. The pavements provided his cover, but they were too crowded, and could conceal policemen. Roots ran out into the street, between two lines of traffic, along the middle. Cars shot past and provided him with intermittent cover. Drivers stared at him with astonishment and curiosity. The police screamed, the rain fell harder, and now he saw the side road in which he had parked the Golf. Still running, he took his car keys out of his drenched jacket, which now clung to his body like a polythene bag around the face. He pressed the alarm deactivator and saw the car's sidelights wink on and off twice at his command.

He saw a gap in the traffic to his left. He careered through, but he didn't see a cycle courier in a jet-black Lycra suit. He had to dive out of the way, and with the speed of his movement he rolled over and over on the wet pavement, coating his trousers, his jacket, his face and hair with city grime. He heard a clink on the pavement behind him, turned and saw Katherine's silver dollar bouncing and rolling away from him. He scrambled to his knees, but then saw the police chasers closing in. He made a grab for the coin, but missed. He figured he could make it to the car, but he didn't want to leave Katherine's coin, he couldn't leave it. He grabbed again, this time forking it awkwardly between the middle and index finger of his right hand. The coin was dry, but his fingers were wet, and it threatened to slip out of his grasp like a bar of soap, but he held on, twisted around, skipped to his feet and got to the car. The policemen had their guns drawn, both of them. The ignition key would not go in. Roots glanced to his right. One of the officers braced himself, legs apart, aimed his gun, prepared to fire. Roots tried again. This time the key went in and the engine exploded into life. He yanked off the handbrake, began to turn the steering wheel away from the police, then imagined them having a clear shot at the back of his head. He turned the wheel the other way, towards the armed men. He pressed his foot on the accelerator and the VW lunged forward. Roots veered crazily in and out of the oncoming traffic, until an officer stood right in the middle of the road, pointing his gun directly at the car. All Roots could hear was the engine revving, though outside the policeman screamed at him so vigorously that the man's lips were pulled right back from his teeth, revealing his gums. A huge lorry blocked Roots's path to the left; to the right the pavement was full of cowering pedestrians. If he stopped to reverse he would be an easy target. Roots accelerated harder. Suddenly the car was right upon the officer. He let off a round. It crashed into the windscreen, shattering it. Glass showered over Roots and he put his hands over his face as the officer dived for cover. He swerved out of the way of the cop's body on the road and turned out of the street on which the bank was located. He had Katherine's silver dollar gripped between his fingers and the steering wheel of the Golf, and as he cut left and right through the City streets his mind quickly calculated the safest way to the derelict site.

CHAPTER SEVENTEEN

Andrea stood outside the front doors of the Royal Courts, from where she could see the rain washing down from the low skies above the Strand but was shielded by the Gothic arch of the entrance. She tried her mobile again, punching in the numbers hard in frustration. The batteries were beginning to run down and the LCD at the top of the phone flashed annoyingly without making a connection. Just inside the doors, the crowds from Court 2 had spilled out into the great hallway and the air crackled with anticipation at the prospect of Hogarth going into the box to give evidence. But while he prepared himself for the contest, Andrea wanted to speak to her son.

On the third or fourth attempt, there was a telltale click at the other end as the line connected. The court usher, with his cheap, ripped gown wrapped tightly around his gaunt body, came through the outer doors.

"Judge wants you in," he said sullenly to Andrea.

"I just need a few—"

"Judge wants you in," he repeated.

In the time it took for this exchange to take place, the phone had rung twice. Andrea glanced at the mouthpiece, urging response. And then suddenly, miraculously, just as she was about to hang up and return to court, it was answered.

As Calvin lay prostrate and vulnerable in the dirt of the building shell, Lifer held the boy's cellular in his huge hands. To the monstrous Yardie it had been like a wake-up call from the real world when the phone had rung in Calvin's pocket. For Lifer had lost himself in demolishing every corner of the room he could lay his hands on, every timber he could tear away from its nails, and the frenzy of destruction had dulled his mind to the presence of his prisoner. But with the call from Andrea, he remembered, principally with annoyance, that the boy was still alive.

Calvin could see that Lifer was covered in dust and cobwebs and mud, so much so that the Yardie's black skin was now ashen grey, like that of the living dead. There were many people who had Calvin's mobile number, but there were only two people who were likely to be calling him. It could be Rufus, if his grandfather had managed to persuade a nurse to bring him a phone. But he knew that the ringing he heard, that he felt as the phone vibrated in his jacket pocket while he lay in the rubble, was his mother, and the thought that his mother could reach out from that dismal court building and touch him in this dreadful place at once comforted him and made his heart plunge in his chest. As Lifer clicked on the mobile, Calvin prayed that he would at least hear his mother one more time.

"Calvin?" Andrea called down the phone.

Lifer's caked face cracked into a hideous smile. He squatted down next to Calvin as best he could and clamped a filthy hand over the boy's gagged mouth. Then he put the cellular to the boy's ear.

"Calvin? Son, is that you?" Andrea cried more desperately.

Tears filled Calvin's eyes as he cried out to his mother as loudly as he could, but his efforts only resulted in him chewing the gag, while his words were trapped inside his head — words he had not uttered since he was a boy, words that represented what he had felt and had never stopped feeling, even when he hated his mother and what he believed she had done to him:

"Mum, I love you, I love you, Mum, I love you."

Standing outside the Royal Courts of Justice, as the traffic in the Strand crept past in the deteriorating weather, Andrea heard nothing except the phone click off.

When she forced her way through the crush in the aisles of the courtroom itself, she saw that Hogarth was already there, waiting in the witness box, but he was not the same man who had taken her on in the Magistrates' court on the day of Earl Whitely's death. Gone was Hogarth's seemingly impregnable confidence. His gaze would not stay still, but flitted from one side of the courtroom to the other, and the massive, immobile bulk of his body, the grave weight that had always appeared to Andrea to give him an impossible strength and conviction, now appeared to be a burden, a drain on his energy, so that she saw him sweating and breathing heavily while he waited within the wooden confines of the box.

The air in the courtroom now was damp, as some people had ventured out into the Strand in the short break and had been caught by the sudden downpour. A young, prematurely balding man behind Andrea shook out his mackintosh, sending sprays of fine droplets in the direction of an elderly woman with salt-and-pepper highlights in her hair. The woman huffed and made murderous eyes at the young man, but said nothing. He smiled back sheepishly. One or two people had umbrellas which were now propped next to their seats, and dripped small, shiny puddles on to the varnished floor. And above the smell of wet hair and clothes, Andrea noticed a strong aroma of coffee. She turned in time to see Dawn Harris sidle into the aisle next to her with a Styrofoam cup sending up little curls of steam. The old usher spotted the offending item and was about to pounce, but Andrea gave him a withering look and he backed off.

"You all right?" she whispered.

"I feel sick," Dawn said.

"Won't be much longer now," Andrea tried to reassure her.

Dawn shook her head and tried to smile. "How do you feel, Andrea?"

Andrea pretended to think about it, though she could have reeled off the answer in a flash. "Oh, pretty shit scared," she said, smiling.

The two women then heard the ominous banging at the front of the court as Mr Justice Malverne made his final entrance. The judge's face spoke of his apparent desire to strike out at anyone who crossed his path. By now the people gathered in Court 2 were so accustomed to the choreography of the ritual that they stood and then sat without the need for the court clerk's promptings.

The moment his body landed on his high-backed chair, Malverne leant forward with his elbows planted on the Bench so that his fists were raised towards the courtroom. "I will have no further outbursts from the public," he said in a fearsome voice. At that moment a line of uniformed policemen came into court and stood against the bookcases along both side walls. "Anyone making any noise will be removed forthwith," Malverne threatened.

From her position in the third row, with Hogarth ahead of her and the uniforms on either side, Andrea felt that she had been surrounded. She tried not to dwell on her attempt to contact Calvin. For a moment, she felt his kiss on her cheek, but she knew that she had to get her argument with Hogarth finished.

Marion Slavin stood to begin her examination, but Malverne held up his hand.

"Miss Slavin," he said. "I am just reviewing a series of authorities that are pertinent to the state of these proceedings. I am arranging for copies to be made for you and for . . ." He gazed irritably at Andrea. "And for your opponent. I am just reviewing what powers remain to me to strike out this case." Then he added, but without enthusiasm, "Or not."

A second usher, a tall, gangling woman, now entered court with two piles of photocopied sheets. She first went to Marion, handed her a pile, then skirted around the front of the court, past the outstretched legs of the reporters, up the right-hand aisle, and to Andrea. Andrea felt the warmth of the underside of the paper, just out of the photocopying machine. Each legal case was separated from the next by a staple, and as the rest of the courtroom watched silently she flicked through five staples. Five cases that Malverne hoped would offer a lifeline to Hogarth. Dawn looked at her anxiously as yet another impediment appeared between her quest and the truth, but Andrea leaned back calmly against the hard wooden bench. She could see Marion in front of her underlining the first of the cases furiously, while on the Bench Malverne did the same. Andrea did not even lift a pen.

"Aren't you going to read them?" Dawn whispered anxiously.

Andrea shook her head just once.

"Why not?" Dawn asked.

Andrea was transported back to the days of hard work she had put in after having served the writ on Hogarth. She remembered fondly her daily runs, her physical preparation, the warm glow she experienced after exercising, how she gradually felt a notch stronger each day. Most of all, she recalled getting caught in the rain, the Catholic church in Chiswick, the clock of remembrance for the two young sons of the parish felled at Inkerman and Sebastopol. Now, while the old clock ticked loudly in the tense silence in Court 2, she smiled to herself.

"They're all crap," she whispered to Dawn. "I've already read them."

Dawn shook her head in disbelief and replaced the see-through plastic lid on her coffee cup. She had not taken a single sip. Andrea felt the weight of Hogarth's gaze and she glanced over at him. His eyes were focused upon her with all their fierce intensity, and she knew that he wanted to dispense with the forms and go head to head with her as well.

Roots Johnson's car raced through the South London back streets, cutting in and out of little-used alleys and one-way systems, always off the main road, always as fast as he could drive in the narrow spaces, and ever closer to the derelict site. He had achieved a sufficient start over the police to make him confident of being able to grab the final item he needed before he returned to Katherine; for all he wanted to do now was to rescue his stash of money and make his way back to her arms. He cursed himself for not having spotted the set-up at the bank before. But what was he to do? Where else could a Jamaican with no credit rating, no references, in fact with no record of actually living in the United Kingdom, go to obtain a huge loan? The point was that it was over. And as he saw the outline of the site in the near distance, he persuaded himself to be positive, to realise that the fiasco at the bank might have been a good omen, not a bad one. It spoke of the treachery he was bound to face wherever he went in this country. It convinced him that Katherine was right — there was no future for them here. He had to leave, to get out before they reached him.

He turned sharply left and the car slid into the forecourt of the derelict site. Roots jammed on the brakes and levered up the handbrake. The car skidded to a halt through the pools of muddy water. He was about to jump out when he saw Lifer's BMW. He clutched the silver dollar, hoping for some inspiration. He could just reverse out now and keep going west towards Katherine. Perhaps they wouldn't need the money. He could work, so could she; tickets were already bought. But then he remembered the name on the passport: John Valentine. He needed money to buy a false ID, and with his rep, it was going to cost him. Maybe Katherine had the money for the documents. But he knew he didn't want to back off. He wanted to leave on his own terms. He remembered how Lifer had tried to kill them both at this very site. He could feel her body under his as they lay beneath the broken wall. He had run from the police, he was going to run off to Canada with Katherine, but he could not live with himself if he ran now from Lifer. He knew what he had to do.

Roots drew the nine-mil from its holster under his seat with his right hand. The fingers of his left stuck slightly to the surface of Katherine's coin as he pressed it into his palm. He slipped it into his trouser pocket and opened the door as quietly as he could, then realised how pointless his precautions were. His car had screeched into the site and Lifer was bound to have heard the noise. But he had seen no sign of movement anywhere, and so he continued to advance, using the sound of the rain drumming on sheets of rusting corrugated iron for cover. He put the nine-mil into the front of his jacket, his right arm crossing to the left side of his body to keep the gun dry, the grip secure. His aim needed to be perfect. He might only get one shot.

Roots advanced to the broken wall. It was here that Katherine had squatted down in the mud to cover her hands in the muck so that she could smear it all over his cashmere coat; here he had seen her cry and had realised that he didn't want to live if she was killed. He knelt down on the street side of the wall, still saw nothing, heard nothing, either from within the shell of the building or from behind him. His back streets and cut-throughs were almost impossible for someone who didn't know the territory, and the cops at the bank, he suspected, were probably the Fraud Squad, or a money-laundering unit. Specialists in white-collar stuff, lost south of the river, no match for the don on his home turf. Roots edged his way to the outer shell of the building. His gun was held firmly, but not too firmly — squeezing too hard made the arm shake, strained the muscles; it meant you could miss.

He squatted at the foot of a smashed window, just a hole in the brickwork with jagged glass edges. The rain continued to fall, while a faint breeze blew off the river and whined through the empty rooms of the building. Roots listened, heard no human sounds from inside, counted to three to confirm this to himself, was about to look inside but decided to count to three again. Three more seconds of his life. Normally it wouldn't have been much, but he knew that somewhere in his wake were police cars and humiliated officers with their blood up, with live ammunition, who had a score to settle with a black man who had out-thought them, so now each second was precious. He counted to three for the second time. Now. He flexed his thigh muscles so that his body scraped up the slimy outside of the building. His left cheek was pressed against the brickwork, the nine-mil in his right hand, and he saw small droplets running down its metal barrel. He kept the gun pointed down, not wanting water to run into the barrel itself. He glanced up, could see now the jagged glass and distorted shapes of the room within — crazy shapes, like the confines of a madhouse. Now he could see into the room, and as his ears strained for sound, he heard breathing. There was someone there.

He adjusted his grip on the gun, felt the sweat on his palm. He closed his eyes and tried to think of Katherine, to imagine her face, to smell her hair, but all he saw was the vivid image of the Jamaican cop slumped in the alley with his intestines pouring out. He fought to clear his mind, but the first man he had killed plagued him with his dead eyes and demanded vengeance. He began to breathe more quickly, through his open mouth, trying not to make a sound. He could still hear the breathing from inside. His nerves began to fray, to splinter, and he knew that he had to act. He pushed up with his thighs, swivelled to his left, pointed the gun directly into the room through the absent window, and saw the boy lying in the rubble, bound and bleeding. Instinctively, he pointed the gun at Calvin's head. Was about to pull the trigger. But stopped himself.

He saw a crushed mobile phone next to the boy's body. Calvin's eyes were huge, filled with terror. He gestured again and again with his head over his left shoulder, to the rear of the building. Roots nodded. He now understood why there had been no sound. Lifer was down by the river. Roots wondered if he had found the stash. Calvin began to buck and shake in alarm, and Roots heard heavy footsteps from the rear of the shell. He squatted down behind the wall again.

He heard Lifer pounding along the exposed timber floors, his footfalls louder and louder. He knew for certain that Lifer would kill the boy. He would not have brought him to the site unless he intended to kill him. Roots put the cool gun barrel to his forehead.

He heard Lifer enter the room. "Now we is going to party," Lifer hissed at Calvin.

Calvin mumbled through the gag, and Roots could hear him struggle. There was then a thud, and the sound of the boy's struggling stopped.

Roots stood up in the window, his gun drawn, pointed directly at the monstrous Yardie, who stood above Calvin with his nine-mil pointed at the boy's head.

"Let him go, Lifer," Roots said.

Lifer raised his gun, but Roots had him lined up, saw the reflection of his barrel at the centre of the wrapround glasses.

"Let him go," he repeated, leaning to his left, against the wall, covering as much of his body as he could.

Lifer hauled Calvin's head up, pulling his hair, arching his back. "No," he said simply.

"This ain't about him," Roots said.

"OK, then I just shoot the boy," Lifer said.

"You hurt him more, I bury a bullet through your eyes," Roots shouted. He felt the muscles in his forearms beginning to quiver and he tried to compose himself, but it increased the strain and the gun barrel began to move. Lifer hoisted Calvin to his feet, trying to deploy the boy's body as a shield. He dragged Calvin to his right. For a fraction of a second, Roots could not see Lifer and Lifer could not see him. Roots moved to his left, into the open space where once a double door had been. He stood facing Lifer, gripping the nine-mil in both hands.

Lifer laughed. "Johnson, you in love with dis boy or something?"

Roots took the jibe in silence, kept the gun pointed. But the end of the barrel trembled, and he secretly began to doubt that he could get a clean shot at Lifer. He feared he would hit Calvin first.

"Ya, man, here how dis goes down," Lifer said. "You leave and me don't shoot you in the back, Johnson. You goin' meet me again. On the street. We both know that one. But not now. Now, the boy is mine."

"No," Roots said.

Suddenly, he heard a wailing from behind him, the muted, distant cries of sirens. Police cars were scouting the area. It would just be a matter of time until they found him.

"Johnson, you bring the heat down on us?" Lifer cried, his gun jabbed in Calvin's cheek just above the gag.

"Looks like," Roots replied.

Lifer shook his huge pumpkin head, trying to figure out a solution. "OK, OK," he cried. "You take the boy. We don't settle you and me now. We both mek escape from Five-O."

The wailing was louder now, and Roots was more concerned, because the sound appeared to be coming from both west and east.

"OK, undo the boy," he said.

Lifer tore at the knots of rope around Calvin's body. One length of the heavy binding fell away. Calvin's arms were free now and he ripped off the gag. Lifer undid the ties attaching him to the chair.

"Undo his ankles," Roots ordered.

But Lifer grabbed Calvin round the neck and dragged him backwards, the boy's ankles still bound together. He stood in the doorway, nearer the river, Calvin still shielding him. The police sirens were louder still. Lifer glanced left, then right, as if deciding which way to make his escape along the corridor behind.

"Give up the boy," Roots cried.

Lifer had the gun under Calvin's throat, to the right of the Adam's apple, forcing his neck upwards. Roots could see that he was panicking.

"Give him up," he screamed.

Police vehicles had now turned into the road, seconds from the site. Roots could hear them accelerating along the front of the warehouses. Now he heard their brakes squealing as they skidded to a halt in the road outside. He turned around, saw the first car. Then suddenly there was a flash. It was followed a fraction later by a booming sound that started in the shell of the building and then echoed in Roots's head as the force of the impact of the bullet flung him backwards. His face was splashed with blood from his upper left arm. Lifer laughed crazily and aimed another shot at his former don. Roots's legs began to buckle. A voice boomed on a megaphone, "Armed police, throw out your weapons, armed police." Roots hit the floor and looked up at the doorway. Lifer threw the boy to the ground, his gun still aimed at Roots. He pursed his lips, almost as if he were tasting the pleasure to come, and Roots fired off one shot, all he could manage through the haze of pain. Lifer sank to his knees, the gun still in his right hand, his left clasping his chest. As he fell he stuck his nine-mil into Calvin's stomach. Roots let go of his gun, helpless to save the boy now as the pain made red-hot loops in his mind, but he heard no shot. Lifer's body crashed against the wall.

"Johnson," the megaphone bellowed, "there is no escape. Throw out your weapon."

Calvin undid the ties around his ankles and crawled over. Blood gushed out of Roots's shoulder. Calvin put his hand over the wound, but blood still seeped through his fingers.

"Johnson, armed police," came the cry from outside. "Throw out your weapons."

Roots saw that the boy's eyes were filled with tears. "Oh, Jesus, what do we do? What do we do?" Calvin whispered.

"You got to be my eyes," Roots said, wincing with pain. It felt to him like a red-hot carving knife had been plunged into the flesh at the top of his arm.

"Eyes?" Calvin asked.

"Tell me what you see out there."

The boy scrambled up the wall, peeked out over the bottom of the broken window. "Oh, Jesus," he cried.

"How many?" Roots asked.

"Dozen. More."

"How many with guns?"

Calvin slumped back down next to Roots at the foot

of the wall. "All," he said miserably.

"You gotta go," Roots said, taking in huge gulps of air, as if he could dilute the pain with oxygen. "They just want me, Calvin."

"No," the boy cried. "You saved my life. I ain't leaving you."

"Go," Roots hissed at him. But he was secretly pleased to see the boy's defiance. He didn't want to be alone.

"Any ideas?" Calvin asked.

"I'm thinking, rude boy," Roots replied. But while he thought about the likely configuration of the armed police outside, his calculations were constantly interspersed with fragmented images of Katherine, of her photograph of Canada, of their child.

CHAPTER EIGHTEEN

After five tense but silent minutes in court, Mr Justice Malverne finally finished his consideration of the relevant law. He addressed Andrea first.

"I note that you did not avail yourself of the opportunity to read the cases, Miss Chambers," he said furiously.

"I didn't need to read them," Andrea said. "I am familiar with both the *ratio* and *obiter* of all of them."

"Well then, perhaps you'd like to enlighten the court," Malverne said.

"No," Andrea said firmly.

"No?" the judge fumed. "This is not an invitation that may be refused, Miss Chambers."

"Why don't we ask DCI Hogarth?" Andrea said. She could feel Dawn twitching nervously to her right, and even as she confronted the judge she was aware of a voice within her saying: What the fuck do you think you're doing, Andy? But she continued to Malverne, "I suspect that the DCI is thoroughly fed up with legal technicalities. I suspect he wants to testify first and ask legal questions later."

Marion Slavin could not hide the fury in her voice. But nor did she wish to. "It appears that Miss Chambers has forgotten just whom she is supposed to be representing. As Mr Hogarth's counsel, I submit that these authorities show—"

"They tell us about the law," Andrea interrupted. "They show us nothing about the truth of this case."

Mr Justice Malverne appeared to Andrea to be on the verge of cardiac seizure. "The truth?" he gasped, as if the mere mention of the word in a court of law were a vile blasphemy.

"Yes, the truth," Andrea pressed on. "Some people in this courtroom are actually concerned with finding the truth. And I am going to suggest that DCI John Hogarth is foremost among them."

Marion bent forward towards the judge in supplication. "I insist on being heard on the procedural technicalities contained in Your Lordship's cases."

"No," came the thunderous reply.

It didn't come from Andrea, nor from the judge, but from Hogarth himself.

The judge turned sharply to the detective in the box. "You don't wish your counsel to argue the law?"

"I'm not interested in the law," Hogarth said, immediately correcting himself. "In these kinds of laws."

"Then, DCI Hogarth," Malverne said morosely, "I have to tell you that you have been accused of the most grievous criminal acts. So I wish to warn you — as I would be obliged to warn any other witness — that under the law you have an absolute privilege against self-incrimination."

Hogarth nodded, but Andrea's distinct impression was that he wasn't listening, that he was lost.

The judge raised his voice. "DCI, you understand, I hope, that in consequence you need not answer any questions from any quarter that might tend to incriminate you." After he had finished, there was silence. Andrea could feel the tension mount in court as people waited for Hogarth's reply. She itched to get to her feet, to deal with the man, to put him to the sword for what he had done to Nicki Harris, for the attacks on her family. "DCI?" Malverne asked more solicitously. "Do you understand this right?"

"I understand," Hogarth said blankly.

"I must also remind you that you are not a compellable witness," Malverne advised him. "You grasp, I think, that no one can force you to testify in this matter. If you wish to leave the witness box, that is your right."

"And if I want to testify," Hogarth said, "that is my right?"

"Yes," the judge said.

It seemed to Andrea that the judge was about to add to his simple reply, but Hogarth spoke again quickly. "Since we are talking about rights . . ." His tone was cutting and vengeful, the bitter tone of a man who believed he alone was privy to some awful truth that had eluded everyone else. "I will testify on one condition," he continued.

"You are not in a position to impose conditions," the judge said, now furious that the case appeared to be slipping out of his hands.

"I want to answer questions from Andrea Chambers," Hogarth said. "Not my counsel. Andrea Chambers."

Marion Slavin was crimson with anger. "This is most improper. My Lord, I need to speak to my client before__"

"I agree," Andrea cut in. "I agree with the condition."

The judge gave way and the old male usher handed Hogarth the Bible. He held the holy book high in his right hand. In his mournful voice he said, "I swear by Almighty God that the evidence that I give shall be the truth, the whole truth, and nothing but the truth."

Andrea and Hogarth stood facing one another. As she thought of the hundred questions she wanted to ask, everyone but Hogarth became mere shapes at the edge of her perception. But before she could ask about Nicki Harris or Earl Whitely or anything else, Hogarth spoke.

"Why did you do this?" he asked her. "Why couldn't you leave it?"

"You arrested my son," Andrea said.

"We had to. He was harbouring Earl Whitely. Whitely was involved in the shooting of Nicki Harris."

Andrea sensed a mistake. "How do you know?" she pounced. "Unless you were there." Hogarth closed his eyes, as if he were trying to rally his energies, to focus on what was important, but if he was now off balance Andrea had to keep him that way. "You were there, weren't you?" she said.

The court was hushed. The clock ticked, more slowly, it seemed to her, more loudly. She tried to block it out, to focus again. "Do you deny that you were there?" she demanded. And when he spoke, Andrea realised that Hogarth wasn't trying to shut his eyes to his predicament; quite the reverse — he was attempting to relive it.

"Whitely ran into a school playground," Hogarth said with such conviction that Andrea was sure he had transported himself back to that dark afternoon.

"Why did he run?"

"He was being chased."

"Who chased him?"

Hogarth paused. His right eye twitched once, and he answered in a pained voice. "He ran into a playground full of children. Then he took out his gun and started firing. With children all around him. This is what your former client did, Miss Chambers. This is what your son's friend had just done when we arrested them both."

There was a mumble around the courtroom at the references to Calvin. But Andrea tried to roll with Hogarth's lashing out at her family. She had to push him her own way, had to steer him back to Nicki Harris. "And who was Earl Whitely firing at?" she demanded.

"Who do you think?"

"I ask questions, I don't answer them," she retorted. She felt as though Hogarth were still snagged somewhere between his doubts and certainties. "I think," she said to him, "that you were there, DCI. But who was with you?"

"Don't you know?" Hogarth asked.

Roots, gun in hand, lay next to Calvin, propped against the outer wall of the derelict building. They could hear more and more police vehicles arriving, then the sound of van doors being thrown open, a dozen more heavy footsteps running for position. The rain came through the dilapidated roof above them, working its way through small holes and fissures. Calvin ripped his white T-shirt from under his cotton jumper. He pulled the torn material taut, then tied it around the wound on Roots's arm. Outside, the police megaphone kept up its droning, warning and cajoling the trapped men in equal measure.

Roots screwed up his face as Calvin tied the ends of the T-shirt into a knot, trying to dress the wound. As his eyelids came down, he began to feel light-headed, as if he were beginning to float an inch or two above the rubbled floor. Despite the pain in his shoulder, there was also a warm, numb feeling in his head. He realised that he was beginning to drift in and out of consciousness with the loss of blood. The gun began to slip from his fingers. He let it go and grabbed Calvin's hand.

"Calvin," he breathed, "I want you to help me some."

"Anything," the boy replied.

"I want you to tell your mother something."

"My mother?" Calvin asked, now confused. "What?"

Roots Johnson stared at him with such earnestness as his failing body could muster. "How Nicki Harris died," he said.

Hogarth repeated his reply, this time more slowly, and Andrea knew that she was almost home. "I was there with Roots Johnson," he said again.

"But why?" Andrea pressed. "Why were you and a

Yardie don together?"

"You will never understand," Hogarth said.

"No," Andrea said, "I will never understand murder."

"You think it's murder? To try to kill a man dealing drugs to schoolgirls? A man like Earl Whitely?"

"He was going to inform on you to Internal," Andrea said. When Hogarth did not reply, she added, "Wasn't he?" Hogarth nodded, and Andrea could have insisted that he put this admission on the record, but she was after a bigger disclosure now. "Wasn't Earl Whitely working for you?" she asked.

Hogarth gripped the front of the witness box more firmly. Then he saw the Bible, still propped on the ledge next to him. He looked away from it, back at Andrea. She could see reporters with their pens in the air waiting for the next response. Malverne looked down, as if he could not bear to hear the answer. The court clerk propped his chin on his hands below the judge. Marion Slavin fingered the back of her horsehair wig. Dawn Harris sat, the calmest person in the courtroom now, caressing the locket containing the pictures of her dead daughter.

"Did Earl Whitely work for you?" Andrea asked again. Hogarth was still silent, and whispering spread around the court until Andrea shouted, "*Did* he?"

"Yes," Hogarth whispered hoarsely.

Andrea tried to ignore the tumult around the court. She had to push on, her task incomplete. "And what was Earl Whitely doing?" she asked, remembering the last frantic words of her former client in the Magistrates'' court.

"Whitely was finishing the job," Hogarth said.

"What job?" she asked.

Hogarth spread his arms widely, encompassing the whole court, from front to back, from the well to the raised Bench. "The job all of you pay me to do." Amid the public outrage, the gasps and shouts, he grabbed the Bible. "Don't you see what this is, Andrea?"

"You tell us," she shouted above the noise.

Hogarth held the Bible out as if he were offering her a sacrament. "Leviticus sixteen," he said. "This case. It's not just a court action. It's an . . . atonement. It's a judgment. On all of us."

"No," Andrea shouted. "On you."

"The Hebrews used an animal. A goat. They poured all the sins of the community on the scapegoat's head. And then they sent it out into the desert. So that they could live with themselves. Knowing the wrongs they had done. Knowing the good they had failed to do."

"So you're just our scapegoat?" she asked him.

"Well, you tell the court." Hogarth's mouth was set into a grimace. "Who really is to blame for the death of Nicki Harris?" he demanded. "Who?"

"The man who pulled the trigger," Andrea shouted. "*You* are."

"No," Hogarth said, feeling her accusation like a sword-thrust in his midriff. He winced and added, "Understand."

"I do understand," Andrea retorted. "You wanted to kill Earl Whitely. He was about to confess to all the killings he had done. You contracted him to kill three Yardie dons."

"They killed and dealt drugs and raped and robbed. With impunity. The law couldn't touch them."

"So you passed sentence on them," she said. "You decided that they should die."

"I was protecting you. All of you."

"We don't want that protection."

"But you need it."

"Who gives you that right?" Andrea shouted. "To kill? To be above the law?"

"You do," Hogarth cried. "You all do. Only you won't

admit it. You want drugs off the streets. Well, you have to fight fire with fire."

"Then innocent people burn."

"Fewer innocent people," Hogarth said.

"And who decides? Who lives. Who dies. Do you?"

Hogarth dropped the Bible. He stared at Andrea with pleading eyes. "You tell me I can't bend the law. And I'm telling you that the law doesn't work. So what are we going to do?"

Andrea tried to answer, but the words would not come. She didn't have the answer. "The facts are," she said, "that you were present at Nicki Harris's shooting. And you wanted Earl Whitely dead."

"Yes," Hogarth said.

"And the fatal bullet came from your police gun, the Carbina SP."

"Yes."

"And you fired the shot that killed Nicki Harris?"

Hogarth weakened now, with guilt, with awful, final realisation. He cowered there, trapped, a man crushed by his principles and actions.

"You killed Nicki Harris," Andrea repeated, and now there was silence in the courtroom. She spoke again, her voice much lower, almost a whisper, a reverential whisper above a sleeping child. "You killed Nicki Harris," she said.

"No," Hogarth replied.

The police megaphone still railed outside the derelict building. Roots saw the horror of his confession reflected in the boy's face — the wide eyes, the slightly open mouth — and the Yardie don felt the dreadful weight of his secret begin to lift as he told the boy the truth.

"It was my law, Calvin," he whispered. "My law. No dealing to kids. Earl knew it."

Calvin instinctively protested, defended his friend. "Earl didn't know what the hell he was doing half the time."

"We all know what we do, star," Roots said. "But that girl? She just ran out. Right into the street. I tried to pull my shot. I tried, Calvin. I tried."

"Oh, Jesus, no," the boy cried.

"I killed her," Roots said, his heart breaking within at the memory of it all. "Oh, God, forgive me."

But what he really meant was: Katherine, please, forgive me. Katherine.

There was total silence in court. Hogarth stood in front of Andrea, finally beaten. A mere shell of the man who had slammed the dripping black-and-white photographs down in front of her, no longer the frightening force of nature who had held her son's freedom in his huge hand.

"It was an accident," he said quietly, looking in the direction of Dawn Harris, who now wept profusely. "Johnson didn't mean to shoot her."

But just then the doors on the left-hand side of the courtroom flew open and Andrea glimpsed the blond hair of DS Stevie Fisher tearing through the packed aisle to Marion Slavin. Hogarth hadn't appeared to notice and still stared at Dawn. Fisher whispered frantically to the barrister, but Andrea could not hear what was being said.

Malverne stirred on the Bench. "Miss Slavin? What is it?"

Marion half rose, still craning her neck towards Fisher, getting the last of the message, getting confirmation. Andrea saw that the woman's sallow face was flushed. "My Lord," Marion said, "there's a police matter of great urgency."

"Well, what?" Malverne demanded, trying to assert

some authority in his courtroom.

"It's an armed siege," the barrister replied. "Involving a wanted criminal, Roots Johnson. He is *the* priority target of this squad."

There were furious voices around the courtroom, voices of hatred at the mention of the man who had shot Nicki Harris. Andrea saw the faces, the loathing. This, she understood, was how lynch mobs began.

"I'll adjourn *pro tem*," Malverne said.

As the court clerk shouted for the rest of the court to rise, people began to push their way out of the rear doors of Court 2 even before the judge had disappeared. Andrea saw Fisher go up to Hogarth and take hold of the shell-shocked senior officer's arm. He kept repeating the name Johnson to Hogarth, trying to provoke a response in his bewildered commander. And then suddenly Hogarth started, as if roused from a dreadful dream, and he rushed out of court with Fisher and a uniformed police escort.

As Andrea watched this from the third row, she became aware of Dawn standing next to her. She said nothing, but she kissed Andrea lightly on the right cheek, and Andrea felt the warmth of her tears.

Moments later, the two mothers walked out into the media frenzy outside the Gothic front arch of the Royal Courts. The rain whipped down from clouds, and camera lights and flashbulbs flickered and flashed in their eyes like lightning strikes. Andrea took Dawn's hand as question upon question was fired at them. Dawn closed her hand tight around Andrea's, and she asked, "Is it over?"

"Nearly," Andrea whispered back.

Calvin went to pick up the gun that had slipped down next to Roots's body, but Roots remained sufficiently conscious to take hold of it himself.

"I'll get Lifer's gun, then," Calvin said unconvincingly.

Roots just stared at the boy and shook his head once.

"No, I won't," Calvin said. He noticed the beginnings of a smile creeping into the side of Roots's mouth and couldn't help smiling as well. Just fleetingly, just something to relieve the fear for a few seconds. "What do we do?" he asked.

"We think, rude boy," Roots said. "They'll have sharp-shooters on every rooftop. They'll triangulate themselves the field of fire."

"What? What does that mean?" Calvin asked fearfully.

"We move, it'll be a turkey-shoot," Roots said. "That's why I say you go."

Calvin sank right back and banged his head against the brickwork behind him. He knew in his heart that he would never abandon this man who had saved his life. But how could the boy save Roots? He closed his eyes and tried to find inspiration. But the only image he saw was that of his mother. His mother's face rose in his mind, not as he had seen it that day in court, but as he fondly remembered it from all those years ago, when he could go to her for any-thing, when he did just that, when she was the stars and the moon and the sun to the boy, a complete and inextin-guishable love.

"Got a burner?" Calvin asked Roots.

"Ya, man," Roots said, wincing as he indicated the inside pocket of his jacket.

Calvin quickly reached in and grabbed the phone, feel-ing the coldness of the other man's flesh through the thin white shirt. He anxiously felt the bandage on the arm. It needed changing. The blood was seeping more quickly through it, and it was impossible now to tell that the strips of T-shirt had ever been white. He flicked the phone open, pressed on the power, but saw to his horror that the LCD was flashing.

"Batteries are dying," he said to Roots.

"Shake it."

Calvin dialled his mother's mobile number, but there was not enough power in the cells. The phone died.

"Shake it," Roots repeated.

Calvin shook the phone hard in his hand, tried again, and looked at Roots with amazement as the phone rang. "Mum?" he cried, as it was answered.

CHAPTER NINETEEN

Andrea drove with insane speed across Blackfriars Bridge and into South London. She overtook recklessly, screamed in and out of bus lanes, while all the time she had her mobile under her chin and tried to ring Calvin back. All she got was the automatic voice saying that no connection could be made. She was haunted during the breathless journey by Hogarth's capitulation in court, and simply could not decide whether it would make him more or less dangerous. Would he try to destroy everything around him? Would he bring down the temple, rage against anything that crossed his path? If so the first of these obstacles would be her Calvin. With that thought, she jabbed her foot on the accelerator, causing the car to lurch forward through the traffic. The buildings and vehicles she passed were a blur in the rain, and the windscreen wipers were metronomes counting out with agonising slowness the beats that separated her from her son.

Hogarth had arrived at the cordon sanitaire around the siege. Uniformed back-up had sectioned off streets surrounding the site, but Hogarth flashed his warrant card and was allowed to drive through. His face a mask, he pushed his way through the ranks to the commanding officer's mobile control post.

As he entered the van, the wind sliced off the river. A large, round-cheeked man whose face bore the scars of a thousand burst capillaries sat by a bank of closed circuit video screens, which gave grainy black-and-white views of the outside of the besieged building. There were telephones, hot lines to HQ, lines of communication with the armed officers in the field, while the megaphone blared noises of appeasement in the background.

"Hogarth," the grim-faced DCI said perfunctorily.

The CO, still dripping from the rain, was given a steaming cup of tea by one of his subordinates, a WPC who pushed herself behind Hogarth into the cramped van.

"Johnson's one of yours, isn't he?" the CO said in annoyance, as if the whole miserable situation were Hogarth's fault.

He did not rise to the bait. "What's the situation?" he asked.

"We've contained it." The senior officer took a hasty sip of the too-hot tea. He winced as the scalding liquid burned his lips. "For the moment," he added.

A dark shadow passed over Hogarth's eyes. "You can't just contain a man like Johnson," he shouted, not respecting the superiority of the ranking officer beside him.

There was a flicker on the screens as the camera equipment was inundated by the downpour. "Damn," the CO shouted, slapping the side of one of the monitors with no effect. "Look," he continued, "containment is the policy."

Hogarth moved in aggressively, his face inches away from the senior officer's. He knew what he wanted. He wanted them all dead. Everyone involved with the case. Everyone who had let him down and betrayed him. "When are we going to let them know this is our city, for Christ's sake?" he shouted.

"We are not vigilantes," the officer shouted back, but Hogarth could see that he was intimidated by the DCI's fervour.

"So what the hell are we? Johnson walks out of here alive? A dozen new gunmen walk into London knowing they've already won." He grabbed the seated officer's shoulder.

"Let go of me, DCI."

Hogarth gripped him more tightly. "The only containment for Johnson, sir," he said with venom, "is a box. In the ground. So let's go in and finish it."

"We've got to wait."

"Why?"

"It's the law."

Hogarth's head throbbed as though a vice were crushing his brain. "We are the law," he shouted.

The CO pushed him aside. "You're crazy," he shouted.

"Johnson killed Nicki Harris," Hogarth bellowed. "He shot the daughter of a serving Met officer. Now, your marksmen out there might not know that, but I'm going to tell them."

"You're insane. I'm ordering you off the site. You leave now or I'll have you arrested."

Hogarth pulled a gun from his jacket. "You get between me and Johnson," he said, "and I'll kill you." With that, he turned and sped out into the rain.

"For Christ's sake," the CO shouted, "there's a boy in there with Johnson."

Andrea's car skidded to a halt at the very limit of the police tape. A WPC in uniform held up her hand behind the fluttering blue line. Andrea dashed out of the car, made her way towards the WPC, realised that in her haste she had left the engine running but didn't turn back to switch it off.

"There's an armed incident, madam," the WPC said.

Andrea began to duck under the tape. The WPC held her shoulder, tried to force her back. "I can't let you through."

"My son's in there," Andrea cried. "It's my son. Do you understand?" With the force of her words, the driven

passion of her whole being, the WPC melted aside and
Andrea rushed through, along the front of the warehouses, her open coat flying in her wake. She ran through the
rain, skidding, slipping, trying to keep her feet as best she
could as she ran past marksmen, squatting behind waste
skips and empty oil drums. She reached the entrance to
the derelict site, the wasteland outside the shell of the
building, and stopped momentarily, wondering where to
go. Then she realised. Each of the high-velocity weapons
was like a signpost, the end of each barrel pointed to
where her son was trapped. She was now in the treacherous no-man's-land between the police guns and their prey.
She stumbled over the rough rubbled ground, splashing in
the muddy pools of oily water. Suddenly Hogarth
appeared, his gun drawn, running along the warehouse
fronts. Andrea felt herself caught between two worlds. She
could not turn back.

"Calvin?" she cried out.

"*Mum,*" the boy screamed from inside. His words
echoed eerily through the building.

Andrea ran towards him, passing the broken outer wall.
She glanced fearfully back towards Hogarth. He raised his
gun, but she couldn't tell whether he aimed it at her or the
building beyond. "Stay down," she cried.

Below the shattered window, still squatting within the
shell, Calvin shook Roots Johnson's arm, careful not to
touch the wound. "She's here, she's here," he whispered to
the Yardie.

Roots tried to smile. "Calvin," he said, gesturing the
boy to his ear. "Tell her, yeah? Tell her you love her." The
boy looked at the older man in confusion. "I never told my
mother, ya know."

Andrea burst into what was left of the building. Despite
his mother's warning, Calvin jumped to his feet and flung
himself at her. She smothered his face with kisses, but

when she tried to hug him, his legs folded. She knelt before him, terrified.

"Where are you hurt?" she cried out, fearing the worst as mothers inevitably do.

Calvin gripped his midriff while his face screwed up with the sharp stabbing pain. "Ribs," he wheezed.

"Shot?"

Calvin shook his head gingerly, but then he remembered Roots. "He's hit. Shoulder," he gasped, the pain preventing him from elaborating further.

Andrea glanced over at the prone and bleeding Yardie, then her eyes were drawn to another figure, on the other side of the room, like a beached whale in a shallow pool of his own blood. She stepped swiftly over the rubble to where Roots lay, his eyes half closed, gripping the wrist of his bleeding arm tightly to stop it shaking. She immediately took off her coat and laid it over him, lining downwards, like a blanket. A thin film of saliva trickled from the side of his mouth and his eyes were glazed with pain.

"Think the bullet went right through," he whispered hoarsely.

"Mum, you've got to help him, you've got to. He saved my life," Calvin said earnestly. "Mum, he—"

"OK, OK," Andrea said, her head swimming.

"Nicki Harris," Roots began to say.

Andrea put her hand on his. "Hogarth told the court," she said.

"It was an accident," Calvin pleaded.

"Any way round it?" Roots asked Andrea, but his voice was devoid of hope.

She shook her head.

"What are you saying?" Calvin pleaded. "How can there be no way round it? It was an accident. He didn't mean to kill Nicki Harris."

"It's still murder," Andrea said, hating herself.

"But why?" Calvin cried.

"I tried to kill Earl," Roots whispered.

Calvin turned to his mother, feeling as if he would burst with the injustice of it all. "Mum?" he asked.

"I'm sorry," she whispered softly.

The Yardie nodded. "Do me one favour?" he asked Andrea. "Take out the boy." She nodded. Then he added, "But slow."

Calvin began to back away. "No," he cried. "I'm not leaving him to the police."

Roots affected a look of mock surprise. "You t'ink me surrendering, little brother? Uh-huh. Ya, man, the don is escaping. I got me an escape route."

Though the tears in his eyes shone brightly, Calvin smiled.

Andrea looked over the bottom edge of the window. She saw a sniper running silently and expertly across a rooftop opposite. She knew that a dozen weapons would be trained on them the moment they left the cover of the building. She knew that Hogarth was outside and more dangerous now than he had ever been. But she couldn't let her son stay in this place of death. It would only be a matter of time, she calculated, before the police made an armed assault on the building, so their only chance of survival was to surrender in plain view.

"Come out with us. Please," she begged Roots. But he did not reply, and she knew that this was as good as a refusal. "Hogarth's armed," she warned him.

Roots lifted his right hand out from under her coat. In it was his nine-mil.

Calvin carefully wiped away the sweat from Roots's forehead. "You gotta come out with us," he said, even as his mother put her arms around his shoulders.

"Nah. I'll check out your vibes later, Mr Calvin MC,"

the Yardie said.

"Please," Calvin cried.

Roots saw that the boy's mother was looking down at her son and that she was on the verge of weeping, too, just by virtue of seeing her son's torment. The Yardie's heart ached.

"One day," he told Calvin, "I'm going to have me a studio in Canada, and we're going to cut some massive disc together, rude boy."

He held out his right fist, clenched, the long ebony fingers pressed tightly together. Calvin touched fists with him. Then he rested his head on Roots's chest and cried. Though it crushed him, Roots pushed the boy towards his mother. "Tell her, little brother," he told Calvin. "Tell her."

The boy nodded, understanding.

"Good luck," Andrea said.

"Who needs luck, counsellor? The po-lice ain't never going to catch me. I'm a Yard man. And there ain't no one faster than a Yard man."

Andrea held Calvin's face in her hands. "Trust me," she said, and he nodded.

She put her arms around his shoulders as they stood and began to edge out of the building, into the field of fire. She squinted through the heavy rain as she tried to make out where the snipers were hidden. Slowly they passed the broken-down outer wall. There was no cover, no obstruction, and now she could just make out the rifle barrels. One on the warehouse roof. Another behind the skip. Still another sticking out through the nearest warehouse door. They were all pointed at Andrea and her son.

"We're unarmed," she cried out.

But there was no reply. And then, to her horror, she saw a red spot on her son's forehead. "For Christ's sake," she cried, "we're unarmed."

Hogarth appeared from behind one of the warehouses.

He had his gun aimed directly at Andrea and Calvin. All
that separated them was a stretch of muddy ground and
the shroud of falling rain.

"Where's Johnson?" he shouted.

Andrea glanced to her left. At the end of the access
road along the warehouse fronts she could see a police van.
She glanced up, down, right. The rifle sights had followed
them. She fought the impulse to run.

"Where's Johnson?" Hogarth demanded again.

"Mum," Calvin whispered, "what do we do?"

Andrea supported him with all the strength that
remained to her, and urged him forwards, slowly, not shy-
ing away from Hogarth, nor from his gun, but directly
towards him.

"Stop," he screamed at them.

Still she edged forward. He had the gun, but she had
beaten him in court, she had the truth, and as she
approached, as she began to make out the contours of his
face, she knew that this huge, frightening man was scared
of her. She moved forward, now five or six feet away from
Hogarth, shielding her son from his gun. He held the gun
out in front of him.

To her left, an overweight uniformed officer rushed
from the van, stood in the middle of the access road and
shouted through the rain, "Drop the gun, Hogarth."

Hogarth kept his eyes fixed upon Andrea, and she kept
hers on him. The gun shook in his hand with the fury that
surged through his body. "You ruined me," he said.

Andrea was two feet away, so close that, despite his
tremors, he could not miss. She could see the dull, dry
metal inside the dripping barrel of his gun. One more step,
a final one. "You ruined yourself," she said.

Hogarth's eyes narrowed as he aimed at her, his eye
sockets now just slits in his face. Still the gun trembled in
front of Andrea, but she did not shy away. "Drugs will

flood into London," he cried, rain and tears and sweat running down his face. "Other children will die."

"But we won't have killed them," Andrea replied. "Not with our hands." Then she said more quietly, as she glanced at her bloodied son, "Not with our hands."

Hogarth's face was molten now, his features slipping, contorting with rage and agony. His mouth fell open, a black hole, and he threw his head back and let out a silent scream. He dropped the gun at Andrea's feet and it splashed into a muddy puddle before disappearing. As it vanished, she saw him for what he was: a man harnessed to his ill-judged actions, a man who, when she had first encountered him, had possessed faith in nothing except his own righteousness, in the higher justice of his actions. But now he was depleted and lost and beaten. Andrea could not bring herself to hate him despite all this, although she was convinced that he hated himself.

She turned to her son, who shivered behind her. Slowly she led Calvin towards the command post, where two uniformed officers held blankets, and she whispered in his ear, "Let's go home."

Roots Johnson had crawled past the dead body of Lifer. He knew that as he hauled himself along the corridors of the abandoned building he was leaving a giveaway trail of blood, but it couldn't be helped. Though he cast Andrea's coat over his back like a shawl, blood from his shoulder wound dripped straight on to the ground as he edged along the rubble, for these moments out of sight of the police snipers. He made his way through the broken remnants of the building, closer to the river, while the police megaphone blared outside: "Johnson, throw out your weapons, there is no escape." He hesitated, turned back towards the source of the noise, then pushed himself through the biting pain, his knees getting scuffed and cut as he moved through the debris, pulling himself along with his right arm. He wondered whether Calvin and Andrea were safe now, and felt sure that they were since he had heard no gunshots outside. And though this pleased him, he also knew that it meant that the police were saving their bullets for him. The breeze blew more strongly through the building, and he knew that he was fast approaching the river. He made his way slowly, steadily, swallowing his pain, until he saw the drain cover.

In a small walled courtyard, Roots sat over the circular disc of metal set into the ground. He found it increasingly difficult to breathe as his wound demanded more and more of his body's resources just to stay awake, not to give in to the pain. With his right hand, he tried to haul the drain cover out of its housing in the concrete courtyard. It would not shift. He recalled that he had always removed it with both hands, and with his full strength. Now, with his body failing and with one arm, it seemed almost impossible. But he thought again of Katherine, and of his painful need to see her, and gritted his teeth. He would have just one opportunity to open the cover. He paused, withdrew into himself, tried to find the core of determination that had kept him alive for two dangerous decades, and then he tugged at the drain cover. It budged a fraction. Immediately he heard a strange whistling from the drainage ducts beneath the ground. His fingers, his forearm, his body trembled with the strain, and he knew he could not pull it open using his right arm alone. There was nothing for it: he used his remaining strength to lift the metal cover a fraction further, then he slipped his legs into the hole. He couldn't hold it any longer. The metal fell back down, crushing his thighs. If the police come now, he thought, it will be the end. He couldn't move. He was trapped.

The megaphone blared: "Johnson, this is your final chance."

Having rested a few seconds, Roots took the cover in his right hand again, lifted it as far as he could, then lowered his right shoulder, edged it under the highest point of the disc and pushed. His legs dangled helplessly in the hole below, but little by little he began to slip through. Right arm under, right shoulder. He craned his head as far to the left as it would go. The rough, damp metal now moved millimetre by millimetre up his neck. It felt like someone running a bread knife along his skin, but all Roots could think of was the pain that would come once the cover reached his open wound. His ear was squashed, now his right cheek. All the time he slipped further and further into the hole below. He fell into a huge bricked drainage pipe. At the bottom of it were six inches of water, so dirty, so slimy, it stuck to his skin, coated it rather than running off as clean water might.

There was total darkness, save for a distant circle of light at the end of the tunnel, through which he could see only water. Roots gave in to the waves of pain that broke through his body and rolled pitifully in the filth. But before the numbness set in, he struggled to shake his mind into action, to orientate himself. He hauled himself to his feet and, standing on the tips of his toes, felt the bottom of the cover above him. He traced out its circle with the fingers of his right hand, then he felt for the bricks just below it, which formed a well, the neck of a bottle, through which he had fallen. Two bricks were loose. He pulled them out and they splashed into the water beside him. The noise of their impact echoed down the tunnel. He had usually done this from the forecourt above, reaching down into the hole, but he managed to remove two further bricks and there it was: his bag of money. The muscles in his right arm ached now, being held above his head for so long the lactic acid burned. He pulled down the bag and then collapsed backwards, leaning against the rounded side of the storm drain. He slid down the wall and rested the bag on his thighs. He began to open the zip. But the moment he felt inside, Roots realised that he did not want it. It was blood money. Each note was washed in Nicki's blood. He flung the bag into the water.

It was strangely quiet in the man-sized brick pipe. As Roots pulled himself through the foetid water and towards the river, he could hear only the increasingly loud sound of the rise and fall of the river, with the rain pattering on it, and his pained breathing. He was now at the very mouth of the drain, and the breeze that flew through the centre of London along the course of the river blew fine droplets of rain on to the Yardie's face. He squatted on the edge. Below him, dividing him from the water, was a thin strand of mud, but his view was restricted by the circular mouth of the drain, and he could see only twenty yards left and right, up- and downriver. The strand was empty. He knew that he needed to gather his strength for his final push, so he waited there a few moments. Slowly, as he attempted to regularise his breathing, he realised that his mobile phone was still in his jacket pocket. He had to contort his right hand into a crab's claw shape to remove it. The rain fell unsteadily, whipped by the wind outside, as Roots Johnson clicked on the phone, shook the battery and dialled. He felt a surge of sheer elation when he heard a click at the other end.

"I'm sorry," Katherine's voice said, "I can't take your call right now, but—"

Roots held the phone against his forehead, devastated. He waited until he heard the faint noise of the three beeps, then he spoke in an urgent whisper with the phone almost in his mouth. "Katherine, it's Valentine, darlin'. You were right. This ain't no country for us. So I want to go, with you, baby, to Canada. So I'm coming for you, Katherine. And everyt'ing's gonna be all right. Katherine," he said, pausing, "I . . ." But the LCD started flashing, and the batteries died. Roots dropped the phone, finished the message alone in the drain. "I love you," he whispered.

With the fingers of his right hand, he took out the silver Canadian dollar Katherine had given him for luck, and he kissed it, his eyes closed. He thought of his child growing within Katherine and he begged that child: Please do not let me be scared, but give me strength, to do my best as a proud Jamaican. He jumped down on to the strand.

His feet plunged into the glue-like mud. The water was only three or four feet to his left. He looked all about. But there was no one around. There was just the river, which now that he was on the mudflat looked vast and alive, heaving under the pull of the tides, sprinkled in a million places with disappearing raindrops. He spotted some kind of dredger, a long flat boat low in the water, anchored just off the bank further downstream. If he could get to that, he calculated, then maybe he could pull the anchor and let it drift with the current to freedom. The rain and the wind washed his face, and he felt utterly alive, despite the wound in his shoulder, despite his predicament. He opened his mouth and he could taste the rain, and it was good. My life is not ending, he thought, now it is beginning truly. He had left the blood money in the drain above, he had killed Lifer, and he was resolved with every sinew of his being to leave for Canada with Katherine. This is the very start of things, he thought with joy, this is how things begin, in an elemental place such as this with water and wind and sky and mud.

He crouched down, checked for signs of other life, saw none, and began to wade through the mud towards the dredger. His shoes were sucked off his feet by the depth of the mud, but after the initial shock of the coldness around his soles he didn't mind losing them, since he knew it would make it easier for him to swim towards the dredger. He moved more quickly now, in bare feet, still holding Katherine's coin in his right hand. Then he heard a dreadful sound.

He saw nothing at first. It was just the sound. Rifles being primed. One after another. Even before he could look around to the bank behind him, he heard the screaming: "ARMED POLICE. STOP OR WE WILL SHOOT. ARMED POLICE. STOP OR WE WILL SHOOT."

Roots closed his eyes. He put his right hand on the back of his head in surrender, unable to lift his left arm with the pain. But even as his fingers touched his neck, Katherine's coin slipped from his grasp and was swallowed by the mud.

"LIE FACE DOWN," the voice behind him ordered.

Roots imagined the rifles, all trained on his body, and the bullets inside them, which would soon be inside him. From the metal of the guns to the flesh of his body. But he was not scared. For he heard a voice, and he could not tell whether it was that of a young boy or a girl whispering in his ear: Run, Daddy, run. They can't stop you now, just run. And Roots did not want to disobey, for although in his time he had disobeyed the letter of the law, the rules of life and the pleadings of his true nature, he now didn't dare disobey his unborn child.

Roots suddenly felt lithe, beautiful, young and strong. He found with curious amazement that he was running well along the strand, splashing along the waterline, his feet just in the river, and he was unafraid, running barefoot and carefree in a way he hadn't done since his mother was alive, playing gospel organ in church. She had told him that if he feared God he could grow into anything. His breathing began to take over, to blot out the other irrelevant sounds around him — the background hum of the

London traffic, the police shouting "Stop or we'll shoot, stop or we'll shoot."

He was running faster now, to Katherine, to Canada, and his breathing was strong and even, an athlete's, and he remembered a young boy standing on a Jamaican beach with his father, watching the palm tree branches sway in the sea breeze. Roots wanted to speak to that boy. He wanted to tell him what he now knew. But it was too late. He heard a distant cracking sound as the snipers fired repeatedly. Bullets ripped into his flesh with such force that he was thrown into the air, upwards, sideways, and fell face down into the water. It was Roots Johnson who was shot, but it was Valentine Johnson who lay floating on the surface of the river, who felt the cares of his wasted life drifting with the swell, who felt the water, dark and inviting and deep. The hopes that he had had for his life were now transferred to that of his child. So it was Valentine Johnson who imagined a net being cast on a distant, sunnier shore in a distant, less troublesome time, a net cast by his ancestors, by his family. He prayed to them now, as the light of the outside world faded, and another light, a faint flaring, quivered inside him. He prayed as his mother had taught him, he prayed that this ancient net would drag him under the water so that he could emerge into another place in the company of fierce, proud, free men, stolen Africans who refused to be slaves, who lived and died as warriors.

CHAPTER TWENTY

The funeral of Roots Johnson could not officially take place until later in the summer, when the coroner finally agreed to release his body, after all the bullets that had torn his flesh had been removed, and metal rods had been inserted expertly into the icy flesh of the Jamaican's back to track their paths. Photographs were taken of the dead body from all angles, black-and-white and colour, and they were presented in neat, numbered bundles to an inquest jury, which agreed that the police had every right to shoot him repeatedly in the back.

Andrea had sat through every day of the inquest, as witness or spectator. So when the day of the funeral finally arrived, all those people immediately around her, who cared for her the most, knew how important the ceremony was both to her and to her son, whom the Yardie had saved. So it was that a small group gathered in an overgrown municipal cemetery in a lost part of South London. That day, according to old Jamaican country tradition, Rufus told them, the mirrors in their houses should be turned to the wall, since no one should be preoccupied with how they looked when they went to commemorate another's death.

Rufus had often wept at night in the intervening months, unable to sleep properly alone in his cold, twentieth-floor flat. Andrea had invited him to come and live with her and Calvin, but Cameron also lived with them, and Rufus did not want to intrude. Rufus Patterson had not wept from grief, but from joy, joy that Calvin and the boy's mother were finally reconciled. This was a bitter-sweet pleasure for the old man, since he realised that his adored grandson did not need him now. To his astonishment, Rufus found himself regularly dreaming with stunning vividness, but never at night. The nights had become for him a slowly passing blackness, but during the days, when he nodded off while fishing by himself along one of London's more or less polluted canals, the old man dreamed of his beloved home in the Caribbean. He remembered how as a young man he had waited impatiently for the sun to drop into the sea so that he could push off in his boat in search of flying fish. He recalled the close, still Caribbean nights, with the sea a flat blanket, shimmering with phosphorus and reflected stars, and even though he would often see nothing for hours on end, he would rush back to port to regale his wife with stories of friendly dol-phins and leaping marlins and circling sharks. He recalled all this with a sad, heavy heart, because he knew he would never see any of it again, that he would die on this colder, far-off island. But he was always cheerful with others, despite these inner longings, for in Andrea and Calvin he had all the family he needed until the end.

Katherine threw the first handful of earth over Roots Johnson's coffin. Then she threw a white rose, in memory of the flower he had left on her doorstep months before. She was clearly with child now and was showing quite marked-ly. She burst into tears as the white rose landed on top of the coffin, bounced in apparent slow motion, then finally came to rest. Andrea put her arm around the pregnant woman.

The ceremony came to a quiet conclusion, and Andrea turned to leave along with the others. She felt that the events had not so much changed her as changed her back. She was a mother again, she had a son's love again, and she had exorcised her dread of the courts. She had imagined that when the case was over she would suddenly be shorn of care and worry, but that had not happened, for other cares and worries about her immediate family quickly replaced the seemingly larger concerns of the Nicki Harris murder. She took no satisfaction from the fact that Hogarth had been dismissed from the Metropolitan Police and awaited trial on criminal charges, but it was just another fact, a closure that she needed to be sure of before she could turn her gaze entirely to the future. She had been offered many other *causes célèbres* — high-profile cases, miscarriages of justice, cases that other lawyers would kill for. She turned all of them down. Now she worried about how well Calvin was doing at college, whether he was going out too often and staying out too late. She worried about whether he secretly smoked the odd cigarette in his room. She found that she was neither happy nor unhappy, but a feeling that she believed to be contentment crept through her body and then laid siege to her heart. She still often quarrelled with Calvin, she could not make up her mind whether or not to marry Cameron, she scolded herself if she did not speak to Rufus at least once a day. She still drank too much hot chocolate, worked too hard for her father, and walled a part of herself away from the world and kept within it her secret doubts about her ability as a mother and a daughter. But the darker days of her life, she fervently believed, had been lived, and she looked forward with hope to a new life — not an easier one, but a life where she strove towards the things she believed to be important rather than ran away from those she feared. That was how it had been. She would never allow it to happen again.

As they walked slowly out of the cemetery, Calvin took her hand, and she looked down at their fingers, black and white intertwining. She gazed at his almond eyes, and he looked back at her full of affection.

"Mum?" he said.

"Yes?" she replied.

He paused, tears brimming in his eyes, and remembered the last words Roots Johnson had spoken to him. "I love you," he said.

They stopped and hugged, and as she looked over her son's shoulder, Andrea could see the workers in the cemetery piling earth on to the coffin of Roots Valentine Johnson. She could feel her son's heart beating quickly against her chest as he cried, and she recalled the lines, she couldn't be sure from where, which said that life was just a sleep and a forgetting — just that, a sleep and a forgetting — and she hoped that the man who had saved her son's life could now sleep.

ACKNOWLEDGEMENTS

I would like to thank the many people whose assistance has been indispensable in the writing of this book. Firstly, my incomparable UK agents Mark Lucas and Val Hoskins, wonderfully assisted by Sally and Rebecca respectively. Also, my other agents, Nicki Kennedy at Intercontinental, David Black in New York and my editor John Pearce in Canada. The entire team at Hodder, but in particular my editors old and new, the two Carolyns. Special thanks to Tony Redston for his unflagging hard work and faith in the project in another context. Nicole for her insight into FMCGs. Readers Antoinette Jones and Jessie Ripley. Sheila Hayler for working so hard at such short notice. Deb Coles of the charity Inquest and Raju Bhatt, solicitor, two legal street fighters, who joined me in the trenches in the case from hell, and reminded me why I went to the Bar a decade ago. The Manning family, whose son and brother, Alton, was unlawfully killed, and whose courage was a constant inspiration to me. My friend, colleague and true Jamaican spar, Courtenay Griffiths. Speedy recovery, Griff. Dad and Mike, who are always remarkably supportive despite their busy lives. Finally, thanks to my three girls. Mary and Lara, in whose house we are permitted to reside — every day with them is a minor miracle. But above all, *Above The Law* owes any merit it may have to Katie, who sat opposite me in a Kings Street restaurant all those months ago and heard a two-line pitch about Andrea and her son, and who convinced me that I should listen to them; who fought fearlessly for Roots and Rufus and their right to exist; and who eagerly read draft after draft when others might have faltered. If the characters on the page are the actors of this small drama, then Katie is its beating heart. Thank you. And *grazie mille* for saying yes.